W9-CHQ-976

"DARING."
—*The Wilmington News Journal*

"An engaging plot…characters who
reward you with their genuine humanity."
—Julia Alvarez

"ELOQUENT."
—*Publishers Weekly*

"[A] fine novel that lovingly evokes a
time in America's past that many people
think of as idyllic but is revealed by the
author to be filled with complexity."
—*Booklist*

"LOVELY."
—*Library Journal*

"What makes *The Saint of Lost Things* so captivating is its marvelous cast of humble yet profoundly individual characters. Beautifully, and movingly, Castellani shows an uncanny empathy for the American immigrant experience. Without ever straying into stereotype, he conveys vividly what it feels like to yearn for a lost, familiar past while striving desperately to create a home and a future in a new world."   —Julia Glass, author of *Three Junes*

"Clear-eyed, unsentimental fiction . . . Fresh and moving."
—*Kirkus Reviews*

"Skillfully captures the Italian immigrant experience at mid-twentieth century . . . a fresh voice in Italian American fiction . . . This lovely, haunting, unhurried story will have readers clamoring for more."   —*Library Journal*

"[An] eloquent, leisurely tale about dreams and disappointments . . . the natural, easy beauty of his prose captures the Italian American immigrant community of a bygone era."
—*Publishers Weekly*

"Tender, touching . . . a richly emotional story of a marriage that needs time to flower in a milieu that values the old ways and fears the new."   —*Chicago Tribune*

"Lyrical and elegant . . . His characters are finely drawn, and he has a keen eye for the subtle dramas of family and friendship."
—*School Library Journal*

"A strong central character . . . complex and daring . . . evocative prose."   —*The Wilmington News Journal*

"A moving evocation of the Italian American experience, told with grace, compassion, and uncompromising honesty. Christopher Castellani is a gifted novelist with a sharp eye and a big heart."
—Tom Perrotta, author of *Little Children*

continued . . .

Titles by Christopher Castellani

The Saint of Lost Things

CHRISTOPHER CASTELLANI

BERKLEY BOOKS, NEW YORK

THE BERKLEY PUBLISHING GROUP
Published by the Penguin Group
Penguin Group (USA) Inc.
375 Hudson Street, New York, New York 10014, USA

Penguin Group (Canada), 90 Eglinton Avenue East, Suite 700, Toronto, Ontario M4P 2Y3, Canada
(a division of Pearson Penguin Canada Inc.)
Penguin Books Ltd., 80 Strand, London WC2R 0RL, England
Penguin Group Ireland, 25 St. Stephen's Green, Dublin 2, Ireland (a division of Penguin Books Ltd.)
Penguin Group (Australia), 250 Camberwell Road, Camberwell, Victoria 3124, Australia
(a division of Pearson Australia Group Pty. Ltd.)
Penguin Books India Pvt. Ltd., 11 Community Centre, Panchsheel Park, New Delhi—110 017, India
Penguin Group (NZ), Cnr. Airborne and Rosedale Roads, Albany, Auckland 1310, New Zealand
(a division of Pearson New Zealand Ltd.)
Penguin Books (South Africa) (Pty.) Ltd., 24 Sturdee Avenue, Rosebank, Johannesburg 2196,
South Africa

Penguin Books Ltd., Registered Offices: 80 Strand, London WC2R 0RL, England

Copyright © 2005 by Christopher Castellani.
"Readers Guide" copyright © 2006 by Penguin Group (USA) Inc.
Translation of "Terra Straniera" on page ix by Allison Adair. Reprinted by permission.
Cover and stepback illustration by Kazu Sano.
Cover design by Rita Frangie.

PRINTING HISTORY
Algonquin Books hardcover edition / September 2005
Berkley trade paperback edition / October 2006

Library of Congress Cataloging-in-Publication Data

Castellani, Christopher, 1972–
    The saint of lost things / Christopher Castellani.
        p. cm.
    ISBN 0-425-21173-8 (trade pbk.)
        1. Italian American families—Fiction. 2. Children of immigrants—Fiction. 3. Philadelphia
(Pa.)—Fiction. 4. Wilmington (Del.)—Fiction. 5. Immigrants—Fiction. I. Title.

    PS3603. A875S35 2006
    813'.6—dc22

                                                                                    2006042813

PRINTED IN THE UNITED STATES OF AMERICA

10   9   8   7   6   5   4   3   2   1

Again, always, for my parents,
Vincenzo and Lidia Castellani—
my favorite storytellers—
vi penso sempre

Terra straniera quanta malinconia
quando ci salutammo e non so perchè
tu mi gettasti un bacio e fuggisti via
e pure adesso te lo confesso non penso a te.

Non mi ricordo più quegli occhi belli
pieni di luce calda ed infinita.
Mi son dimenticato i tuoi capelli
e la boccuccia ch'era la mia vita.

Ma sogno notte e dì la mia casetta,
la mia vecchietta che sempre aspetta.
L'amore del paese e della mamma
è una gran fiamma che brucia il cuor.
Questa tristezza, questa nostalgia sono il ricordo dell'Italia mia.

Ma sogno notte e dì la mia casetta . . .

Strange land, such sadness
when we saluted one another, and I don't know why
you threw me a kiss and fled
yet now I confess I do not think of you.

I no longer remember those beautiful eyes
full of warm light and endlessness.
I've forgotten your hair
and the full mouth that was once my life.

But I dream night and day of my little house,
my gray darling that always awaits.
Love of a country as of a mother
is a grand flame that burns the heart.
This sadness, this homesickness is the remembrance of my *Italia*.

But I dream night and day of my little house . . .

—Traditional Italian song

Every man supposes himself not to be fully understood; and if there is any truth in him . . . I see not how it can be otherwise. The last chamber, the last closet, he must feel was never opened; there is always a residuum unknown, unanalyzable. That is, every man believes that he has a greater possibility.

—Ralph Waldo Emerson

The Saint of Lost Things

Christopher Castellani

PART ONE

Games of 1953

I

The Little Ladies of Wilmington

FOR A TIME, Maddalena knew so few English words that each carried memories from the day she'd learned it. The words were common and unrelated: vacuum, headlight, mouthwash. "Take an umbrella," her husband, Antonio, would advise, and suddenly she found herself back on the boardwalk in Atlantic City, making her first purchase with American money. "One *uhm*-brell-*ah*, please," she'd repeated as she approached the vendor, a fistful of dollars in her hand, Antonio a few steps away, guiding her with his eyes. The vendor had taken her money with a disinterested nod, not seeming to notice her accent. To celebrate this success, she and Antonio had spread a blanket on the sand and watched the storm clouds gather over the pier. When the rain came, they'd huddled under the umbrella until the lightning scared them off.

With the word *apple* came the opening and closing mouth

of Maddalena's night-school teacher, Sister Clark, a woman so committed to training her students in proper pronunciation that she offered free private tutorials at the convent. *Ah-po* is the sound of the immigrant, Sister Clark had said, her lips in an exaggerated O; until you master your speech, no one will show you the respect you deserve. That's all it takes, she'd said: your tongue in the right spot between your teeth, a little concentration, and practice practice practice. Then America will smile and open her arms, loving as a grandmother.

Seven years have passed, and Maddalena has mostly forgotten the histories of the English words that come to her. On the bus today she thinks, Why do we keep lurching? then wonders where she learned this verb. Did she see it in a magazine? On a billboard? She practices, in honor of the recently deceased Sister Clark: I lurch; you lurch; the bus never stops lurching. Unlike most words, this one at least sounds like its definition. There are no extra letters, silent for no reason, to confuse her. In Italy, the country in which she was born, they'd pronounce the word "lurk," but lurk means something different here. Lurk is what the men do in the alleys near the bus stop, what Antonio does in the doorway at night before he leaves her.

The driver brakes hard and jolts Maddalena forward again. She looks up from her book, grabs the armrest, and snaps back against the seat. Her stomach has gone sour, and a dull ache spreads like a stain from one side of her abdomen to the other. She holds her breath. Ida, her sister-in-law, dozes beside her. Ida can sleep on these morning rides, but Maddalena cannot, even though she has lain awake most of the night. She can never sleep when she is keeping a secret.

She tries to determine whether the sourness in her stomach feels different from the everyday sourness caused by the lurching. Her skin looks puffier than normal, of that she is certain, but maybe the recent drop in temperature—Indian summer to crisp fall in twenty-four hours—bears responsibility. Among these extreme changes she seeks the third sign, the one that will convince her she is finally carrying a child.

The first sign occurred this past Sunday, when two deer strayed into the empty lot across from her house. The bigger one—the mother, Maddalena guessed—chewed on a white paper cup as her baby nuzzled at her side. They'd stood together in peace, content with the trash and the dead patches of grass at their feet. Then suddenly the mother looked up at Maddalena in the window. She stared at her for a long moment, cocked her head, nodded twice, then dashed back into the woods. The baby, lighter in color, its legs delicate as matchsticks, trotted after her in no hurry to catch up—as if it wouldn't have minded lingering a while. Until that morning, Maddalena had not seen a single deer in that lot.

The second sign occurred just yesterday, the start of the sixth week since her last monthly bleeding. She heard music in the factory, sweet chimes in the tune of a lullaby. Ida and the other ladies kept sewing unaware. Minutes later, their boss, Mr. Gold, walked past carrying a mobile of plastic daisies, which played the lullaby when he pressed a button on one of their golden eyes. A gift for his newborn niece, he explained. But since when did Mr. Gold walk around showing off baby gifts? And why was Maddalena the only one who'd heard the lullaby over the chattering women and the din of the machines?

Despite all this evidence, Maddalena will not allow herself to be sure. She and Antonio have been wanting a child for the seven years she has lived in America, and the signs have failed her again and again. All she knows of babies is the What that makes them; for the How and the When and the Why Not she must guess. She and Antonio have tried the What so many nights, followed always by his assurances, "We are becoming mother and father, my beautiful Maddalena; I feel it this time." As they lay beside each other, he'd tuck her hair behind her ear with trembling fingers and promise they would not be childless much longer. He repeated what Dr. Barone told them: you are both young and perfectly healthy; it is just a matter of time; the woman's body will act only when it is ready. Then, four months ago, without a good explanation, Antonio gave up hope. He decided that if Maddalena wasn't going to bring in a child after all, she could at least earn some money. And so, since early summer, he has cashed her paychecks from her hours in Mr. Gold's factory. They hide the bills in a pocket she sewed into the cornice of the drapes.

The bus stops in Chester, where dark-coated women wait in line in the rain. Maddalena waves good morning to Gloria, the Cuban, as she steps on clutching an enormous package wrapped in brown paper. If Maddalena feels chatty—today she does not—she can struggle through a conversation with Gloria, who speaks an unpredictable jumble of Spanish, English, and half-guessed Italian. Instead she closes her eyes and pretends to nap. As the bus nears Philadelphia, she puts her book—an Italian romance called *Il Sogno della Principessa*—in her purse and elbows Ida awake. It is 7:20. They have ten minutes to punch their cards.

The streets are more crowded than usual as the three women make their way. The late October air blows gusty and cold, shaking the half-naked solitary trees in their square grates along the sidewalk. Children in blue and white uniforms race past them, the girls with ribbons in their hair, the boys' shirts untucked and hanging below their sweaters. The rain has coated all the stone and asphalt in a slick sheen. Red and yellow leaves stick to their shoes, and Maddalena skids, nearly falls, as she makes the right onto Passyunk Avenue. Ida, in her clear plastic bonnet, yawning, takes her arm.

With three minutes to spare, they stand outside the front door. THE GOLDEN HEM, EST. 1948, says the newly painted sign above the arch. Ida refuses to enter the building until the second hand on her watch reaches 7:29. Maddalena finds this dangerous. If Mr. Gold sees them, he might think they do not value their jobs or need the money. The other ladies—not Gloria, who is on their side—shoot them looks on their way in. Maddalena makes no protest. After her husband, Ida is the most stubborn person she knows.

They work at adjoining tables, Ida and Maddalena in one row, Gloria and a Greek woman named Stavroula across the aisle. Stavroula, in her miniature black glasses and white hair, arrives on an earlier bus from New Jersey and rarely speaks. They are four of fifty women, arranged in rows on the first floor of an enormous windowless warehouse. They sew blouses and robes mostly, fashionable garments sold in stores they rarely visit, and make seventy-five cents an hour no matter how many they finish.

Maddalena and Ida have just switched on their machines when Mr. Gold appears for his morning promenade among the tables. Bits of thread cling to his pants. He wears his short-sleeved shirt buttoned to his neck and carries the yardstick that he rarely uses or puts down. He has a thick mustache, hairy arms, and a kind face with wrinkles on his forehead and around his eyes. But you can never count on his mood. Maddalena once saw him charge up and down the aisles, slap each woman's table with the yardstick, and screech, "Wake up!" Then, not a minute later, he was speaking sweetly again. This explains the wrinkles on a man no older than forty.

"Good morning, my little ladies," he says.

"Good morning, Mr. Gold," they say in unison, keeping their heads down.

"Let's do eighty today, yes?" he says, and holds up a piece of paper with the numbers *8-0* written in black marker. "What do you think, Ida? Yesterday I asked for seventy and you did thirty-six."

"I'm trying," she says, a pin between her lips.

Maddalena will have no trouble with eighty. Unlike the English language, sewing has come easily to her, and often she must slow her pace so as not to shame Ida or Gloria.

"I'm telling all my ladies some news," Mr. Gold says.

Ida looks up.

"Keep working while I talk," he continues, "and if you don't understand me"—here he glances at Maddalena, who loses track when he speaks too quickly—"make sure someone explains it to you." He sighs and rubs his forehead. "The sad truth is that I must let go of five of you by the end of next week. Business is not so good. The five who produce the least I must lose. This does not make me happy, believe me, but it is what I am forced to do."

"But I need the money more than anyone!" Ida says. She pushes herself away from the table and looks at him. "I have two little girls at home. Some of these ladies have no children at all."

"I have babies in two countries!" Gloria says.

"Then do the work of two women," Mr. Gold tells her, as he moves to the next set of tables.

Maddalena has followed most of this. At lunch Ida fills her

in on the details. They talk low, though the other Italian women—snobs from the North, who would like nothing more than to see Maddalena and Ida sent away—sit far across the other end of the room. "Mario will kill me if I lose another job," Ida says. She has been dismissed from four places before the Golden Hem. At the most recent dress shop, she set a bridal gown on fire after leaving the iron on it too long. "Mario and I make just enough as it is, and we have to pay back all that money from the restaurant."

"This is not fair to us," Maddalena says.

"Don't even pretend you're worried for yourself."

Maddalena shrugs. "One of the five doesn't have to be you," she says, folding a piece of wax paper into a square. She stuffs the paper in her purse to reuse and reaches for the extra piece of fruit that Mamma Nunzia, their mother-in-law, throws in "for health." Lunch was a few pieces of roasted chicken and spinach between thick slices of bread, eaten without an appetite.

"You have it easy," Ida says. "We have Nunzia and Nina to worry about. And whatever happens, Papà and Mamma will take care of Antonio. You think they would have given Mario the money to go find a wife in Italy? For the younger son, their pockets are always empty."

Maddalena listens, though she has heard this song from Ida many times before. She and Mario believe that Antonio, the oldest, is the family favorite. Nothing anyone says can change their minds. Mario has invested in one failed family business after another—the Pasticceria Grasso, the Grasso Grocery, Café Grasso—while Antonio has chosen the steady work of the assembly line at the Ford plant. Maddalena does not dare ask Ida why her husband should be punished for making the safer choice, especially since someone has clearly put a curse on the Grasso name.

For now they all live together in a narrow, three-story row house on Eighth Street, in the city of Wilmington, Delaware. The room on the other side of the wall from Maddalena and Antonio's bed belongs to Ida and Mario and their two little girls. Down the hall, out of earshot but never far from Maddalena's thoughts, sleep Mamma Nunzia and Papà Franco. Maddalena has no blood relations on this side of the ocean. For the first eighteen years of her life, she lived in the village of Santa Cecilia, in the mountains of central Italy, with three sisters and three brothers of her own, in a house no smaller than the one that waited for her here. Antonio appeared in Santa Cecilia after the war, started coming around and staying for dinner, sweet-talking. Her mother and sisters told her, "That man will take you to America, stuff your purse with money, and drive you around New York City in a Cadillac," and Maddalena believed them.

"Look in my purse," Ida says now, as Maddalena peels a pear. "Only one piece of fruit for me."

"Don't worry." She cuts the pear in quarters and hands one to her. "Between the two of us, we'll make two hundred. Easy."

Just to be sure, Maddalena works twice as fast. After Mr. Gold passes their tables, when Gloria and Stavroula aren't looking, she slides a pile of material over to Ida's side.

Precisely at three-thirty—the hands of the clock above in exact position—comes the third sign. A sudden cloudiness fills Maddalena's head, and before she can bring her hand to her brow a nausea unlike one she's ever felt bubbles in her stomach. The significance of the time of day strikes her, briefly, as she stands, lets fall the fabric on her lap, and rushes down the aisle to the ladies' room. She makes it in time to vomit into the toilet, crouching so the greasy floor doesn't stain the knees of her stockings. When this happened to her as a child, her mother would kneel beside her, palm her forehead, and smooth her blonde curls around her ear. "Get all the poison out," she'd say; "this is your body cleaning itself." Now her mother sends advice in letters a month too late for it to matter. Now it is Gloria, wheezy and fat, who follows Maddalena into the bathroom and squeezes herself into the stall.

"*Tutto bueno?*" she asks. "You A-OK?" She flushes the toilet and hands her a wad of tissue.

Maddalena wipes her mouth and gets to her feet, keeping her head down. Her legs shake. She is too happy to look at Gloria. She has a new body now, possessed by something holy and powerful. The joyous transformation numbs her. She wants to keep it to herself for as long as she can. As soon as she reveals it—to Gloria, to Ida, even to Antonio—it will no longer belong to her.

But of course Gloria guesses. "You did not eat bad food, I can be sure. You are—" she places her hands over her belly, then brings them out slowly as if the belly is expanding.

Maddalena nods, then looks up. She has prayed for this moment long before the deer and the plastic daisies, and now, finally, it has come.

"How *bella!*" Gloria says, then bursts into a fit of Spanish that Maddalena cannot follow. She wears a thick coat of makeup on her brown skin, big gold earrings that jangle when her head bobs. She guides Maddalena toward the sink and pulls from her sleeve the photos of her two boys—Carlos and Eduardo—that she has already shown her a hundred times. "*Morning* sickness," she says, laughing. "With Carlos it's sickness all the day long." Then she wraps her arms around Maddalena and pulls her close.

She rests her head on Gloria's ample chest. The numbness breaks, and she sobs into her silky blouse, her strong, sweet perfume. Her hunger returns with great force. How she will finish out the day, the week, the next seven months at work, she does not know. Already she is impatient and longs for the baby to hold in her arms and present to Antonio. Already everything has changed.

Gloria strokes her hair. "How much did you sew today?" she asks.

"Sixty-five," Maddalena answers, though the real number is over eighty, not including what she's done for Ida.

"Then relax! Say your prayers. Give thanks to God."

She does. She works the needle slowly and devotes the extra time between stitches to things that, for superstitious reasons, she has not yet allowed herself to consider: the exact words she will use to tell Antonio, names for boys, names for girls, and—at this her hands fail her—the love of someone who belongs to her, someone of her own blood, in this country of strangers.

UNTIL NOW, MADDALENA has not found much beauty in America. But this evening, on the 5:55 back to Wilmington, everything charms her. The streets jammed with cars, the smoke gushing from the engines into the drizzle, the rhythm of wipers on windshields—it is all a symphony composed for her pleasure. Rows of brake lights fade from bright to pale red as the traffic lurches forward. She opens her window halfway, for air, and welcomes the spray of cool rain on her face. The men below stare straight ahead over their steering wheels, then—like the deer—suddenly turn and look up at her as if to catch her watching them. They smile and tick their heads. She wants to know each of them, these hardworking men, and their wives, and their children. She wants to walk across their green lawns. She wants to sit with them at a picnic table under the trees at Lums Pond, bouncing her baby on her lap as they trade stories and jokes and memories of years gone by.

This time of day, Ida can't sit still. She chats with Gloria, who has agreed to keep Maddalena's secret until Antonio hears it for himself. After Gloria's stop, Ida turns all her attention to Maddalena. The Golden Hem is a cage, Ida informs her, and we are birds who need to fly. God did not create women to work in factories; He wants them in the bedroom with their husbands, in the kitchen with their daughters, in the garden with their hands in the soil. Despite this belief, Ida says she will fight to keep her job. If she and Maddalena can't keep up the system they began this morning, she will tell Mr. Gold that Nina, her younger daughter, is going blind and needs an expensive surgery. "God save my soul for lying," says Ida. "But I'll do what I have to do."

Maddalena half listens. The traffic breaks and they cross into their home state of Delaware, different in not one single way from the state of Pennsylvania. The same little brick houses, squat and square, divided by chain link fences, go on for miles. Tall wooden poles, strung with thick black wires and iron bolts, run alongside. If someone had not put up the sign WEL-COME TO DELAWARE, nobody would notice a change. In Italy, Maddalena has said many times, every town has its own distinct face. The church and the piazza are the eyes; the streets and houses are the nose and mouth; and each person is a freckle—or a mole, or a sharp tooth, depending on his personality—that makes a village different from its neighbors. Antonio, who'd eat the dirt from the gutters in America and call it delicious, finds this silly. Maddalena has told him it is because he himself is a pimple.

It surprises her how familiar the landscape has become, how the memories of her village have faded. She reads *albero* in *Il Sogno della Principessa* and sees not an olive tree, but a spruce. Though horses—donkeys, at least—were common as dogs in Santa Cecilia, she takes great delight when a mounted police-man approaches the bus. Any other day, these thoughts of home would sadden her. Until this afternoon, she has felt like the girl on the deck of the ship, weak-kneed and seasick, afraid to let go of the railing.

But that was another autumn evening, colder than this one, seven years ago to the month. October 1946. She watched the sun set on the immense Manhattan buildings and light up the windows bright gold. She longed to share in the joy of the pas-sengers around her, who blew kisses and sang songs, and waved to the shimmering buildings as if they were old friends. Instead she kept silent. She had promised her mother that, no matter how hopeless she felt, she would never let her husband see her cry. They had met less than three months before, and it was still too soon to trouble him.

In New York harbor, Antonio gleefully pointed out land-marks: the Empire State Building, the Chrysler Building, the Brooklyn Bridge, the flurry of names strange and German-sounding. Everything terrified her: the waves licking the side of the boat as it slowed; the birds gathering high in the air then darting down ten at once for the decks. Antonio talked on and on. Look, there was a famous battleship; there was the state called New Jersey; there was the Statue of Liberty on her little island. Maddalena gazed at this statue, the one landmark she recognized from films and postcards. She was like the *Mona Lisa*, she told Antonio a few years later: look at her face when you're sad, and you see sadness in her expression; look at her when hopeful, and she gives hope back to you.

In the car on the way to Wilmington that first day, Maddalena discovered that her new country was, in fact, a land of green, just as Antonio had described: lawns and fields, hills, thick stretches of trees, rows of hedges under windows. Every house, no matter how modest, seemed to own a share of grass and tend it like the plot of a grave. The roads were wide and paved, and the cars rolled over them in patient, orderly rows. In Santa Cecilia, Maddalena's family had owned the only store for miles; here, every block was lined with little shops, each proudly displaying signs with big letters that screamed s-a-l-e!

As Maddalena passed sign after sign, some large and some small, all announcing the same one product—*sale*, salt—she tried to figure out why a country so wealthy would be this proud of such a common ingredient. Then she grew worried. Was salt very expensive here? If so, how would she cook? Or was salt so cheap that everyone tried to give it away? Did Americans use more salt than Italians? She considered asking Antonio, then changed her mind. After he and Mario stopped laughing at her, Antonio would tell some long story about the history of salt in the United States. It occurred to her that she had no one to ask. She kept silent in the backseat, her head against the glass of the window and her hands folded in her lap, panic rising in her chest, and then, for the first time of many, as the SALE! signs flashed by her faster and faster, and Antonio argued with his brother over the best route home, she wept.

"*Ecco*," Ida says now, as the bus makes the turn onto Union

Street. She buttons her coat. "So what do you think, then? Peas?"

"Peas?"

"Or spinach? For dinner."

"Whatever Mamma Nunzia wants," says Maddalena.

"So it'll be cauliflower with vinegar again," she says, with a snort. "One day, it will be me deciding what to cook in my own house. And my Nunzia will have to like it. Don't you look forward like that?"

"Sometimes."

They are up and off the bus, sloshing on the pavement toward Eighth Street. They walk quickly, arm in arm, past the storefronts on Union: the pharmacy, the beauty salon, the shoe repair. At this hour they are all closing, and most of the bread in Lamberti's Bakery has been sold. If she and Ida time it right, though, Signor Lamberti will offer them a bag of leftover rolls to use for their lunches.

After the old man tells them he has not even a burnt loaf to give them tonight, Maddalena says, "Good for him. Someone should make money."

"Why him and not us?" is Ida's reply.

"Him now," Maddalena says. "Us later."

Ida shakes her head. "You are too patient."

Birds circle the bell tower of St. Anthony's, as if waiting for it to ring the hour. The church sits at the top of a broad hill, no wider than a half mile, and looks down on the ten square blocks that form Wilmington's Italian neighborhood. In forty years, long after most of the immigrants have left, a group of merchants will officially designate these blocks "Little Italy." They will commission an archway to demarcate the entrance at Fourth and Lincoln. But in 1953 these blocks are merely a scattering of Italian families who have paid for their relatives to move into the row homes and apartments surrounding them. Antonio calls Wilmington a half city, Philadelphia a real city, New York *the* city. *La Città*, he says, with reverence, never in English. Roma, Milano, Genoa, to him these are dead cities, and Italy the land of dead cities. For the time being, Maddalena finds Wilmington city enough.

She knows the route from the bus stop to the house on Eighth Street, from the house to the church, from the church to Angelo's Market, from the market to the butcher and the produce stand, and home again. She has never set eyes on the four other blocks in this neighborhood, but she imagines they do not differ much from the six she's familiar with: long brick buildings on both sides of the street, each divided into tiny row homes with white wooden columns and concrete stoops. Dormers peek up from the roofs of the nicer houses. The view from Union Street to the church is one unbroken line of red brick. If she wants to see a stone house, Antonio must drive her to Rockford Park, where a wealthy American family has constructed a mansion with a terra-cotta roof. Sometimes, while they sit out front in the parked car with the engine running, admiring the stonework, the American lady comes onto the terrace for a cigarette and waves to them.

But Antonio has not taken Maddalena on a drive for many months, not since she started at the Golden Hem. Her failure to become a mother changed him. He has talked less and less—to everyone, not only to her—and worked longer hours at the plant to earn overtime. When he does talk, it is mostly to argue with his father over how little money he has managed to save. An hour after dinner, Antonio is either asleep or out for one of his long walks. Though she knows where these walks lead—to

Renato's Pizzeria, to play cards and drink whiskey—she also knows how important it is for men to have their secrets. So she plays along. She even went so far as to sew extra padding into his shoes. "So your feet don't hurt," she told him.

She decides to wait until they are alone to tell Antonio the news. She wants the privacy of their bedroom and the rest of the house asleep. He won't arrive home for another hour, but still Maddalena's heart races as she and Ida shake out their rain bonnets on the porch. She walks through the door, and already her mother-in-law is calling her to the kitchen. She has enough time to run upstairs, throw her purse on the bed, then rush back down to help prepare dinner.

The next few hours pass quickly with the night's work. This is the beginning of happiness, Maddalena thinks, as she ladles the minestrone and slices the day-old bread and sweeps up the onion skin that has fallen onto the floor. She says little. Her secret is like a ruby in her pocket; if she looks at her family or her husband too long, she will give it away. And so she is too distracted to notice that Antonio is not himself tonight. Before she can clear his coffee cup and ask him to come to bed early, he is gone.

2

Dirty Eyes

So the girl, Cassie, has returned to Fourth and Orange. She sits barefoot on the counter of the pizzeria in a pair of shorts and one of Renato's white T-shirts. No brassiere. When she sees Antonio, she lifts her leg and wiggles her toes hello.

Just what I need, Antonio thinks. He considers turning back. But it's too late, and he has nowhere else to go.

"Look who it is," he says, and kisses her on both cheeks. She has not changed at all in two years: same skinny frame, lips thin and pale, stringy red hair to her shoulders, those strange V-shaped indentations—like bird tracks—on her neck. The T-shirt covers most of the tracks, but Antonio and Renato and at least two other men who work here have seen how far south the bird has hopped. More than once, Antonio has traced the pattern down to her navel with his tongue.

"I'm back for good this time," Cassie says. "Right, Renato?"

She swings around and catches him between her legs. He flicks some flour at her face, then kisses her.

"Open up," he says, with a laugh. He still wears his apron. "I have work to do."

Cassie releases him, but not without a playful kick to his behind. Renato walks to the front, flips the sign to CLOSED, and locks the door. It is 9:30. On his way up the aisle, he shrugs and raises his eyebrows at Antonio as if to say, "I'm as surprised as you are."

I give it a week, Antonio thinks, and flashes Cassie a friendly smile.

Antonio does not want Maddalena to know he still comes here. It means little to her that Renato Volpe has been his best friend for more than ten years, that he trusts the man more than his own brother. According to Maddalena, Antonio does not need a friend who still lives with a roommate at thirty-five, refuses to get married, and spends Saturday nights driving up and down Market Street in his big white car. "Lucky for you those days are over," she has told him, matter-of-factly, on more occasions than he cares to remember. "You need more friends like Gianni Martino."

But Gianni Martino is asleep by nine o'clock, about the time Antonio finishes his dinner and announces that he's going out for some air. Gianni is in bed with his wife, snoring and getting fat, as Antonio passes his little brick duplex on the way to Fourth and Orange. Gianni will not pour Antonio a shot of whiskey and tell him stories about the three Polish sisters who share a house in Browntown. He will not have a new girl every week to remind Antonio how it felt to be twenty-three and single, when, in charmingly broken English, he'd convinced more than a few of them to follow him up the back stairs of the pizzeria. It is not a crime, at thirty-two, after a long day at work, to talk and drink with your friends and tease the girls for a few hours. If it costs him no money and settles his nerves, if it does not diminish his love for Maddalena, he sees no harm in it.

"Cassie has a job now," Renato says. "She's learning the cash register."

"The first Irish girl to work in this place, to be sure," she says.

"Downstairs, at least," says Buzzy, under his breath. Buzzy is a German Jew brought over by the Federation after his parents were killed in the camps. Antonio and Renato met him at Wilmington High School, where they took night classes in English. Now he works half-time at Kaminski's Furniture on Route 13 and the other half in the pizzeria doing the books. He splits the rent on the upstairs apartment with Renato.

"She's going straight," Renato says, from behind a stack of trays he's wiping down behind the grill. "As of tonight, so am I."

"It's a new era for us all," Buzzy says. "Just last Saturday I was telling the three girls in my car, 'One of you lucky ladies might be the first Mrs. Bernard Fisher,' and for most of the night I actually believed it. We all want to be family men like you, Antonio."

Buzzy is short, with perfect curly hair. According to Renato, he spends an hour each morning trimming his beard and fingernails. Once, Renato caught him applying some sort of cream to his knees and elbows. No one has ever called Buzzy handsome, but he has had more women than Antonio can count. One— whose name might be Marcie—stands beside him now, taller by a head, and gently rubs the back of his neck as he speaks. Somehow, Buzzy has convinced Marcie they have a future together.

Antonio has never cheated on his wife. Maddalena's body— her skin smooth and unblemished; her shy compliance, which, with just a little encouragement, gives way to a restrained eagerness—still thrills him. Next to her, American women are cheap and loud; there is something coarse about them. They sit backward in their chairs, smoke cigarettes between their thumb and forefinger, swing their arms too wide when they walk. They are like horses, Antonio has said, while Maddalena—most women from Italy, but Maddalena in particular—is graceful as a deer. *Elegant* is the word. He has an elegant wife. She has made it easy these seven years to honor the vows he made to her in the church of Santa Cecilia. They had both been born in that village, seven years apart, and whenever he's tempted by another woman he reminds himself that Maddalena alone has tasted the mountain air of his boyhood. No American girl, however pretty, has eaten olives from the grove outside his bedroom window or played hide-and-seek among those silvery leaves; she has not climbed to the top of the chestnut tree to snicker at old Don Paolo sunbathing in the wheat field; she does not know anything at all about where he came from. Most of the time, these reminders are enough.

Lately, though, a restlessness has plagued him. His trips to the pizzeria three or four times a week, once a luxury, have become necessary. He does not want to admit his pang of disappointment upon seeing Cassie back with Renato. He worries about what he might have done if Cassie offered herself to him instead, what he might still do one night if he drinks too much and one of Buzzy's girls puts her hand on his knee.

He traces the start of this restlessness—the quick temper, the sleepless nights, the lure of girls he'd once dismissed—to the day he sent Maddalena to work. It seemed wrong from the first, his wife on a bus with strangers and coloreds, in a factory taking orders from another man. None of this bothered Mario, whose wife had been finding and losing jobs for years, but it weighed on Antonio. He applied for the late shift at Bancroft Mill so Maddalena could quit, but the job was not offered to him. Mr. Hannagan, his supervisor at Ford, refused to give him additional overtime. It was then when he began to dread those useless hours between dinner and sleep, caged in the living room with his father, the only sound the kitchen chatter and the drone of the radio. When he could escape his father's constant questions—what did he think of Eisenhower? this year's new Chevrolet models? the price of gasoline?—he'd rest his elbow on the counter beside Maddalena as she dried dishes and tell her with his eyes to come upstairs. He'd make love to her with an aggressiveness he had not shown in the past, as if to convince her that he was doing more than his part to make a baby. Afterward, while she resumed her work in the kitchen, he'd lie on his back with his arms behind his head, wearing only his socks and shirtsleeves, and blame himself. After all, it could be his own defect that prevented the pregnancy, since Dr. Barone had conducted a series of tests and found nothing wrong with Maddalena. Antonio would examine his body, bring the hand mirror to the curious discoloration on his inner thigh for closer inspection, and wonder fearfully why he had been put on this Earth if not to bring forth children.

He could take little more of this, so that summer he paid his first visit in three years to Renato and Buzzy. They welcomed him back with a seat at their card table and tales of the single life in Wilmington. Their greatest joy came from picking fights—over politics, family, girls, anything to get Antonio's blood to boil. It didn't take much, and Maddalena was their favorite target. They teased him for setting her loose in a city full of men, asked him how often she mentioned her Jewish boss, how long she took to put on her makeup before she left for work. "You think Italian men are bad with women," Buzzy told him, "but the Jews are worse. We can't get enough. It's like a sickness. If I ever get married, I won't let any Jew near my wife."

"The kind of girl who'd marry you," said Antonio, with a grin. "I'm sure it won't be hard to keep them away."

On only one occasion did Antonio bring Maddalena to Renato's Pizzeria. It was early in their marriage, not long after she'd arrived in America. She wore a hat, one of her fancier dresses, and a long coat with fur on the collars. She clutched her purse and stood stiffly beside Antonio as he guided her around the tables packed with teenagers in jeans and leather jackets. Renato rushed out to greet them and kissed her hand. "The famous Maddalena," he said in Italian. "What an honor! Nobody here thinks you can be real, the way Antonio describes you. But now we must apologize for calling him a liar." In the corner booth, a group of teenaged girls—Cassie among them—kept whispering and giggling, as Maddalena stared at the floor. Afterward, though Renato fixed them a generous plate of antipasti then insisted they return for a proper dinner in his apartment, Maddalena declared that she did not trust him.

"He has *occhi sporchi*," she said. Dirty eyes. "Tell me you won't go back to that place too much, not as long as we're husband and wife." He promised he would not and assured her that he had no need for Renato now that he was a married man. He'd taken her to visit the pizzeria only out of respect for their friendship, he explained. They walked arm in arm down Orange Street, had a good laugh at it all, and for a while Antonio believed he'd never see Renato or Buzzy again.

But now here he is, in his usual seat at the table behind the counter. He arranges his coins in neat stacks, Buzzy shuffles the cards, and Renato leans back in his chair with his hands on his stomach like he's just eaten a juicy steak.

Cassie sets down a whiskey and water for Antonio. "I've been looking for you at Mrs. Stella's" she says. "Your brother doesn't give you my regards?"

Mrs. Stella's is Mario's latest adventure, an Italian restaurant he opened that spring with two men from the neighborhood. He could not invest enough to get Grasso in the name, and that simple fact may explain its success.

"I don't go there too often," Antonio says.

"The food's not so hot," Cassie says. "No offense to your brother, but Renato here serves the best Italian food in Delaware. What Mrs. Stella's does have, though, is a bar."

"And a crowd," Renato says. "Makes my heart sick." He shakes his head and looks at Antonio. "I hate to repeat myself, my friend, but your brother has become the enemy. If he puts me out of business—"

"I hardly go there anymore, baby," Cassie interrupts. "I'll tell all my friends about the roaches in the kitchen."

"There are roaches in the kitchen?" asks Antonio, his eyebrows raised.

"Don't get too excited," Cassie says. "I made it up."

Antonio does not want his brother's restaurant to fail. He simply distrusts any success that comes too quickly, before it is earned. He is not jealous, no matter what anybody thinks. He believes in balance, that each member of a family should have as much money as another, that any disproportion only causes problems. Antonio's pride will not allow him to work for Mario, though he has offered many times. Not even to spare Maddalena her job at the factory will Antonio put on an apron or wash dishes for his brother.

"Antonio wants Mrs. Stella's for himself," Renato says, as he studies his cards. "Am I wrong?"

"Yes, as a matter of fact you are."

"I don't think so," Renato says. He picks up a four and a three of diamonds with the seven of spades. Always lucky. Antonio has little respect for this Italian game, *scopa*, which he's played for as long as he can remember. Anyone who gets the right cards can win. He prefers poker, learned only recently, which requires strategy, discipline, and more than a passing attention.

Antonio turns to Cassie and Buzzy. "Now Renato will tell you how we almost went in together on this pizzeria," he says. "Because you've only heard that story a thousand times. He forgets that was ten years ago, when I was young, when I had no wife or children." He takes a sip of whiskey.

"You don't regret not owning half of this dump?" asks Buzzy.

"Not a bit."

"You should have seen this man, Cassie," says Renato. "He never slept. He had all the best ideas. He used to draw diagrams of the restaurant with crayons and tape them to my walls. He wanted to call it La Bella Trattoria: Renato Volpe and Antonio Grasso, Proprietors."

"La Bella Trattoria, for short," says Antonio.

"What about Bella T's," Cassie suggests, "So people could pronounce it?"

Renato ignores her. "Then, when it came to sign the papers, his feet got cold. So I put up one hundred percent of the money myself, and now"—he winks at Cassie—"we all know who gets one hundred percent of the profits. And his name on the sign."

"And one hundred percent of the glory," Buzzy says. He opens his arms, and they laugh.

The cinder-block walls of the pizzeria are painted white and covered with various maps of Italy torn from encyclopedias. The dining area is crowded with cheap wood tables, most of which tip when you rest your elbows on them. The only luxury lies in the newly installed leather of the six booths along the far wall, but the leather has already faded and torn at the seams. The customers don't seem to mind. Day after day they sit, eat their slices of pizza, and wave to Renato and his cooks as they stand sweating in the open kitchen.

"You call it a dump," Cassie says, "but to me it's a palace." She leans across the table to plant a kiss on Renato's lips. "There's nowhere else I'd rather be. Not even the bar at Mrs. Stel—Mrs. *Roach*'s."

"So loyal these days," says Buzzy, under his breath.

Antonio has grander visions—far beyond this place, beyond Mrs. Stella's, beyond even the crayon diagrams from ten years ago. He has not told anyone about them. He sees a band, a dance floor, a flagstone courtyard. He sees white linen tablecloths on tables under vases of fresh flowers, wood floors shiny enough to give back a reflection. The men wear sport jackets; the women remove their fur wraps to reveal glittering jewelry; they know Antonio by name and ask for their usual tables. No such place exists in Wilmington, but the city is crying out for one.

"You still working at the car place?" Cassie asks.

"Good memory," says Antonio. "Ford Motor Company. Fifteen hours a day fitting armrests on next year's models."

"What a waste of time," Renato says, shaking his head. "And you know it. Yours is a sad story."

"Do I look sad?" Antonio says, defensively. Then he steadies himself. Renato is baiting him, and he does not want to give him the satisfaction of falling for it.

Cassie reaches across Renato, thrusting her chest in his face, to turn up the Julius La Rosa record. They play a few tricks of *scopa* as she hums along to "Anywhere I Wander." One by one they express their solidarity with La Rosa, who was recently fired live from the Arthur Godfrey Show by Godfrey himself. Only Antonio saw the actual broadcast. "Talk about someone who should be sad," he says. "But did he let it show? Did he start blubbering there in front of the audience? No—that's what you call class."

"Class and elegance," says Cassie. "*That's* what I remember most about you, Antonio Grasso. You talk more about class and elegance than any man I ever met."

Antonio shrugs. "Do I?"

"I've got my eye on a new place," Renato says, to no one in particular. "Corner of New Castle Avenue and Riverview Drive." He marks the score on a guest check and shuffles the cards. "It's got two big rooms, with marble columns in the middle. Elegant. Very much in the style of Antonio."

"You're not moving the pizzeria?" asks Antonio. "Or is this a new place all together?"

"That's up to you, maybe," says Renato. "Listen. I have an idea I think you'll like." He deals the cards, three to each player. "We all know the time has come for you to quit being a slave to Ford Motor Company and work with me. Two thousand dollars is all I need for this place on Riverview, this place that's more Antonio than Renato. Two thousand dollars and it's mine. Ours. Trattoria Renato. What do you say?" He holds up his hand. "And before you make a stink about the name, let me tell you we have to keep Renato in there somewhere for a reason, so people know to expect the same quality they get here. I learned that from a magazine. Plus, it's common sense."

Antonio stares at his cards. He knows this space on Riverview; Renato brought him to it five years ago, the first time he considered opening a second location. It had a parking lot, a stone front and brand-new ovens. The back windows faced an empty lot, which could be landscaped with a little effort. His heart races. Can Renato be serious, or is this just sweeter bait?

He drops a three of spades, and Renato immediately snaps up another seven, diamonds this time. Finally Antonio says, "Sure, *uaglio*. I'm in. Do you want the cash now—it's right here in my pocket—or should I bring a check over in the morning?"

"Joke all you want," Renato says. "But the offer is real."

Nobody says anything. The record ends, and the only sound is the slap of the mop on the tile floor. Paolo, Renato's teenaged nephew, pushes and pulls his way around the front room, looking up only now that the conversation has stopped.

As Buzzy deals the next hand, Antonio breaks the silence. "It's a temptation, my friend. I admit it. But those days are over for me. I need work that's more steady."

"What do you think this is?" says Renato. "Once we get the customers, the money pours from the walls like a fountain! We'll set a schedule for you, no more than fifty hours a week. You'll have to work some nights, some weekends, holidays, but come ten o'clock, aren't you here anyway? You might as well get paid to sit and lose at *scopa*."

"He's right, you know," Buzzy says. "You can't go wrong with this one."

"Then where's your money?"

"Renato asked me the same thing. I told him—Marcie was

there, you remember, gorgeous?" The girl nods as she continues to massage his shoulders. "I said, 'Renato, my dear friend, I'm a worker, not a leader. The last thing I want in life is more responsibility. Tell me what to do, I'll do it right, then good-bye. I want to leave at the end of the day with nothing on my mind.'"

Renato listens, chewing on a toothpick. "So now I know," he says.

"Well then, I am the same," says Antonio.

"Bullshit," Renato says. "In your heart, you're a boss. You have ideas. Like me. A supervisor. I see that very clearly. And I bet if we asked the lovely Maddalena, she would agree."

Antonio laughs. "She can't stand me here for one minute playing cards," he says. "I want to see her face when I tell her Renato Volpe is now my business partner."

Cassie points at him. "That's the real reason, I'll bet. Otherwise—"

Blood rushes to Antonio's face. "There's no real reason," he says. "There are a hundred reasons. Two thousand reasons!"

"Let's drop it for now," says Renato, handing him a cigar from the front pocket of his shirt. "I'm not trying to make you angry. Give yourself some time to think. Have a smoke. Talk to your wife, maybe, maybe not. I'll say this, though—" He leans forward. His eyes are wide and hopeful as a boy's. "It's not every day your dream falls into your lap."

An hour later, Antonio is too drunk to focus on his cards. He declares it time to leave, kisses Cassie and Marcie on the cheek, then takes the long way home to walk off the whiskey. The downtown streets are quiet. A man unloads boxes from a truck in front of Angelo's Market; another walks his dog through the gated park near St. Anthony's. Antonio coughs to get the man's attention, then waves when he looks up. No response. Shadows move, as if in a procession, across the dark windows of the rectory, and Antonio wonders if it's some midnight ritual for the priests. He stops on Union and peeks into Mrs. Stella's, but the lights are off and even Mario has gone. A gust of wind shakes the two evergreen bushes planted on either side of the stoop, and a Coca-Cola bottle rolls in circles on the sidewalk. Antonio picks up the bottle and stuffs it onto the top branch of the bush. "Merry Christmas," he says, and turns for home.

What might this little half city become, with his help? Maybe it is the whiskey, but Antonio is suddenly filled with love for these ten square blocks of brick and concrete. It is all his for the taking. He loves the broad slope of the hill, the hundreds—maybe thousands—of Italians who've become his neighbors since he moved here in '36. He loves the smell of bread from Lamberti's; the red, white, and green flags that hang in the storefront windows. At sunrise, not long from now, the old men will set up their folding chairs on the street corners and spend the morning arguing politics in their *campani* dialects. Whenever he wants to, Antonio can shut his eyes and easily pretend that this is the village of his childhood, and then, better still, he can open his eyes and find not donkeys or dirt roads, but highways and cars and department stores. And possibility. With the right people and enough money, he can turn a place like Renato's or Mrs. Stella's into a destination for people as far away as Philadelphia or New York. It can all start right here, with his own people. If he doesn't try this now, when he's still young, then when?

He sits on the curb across the street from his house and tosses cigarette butts into the sewer grate, too restless, his mind at too fast a gallop, to lie beside Maddalena and risk waking her with his anxious fidgeting. He gazes up at the light in their bedroom window. The rest of the houses on their street are dark. Maybe she is waiting up for him. He breathes into his cupped hands to check his breath. Only a faint trace of whiskey.

Two tall shadows walk toward him in the glow of the city. They slow as they get closer, then stop and turn back the way they came. Their cigarettes flicker. Another man with a dog crosses in front of them. A car circles the next block, then appears twice more. He wonders if God is testing him, if He has sent this car around and around to say, That's you, Antonio Grasso, stuck, like your friend Gianni, on the same dizzy loop. Renato can help you escape.

If Antonio does this, he will have to move slowly. The next time he is alone and sober with Maddalena in their bedroom, he will confess his dream of owning a restaurant. At dinner soon after, he will mention the space on New Castle Avenue, in passing, to test the reaction of his family. No doubt Maddalena will start asking questions, at which point he will pretend not to have given the matter much thought. He will drop more hints, and soon she will think the idea is hers, and beg him to take the money from the drapes and put it toward the trattoria. She will quit the Golden Hem and work as a hostess. The place should be elegant enough for her, somewhere to show off her shiny dresses, the gold jewelry her mother sent, her charmingly broken English. She will be proud of him and this gift to the city. At this moment, as Antonio crosses Eighth Street toward his father's house, it seems their best chance for a happy life.

3

The Silence Game

MADDALENA WATCHES ANTONIO from the window. For the past half hour, he has sat on the curb in front of the sewer, his head in his hands. She will soothe whatever troubles him, whatever drove him from the house without a good-bye. He worries too much about money, she thinks: what to spend it on, how much to save, how long before they can move out of these six little rooms. Money has worried her, too; but if only he'd come upstairs, she'd tell him how little it matters anymore. She inches away from the windowsill, crawls back into bed, and waits.

The smell of cigars reaches her before the man himself. Another night at Renato's, she guesses, with whiskey and cards and loud cursing over politics. The only resistance she has shown to this has been to tell him that his shirts stink and should be aired out before he puts them back in the closet. Secretly, she has felt relieved not to be forced to entertain him during those long after-dinner hours. She can take her time with the dishes, sit for a while and talk to Mamma Nunzia, write letters, then turn the bedroom radio on low and fall asleep to the music.

Antonio seems surprised—happy, even—to find her awake. He kisses her forehead and sits beside her on the edge of the bed, still in his coat and hat. She wears her best nightgown, an ivory satin to which he pays immediate attention. He runs his hand over the sheer fabric, then under it, from her knee to her thigh. "How can it be that every day you get more beautiful?" he says.

"Because you're getting old," she says. "Your eyesight's not so good."

As he disrobes—throwing his shirt in one direction, his pants in another—he declares the weather too cold for October, the bedroom too drafty, and the city asleep too early. Even in the village, he says, the Al Di Là Café stayed open for hours past midnight, and the people kept coming.

He repeats the same story he told at dinner, about a man he works with at the Ford plant. The man was joking around with a blowtorch, waving it above his head as if it were a flag, and by the end of the joke he'd burnt off his left earlobe and half an eyebrow.

"I tell you," Maddalena says, thinking, this is one of his talking nights. "Americans have no common sense."

He climbs into bed and immediately starts another story, this one about his boss, Mr. Hannagan, who took his wife to Mrs. Stella's last week for her birthday dinner. After the wife spent the rest of the night with her head in the toilet, Mr. Hannagan demanded his money back. Mario refused, saying it was not his fault his wife had an "overdelicate constitution."

"Whatever that means," Antonio says. "So now I have to pay the whole bill myself and pretend Mario changed his mind. Just to keep in good with a boss at a stupid going-nowhere job." He turns to Maddalena. "You know, if I ran a place like Mrs. Stella's, we'd get one complaint only: not enough tables. Or: the food's so good, I can't eat at home anymore. Sometimes I wonder how my brother got so lucky."

Before he can start another story, Maddalena takes his hand. "You don't wonder why I waited up?" she asks.

He looks at her. "You missed me?" he says, and laughs. "You thought, 'I want to hear that story about the blowtorch again?'" Then his face changes. "Nothing happened, did it?"

"Yes," she says. "Something good. Mario is not the only lucky one." She squeezes his hand, guides it to her stomach, and nods. "We don't have to worry anymore."

A flash of joy, the corners of his mouth in a natural smile. His eyes brighten. The room, too, seems to fill with light.

Then his face freezes. He narrows his gaze at her and sits up against the wrought-iron bars of the headboard. "Now?" he asks.

She hesitates. "I'm almost sure." She starts to recount the signs, the most recent one first. The bathroom. Gloria. The lullaby. But they sound silly, unconvincing. She stops before she gets to the deer.

He turns his face toward the opposite wall. For a long time, he does not move or speak. Maddalena focuses on the birthmark on the back of his neck, a pink blotch in the shape of an almond. When he's angry, the blotch turns red.

He is angry.

"You're my wife for seven years, and no baby," he says. "Then you go to work for the Jew and *poof!* there's a baby now?"

Maddalena pulls the sheet up to her waist. "What do you—" she starts to ask, then stops herself when she realizes the implication. She almost laughs, but Antonio's face has gone dark. "I think I'm more relaxed," she says, remembering what her mother told her in her letters: *every nail you bite is one more month without a child*.

Antonio does not wrap his arms around her the moment he hears the news. He does not throw open the window and sing to God and wake the neighbors. He does not run downstairs to get the bottle of *spumante* they have kept in the refrigerator for just this occasion. Instead he stands in his shirtsleeves and underwear and paces from the bed to the window, hands on his hips. "I have to think," he says. "I wasn't ready for this. Not tonight."

"I don't understand," she says. "How can you not be ready?"

He puts his fingers to his temples as if to stop a sharp pain.

"Whatever idea you have, I can tell you right now it's crazy." She laughs. "If this is one of your jokes—"

"Do I look like I'm joking?"

"But it doesn't make sense."

"You're right," he says, standing against the far wall. "It doesn't at all. For so many years we want a baby, and there is no baby. Then, just when we give up, when we think, 'maybe it's not meant to be,' and we start to dream of something else, a different kind of life, here comes the baby."

He has not slapped her. In fact, he has kept his distance and spoken barely above a whisper. But she feels as though his hand has struck her face.

"I didn't know you gave up," she says. "What kind of life are you dreaming about? What kind of life doesn't have a child in it?"

"Never mind," he says. "What's done is done." He goes to the drapes, stands on his toes, and pulls out the wad of bills wrapped in a rubber band. He divides the bills into stacks on the dresser. "All this—we'll need every dollar—more—"

"That's what we decided," says Maddalena. "Right? We save enough for the baby, and then whatever is left we use on a house."

He counts the stacks again. "I don't remember anything being decided," he says. "Except now I decide you'll never step foot in that factory again. You're staying home like a normal wife. Ida will tell the Jew tomorrow."

Until this threat to keep her from the Golden Hem, Maddalena has never considered that she might miss it. She thinks of the competition, which Ida will surely lose without her. Then, evenly, she says, "I have to work." She looks up at him. "Ida needs me. And we need the money. And I'm good at it."

He stands motionless at the foot of the bed, looking down at the length of her body the way he looks at meat when she undercooks it. Antonio likes everything burnt through, with a charcoal crust, and when it doesn't turn out right, he glares at it until it is taken away.

"Tell me what kind of life you're dreaming about," she says, but he does not respond. His gaze pins her in place. "Talk to me." After a while, she adds, "Please."

But Antonio, like most men, fights best with silence. In recent years, Maddalena has worked up the courage to scream at him, call him *disgraziato* and slam the door just as he approached it. She has locked herself for hours in this bedroom and cried. She has even caught the shoe he pitched at her from across the kitchen, thrown it back at his face, shaken her fists; but she has never won the silence game once he began it. She has only outlasted it. And now it begins again.

He puts on his pants. His belt jingles. He puts on his shoes without sitting down, and keeps his back to her. He kicks a pillow out of the way to get to the door.

"Where are you going this time?" she says. "Back to that dirty pizzeria?"

She closes her eyes and listens to his footsteps on the stairs and the slam of the front screen door. She hurries to the window to see which direction he's walking, but she sees only the two colored boys. They have taken their usual spot on the curb, where Antonio sat not long before, and pass a cigarette back and forth. She waits at the window until it grows too cold, then returns to the bed and wraps herself in the covers. It is past midnight. In five hours, she will have to rise and dress for work.

If she were back in Santa Cecilia, if this joy had happened there, her mother and sisters would be sitting around her, weighing down the bed, not letting her sleep. They would put on some music. Teresa would feed her beef from her husband's butcher shop, for strength; Celestina would say how much better men liked their wives once they got fat. Her mother would refuse to admit she'd felt pain delivering any of her seven children, and remind Maddalena of the beauty of bringing life into the world. Now her mother and sisters exist only in letters, in the few photographs they send after weddings and baptisms.

She reaches over and switches off the lamp. What good do comparisons do her—the new country, the old; his family, hers? She is cursed with comparisons. She has one country now, one family. She does not even have memories anymore, only these fantasies of what might have been if Antonio had never come for her. It no longer matters that she had another man—a boy really—in Santa Cecilia, someone who loved her and whom she loved in return. It no longer matters that, had she chosen him, she would not be here, alone in a bed by a drafty window, longing to hear his footsteps on the stairs. She has prayed to God to wipe her mind clean of the boy and every memory of the village—to give her a moment, at least, of rest—but so far He has not answered. Now, maybe, the child will help.

As husbands go, she reminds herself, she is lucky with Antonio. He works hard. He does not beat her, unlike many husbands she knows here and in the Old Country. Once this storm ends, he will make a devoted father. He knows about things of which she is ignorant: politics, geography, the price of electricity and heating oil. She cannot even write a check or remember their phone number. Most of the time, Antonio has a calming, confident voice, which he frequently uses to brag about her beauty. Just last week his friend Gianni described Maddalena as an Italian Marilyn Monroe, and Antonio had blushed with pride. (She has to admit a resemblance, in the hair and face at least; God has not been as generous with the chest.) Then later, after too much wine, Antonio called her "my Marilyn" and grabbed her by the waist as she cleared the dishes. "Don't go back to Hollywood, Signora Monroe," he begged, and buried his face in the small of her back. She stood trapped at the table with her hands full, smiling, and shook her head at his family gathered around them. "Stay with me in this humble house."

She calls that evening to mind, then, here in her satin nightgown: shimmying free of his hands on her hips, her quick flirtatious look back, catching his eye as she turned the corner into the kitchen. She replays this scene until sleep takes her, and when she wakes she will join in the silence game for as long as she can bear it.

ANTONIO MOVES SOUNDLESSLY through the house. He does not insist that Maddalena stay home from work. He does not say anything to her at all. She sets out his clothes as usual, but does not ask him which shirt he prefers. He dresses and undresses without a glance in her direction. With the rest of the family they act as if nothing has changed, and for two days no one seems to notice the wall of ice between them.

"When did you plan to tell me?" Ida asks Maddalena on the third day, as the bus turns off Union, and suddenly everything is out in the open. "I'm not the smartest lady in the world, but I think I'd notice sooner or later. Maybe when you started stealing my maternity clothes?"

"I'm sorry," Maddalena says. "How did you—"

"Last night Antonio went to the restaurant and kept Mario at the bar for an hour, talking and asking questions. Then this morning, when you were downstairs, he asked me, out of nowhere: 'How tall is this Jew boss of yours? Where does he live?' He asked me how much he talks to you, and I said 'not much.' He thinks if he asks me enough times I will slip up, that I know what's going on but won't tell him."

"What's going on," says Maddalena, with a roll of her eyes. "Nothing is going on! When I tell him that, he looks right through me. I don't know what I'm supposed to do. I can't stop him from thinking something so crazy."

Ida shakes her head.

"He sends me to work, but doesn't trust me," Maddalena continues. "And Papà is on his side, I'm sure. He always thinks the same as his son, and even if Mamma Nunzia disagrees, she can do nothing. So I'm all alone."

"You're not alone," says Ida. "You just don't know what it's like for him. When he sees his son or his daughter, he will change. You wouldn't believe it was the same Mario before I had my Nunzia. I was like one of his hats—if you didn't remind him he had one, he'd get all wet. Believe me, sooner or later Antonio will talk to you again, and you'll remember the days when he didn't talk, and you'll think, that wasn't so bad after all. He's just embarrassed now."

Maddalena removes her coat and settles it on her lap. She is sweating in the overheated bus and the glare of the window seat. The morning is bright and cold, and the last leaves of the season cling to the roadside trees. The frost crusted along the bottom edge of the windows begins to melt.

When they reach her stop, Gloria enters with another large package addressed to her mother in Cuba. She takes a seat across from them, looks quizzically at Maddalena and asks, *"Tutto bueno?"*

"Sì, sì," Maddalena says, with a wave of her hand. She nods toward Ida. "She knows."

"Finally!" Gloria says. "It's bad luck to hide happy news."

Ida turns her back to Gloria. "He wrote to us from Genoa," she continues in Italian, "when you were on your honeymoon. He said that when you finally came to live with us, you'd be carrying the baby you made in the Old Country. He wanted the baby more than the wife—excuse me for saying the truth. And he still believed there was a baby, even when you stayed skinny. He told everyone at his work. For six years they've been teasing him, 'Antonio, where is this son of yours? You still hiding your daughter from us?' Men get embarrassed easy; you're smart enough to know that."

"But do I know how to have a baby?" Maddalena says. "Do I know why God waited this long? I think, 'It's because you don't like it enough when you're in bed together,' so I try to like it more, but I'm not—" She stops, sure she's said too much, not sure she means it. On Ida's face is the look of someone not used to hearing ugly things. In English, Maddalena says: "I love my husband, Ida. I can't love him more than I already do."

"Of course."

Maddalena learned early on that, though Ida is her one sister-in-law and closest friend in this new country, she cannot rely on her for comfort. She can tell Ida half, at most, of what she feels, and hope her dim mind prevents her from guessing the rest. In the House of Ida, Antonio has said, there is no furniture or lights or decoration. Only double-thick walls and a front door that sticks. La Genia, Antonio calls her. The genius. Sometimes Maddalena envies her—this woman who never swims below the surface of life, who believes whatever she is told.

"So I work," Maddalena continues, "and I calm down a little because it feels good to make some money, and it's nice to see the city every day and to sit with you on the bus and watch the people go by, and now, all of a sudden, that's too much for him. When do I have time for another man, Ida? When? It doesn't make sense!"

"Please keep your voice down." She looks around the bus. Gloria raises her eyebrows, makes an exaggerated frown. "I believe you, but, as you know, I don't count."

"It's strange," Maddalena says, her face turned toward the window. "I don't want to quit my job. I'm used to it. Did you ever think I'd say that?"

At the Golden Hem, Maddalena works as quickly as her hands allow. It is the only way to occupy her mind. The week of competition passes slowly. Mr. Gold walks up and down the aisles, quiet and serious as a judge now that he's made rivals of his little ladies. He looks twice at the pile on Ida's table but won't admit his pleasant surprise. Or maybe it is obvious what they are up to, and he is giving her false hope. Whatever the case, Maddalena does not care. She will play along until he tells her otherwise.

The race ends on Friday, two weeks before Thanksgiving, when word ripples across the rows of tables that Mr. Gold has fired two Polish women, two new Americans on the other side of the room, and Gloria.

He stands at Gloria's table with his head down, shifting his weight from side to side.

Before she starts to cry, he hands her a tissue from his shirt pocket. "Now I have nothing," she says. "Now I jump off the Memorial Bridge."

"My situation could change after Christmas," Mr. Gold tells her, with a softness he's not shown in the months Maddalena has known him. His hand rests on her shoulder. "If you're still looking for work in January, don't forget me."

Before she leaves, Gloria writes her phone number and address on a slip of paper, hands it to Maddalena, and wishes her and the baby good health. She makes Maddalena promise to visit her. "Come cheer me up," she says, "before the little one comes. And after, too. You'll be fat and I'll be skinny from starving." To Ida she says nothing.

"You'll find a job before December," Maddalena assures her.

Each morning now, when the bus reaches Gloria's stop, Maddalena crosses herself and says a prayer. She still expects Gloria to walk down the aisle balancing one of those giant packages on her hip. People disappear so quickly, she thinks, as the strangers take their seats, the doors snap closed, and the bus charges ahead in a cloud of smoke. She is never prepared for it, though it has happened to her again and again, in two countries, with and without warning. And she never remembers, from one person to the next, how much easier life would be if she didn't care.

4

Giulio Called Julian

"GIULIO!" CALLS SIGNORA Stella, from his front porch. She carries a pan of lasagna, enough to last him a week. It is just past ten in the morning, and she has woken him from a particularly mysterious dream.

"Giulio Fabbri!" she calls again. She bangs her fist on the door, tries the broken bell, then shakes her head and leaves the pan on the top step. He watches her shuffle down Seventh Street in her winter coat and slippers. Not until she crosses Lincoln will he dare retrieve her gift.

For nine full months he has been an orphan, and still the old ladies bring him food. Now he will have to pay Signora Stella a long, somber visit to return her pan. She will sit him at her kitchen table and brag about her daughter's house in New Castle and the successful restaurant her son Gino has opened in her honor. "Forty is still young," she'll tell him, and point her finger at his face. "Don't let anybody tell you your life is over."

To avoid all this, a few days later he writes *Mille Grazie* on a slip of paper, signs it, and tapes it to the empty pan. When the neighborhood goes dark, he sets out for the Stella house, leaves the pan at the front door, and sneaks back home. He wonders if Signora Stella will even notice the new name, Julian, that he has used on the note. All year he has practiced the bow-tie loops of the American *J*, first on thank-you cards for the guests who'd attended his father's funeral, then on the checks he mailed to the power company and the government. He wants everyone to see hope—rebirth is the word—in the flourish of the American letter, in the embrace of the new country. Not betrayal. Not a rejection of his parents or the good Fabbri line. He has been a good son. He cannot be accused of disrespect.

No, Julian did not bang his fists on his father's casket, after the lid was closed and he'd seen his face for the last time. He believes that grief, like love, should be a private thing. Calmly he shook the hands of his family friends, endured the women's cold, wet cheeks pressed to his face, and invited them all back to the house for lunch, the whole time keeping in mind the words of his favorite American thinker, Ralph Waldo Emerson: "I grieve that grief can teach me nothing." Impassively Julian listened to Gino Stella's long, jumbled, half-remembered story of his father's winning fifty dollars on a horse called Fly Me Home. "Any name that reminded him of an airplane, your father would bet on it," said Gino, to a chorus of agreement among the other men in the room. "Don't ask me how much he lost on that stinker Sky's the Limit. I tell you, the only tragedy in the life of Ernesto Fabbri was that he never saw an airplane from the inside. He had a good wife, a son with intelligence, a decent job, plenty of money—but he'd have given them all up to fly cross-country in a Connie." Julian nodded and scratched his beard. He put his arms around Gino and thanked him for his words. Not until the last guest departed did he stand at the open refrigerator, rest his head on the cool vinyl door, and weep.

His parents lived long and died painless deaths in their sleep within a year of each other. Julian took some comfort in that. But he vowed not to wear black—inside or out—for the rest of his life, like the widows in his neighborhood. He was grateful for the end of summer, when they stopped bringing so much food, and he believed he'd finally exhausted their pity. But apparently he still deserved it.

The first months of solitude in his house on Seventh Street, Julian donated his grandparents' little porcelain sculptures to the church and stocked the bookshelves with history texts and albums and collections of American literature. He moved his accordion and guitar and boxes of sheet music from the basement to what had been his father's bedroom. He took down the ghostly photos of his mother from the living room wall and hung in their place a poster of the Manhattan skyline. In a gold frame on the end table he displayed a single family photograph: father, mother, and son at Rehoboth Beach, the man's arm around the waist of his pretty young wife, the baby named Giulio behind them digging in the sand. All of them were gone now.

"I won't rest until you're settled," his father had once warned him. They'd been sitting at the kitchen table, just a few weeks before his mother's stroke. "Not for one minute. Not on this earth and not after I'm dead. And your mother won't, either. If you remember us, think of that."

"Think of you very tired, you mean?" Giulio replied. "Walking around heaven with bags under your eyes?" He knuckled his father's bald head.

"You're like a big kid," said his father. He slapped his hand away. "No job, no wife, nothing to do all day. What'll happen to you when I'm gone?"

Every Sunday, Julian visits their graves, side by side in Cathedral Cemetery. He fills the vases with fresh flowers from DiNardo's on West Eighth Street, the one Italian-owned florist in Wilmington. Afterward, he walks the ten blocks to Renato's for an espresso, a slice of pizza, and the newspaper, which he reads in the corner booth. Then he sits on his porch. Neighbors walk by and stop to talk. Sometimes he plays his accordion and sings a little, under his breath, unsure of his voice but overcome with the beauty of "Vivere" or "O Sole Mio." For dinner he chooses from one of the pans he keeps in the icebox. On the days between deliveries, he cooks pasta and a half-price cut of meat from Angelo's Market. He can live this way for twenty more years on the money his parents saved for him, longer if he switches to silk flowers, even longer if he sells the house and moves to an apartment. But this is how Giulio would have lived. Julian has promised himself to take a different path. Each night, standing at his bedroom window in his underwear unable to sleep, watching the men walk home from shift work in the city and the lights go out in the streetlamps on Union, he promises to start making good on his new name.

But then he sleeps until eleven, his mind heavy with dreams. He wakes exhausted, and by the time he's out of bed, shaved, dressed, and has finished his lunch, it's midafternoon—too late in the day to make even the smallest decision. There is the newspaper to read, the library books to return, the porch to sweep, dinner to worry over. No plan begun at three o'clock can ever succeed; it must be set in motion before noon to have a chance. The months have gone swiftly by, and now it is not only late in the day, but late in the year—November—and Julian feels 1953 slipping away. Better to put off the next stage of rebirth until January, he thinks. A new year for the new man called Julian Fabbri. Better to fill his lungs with the fresh air of 1954 than to contaminate them with the staleness and grief of '53.

So he walks up and down the neighborhood, wanders the aisles of the library, or brings his folding chair to sit with the men at the corner of Seventh and Union. With them he argues over the so-called end of the Korean War, which Julian worries is not an end at all. He has read too much history not to see the decades of unrest to follow. The old men, in their camel coats and striped ties, smelling of cigars and woodsy cologne, disagree. Julian can barely stomach their dangerous optimism, their belief that, slowly but surely, the world is losing its taste for war. Now that their own government has electrocuted the little Jewish couple on no evidence at all, and Russia has exploded the H-bomb, and even Marilyn Monroe has disgraced herself, how can these old men think the world is headed anywhere but disaster? He counts off these examples and more for them, one for each finger on both hands, but they stare back at him blankly. One of them always changes the subject. Leaves blow around in little tornadoes at their feet, and the debate becomes whether or not this November feels warmer than last year's, whether or not the winter will be snowy. Julian gives up on them.

Instead he watches the people getting off the bus and imagines what compels them to walk so briskly. Who waits at home for the woman in the purple hat? Does the teenaged boy, carrying a bucket and a washcloth, need to earn money after school now that his aging father—in bed with a broken back—can no longer support his family? And what of the man Julian has named Dr. Z, who waits for an hour every day on the opposite corner, checking his pocket watch and digging into his black bag? What does he keep in there? What is he plotting? Julian can entertain himself for hours with these inventions.

On a Sunday morning in mid-November, he wakes earlier than usual and walks to the park to feed the pigeons. It is a chilly, gray day after a week of sun, and Julian fears this may be the last of his walks until spring. His body has always rebelled against cold weather. Itchy red spots form at his fingertips, toes, and neck, no matter how well he covers himself. For the first time this season, he wears the blue scarf his mother knitted for him. It smells like her—her hairspray, at least—and he stops for a moment on the sidewalk to breathe her in. In the last years of her life, her hair had begun to thin. She used to sculpt the remaining wisps into a hollow bun, then coat the bun with the spray until it hardened. She'd emerge from the bathroom in a mist, and soon she herself took on that chemical smell of wood smoke and wildflowers.

The park is small, less than half the size of a city block. It is all grass and trees except for the wide circle of cobblestones in the center, which will be a fountain if the church raises enough money. Presumably St. Anthony's spent the bulk of its donated funds—a percentage of which had come grudgingly from Julian's parents—on the elaborate wrought-iron fence that encloses the park. Atop each slat of the fence sits a sharp spike to keep out visitors after dark. What damage they could do to a bunch of trees, Julian can only wonder—carve their initials into the bark? Make love on the already dying grass? If anything, the church should encourage parishioners to spend time here. Most days Julian sits alone on one of the six wooden benches bolted along the walking path.

Immediately the pigeons descend on him from all sides and fight for space on the cobblestone dinner plate. He clucks his tongue, lets them eat from his palm. They amuse him, these silly creatures cooing and crashing into one another, and he can use a laugh on this bleak Sunday, with the wind swirling the dead leaves and rattling the windows of the rectory. He has been awake for only two hours, but already his limbs ache with fatigue.

The Negro man, Abraham Waters, walks on the sidewalk along the fence and stops at the corner of Tenth and Lincoln. He wears a long coat and dress pants that drag along the ground. No hat, though he's bald everywhere but around his ears. He doesn't cross the street. He sways, rubs his face, and looks up and down the block. Drunk, thinks Julian.

When he pushes through the heavy gate into the park, Julian's back stiffens. He considers leaving, but he's barely halfway through his bag of birdseed, and he doesn't want the man to think he drove him from the grounds of his own parish.

Waters sits on the opposite bench, rests his elbows on his knees, and covers his face with his hands. He stays this way for a long time. He does not seem to have brought anything for the birds. He snorts, coughs, and cups his freezing ears, all the while slumped so far forward that his back is parallel to the ground.

Unlike every other Italian in this neighborhood, Julian does not hate Mr. Waters. He does not fear him or his family of six, who have moved into the house across the street. What's to fear from a man who keeps his yard free of trash and his gutters clean? Yes, he'd rather Waters lived on the East Side, or in that new colored development behind the bridge, but only because life might be easier there among his own people, away from the ignorant *cafoni* who think his black skin might rub off on them. On the East Side, Waters wouldn't be forced to keep his wife and kids dead-bolted in the house with the shades drawn. As it is, they go in and out so quietly that Julian sometimes forgets that anyone at all lives at 1932.

The day the Waters family appeared, late in January of that year, Julian's neighbors stood on their porches with their arms folded and shouted at them as they unloaded their boxes. Angelo Montale spit on their lawn. A group met that very night in the back room of Angelo's Market to devise a plan to force them out. Rosa Volpe, mother of Renato, who lived next door at 1930, refused to leave the safety of her house for a month. Angelo convinced even Julian's father, who had had no opinion about anything other than horse racing, the saltiness of his soup, and his son's unhealthy attachment to books and solitude, that Waters must be run out of this neighborhood that he and his fellow Italians had built. He'd returned from Angelo's in a breathless rant about self-defense, land rights, and the immediate need for a gun. A week later, he died.

The morning of the funeral, Waters left a small bouquet of flowers at Julian's doorstep. On the card was signed: "Many Condolences, Your Neighbor, Abraham Waters & Family." Since then, Julian has waved good morning to him from his porch on no fewer than five occasions. Once, he walked across Seventh and delivered a letter sent to him by mistake. It turned out to be a short visit. One of the boys pulled open the door halfway and peered around it; he snatched the letter from Julian's fingers and slammed the door without a thank-you.

When a pigeon grazes Waters's shoulder, he finally lifts his head. His face is leathery, pocked with tiny dark freckles that might be moles if Julian could see them up close. He wipes his eyes.

"Cold day," Julian says. "Summer to fall to winter in one shot, looks like." It is the most he has ever said to the man.

Waters doesn't answer. He sits back, folds his hands in his lap, and stares at the sky. His fingers and legs are trembling.

"You feeling all right?" Julian asks.

Waters shakes his head, his eyes still fixed on the clouds. "Nothing of your concern."

Julian shakes out the nearly empty bag of seeds closer to Waters's feet than he intends. Suddenly the pigeons rush across the pavement and dive at him from the lower branches of the trees. "Sorry about that," Julian says.

He scowls. "I hate birds," he says and slides to the opposite side of the bench. "Filthy pests." He holds up one of his trembling hands. "No offense to you."

"Do I look like a bird?" Julian says, and smiles. "I like to feed them, that's all. Good way to pass the time."

"Pass the time," Waters repeats. His face goes blank. The pigeons finish their course and scatter. Only a determined few remain to hunt and peck. Julian is about to rise—nearly ten minutes, an appropriate amount of time, have elapsed—when Waters asks: "What kind of work you in, anyway? You're always home."

"Me?" says Julian. He has not been asked this in years. Everyone he talks to has known him since he was a boy. "I'm looking for work right now, as a matter of fact. Something with numbers. I've always been good in that department." He has no idea why he tells this particular lie. Numbers confuse and frustrate him. When he does start looking for a job—the second day of January—he will not consider any position that requires knowledge of math. Nor will he be any use at a job that requires "good hands": stonemason (like his father), barber, electrician. He will inquire as to the qualifications of a librarian, a newspaper reporter, a teacher of history or literature. He has four years of high school to his credit and twenty-five years with his nose in books. If they are not worth something, he is out of luck.

"I drive a cab," Waters says, though of course Julian knows this. Between fares, he parks in his driveway and waits. Once, he spent an entire afternoon in the front seat with the engine running, listening to the radio. "You gotta be good at arithmetic to make a good cabbie."

You must also know how to drive, Julian thinks. He won't confess that he's never learned. His other plan for the new year—the third of January—is to get his license and purchase his first automobile. He dreams of making it all the way to Florida, where he'll spend a month going from beach to beach, sleeping on the sand, drinking rum punch in a big wicker chair. "That a good business?" he asks.

He shrugs. "Some days yes, some no. But I'm grateful for the work."

"Times are tough," Julian says, brightly.

Again the blank stare.

Julian averts his eyes. On the other side of the park, two boys in hooded jackets jump from a tree stump into a pile of leaves. They roll around, yapping and laughing, until the leaves are flattened. They lie on their backs on the grass and kick their legs. Julian can see their breath from here.

Waters maintains his fixed stare. A trickle of sweat rolls down Julian's neck under his scarf, but he won't let the man think he's afraid. He watches the boys gather the leaves and rebuild the pile.

"My oldest ran off," Waters finally says. "How do you like that? Sixteen years old. Gone two weeks without a word. Don't know if he's alive or dead." He shakes his head. "Shit—" He reaches down, pries a rock from the crumbling pavement, and throws it into the trees. The birds scatter. He bites the corner of his lip, and for the first time Julian notices his missing front tooth, his bright pink gums.

"Ran off?" Julian asks. "Out of nowhere?"

Waters shrugs. "Kidnapped, run off, no idea."

"I'm very sorry to hear that," Julian says. What else can he say? "And the police?"

" 'If the boy's dead, sooner or later he'll get found,' they tell me. 'If he's alive, he don't want to be found.' You think they care one way or the other? Sixteen years old. Made good grades. Never hurt a soul. I drive all over Wilmington looking for him, on my own dime. I can't sleep, can't eat." He takes a breath. "His mother's flat out in bed, can't move her arms or legs. Some kind of fit."

"I wish I'd seen him," Julian says, lowering his head. But would he recognize him if he did? Was it his hand that reached out and grabbed the letter? He doesn't even know the boy's name. Young Negro men all look alike to him—thin as flag-poles, shiny skin, wide noses, hair thick as a helmet. He's never seen one up close long enough to register a difference. Lately, walking through downtown, he notices more of them, walking fast by themselves or huddled on the street corners, not bother-ing anybody but not doing much good either.

Though Julian had his own doubts about integration, espe-cially when it came to schools, he was a passionate advocate for rights and compassion within the walls of 1935 West Seventh Street. America had given every other immigrant a fair shake, he used to argue; why not do the same for people they'd treated with such blatant cruelty? To his father, though—to most men Julian knew—blacks did not fall into the same category as Irish or Greeks, and they only half believed that any undue cruelty had taken place. God had given that race a distinctive color to mark them as different, to signal that they were put on the earth for other reasons. No, not like animals, Ernesto Fabbri would say to his son—though those people did, in fact, need to be tamed; and you didn't tame people by handing them jobs other people had worked hard to earn.

"My son," Waters says, looking up at the trees. He makes two fists and presses them against his waist. "My little Abraham."

Why are you sitting here? Julian thinks. If you're so worried, why aren't you out looking for him? It feeds Julian's fears—which he never admitted to his father—that maybe the blacks are, at their core, lazier than the other races. Right now, little Abraham could be lying in a ditch under the Delaware Memorial Bridge, hit by a car and left bleeding, robbed, desperate for someone to rescue him, and here was his father uselessly broadcasting his grief to a stranger. These *are* tough times. Julian was right to remind Waters of that. You can't rest for one single second. The country survived a depression and a war, but in Julian's mind America is still hungry, still at arms. Everyone is fighting their private battles for the same thing: a little square of land, a steady job, a child to pass his name to; but if they win, something invariably goes wrong. The land is in the wrong place; the job doesn't pay enough; the child disappears.

How many times in the past two years of mourning has someone told Julian, "This too shall pass"? The consolation works every time: he imagines himself in the middle of a dark, dripping tunnel, stepping slowly toward the distant light. He believes in the light, that time will heal. But then he sees the happy fathers playing bocce in the street, the kids in the pile of leaves, the mothers at the grocery flirting with Angelo, and he fights the urge to shake them. "There's another side of the story!" he could yell. He could say, "This peace in your heart right now, this uncomplicated joy, *this too* shall pass." His parents had once been young and untouched by sadness, but then Caterina, their first child, died in her crib a year after she was born. They had thought themselves safe, just as Giulio had never truly believed his mother and father would leave him, just as most people believe they have been spared until the hammer comes down. Even after he changes his life—January, January—any happiness Julian achieves will be short-lived. The only difference will be that he'll know to appreciate it.

The two men sit in silence. When Waters gets up to leave, it is nearly noon. "You heading back?" he asks, and Julian says no, though he's shivering and needs to urinate.

"Church," Julian says, and ticks his head toward St. Anthony's. He's had no intention of attending, but he certainly cannot walk with Waters back to Seventh Street, not unless he wants a lot of questions from his neighbors. "I will pray for your son. If that does any good."

"Can't hurt," Waters says. Then, just before he passes through the gate, he stops. "You know what else? Sing a song for him, too. A good one. He used to mention your voice."

A rush of heat to Julian's face. "*My* voice?" he says. "I don't understand."

"We listened to you across the way, this summer, with the, uh—" He pumps his arms in and out.

"The accordion?"

"Yeah. It was nice. My Abe would make remarks about it.

He's got some pipes on him, too. From his mother, no doubt. Not from me. He used to mention wanting to sing and play guitar."

"I—I didn't—" Julian responds, but Waters has already reached the sidewalk.

Julian sits up straight on the hard bench. His lower back throbs. He is sweating. The church bell strikes the hour, and the Sunday morning congregation begins to climb the hill. He knows most of the families—Gaetano DiNardo, the Arienzos, Emidio and Evelina Castellani, Gianni Martino and his round little wife. La Polpetta, the meatball, his father used to call her. Women in fur shawls walk arm in arm, their men lagging a few steps behind. Father Moravia, the pastor, stands outside in his white robe to welcome his flock.

It's bad luck to lie about Mass, Julian decides, and guilts himself into attending. In his faded corduroys and a cardigan with a coffee stain on the sleeve, he is not dressed properly, so he buttons his coat to the neck and makes his way unnoticed past Father Moravia. He uses the men's room, then sits in one of the pews in the far back. Thoughts of the Waters family fill his mind. He lowers his head, in no mood to make conversation with the neighbors.

St. Anthony's is a beautiful church, with panel after panel of stained glass on both sides of the aisle. Behind the altar, the fading light shines through the enormous rose window. It inspires him, this castle of stone, with its shiny gold sunburst and thundering organ. Whisper, and your voice echoes across fifty pews. Julian should come here every morning for the early service, if just to coax himself out of bed. He gave up on God after his confirmation over twenty-five years ago, to his mother's great sadness and shame; but maybe now that she and his father are gone, it is time to return to the Lord. If he begins every day, not just Christmas and Easter, with Jesus, maybe He'll help walk Julian through this strange afterlife.

At the Offering, in his litany of private remembrances, Julian prays for the soul of his mother, his father, baby Caterina, the grandparents he never met, and his cousins back in Italy who died in the war. He prays for President Eisenhower, the rebels in East Berlin, the soldiers returning from Korea. Lastly, he prays to St. Anthony to find little Abraham Waters. He has no face to put with the boy's name, so he calls to mind the glowing eyes in the dark sliver of doorway, the skinny arm that reached for the letter.

He has always loved hymns. He sings each more loudly than the one before it, caring less and less that people can hear him. The words come easily from memory, like the stanzas of his favorite poems and lines from Emerson. By the recessional— "Joyful, Joyful, We Adore Thee," one of the most beautiful songs he knows—his voice is booming, carried high over the heads of the droning congregation, up to the ears of the Son of God Himself. Ten rows up, an old lady with sparkling eyes turns to smile at him, wondering—probably—why that silver-throated gentleman in the bright scarf has not joined the choir.

JULIAN'S FATHER USED to say that dreams should never be discussed, not even among family. They were a kind of pillow talk between God and man, spoken in a language that only God understood fully. Whenever he heard someone begin to recount a dream, he'd cover his ears, say, "Keep it to yourself!" and warn the person not to give away his secrets and humiliations. It was like kissing and telling; the story went on too long, and the details were interesting only to the person who'd done the kissing. He claimed to dream once a year, on average, and always the same vivid, illogical set of scenes, like a film spooling backward. He believed that, in heaven, he'd see the film from the beginning, and he'd get to ask God what He'd been trying to tell him.

Julian and his mother knew each other's dream lives as well as they knew their own. As soon as Ernesto left for work in the morning, she'd sit for a moment in the kitchen, fold her hands on the table, and report all that happened to her in the night. From an early age until the day she died, Julian heard over and over the dream where her teeth grew too large to fit her mouth, or she fell down a flight of stairs and landed safely in a lemon tree. She heard his tales of speaking perfect German to Hitler and eating a cheesecake filled with gold coins. Sometimes he made up the dreams just to give her a laugh, and maybe, he thinks now, so did she. These days, he has taken to writing his dreams in a notebook beside his bed. Every once in a while, he tells the best ones to her in the living room photograph, though his father is standing right there beside her, and Julian can almost see him scowl and bring his hands to his ears.

It does not take long for little Abraham Waters to appear in Julian's dreams, but of this he does not speak, not even to his mother. The boy floats facedown and naked in the Delaware River, bobbing on the waves. Julian watches him from the top of the Memorial Bridge, which is cut off, for some reason, midway to New Jersey. The steel beams are jagged where the bridge stops, as if a giant saw has zigzagged through them. Beside Julian stands a fat construction worker in a hard hat. He wears a shiny gold necklace around his neck. The construction worker dives into the water, straps Abraham to his back, and drags him to shore. He lies on the sand, his face smooth, his eyes open and bloodshot. There is not a scratch on him. Then suddenly Julian and the other construction workers are standing in a circle around him on the bank. They see Waters jump out of his taxi and run toward them. His eyes are fixed on his son, but he charges at Julian. Before he can reach him, Julian wakes.

TWICE THAT WEEK, Julian lingers on the opposite side of Union, watching the customers go in and out of Mrs. Stella's Ristorante Italiano. They arrive in a rush, but leave more leisurely, clutching leftovers wrapped in brown paper bags. Up and down the sidewalk Julian goes, hands in his pockets, telling himself things like *When the man with the blue tie comes out, you will go in.* But when the man with the blue tie comes out, Julian loses his nerve and heads home.

Then, that Friday, late in November, more than a month ahead of schedule, he finds himself awake and fully alert at eight o'clock. It is a sign. He puts on his good suit and carries his accordion, in its heavy brown case, down the block to Union Street. He makes it to the door of the restaurant, then turns around, comes home, and sits on the edge of his bed. The accordion stares at him from the other side of the room.

By the time he finally steps into Mrs. Stella's, it is the dead hour of the afternoon between lunch and dinner, and the restaurant is dark. He asks for Gino, and a boy in a white apron greets him and tells him in Italian that Mario Grasso will be with him instead. "Sit," says the boy, pointing to the bar, and offers a glass of wine that Julian accepts.

He sets the accordion on the floor. He thumbs the waist of his pants and breathes more deeply. He has been inside Mrs. Stella's only once, for a small gathering after the funeral of his great-aunt. Since then, he has pictured himself many times among the crowds who gather here for dinner. In his mind, he sits elbow to elbow for hours in the bar area with patrons waiting for a table; the waiters in tuxedos rush past him carrying plates covered with stainless steel lids. Julian has heard a rumor that some people eat at home and come to Mrs. Stella's just to drink cocktails. They spend their Saturday nights on these stools talking to strangers, making friends.

Mario walks through one of the swinging kitchen doors, wiping his hands on a dishtowel. Julian has met him once or twice at Renato's, before he grew the thin mustache just above his upper lip. He looks young, thirty at most, and carries himself like he has something to prove: shoulders square, arms stiff, eyes narrowed in suspicion. Or maybe Julian just imagines this. When Mario notices the accordion, then offers his hand, he does it with a pleasant—almost eager—smile.

"Julian Fabbri," he says, rising, with a smile equally broad.

"Of course," Mario says. "Giulio. Your father worked with my father at Bancroft Mill." He bows slightly. *"Condolianze."*

"Grazie."

"What can I do for you?" He walks behind the bar and pours himself a glass of red wine. "If you'll forgive me, I don't have a tremendous amount of time. Friday night, you know. Busy busy." He sits beside him on one of the stools.

"I understand," Julian says. He asks about his family, his two little girls in particular, and tells him to please send his regards to his father. Then he runs out of small talk, and Mario glances at his watch. "What I want to bring up with you is—I have heard so many wonderful stories about your restaurant. All the life here and the food and the happy customers." He waves his arm around. "I came here only once, I'm sorry to say, but I have wanted to come back, and then my father—I play the accordion sometimes, at home; I practice Italian songs, the ones you hear on the radio and ones from the Old Country too—'Santa Lucia,' 'O Sole Mio,' songs like that—and I sing a little, not great but not terrible—this is what they tell me, at least, and so I was thinking—" His throat catches; he swallows, breathes; Mario squints at him. "I was thinking Mrs. Stella's might like someone to play—not sing if you don't want me to, just play a little, very soft, in the background—while the customers wait for their tables—maybe starting in January after the New Year, or on Saturdays, or once a month, or one night in the summer when you're not too busy—" He reaches down and touches the handle of the accordion case, as if it might run off. The wine makes red streaks in Mario's empty glass. "Or maybe it's not best for the restaurant for a musician to take up space."

Mario looks around, twirling his wedding ring around his finger. He walks to the narrow corner by the back of the bar. He stretches out his arms, then pretends to play an accordion. "Is this a big enough space?" he asks. "Would you need a stool to sit on? Or could you stand?"

"Stand, sit, whatever you want," says Julian. "Usually I sit—but whatever you want."

Mario scratches his upper lip. "I have to hear you first. Can you play me something now, very quick? Live music is a tremendous idea, something I've thought about many times. We have a record player and a few albums, but that's it, and the same opera songs over and over get under my skin. I can't pay you, though, not right away. Maybe later, if the customers like it—"

"I don't care about money," Julian says, already squatting on the floor in front of the open case. "I just want a change." He pulls the straps around him and with his sleeve wipes the sweat from his forehead. He takes Mario's place in the corner. He tests the keys.

"How about this: the nights you play, we give you dinner and lunch on the house," says Mario. He moves to the end of the bar and refills his glass. "Of course, I'll have to talk it over with Gino before anything is decided. He's not an easy man to convince, so—"

"I understand."

"Do you know 'Serenata Celeste'? I love 'Serenata Celeste.'"

Julian nods. He plants his left leg firmly in front of his right, lifts his head, and begins.

5

The Dream of the Princess

AT WORK, MR. Gold lingers at Maddalena and Ida's station. He sits at the edge of the table and taps his yardstick on the warped linoleum floor. He asks them about their family traditions and records the details in the little notebook he keeps at all times in his shirt pocket. "I am a student of the world," he tells them. "Everything interests me. I want to understand all the many cultures in my shop. For example, you say you will serve seven types of fish on Christmas Eve, but why seven? Why not three or six? And is there any significance to the types?"

Maddalena waits for Ida; Ida waits for Maddalena. Neither of them knows. All Maddalena can say is that the seven fishes have been prepared for generations in Italy, since long before their grandmothers were born, and that it probably has something to do with Jesus. Still Mr. Gold nods and scribbles in his notebook.

With Gloria gone, Stavroula has an entire table to herself. Queen Stavroula, Ida calls her. She mutters in Greek as she stretches and rests her foot on Gloria's old chair; she spreads the stockings she's sewed across the length of her station as if to air them out. She removes her earplugs to eavesdrop on Mr. Gold and the Italians, and every once in a while interrupts them with a snort or a sigh. Today she says, "In my country, we take a sprig of basil and tie it above the fireplace, to keep away the hooved ones, the Kallikantzari—"

"Is that so," says Mr. Gold, blandly.

Maddalena has been taught that Greeks are good people, like Italians when it came to keeping their families close, but that you'd never want them to cook for you. According to Antonio and Papà Franco, they care more about dancing and poetry than cleaning their kitchens. But there is no dirt under Stavroula's fingernails, Maddalena has noticed, and more than once she has witnessed her vigorously washing her hands in the bathroom. Still, made with dirty hands or clean, the contents of Stavroula's lunches turn her stomach: yogurt oozing through a cakelike ball of ground beef, chunks of soggy eggplant on which she squeezes a browning lemon.

"I should write a book," says Mr. Gold, over the whirr of the machines. "In Poland, I would have been a professor of literature, like my father and uncle."

"A professor!" says Ida. Since the competition, she has taken every opportunity to fawn over her boss.

"My problem is I've seen too much," Mr. Gold continues. "Too many horrible things. No one would want to read about them. Compared to where I've been, this shop is paradise."

"Ask me how many books I've read in my lifetime," says Ida.

Mr. Gold raises his eyebrows.

"None." She beams at him. "On sewing I have focus, but I can't concentrate on words for more than five seconds. Even when I was a girl. My sisters and brothers were all the same. Maddalena is the professor in the family. She likes her romances." She reaches under the desk, pulls out *Il Sogno della Principessa* from Maddalena's purse, and hands it to Mr. Gold.

"Ida!" Maddalena reaches for the book, but it's already in Mr. Gold's hands. On the cover is a watercolor drawing of a castle and moat, with a man crossing the drawbridge on a white horse.

"How does the title translate?" he asks, as he thumbs through it.

"The Dream of the Princess," says Ida.

Maddalena blushes. "It's about a princess," she says. Mr. Gold hands it back to her and winks.

"Reading is very important, Ida," he says. "The secret to a long life is to escape it as often as you can." He thinks a moment, then takes out his notebook and scribbles. "My heart is with poets and historians. Not dressmakers. Not accountants and shopkeepers."

"My heart is still in Kavala," says Stavroula, tossing a handful of stockings onto the far side of her table.

"My heart is with my babies," says Ida. "May they outlive me!"

They look to Maddalena, but she offers no report on the location of her heart. It lives in many places, she could tell them, if she wanted them to know. It beats with the child's inside her; it tumbles down the hills of Santa Cecilia; it quickens when Antonio lays his hand on her hip. To try and catch up with it leaves her breathless. When she first arrived in this country, she thought her heart had broken, but no broken thing can propel itself so forcefully in so many directions. At work the demands of the machines and the endless yards of fabric numb her; for hours she forgets she has a heart at all. Then, without warning, it leaps inside her, and a daydream begins: Antonio kneels on the thick living-room carpet in their new house, his arms outstretched to welcome the child as he wobbles toward him; she turns on the record player, and the three of them join hands and dance in a circle around the coffee table. If Ida has this much, why can't she?

"And so my wish is to live long enough to learn every fact," says Mr. Gold, the end of a speech Maddalena has missed. He hops down from the table and walks toward the next group of ladies. "Imagine that! Every fact!"

"What a *chiacchierone*," Ida whispers, when he's out of earshot. She's got a pin between her teeth. She fluffs her pile of stockings, and for a moment, it looks as tall as Maddalena's. Then it deflates. "He talk-talk-talks like this is a party, but he expects us to get done the same work?" She stands, grabs a handful of stockings from Maddalena's side and transfers it to hers. "I don't know how you keep up," she says, shaking her head. "But I'm glad you do." She kisses Maddalena on the back of the head. "I'll be in the ladies' room. All this talking makes me have to go."

THAT EVENING, MADDALENA and her family stand at the corner of Union and Eighth, gazing at a glorious display. The lampposts on both sides of the street are wrapped with gold garland and strings of colored bulbs. At the top of each lamppost, a plastic Babbo Natale, his white beard illuminated, waves his red-gloved hand and smiles. If they stand in a certain spot and look at him, he grows brighter and blurrier as the street curves out of the city, as if refracted through a mirror. In the twenty years the Grassos have lived in Wilmington, no one has decorated Union Street so elaborately. A few lights on trees here and there, a plastic star atop a chimney maybe, but nothing like this. Maddalena takes it as a sign that her daydreams, which seemed impossible as recently as this afternoon, might come true after all. Amid this beauty, maybe Antonio will forget the crazy game they're playing.

Maddalena loops her arm through her mother-in-law's and rests her head on the fur collar of her coat. For a long time they stand motionless, gazing up and down the street. Nobody says anything. Antonio rubs his chin, his eyes wide as a boy's. Then he reminds them they are already late for dinner, and suddenly he's rushing everyone across the street to avoid the oncoming cars.

As an early Christmas gift, Mario has invited them to dinner at Mrs. Stella's. Maddalena is grateful for the night off, if not for the menu that awaits her: large bowls of overcooked pasta in watery tomato sauce, fatty lamb chops roasted in a brick oven, pizza with a bland, soggy crust, and a few American dishes like French fries and hamburgers that Papà forbids them to order. Most nights Mario works the floor or the kitchen to earn back what he owes Gino Stella, the principal owner. Gino writes the checks for rent and utilities and supplies, and each month pays protection money in cash to a man named Roberto Fante. Every once in a while, Gino brings in his mother to greet the customers and walk among them in her apron. She is here tonight, a round woman no taller than Maddalena's shoulders. "What a beautiful family you have, Mario!" she says as she takes their coats and leads them to the large table by the window. When she smiles, dimples appear on her cheeks.

Mario can't sit still. He refills the half-full wineglasses and polishes the unused silver with a linen napkin. Before his father finishes chewing his trout, Mario asks him, "Top quality, Papà, don't you think? Cooked perfect? You know this afternoon that fish was swimming in the Atlantic?" He wears a tie and has recently clipped his nails. He crouches beside his mother as she brings a forkful of rubbery pasta to her mouth and claps when she proclaims it as good—no, better—than her own. Antonio sits beside Maddalena, but he does not look at her, does not see her move the food around her plate.

"This place will make us a fortune," Mario says, lowering his voice. "Pretty good, Antonio, don't you think? Not too bad for your old *fratello*. Soon you'll come work for me, make this a real family business. I'll get Grasso in the name if it kills me."

"I wish you luck," Antonio says and raises his glass.

He has had too much wine already. He rolls his eyes whenever Mario turns his back, and twice complains to the waiter that the sauce has no taste. Mamma Nunzia kicks him under the table, and for a while he manages a neutral expression.

Mario puts his arm around Maddalena and Antonio. "This meal is my Christmas gift to all of you," he says, and squeezes her shoulder. "But if you ask me what I want under the tree this year, what will make me and Ida and my girls the most happy, I'll tell you: I want my brother and his wife to kiss and make up. Fill this Christmas with joy. What do you say?" He looks back and forth between them. "If not for me, then for the little baby?"

Maddalena lowers her head.

"Sit down, Mario," Antonio says. "Nobody's kissing tonight. There's nothing to make up about."

"Mind your own business," Papà tells Mario.

As a sign of comfort, Mamma Nunzia removes her shoe

and rubs her foot along Maddalena's calf. "What's for dessert?" she asks.

Maddalena excuses herself. In the ladies' room, she slaps her cheeks to bring back the color, deflate the puffiness. She tugs at the fabric in the waist of her dress. A young woman, thin and pretty, stands beside her, woozily applying lipstick. "Can you tell I'm drunk?" she says to Maddalena's image in the mirror, and straightens her shoulders.

"A little bit," Maddalena says, and smiles. Then her stomach growls, loud enough for the woman to hear.

"Your food slow, too, huh? We've been waiting an hour. No wonder I'm so light-headed."

Maddalena nods, washes her hands. Until Antonio speaks to her again, she refuses to eat a healthy meal. Certainly not tonight, here in this tacky restaurant with its cartoon murals of Venice and its chalky bread, with Ida twisting her napkin praying for more customers. In a few days they will have Christmas Eve guests, and Antonio will be forced to put on a better act than the one he's performing tonight.

"Well, good luck," Maddalena says to the woman, on her way out.

"Oh, he won't mind," she says, still looking in the mirror.

Maddalena returns to find her plate of pasta and veal cutlets—uneaten but cut-up and rearranged—still on the table after the other plates have been cleared. Gino Stella sits in her chair. "My cooking's not good enough for you?" he asks her in Italian, with a grin. He does not stand.

"I—"

"Food is like poison to her lately," says Papà. "Don't pay any attention."

"Don't worry, Maddalena," Ida says. "The hunger will come."

She tries to smile. "I'm sorry, Signor Stella," she says, as Mario rises and offers his chair. "Settimio's a very fine cook."

Antonio gives her a quick, empty glance.

"I have good news," Signor Stella says to Mario. "We have no reservations left in December. Not a single table will be empty. Have you ever heard of such a thing?"

"You hear that, wife?" Mario says. "You're going to miss me. You won't see me at all, not even Christmas Eve dinner. I'll come home just to drop off the bags of money. Then I'll leave again."

"And she'll spend it all by the time you get back," says Signor Stella.

Ida crosses herself. "Keep talking like this, then for sure it won't happen."

The record player stops in the middle of "Be My Love," and out of nowhere comes a string of notes from what sounds like a live accordion. The customers turn their heads toward the bar. "Look at this!" says Mamma Nunzia.

Maddalena cranes her neck. A man in the corner wipes his forehead with his sleeve, bows slightly, and starts to play. He's older, in his forties at least, with a long face and thinning hair. His suit jacket hangs off his shoulders as if he were still expecting to grow into it. She does not know the song, but he plays it beautifully, and before long the crowd nods and sways. Everyone is watching him. At the next table, a man reaches across to join hands with his wife. When the song ends, the accordion player clears his throat and whispers his name into the microphone, but Maddalena can't make it out. Everyone claps, and he bows again.

"Not bad, no?" says Gino. "For free this man plays, just so he can spend a few hours in my restaurant and get a good meal. Our Mario here discovered him off the street."

"I felt sorry for him," Mario says. He leans forward over the table. "Never married. Father and mother dead. Broke my heart, if you want to know the truth. I think of it as my good deed for the year." He sits back and takes another drink, closes his eyes as another song begins. "You see what I mean, *fratello?* Life is hard. You should be dancing with your wife, not holding some grudge."

Antonio stops him with a look.

Maddalena pushes her chair away from the table to get a better view of the man with the accordion. When he plays "Tu Scendi dalle Stelle," she folds her hands and says a prayer for her family back in Santa Cecilia. They used to sing this song at the end of Midnight Mass, and afterward everyone would spill out onto the streets still singing, repeating the verses over and over. The fire in the torches they carried seemed to flicker to the rhythm of the music, or possibly this was just how she perceived it. She remembers the sadness of finally reaching home, when she had to break from the procession and let the other villagers walk on. She would run to the terrace and listen to the song echo over the hills. Then it would fade, and she'd join her sisters for a game of *tombola*. How little of the world she knew then, to get so excited over a song she could sing any day of the year if she'd wanted! She'll have to tell Mr. Gold about this, she thinks; he'll put the torches and the midnight parade in his little book of traditions.

Tonight, only Maddalena and a few customers hum along to "Tu Scendi dalle Stelle." It must not be a song familiar to Americans. The accordion player moves his lips to the words. "You don't let him sing?" Maddalena asks.

"He's too shy," Mario says. "Says maybe he'll join the church choir one day, but that's it. We tell him he has a good voice—it's the truth—but he shakes his head. 'One day,' he tells us. We're still waiting. But for now, the accordion is good enough."

"He wants to sing," says Maddalena. She notices how he lifts his chin and flutters his eyelids on the high notes. "You can tell."

"I have an idea," Ida says. "Another good deed. Let's invite him to our Christmas Eve." She turns to Mamma Nunzia. "What do you think? Is there room?"

She shrugs and makes circles with her hand. "What's one more?"

"Christmas Eve he's working," says Mario.

"So, you have to close sometime," his mother says. "We won't be awake?"

"I'll mention it to him," Mario says, and takes a sip of wine.

"He has no family at all?" Ida asks.

The song ends. During the applause, the accordion player keeps his eyes closed and stands motionless, as if in prayer. After a few moments, he opens his eyes, gives an embarrassed smile, and bows.

"You're very kind," he says, so quietly the microphone doesn't pick it up. But Maddalena can read the words on his lips.

AFTER DINNER, THEY walk down Union Street to spend more time among the lights—the women arm in arm, the men in front. They lead them uphill through the neighborhood, where fat red and green bulbs hang from the eaves of the row homes and on the bushes in the front yards. People wave at them from their windows, through the branches of their glittering Christmas trees, all Italians they know from somewhere: Alessandro the produce vendor, Elena from the bakery, Dellucci the electrician. Whatever a family needs, it can find on this wide hill in the shadow of St. Anthony's.

Ida shivers and pulls Maddalena closer. "Listen to me," she whispers. "You have to eat. Antonio is worried about you."

"He doesn't look worried."

"Well, he is." She guides them over a frozen puddle. "OK, it's really Mario who's worried, but Antonio got him thinking."

"I'm the only one who understands Antonio," Mamma Nunzia says. "He's got a problem, that one, and the problem is that his wife is too beautiful. He doesn't know how to live with it. He thinks he doesn't deserve you, that someone will steal you. He's been worried since the day he brought you here."

"That's crazy," says Maddalena.

"And not talking to her, that will help?" Ida asks.

"Yes," Mamma Nunzia says. "It makes sense to me somehow. If he doesn't talk, then nothing happens. Everything stays the same until he figures out what to do."

"The baby will change him," Ida says. "You should have seen Mario before I had Nunzia—"

"We know," says Mamma Nunzia. "I was there. And I lived with Mario twenty-two years before you came. No man is the same as another. Maddalena has to plan what she will do if Antonio behaves more like his father. I don't think he carried Mario in his arms once until he was two years old."

Ida pinches Maddalena, as if to say, "You see? Never the favorite."

Maddalena rubs her eyes. She feels dizzy. This is what women do, she thinks. Night after night, we examine our men. We look for patterns in the same stories to predict what they will do next. In the meantime, they play cards and keep secrets, surprise us with a joke when we expect anger, a slap when we lean in for a kiss. After seven years with Antonio, she has yet to learn all the rules, and the few she's learned so far have already changed.

"Think about it like this," Mamma Nunzia tells her. "If you have Ida and me, you don't need Antonio so much. Even the good fathers are never much help with a baby. They pick him up, kiss him on the forehead when he has a fever, and say, 'Wife, you know my son has a fever?' All you have to worry about is whether Antonio has a good job. And he does. The rest you put up with."

They walk to the top of the hill and stop in silence before the *presepio* at St. Anthony's. Maddalena's legs are weak, her stomach hollow. She kneels in front of the statue of Mary and rests her forehead on her folded hands. She closes her eyes and prays again—for a healthy baby, a son if she's allowed to choose; for Antonio to surprise them all with a change of heart; for the health of her family in the village. In her mind, she sees her mother carrying the wash up the hill from the river. Then a field of olive trees flashes before her, then children running over cracked stone steps. There are torches, a donkey kicking its legs. She smells rosemary and smoke and snow.

A hand shakes her shoulders. She wakes to a red and green blur, the Christ Child's chubby face, the stare of the plastic animals. Ida helps her to her feet. But it is not until she says, "I told you—you have to eat!" that Maddalena remembers which country she is in.

MADDALENA'S BODY IS changing. Once thin and taut, it has softened noticeably in the last month alone. She can do nothing to hide this, she thinks, as she turns from side to side in front of her bedroom mirror. When she was a teenager, people said she could have been an actress or a dancer with legs like hers, but look at them now: trunky and bloated and mannish. Overnight. Even her neck and cheeks are fleshy. Her straw-colored hair has darkened over the years, ordinary as any other Italian woman's.

She lies in bed, another night without Antonio, and remembers a time when she knew she was beautiful. There was a Sunday afternoon three years ago, not long after their fourth Christmas together, when Antonio sat in the kitchen reading the newspaper out loud. Maddalena sat beside him and looked over his shoulder, trying to follow the sentences as he spoke them. It was another of Sister Clark's suggestions, a way to meet new English words "where they lived and breathed," to get to know them so as not to fear them. It didn't work. How could it? Maddalena was continually confronted with words like "enough," at which she stared utterly baffled. Only the *n* was where it should be, and maybe the *u*; the other letters existed only to mock her.

"Pain and Loneliness Only Reward to Hero of Auto Explosion," Antonio announced and proceeded to read an article about a forty-four-year-old bachelor named Orville, who rescued three strangers from a burning car, then spent eleven days in the hospital without a single visitor. He had burns all over his body, no insurance, and no one to help him, but still, he said, he'd "do it again in a heartbeat." Antonio admired this. Maddalena wouldn't have done it in the first place, she said, let alone a second time, but like her husband, she was grateful for the Orvilles of the world, good, selfless people God rarely rewarded on earth but would shower with riches in heaven.

Her mind wandered as Antonio read, but this Maddalena remembered very clearly: beneath the explosion article was a photo of a pretty young woman with a flirtatious grin, her hair arranged in a bun, her hand resting lightly at her throat. Above the photo was written *Bianca*—the Italian word—and other words Maddalena didn't recognize.

"Who is Bianca?" Maddalena asked. "An actress?"

"I don't think so," said Antonio, and read: "'Bianca Talent Agency. Think You Have What It Takes to Become a Professional Model? We Will Teach You How to Make It in New York and Hollywood. Free Consultations.'" He snapped the newspaper, folded it over, and set it on the table with the photo facing out. "You're better-looking than this girl."

Maddalena studied her. She had a superior nose (without the bump in the middle that Maddalena had inherited from her grandmother), long lashes, and a slim heart-shaped face. But she did not have Maddalena's full lips or wide, deep-set eyes. If she received as much help with her hair and makeup as this woman had, it was possible Maddalena could defeat her in a beauty pageant. The race would be close, at least. Still she said to Antonio, "Oh, I don't think so."

"I do," he said. He pointed to the photo. "Look at her. If she's the best the Bianca Talent Agency has to offer, they'd faint if they saw you."

Maddalena shook her head, dismissing Antonio's exaggerated faith in her beauty, but he went on to explain the meaning of "Free Consultation" and told her nothing would please him more than to show her off to Bianca herself.

Then, the next day, without telling anyone, he called the number in the newspaper and scheduled a consultation for the following weekend. He told Maddalena that they'd been invited to his friend Giovanni's house for an early dinner. He bought her a new dress, black with strips of crinkled red velvet at the sleeves and waist, and though she found it overly showy, she agreed to wear it as long as they were only going to Giovanni's. From the doorway of the bathroom he watched her apply her makeup and remove the curlers from her hair, more anxious than usual about arriving on time.

She had not paid much attention during the short drive, but when he pulled over and parked on Delaware Avenue, she realized she'd been tricked. There, on the second floor of an office building, between a hair salon and a dentist, was a small sign for the Bianca Talent Agency. *Since 1934,* it said. Its logo was a pink cartoon of a Greek goddess wearing cat-eye glasses.

"O Dio!" Maddalena said. She saw Antonio's grin, shook her head, and gripped the edges of her seat. "I'm not going in there!"

A group of women in fur coats passed in front of the car. One paused, peered through the windshield, and gave Antonio a curious look before rushing into a dress shop called Minuet.

His face softened. He reminded Maddalena of the promise he'd made to her parents in Santa Cecilia: that he would take their daughter to the United States and give her the chance to become an actress. Wilmington wasn't Hollywood, but it wasn't a nowhere village either; it was still America. Everyone had to start somewhere, and, according to the woman he talked to at the agency, Maddalena would probably start with modeling, for the Sears or Wanamaker's catalog, or ads in the *Wilmington Morning News.* In the meantime, she could learn English well enough to read and understand her lines. She was only twenty-three years old, with most of her career ahead of her. The agency girls performed on a regular basis in Philadelphia, for big money, and one of them had emigrated all the way from Russia just to study with Bianca herself. The best part, said An-

tonio, was that the modeling and acting classes didn't cost a
penny. The agency got a reasonable cut of every dollar their girls
made after they finished their training, which seemed like a
small price to pay for making them stars.

Maddalena listened. It sounded like a good system—fair,
without risk. She relaxed her grip on the seat. Now that she was
here, in a new dress she wouldn't have chosen but which flattered her chest and waistline, the appointment made and confirmed, she had no excuse not to try. She imagined them sitting
her in front of a mirror, admiring her cheekbones, parading her
into a studio in Philadelphia with the declaration: "Meet the
next Anna Magnani!" If she never learned English well enough
to earn a part in a play, that would be fine; she could live with
that; modeling the newest fashions in Philadelphia came close
enough.

It was the walk from the car to the office that she dreaded.
The ladies in their minks, the policeman in the window of the
coffee shop, the snobby clerks at the Minuet—what would they
think of her? Would they laugh when she walked not into the
hair salon, but the agency? Would they shake their heads and
say, "*She* thinks she has what it takes to become a professional
model?"

So she kept her head down—a habit of hers Bianca would
surely attempt to break. Antonio took her hand and led her up
the stairs, making nervous small talk about the new asphalt on
the street. It was a windy day, bleak and cold, the sun a sliver of
lemony yellow hanging low in the sky. On the top step Maddalena stopped, took out her bottle of Nina Ricci perfume, and
sprayed a quick mist on her neck.

The waiting room was small and empty. They were the last
interview of the day, or so the pretty young receptionist in-

formed them, and a woman named Lorraine would be with them in a moment. They sat on a leather sofa between a tasteful imitation fern and the door Lorraine would eventually open. On the end table lay a stack of *LOOK* magazines, from which Ava Gardner watched them in her strapless black dress, beside the headline "Divorce: A Woman's Tragedy." The walls featured wood paneling and, just above eye height, a row of framed glossy photographs. Some were black and white shots of beautiful women and a few handsome men, all with perfect teeth; they smiled or stared seductively at the camera. Other shots were taken directly from plays or films: an adorable child in a bunny suit; an older woman peeking menacingly from under the hood of a cloak; a man holding a football above his head, his arm flexed to display his muscles.

"You'll be up there someday," said Antonio. He nudged her in the side with his elbow. "And we'll have a house on Easy Street."

Maddalena crossed and uncrossed her legs. The appointment was for four o'clock, and it was now nearly quarter past. It felt like waiting at the doctor's office: the same powerlessness, the threat of awful news, of being told the specifics of your body's many failings. Every time the door opened, Maddalena's chest tightened. But for the next twenty minutes, no Lorraine; only a succession of skinny girls in heavy makeup and heels clacking toward the exit, not bothering to acknowledge the receptionist or glance in Maddalena's direction. The best she could tell, none was dramatically prettier than she.

Close to half past, a woman in her fifties, wearing a pink double-breasted business suit and nail polish to match, appeared in the doorway. "Mr. and Mrs. Grasso," she said, and held her arms out as if she'd known them all her life and merely lost touch. She kissed them on both cheeks, said "Follow me," and led them down a narrow hallway lined with more framed photos. Lorraine was a few inches shorter than Maddalena but carried herself well; there wasn't a single crease on the seat of her skirt. She wore her thick auburn curls in a chignon, and a pair of tinted tortoise-shell glasses.

Her office had a view of Delaware Avenue, now softly lit by streetlamps. The radiator knocked awake and began to hiss. Lorraine sat behind a metal desk covered with a scatter of papers held down by coffee mugs, and Maddalena and Antonio faced her from the two chairs that had been set out for them. Lorraine folded her hands in front of her, unleashed a big smile, and looked back and forth between the two of them. "Wonderful, just wonderful," she said. "Tell me you brought the pictures."

Maddalena shook her head, then watched in surprise as Antonio pulled two snapshots from his blazer pocket. She recognized one from their wedding—a profile of her bending to sign the register—and the other from a rainy trip to Atlantic City two years before. She'd worn a one-piece striped bathing suit and stood awkwardly under the boardwalk, one hand on a post, the other on her hip. In both pictures she looked bony and plain, though in the beach shot her legs did appear smooth and supple.

"Not those!" she said, as Antonio handed them to Lorraine. "We must have better ones."

Lorraine set them side by side on the desk before her and removed her glasses. "But these are stunning!" she said. Then she placed a small cylindrical object on the wedding shot and peered through it. "Yes," she said. Then the other. "Yes. Yes!" she repeated. She gazed across at Maddalena and shook her head as if in disbelief. "She has better ones, she says. And here I am asking myself, 'Lorraine Stetson, is it possible you can be this lucky?'"

"Really?" said Maddalena.

Antonio was beaming. "I tried to tell her, but you know a woman never believes her husband."

"Most shouldn't," Lorraine said. "But in this case! You photograph very well, Mrs. Grasso. *Very* well." She looked again, with that same amazement, at the pictures. "And these aren't even quality shots. Not taken by a professional, I'm assuming."

Simultaneously Maddalena and Antonio shook their heads.

"I have this Russian," Lorraine said. "Came from Siberia. Siberia! Lived in an igloo or something. Didn't see a citrus fruit her entire life. Anyway, during the war an Italian soldier falls for her and steals her away from that God-forsaken country. The soldier gets killed, but she makes it to a boat and winds up here in the Promised Land. We found her on the street like a hundred-dollar bill in a sewer grate. Spiffed her up, took some pictures, and now you want to know what she earns? Fifty dollars an hour, almost as much as Dorian Leigh. Lives in Society Hill, Philadelphia, in a penthouse, with a balcony!" Here Lorraine leaned forward and dropped her voice to a whisper. "And I tell you: she's not half as pretty as you."

Maddalena blushed.

"She didn't know Bianca before she got here?" Antonio asked. "On the phone, you said she came especially for her."

"That's a different Russian girl," Lorraine said. "You'll find we work with many internationals. It's what distinguishes us. The exotic look is always in fashion. Ava Gardner, Gina Lollobrigida, always *la moda*. And they're not even blonde! Italian women are world-renowned for their beauty—especially the sort of rustic beauty that comes through here." She pointed again to the pictures. "Your husband told me you once lived in one of those charming villages?"

"Yes," said Maddalena, confidently, and smiled. That was an easy question. But Lorraine raised her eyebrows as if expecting her to elaborate. She stammered a bit, then came up with: "It was very small. We had three streets, that's it, and no cars or trains. Only an olive grove and a church and a small café. I didn't know any different, so to me it was beautiful. It was the center of the world." She paused. The sparkle in Lorraine's blue eyes encouraged her. "Every morning it was my job to carry the milk in two big buckets back and forth from the farm to my house. Our family owned the one grocery store, so we weren't poor, but still we had to have milk like everybody else. I was always the last one to pick it up, though, because I slept too late, and sometimes the cow ran out before I got there. My mother used to get so angry at me!"

Lorraine looked at Antonio. "It's not Siberia," she said. "But that's exactly what I'm talking about. Rustic beauty. You can't buy it for a million and a dime."

Antonio was proud of her. Maddalena could see it in his puffed-up chest, his confident slouch, his right foot dangling over his left knee. He, too, might have had model looks: a strong jaw, hair velvet black. He was tall and usually had good posture. "So, where do we go from here?" he asked.

Lorraine stood. "We see her walk."

She led them both into the hall and asked Maddalena not to think about the fact that they were watching her. "Pretend you're at the market," she said. "You're going up and down the aisle like a normal person. No one's bothering you."

Maddalena strolled slowly between the rows of photographs, stopping every few steps to reach out and touch one as if it were a box of detergent.

"No!" Lorraine said, not unkindly. "You're not *really* in the market, sweetheart. It was just an example. Just walk like you're walking down the street."

Stiffly, embarrassed, Maddalena made her way to the end of the hall. She turned just before the door to the waiting room and came toward Lorraine and Antonio at the other end.

"One more time," said Lorraine. "More natural, OK? I'm not here." She covered her eyes.

Obviously she was flunking. It had always been a point of pride that she carried herself well and that, like a mannequin, her body had been built to show off clothes. According to the reaction of Lorraine Stetson, though, she walked with the grace and sophistication of a donkey. She was shaking, and felt tears coming on. Antonio handed her his handkerchief, and she quickly dabbed her eyes.

She was then led into a room of mirrors. There, Lorraine pointed out the tiny mole on her left ear, ran her finger down the length of her nose, and examined all angles of her profile. She made notes in a little pad of lined paper. Antonio watched from the doorway as she sat Maddalena in front of a powerful makeup mirror and commanded her first to smile, then frown, then get angry, now look sad. With every new face, she pressed a button on the mirror to change the light: day to dusk to evening to office. "Let's see your teeth," Lorraine said, and nodded as Maddalena held her mouth open wide. "Good," she said. "Not too European."

Back in the office, they sat in silence as Lorraine shuffled papers. Her large hoop earrings, gold choker, and assortment of brilliant rings seemed gaudy at first; now Maddalena realized she herself must be out of touch with the times, a simple village girl after all, with no sense of style. Her own jewelry was understated: two small posts in her ears, a thin gold cross attached to her necklace, her wedding band, no bracelets.

After two long minutes, Lorraine folded her hands, looked directly at Maddalena and said, "It would be our honor to work with you, Mrs. Grasso."

She covered her mouth. "Are you sure?" she asked, through her hand, then dropped it. "I didn't think I did very good. The walking—"

"I trust *these*," Lorraine said, and again held the photographs. "These don't lie. My job is to train my eye—to see through imperfections, beyond inexperience. To see the future, if you like. But the camera's eye is pure; it sees only the truth of the here and now. In these pictures the camera tells me, 'I'm in love with Madeline Grasso,' and now so am I!"

Antonio clapped his hands. "So you think she can make it big?"

"Oh, yes," Lorraine said. "With our help, absolutely. Just look at her!" She gazed at Maddalena with the ardor of a mother at her newborn baby, astonished by the miracle of her existence. "I'd be a fool to let you out of here without signing some papers."

"I've got my own pen!" Antonio said, and pulled one from the pocket of his blazer.

Things were moving very fast. Three days before, Maddalena had sat in an office much different from this one, hands folded, listening to Dr. Barone tell her there was nothing physically wrong with her or Antonio, that it must be her obviously frazzled nerves that prevented her from getting pregnant; three hours before, she'd dressed for a dinner party at the home of

Giovanni Vitale and his sweet but scatterbrained wife; now a kind stranger in a pink suit was grabbing hold of her life and steering it in a new direction.

"Two *d*s?" she asked Antonio, her pen on the lip of the folder. "Spell it for me again, please. Slowly."

What a thrill it was for Maddalena to see Lorraine print her full name, date of birth, and address on the complicated form and hand it to Antonio. It was an official document: the words small in places, bold and oversized in others. As Antonio looked it over, Lorraine reached into a drawer with her free hand and pulled out a stapler and a stack of colored folders.

"I don't know anyone else in America with my same name," said Maddalena, but Lorraine was not paying attention.

"Now, just to make sure," Antonio said, the tip of his pen on the bottom line of the form. "There's no risk to any of this. If she decides she can't do it, or you think she's not good enough, she can just stop?"

"Of course," Lorraine said. "We're not running a prison here. You owe us only the cost of materials, which is only fair."

"Materials?"

"Photographs, postage, cosmetics, various out-of-pockets. The usual."

Antonio looked up. "She pays this only if she quits, though, right?"

"Well, no," Lorraine said. "It's all in there." She pointed to the form. "Our fees are extremely reasonable, when you consider the guaranteed success we offer."

Antonio narrowed his eyes and kept reading. Maddalena looked over his shoulder, but she couldn't decipher enough of the words.

He turned the page over. It was blank. "I don't understand," he said. "On the phone you told me the agency pays for everything. That you get a cut only when the girl makes money."

"Oh, no," said Lorraine, gently. "If that was true, we couldn't afford the rent on *this* place." A look of concern fell over her face. "I'm afraid you misunderstood? Maybe I spoke too quickly, or something got lost in translation?"

Antonio rubbed his forehead. "How much would they cost, then, these materials?"

"It's extremely reasonable, as I said. But every girl is different, so the expenses will vary. Your wife will need to take a walking class, and experiment with a few skin products, and take a color test. After that it's hard to say. Her teeth are good, so you're saving a lot of money there—"

"The Russian paid for all these classes and tests?" Antonio interrupted.

"Irina was a special case," said Lorraine. "And even so, it's our policy not to discuss the terms of our clients' contracts. Rest assured: no one will know how much it takes to get Madeline some work."

"Maddalena," he said.

"Yes," said Lorraine. "It's a beautiful name. Unique enough to stand on its own, don't you agree? Like 'Valentino' or 'Sinatra.' I'm already thinking." She tapped her right temple with her finger. Then she got serious, pulled her chair closer to the desk. "Let me reassure you, Mr. Grasso. Once the work comes through, which it undoubtedly will, the fees won't hurt one bit. We have a very extensive network of opportunities. And a payment plan."

"Well, we're not paying a dime up front," he said.

"Antonio," said Maddalena.

At that moment, a woman passed in front of the open door. "Bianca!" Lorraine called. "Come in here!"

Not surprisingly, Bianca was a blonde. She had a thin frame, narrow hips, and an incongruously large rear end. Her entire body was on display in the black leotard she wore—the kind you might see on a dancer or a cat burglar. "Yes, darling," she said, in an accent Maddalena could identify only as British, but which may have been something more exotic. She grabbed the doorjamb and stood half-in, half-out of the office.

"You must see these photographs," Lorraine said.

Bianca held them at arm's length, in both hands, then brought them closer. She set them on the desk and examined them through the little looking glass. "Extraordinary," she said. "Absolutely extraordinary. The *presence*."

"That's exactly what I saw," said Lorraine.

"She's going to go very far in this business," Bianca said to Lorraine, as if Maddalena weren't sitting across from them. "When can we get her to see Ellie?"

"Actually," Lorraine said. "Mr. and Mrs. Grasso are having some second thoughts about us."

"Oh?" Now she turned to Maddalena. "With photos like that?"

"We're hoping you have some other plan," Maddalena said. "For poor people who can't afford to pay right away?"

"Hmm," Bianca said. "I'm sure something can be worked out. Lorraine?"

Lorraine ticked her head toward the door, and the two of them left the room to talk in private.

"*Andiamo*," Antonio said, and stood. "Let's go. This was too good to be true."

"We can't leave now," said Maddalena.

He rubbed his face. "They're lying to us, *tesoro*. You don't see that yet? They just want our money."

"How do you know for sure?"

"I don't have to. It's obvious."

She shook her head. "We have to wait for them to come back," she said. "It would be rude to just run away." And what was more, she thought: if Antonio refused, she'd grip the edges of her chair the way she had in the car. She would show him he couldn't hand her this new life, precious and dazzling as a ruby, just to snatch it back.

Lorraine returned alone. "Good news," she said, sat down, and gleefully blotted out a few of the lines on the form with a marker. Above the marker she wrote a figure that reflected a 15-percent discount on their training fees, valid only if they signed the papers today. She reminded them that it was their policy never to offer discounts, and that the office closed in twenty minutes.

Even with the discount, the fees were unmanageable, and though they could be paid in increments, the increments incurred interest. When all was said and done, Maddalena's instruction at the Bianca Talent Agency would cost more than three times Antonio's monthly salary.

"I know it seems like a lot at first," Lorraine said. "But I'll be very honest with you. Some girls walk in here, and I can see in two seconds that they'll never make it in this business. I could take their money, put them and their rich mothers through a lot of heartbreak, years and years of classes and shoots, and make life easy for me and my husband—we run the agency with Bianca, and between the three of us we have four children to raise—but I don't. I take only a few girls who come along." She sat back. "You're one of the few, Mrs. Grasso. And with the Italian angle—it's a lock."

She was begging her, Maddalena thought, the way a friend

would if she were about to make a terrible mistake. She believed no woman could look another woman in the eye like that and lie. It heartened her. So she said, "I was just thinking. Maybe I could work here in the office a few times a week." She glanced at Antonio. "I can't read or write English so good yet, but I could clean and dust and straighten up. Maybe do some sewing for the costumes?"

Lorraine looked closely at her. "We have an old Spanish lady who does that," she said. "Besides, we can't have one of our best girls mopping the floors. Can you imagine? What if Mr. Wanamaker walked in?"

Maddalena looked down. "So there's nothing else we can do?"

"You can have faith in yourself," Lorraine said. "You don't have to trust me, that's fine; but you do have to trust these pictures."

Antonio stood, shaking his head. "I don't believe you people," he said. He reached for Maddalena, but she remained in her seat, her eyes fixed on Lorraine's sculpted fingernails, the gloss of the polish, her creamy skin. "Come on, Maddalena."

This chance was passing, she knew, and she would never get another. Would it kill Antonio to give her the rest of her twenty minutes, if just so she could hear Lorraine continue to beg them to change their minds? Did she not deserve to hear who she might have become if she'd had more money, more faith, a dreamer for a husband?

"If they really want you," Antonio said, "they'll call us on the phone first thing Monday. They have our number."

Lorraine folded her hands. "I'm sorry," she said. "This is the best we can do. We won't call you."

Antonio took Maddalena's hand and lifted her from the seat. Head bowed, she was led out of the office, down the narrow hallway of women flirting and frowning and baring their teeth, through the empty waiting room, into the night.

They had nowhere to go. Without a good explanation for why they'd leave Giovanni Vitale's at six o'clock, they could not go home. Neither of them felt like coming up with a good lie or enduring his mother's thousand questions. So they drove around aimlessly downtown, hungry and disappointed and uncomfortable in their nice clothes.

After a while, Antonio headed out of the city, past the cemetery, where his parents had already purchased their plots, past Wilmington High School, where night classes were held. They passed the mansions of Westover Hills, with their stately pillars and round front windows that showcased enormous gold chandeliers. "Old Money Town," Antonio called it.

Then he looped back around, and they found themselves in the budding developments of New Castle, where people with seventeen thousand dollars of new money could buy a two-bedroom home of fifteen hundred square feet. The streets were wide and quiet here compared to what they were used to, with strips of mown grass between the sidewalk and the curb.

They fell into a familiar game: pointing out which of the houses they preferred. Most looked alike—a brick front, white wood shingles on the sides, black shutters—but every so often they'd come upon a bay window or a hip roof or a double door. Generally they favored ranches over split-levels, but they'd take either one on a corner lot. They decided they would never let their children junk up the lawn by leaving their bicycles out after dark. They'd plant tomatoes and zucchini and lettuce in a small backyard garden, which they'd shield from the road with an inconspicuous fence. There would be no grape arbor, no stone lions, and no statue of Mary on a circle of pine needles

(God forgive them). Nothing about their house would announce, "We're immigrants!" except the aroma of garlic and basil floating from the kitchen window. In the city, on Eighth Street, they were Italians; in the suburbs, on a place like Myrtle Avenue, they would be Americans, no different from anyone else. Their neighbors would stop in for coffee and cake; they'd trade recipes and borrow tools and water the plants for them if they ever took a vacation.

They talked like this, agreeing mostly, until nine o'clock. Then they drove to Fourth and Orange, and Maddalena waited in the car as Antonio fetched a free pizza and two small sodas. They parked in an empty lot off Glen Avenue and ate in the warm car, on paper plates, trying not to drip grease on the leather. The Brandywine River flowed just beyond the edge of the lot, fifty feet down, but they could not see it through the thick trees.

"I'm sorry," Antonio finally said, his features ghostly in the light of the streetlamp. "You know I'd give you the world if I could."

"Let's just pretend it never happened," said Maddalena.

"There's a small chance I'm wrong, you know," he said. "They might still call. If they do, I tell you, I'll start going to church again. But if you ask me—"

She covered her ears.

"They're smooth," he said. "That much I'll give them."

They stayed in the lot for a while. Antonio switched off the headlights, raised the volume on the radio, and put his arm around her shoulders. Nat King Cole sang "Mona Lisa." She laid her head on his chest, closed her eyes, and imagined herself at the kitchen window of their ranch house in Collins Park. She's drying dishes, watching her baby crawl across the grass. Her middle is fat and round with another one on the way. How quickly, she thought, how quietly one dream replaces another. How lucky it is, sometimes, when the ruby falls irretrievably through the sewer grate; only then can you let go of the nagging wish for someone to press it into your palm.

Antonio kissed the top of her head. He tucked her hair back to reach her ear, her neck, her lips. "We're the only ones here," he said. She nodded. The parking lot was empty. She let him pull down the straps of her dress— that flashy dress she'd loan to her neighbor and never want back—and spread her legs there in the cramped front seat of the Chevy, miles from Mario and Ida and their light-sleeping daughters. She relaxed, breathed easily, though her elbow smacked against the door and a sharp pain shot through her back when she arched it. And it occurred to her then—as Antonio fumbled to undo her zipper—that when Dr. Barone said she had a problem with her nerves, he may not have been referring to the sadness she'd felt every moment since leaving Santa Cecilia, or to her anxious failure to love her husband enough to forget she gave up her family and her country and another man for him. Maybe by nerves Dr. Barone meant something as simple as her fear of making even the slightest noise when Antonio made love to her, the rush of panic she felt when the mattress squeaked or a whimper escaped her mouth, the ever-presence of the eavesdroppers just beyond the bedroom wall. So here, in the empty parking lot, for the first time in her four years of marriage, she let out a wild cry—of surrender, of pleasure, of relief—and didn't care if anyone heard. Her cry provoked a similar response from Antonio, and soon they were both howling loudly, and laughing, and sticking and unsticking themselves from the sweaty leather; and after it ended, she thought, breathlessly, that if this abandon brought forth a child, then the disaster at the Bianca Talent Agency had a purpose after all.

6

Common Sense

EVERY CHRISTMAS, ANTONIO relies on Renato and Buzzy to steal him a beautiful gift for Maddalena. If they don't have an arrangement with someone on the inside of a department store, they show up in the middle of the day, and one of them distracts the salesperson with his broken English while the other stuffs his coat with a nightgown, a dress, a necklace. They store everything in the upstairs apartment, in what they call the Insurance Closet: stacks of jewelry boxes and eyeglass cases, silk blouses and fancy gowns on hangers. They have shoes in all sizes, hats, even a blender or two for their more domestic girlfriends. In return for the free gifts, Antonio gives them discounted bottles of whiskey and wine from Ida's brother's liquor store and helps in the pizzeria on holidays. His chief function, though, is to troubleshoot their more elaborate schemes—most of which are full of holes—so they don't get caught and ruin the system that has worked so well for nearly a decade.

"Time is running out," Antonio says. He stands in front of the enormous back sink, which steams from the dishes he's been washing. His apron is splattered with soapy water. He's worked at least twenty hours here since the first of December, more than enough for this year's worth of gifts. "What will Santa Claus bring my wife this Christmas?"

"Take your pick," Renato says, wiping down the prep table. "The Closet is full."

Antonio unties his apron. Water has soaked through to his shirt and wrinkled the tips of his fingers. Honest work for dishonest wages doesn't bother him one bit. In fact, it gives him great satisfaction to punish Sears and Roebuck and its kind for overcharging. He knows better than anyone the wholesale price of parts and ingredients: armrests at the Ford plant, tomatoes at Renato's and Mrs. Stella's, yards of fabric at the Golden Hem. The markups from assembly to sale enrage him. In stores, he often can't bring himself to purchase the product he's brought to the counter. So he looks for ways to barter, to get around the evils of commerce. In his own restaurant, he tells himself, he will charge a fair price for food and entertainment. The profits will be just enough to pay his family's basic expenses, nothing more. He won't be greedy. Customers will recognize this and come to a place like La Bella Trattoria not only to eat the best food in town and dance to beautiful music, but to support his philosophy, to show him respect.

Halfway up the stairs to the apartment, he hears voices. He steps back down. "Is somebody up here?" he calls to Renato.

He rushes over. "Officer Stanley!" he whispers. "I forgot! Tonight he breaks it off with the Puerto Rican girl."

"How long does that take?" Antonio checks his watch. "I've been here two hours."

"Who can say?" is Renato's reply. He twirls his rag around his index finger. "Maybe she changed his mind. They could be making up."

Officer Stanley—the old Irishman who treats Renato's like a cheap motel—is fully aware of the Insurance Closet. He has used it more than once this year on this same Puerto Rican girl. In exchange for his privacy, the officer makes sure the sidewalk and alleys around the pizzeria get swept and plowed and that an extra police car drives by each night.

"Maybe you should wait," Renato says. "Come have a drink with me. We'll talk business."

Antonio tenses. Renato hasn't mentioned Riverview Drive since that first night, now more than three weeks ago. Maybe the property has already sold to another "wop with a shop," as he likes to say, and he and Buzzy want to sabotage it. Or he has found another investor, a young man unattached to a wife and child. Antonio has too much pride to ask what's going on, to suggest a compromise plan to keep him involved; he must wait for Renato to make another offer. He has not admitted to anyone the new restaurant designs he's sketched on the backs of envelopes and napkins. Nor has he told Renato or Buzzy that Maddalena is finally expecting a child. He cannot bear the conclusions they will draw, the teasing that will follow.

Renato heats up two sausage rolls. They eat them with their hands, and afterward the outsides of their whiskey glasses are coated with grease. Renato doesn't mention Riverview Drive at all. He tells Antonio he wants to take Cassie to Italy for a vacation, then changes his mind and decides the Poconos are good enough. "Makes me sick to my stomach," he declares, on the topic of the colored family who has moved into the Seventh Street row home adjoining his mother's. He complains that the price of cigarettes has gone up.

When Renato gets up for another drink, Antonio's pride buckles. "And the new restaurant?" he asks, trying to sound as though it's just entered his mind. "What's the story?"

Renato shrugs. "What can I say?" He looks him in the eye. "You broke my heart, and we lost the space. End of story."

"You asked me one time," Antonio says. "One time only. I didn't know you were serious. If I knew——"

"Bullshit," says Renato. He smiles, not playfully, and tosses the empty whiskey bottle into the trash. "I have to ask you over and over, like you're some girl I want to take to bed?" He shakes his head. "It's better if we drop this conversation."

But Antonio has to know. "Who'd it go to?"

"Some Greek," Renato says. "He's already got the contractors in there. My man at the bank says he's going to sell steak dinners."

"I was the only one you asked?" Antonio says, but Renato doesn't answer.

They are quiet. The pipe drips under the sink. Antonio finds a rag, ties it around the leak, and now the only sound is the buzz of the fluorescent lights above them. "It's not a small decision," Antonio says. "Especially now. I can explain better——"

"I already know your reasons," says Renato. "Your wife, your job at Ford. Security. It all makes sense to me. I'm not angry with you, Antonio. What I am"—here he sits back in his chair and lowers his head—"is very very sad. Disappointed. You're like a brother to me. You and Mamma are my only family in this

country. I thought, maybe, if we opened the trattoria together—
like we wanted ten years ago—I would feel—I don't know—
settled. And with Cassie back, it starts to look like a life. I had
dreams like that."

Antonio avoids his eyes. He wipes his hands and listens to
the movement that has begun upstairs. It sounds as though a
bed is being dragged across the floor. A radio comes on, mur-
murs staticky jazz for a while, then settles on Patti Page singing
"Come What May."

"In five years, you think I want to still be living here with
Buzzy? With the policeman and his *puttane?*"

"It's not such a bad life," Antonio says. What he really wants
to say is: What about me? Where will I go if you become another Gianni? Can you promise we'll get another chance at the
trattoria when my life is more settled? "You have all the freedom
you want, your own money, nobody holding you down. Be sure
before you throw it away."

"I'm sure," says Renato. "One hundred percent. And you
know Cassie better than anybody. She's like a wildcat. If I don't
marry her soon, some other man will tame her. And she's too
good to lose."

Can Renato see the shock on Antonio's face? Marry Cassie
Donovan? He'll never go through with it. Antonio gives him
ten years at least before he gives up the bachelor life. Then he'll
find a wife in Italy, the way all smart men do. Renato would
never poison a church marriage with Cassie's dirty history, her
nights with Antonio, Buzzy, and God knows how many other
men. Even little Paolo has tasted her. The absurdity convinces
Antonio that Renato is testing—or, worse, tricking—him. He
takes the bait and says, mockingly, "You're lucky she took you
back, *uaglio.*"

"Lucky is right," Renato says. "Most girls I'm with, I think: Look at me. I'm a know-nothing immigrant. I came to this country when I was eight, but I never finished the sixth grade. And still I'm smarter than you." He laughs. "But with Cassie— that girl is sharp as a whip. She has ideas. The way her mind works sometimes, I can't keep up. I can't get away with anything."

"That's good?" Antonio asks.

"That's very good," says Renato. "That's the best. It's like— the same feeling I get when I'm walking around the jewelry store with a gold necklace in my pocket. They can catch me any second. My blood is pumping. I'm short of breath. That's how it is with Cassie all the time." He laughs again. "It's like I can feel her eyes following me, but I think I'm home free; and then just before I walk out the door, she sticks a gun at my back and says, Gotcha."

Antonio considers this. Maddalena lets him get away with everything. He is seven years older, has seen more of the world, can speak two languages without much trouble. He reads the newspaper. He can argue his way out of most of their disagreements, sometimes by inventing statistics, historical events, and laws to prove his point. "How can you want to vote?" he said to her last November. "You can't even spell *Philadelphia*. You think Eisenhower should be president because he has a nicer face, and you're tired of looking at Truman." Though this brings on a wave of guilt, it is the quickest way to win their fights. She gives him a fierce look, her eyes welling with tears, and tells him he may have read more books, he may know fancy words and ideas, but she has something he'll never have: *common sense*. She enunciates this term in English, with great care. She has taken it to heart. She believes common sense is her greatest strength, and she may be right.

Officer Stanley appears on the stairs, the Puerto Rican girl at his side. He kisses her forehead before she slinks out the back door. He tucks in his shirt and checks his face in the cracked oval mirror above the sink. "Thank you, boys," he says as he approaches. Renato offers him a drink, but he declines. He is on duty.

"How did she take it?" asks Renato.

He shakes his head. "I'm a weak man," he says. "We'll be back tomorrow."

After he leaves, Renato takes Antonio up to the Closet. They are not surprised to find it ransacked, shoeboxes and hangers strewn across the floor. Renato picks up the one empty box and says, "Looks like Prince Charming found his Cinderella," and Antonio laughs along, though he does not know the reference.

"I need something special this year," Antonio says. He picks through the hangers one by one, holding up blouses and scarves to the light. In the jewelry boxes are diamond pendants, plain necklaces, Italian horn charms, and gold crosses in various sizes—all of which Antonio has rejected before. He sighs and tosses a cheap silver bracelet onto the heap. "When's the next shipment?" he asks.

"Buzzy's in the clouds with love," says Renato. Then, after a pause, "Maybe I am, too. Who knows? We don't have any jobs lined up before Christmas. Not for more gifts, at least." He stifles a mischievous smile.

"What am I supposed to do, then?" says Antonio, ignoring the smirk on Renato's face. He sounds like his niece, Nunzia, whining to her father. He sits on the edge of the bed. Last year, he took a gold ring with one bright ruby in the center. He hid it under Maddalena's pillow after she fell asleep, then woke her an hour later because he couldn't wait for her to find it. This year he must outdo himself, in honor of the baby.

He is impatient for the Christmas Eve festivities to start, if only to break the silence between him and Maddalena. To reconcile before then would be to admit defeat, to signal a shakiness in his authority. Surrender even a little bit to your wife, he knows, and her voice gets louder and louder until it drowns yours out completely. It happened to Gianni. It was about to happen to Renato. Antonio already allowed Maddalena to return to the Golden Hem, a decision she must consider a victory. She did not know he needed her to make all the money she could—not only for the child, but for the trattoria.

"I'm very sorry the Closet disappoints you," says Renato. He digs through the pile and uncovers a heart-shaped locket on a chain. He snaps it open and shut. "What about this? It's real silver. You put a little picture inside—what could be more romantic? Buzzy gave one of these to Marcie, and she fell down on the ground crying. I even have a little pink box for it somewhere—"

Antonio rolls the locket around in his palm. It feels heavy enough. If it were gold, it might make the perfect gift. "You don't understand," says Antonio. He cups the locket in both hands and shakes it like dice. He lowers his eyes. "Maddalena—she's going to have a baby."

Renato raises his arms above his head. "Well, *grazie Dio!*" he says. "We thought the day would never come."

Antonio braces himself for the teasing. He's already prepared his responses: they made love at a different time of day; the pregnancy is a sign from God that Maddalena should not work; the doctor prescribed her a new kind of pill. He has yet to convince himself fully that any of these might be true, that that man in Philadelphia has not made him a *cornuto*. He keeps the address and phone number of the Golden Hem in his wallet, just in case. And though he believes the impossible can't be true, he cannot stop imagining the worst. In his mind, he sees the man force Maddalena against the wall of his office. He sees the shame on her face and her desperation to hide the truth from her husband. For this he blames Buzzy, whose stories of Germany and his many women have alerted him to the wickedness of men. Then he blames himself for not making enough money to keep his wife at home where she belongs, where she is protected.

"When did you find out?" Renato asks.

"Last night," Antonio lies.

"Just in time for Christmas!" He takes Antonio's hands in his and holds them. "Congratulations, my friend. Always one step ahead of me. Two steps now. I wish you and the beautiful Maddalena all the luck in the world."

They sit on the couch, which for some reason Officer Stanley has pulled into the center of the room. The apartment is sparsely decorated: one crucifix on the otherwise bare white walls; a tall lamp in the corner that emits a dull, flat light; a pair of swinging saloon-style doors that lead to the kitchen. The radio spits static at them from the windowsill. The bedrooms consist of one bed, two dressers with the drawers half-open and overflowing, and floors covered with clothes and damp towels. For drapes they use sheets secured to the rods with clothespins. The bathroom, however, is immaculate. Buzzy scrubs the sink, shower, toilet, and wall tiles once a week. He arranges the toothbrushes and soaps neatly on the countertop, a gleaming speckled Formica. As for his skin creams, he hides those in a plastic bag under his bed next to his boots and dirty magazines, but everyone knows they are there.

"I don't think I'm a step ahead of anybody," says Antonio. He leans over and switches off the radio. "This should have happened a long time ago, the way I see it. But what can you do?"

"If I were you, I'd be singing up and down the street."

Antonio shrugs. "A child is a lot of responsibility," he says. "A lot of money, if you want to do it right."

"Money!" says Renato. "Oh, I wish Buzzy could hear you. Money is the first thing on your mind always, Antonio. Everything costs too much. Everyone's trying to screw you out of a dollar. You want a beautiful present for your wife, but you don't want to pay for it. You'd rather waste twenty hours of your life washing dishes than write a check to the jeweler."

"I don't want to work as hard as I do for nothing," he says.

"Who does?" says Renato. "But you have to live, too. To take pleasure. Why work so hard if you can't enjoy it? Why have a baby at all?"

"Sometimes I wonder," says Antonio. He thinks a moment. They do not face each other. They cross their legs and stare straight ahead, talking to the empty room. "To pass on your name, right? Isn't that the reason? To play with on the beach. To take care of you when you're old."

"I was teasing, Antonio," Renato says. "A baby is—is God's miracle! It's a blessing from above." He shakes his head. "I almost had my own once, you know. A long time ago."

Antonio turns to him. "When?"

"With the girl—Angelina—but we got rid of it. I never saw her again."

"I don't know any Angelina," Antonio says. "Where was I?"

"You weren't paying attention," says Renato. "But it doesn't matter anymore. I have another chance with Cassie." He digs between the cushions, pulls out a white sock, and throws it across the room. It lands on the top rung of the coatrack. "You don't know how good your life is. You walk around here half-asleep most of the time. Buzzy and I see it. Even Cassie sees it. We say to each other, 'Poor Antonio. So rich and so stupid.' The only thing that goes wrong in your life so far is that it takes Maddalena a few years longer than usual to have a baby. I don't call that a tragedy."

"Who said tragedy?" says Antonio. "Tragedy is war. Hunger. Poverty. The last twenty years—in Italy, in Germany, in Korea, even here—all tragedy." Then he lets this go. It is beside the point. He does not say how easy it is to see richness in another man's life; the trick was to see it in your own. One step ahead of Renato and Buzzy, he knows, means one step closer to Gianni, to old age, to death. Yes, he has wanted a child since the moment he saw Maddalena in the village. He has longed for the baby, imagined again and again the moment he'd first hold him in his arms. But now that the time has come, he feels a gathering fear. "Where's that pink box?" he asks Renato.

They stand, and Renato hands him the gift. He kisses him on both cheeks and again wishes him luck and congratulations.

The fastest route home from the pizzeria is to take Fourth Street down and up the hill to Union, then make a left on Eighth. Two turns. Instead, Antonio cuts across Washington to Pennsylvania Avenue, then zigzags through the neigborhood. Such is life when you're young, he thinks: taking the long way for no good reason. Then you get old, and one by one the streets close around you, and before long you're stuck on the same one route from home to work, work to home, with no means or cause to step off track. You wait for your son to live the better life you failed to provide. This is the story of his father, of most of the men at the Ford plant, and soon of the great playboy Renato Volpe.

He spits onto the sidewalk. At the corner of Clayton and Fifth, he takes Fifth, though it's in the opposite direction of his house. On this block once lived a family of three brothers, friends of the Grassos, who came from a village in Abruzzo not far from Santa Cecilia. Not one of them saw fifty years of age. At forty-six, the oldest dropped dead on the dance floor at his niece's wedding. The middle went while throwing a bocce ball; the youngest in his sleep. They had weak hearts, the doctors said, and now their widows live together in a home paid for by the church, three young single ladies who will never again be kissed or loved or given a locket in a heart-shaped box. In a few years, Antonio will turn thirty-five. He has a good decade to spend not worrying over the strength of his own heart. He is a young American, smarter than his brother and Renato put together. If he reminds himself of this more often, there is no telling how his story will end.

THE NIGHT BEFORE Christmas Eve, Antonio receives a rare telephone call from Renato. Something has happened. He leaves immediately, after a hurried and unconvincing explanation to his family. If she'd been a different woman—more suspicious, or maybe just less busy—Maddalena might think he had a girl on the side, but, as far as Antonio knows, she trusts that whatever road he takes at night, it always leads back to her. His last glimpse of her on this cold and rainy December evening is from behind: her apron crisscrossing her waist, her elbows thrust back as she kneads dough. She turns her head to the side and ticks it upward as he mumbles his good-byes. There's a smudge of flour on her cheek as if from a paintbrush, and he feels the urge to wipe it clean.

Renato has locked the whiskey in the cabinet, put on a pot of espresso, and gathered everyone around the back table. Cassie bounces on his knee, though there's a perfectly empty chair beside him. Though the air outside is below freezing, she wears a tank top and jeans, her hair in a ponytail. "This girl's our secret weapon," Renato says. He kisses her bare shoulder, which is inexplicably tan.

"We've been working on a plan," Renato says, and explains that this one requires concentration. It is much more serious than stealing necklaces from Wanamaker's. It is so serious, in fact, that he trusts only Cassie, Buzzy, Antonio, and one other man—whom he hasn't yet named—to hear the details. He sends little Paolo home early, Marcie upstairs.

"Should I be nervous?" Antonio asks.

"Yes," says Renato. "But don't worry too much. You won't be involved. Not completely. But I need your mind. And your brother's restaurant."

"If my brother's involved, then I'm involved," says Antonio.

"Mrs. Stella's plays a very minor part," Renato says. "Listen first, ask questions later." He takes a breath, stirs some sugar into his espresso. "You know what lives next door to my mother now. I can't stand the sight anymore. Every day I visit her, and every day there they are in the backyard. Talking. Smoking. Throwing a football back and forth. Anything but working. More and more and more of them, like the roaches in Mrs. Stella's kitchen." He nudges Antonio with his elbow, but Antonio's blank expression does not change.

"This much I know," he says. "Everybody knows. But what can you do?"

"You can't keep track of those people: the big fat ones, the screaming little babies, they go in and out like it's a hotel. We go into our kitchen, there they are through the windows. Last night we ate in the dining room, and we could hear them like they were sitting in our laps. Yelling at each other, crying, banging on the wall. Like animals. What's that house going to be worth in twenty years when Mamma's gone?"

"Less than dirt," says Cassie.

"Less than dirt is right," says Renato. "If they keep their hands on it. So I have to take steps. Big steps. To protect Mamma. She has nightmares. Thank God Papà didn't live to see it. But if he was alive today he'd kill me for doing nothing to protect her—and his investment."

Cassie cracks a smile. "I told him he should be a good son and move back in with her." She pinches his cheek. "Then we get married, and I come to live there, too. One big happy family."

Renato leans over in his chair. He looks each person in the eye. "I tell you: big steps. Soon. It's gone on too long already. Here's the plan. Cassie's going to stop into the bar at Mrs. Stella's just before it closes. She'll drink a little too much—not hard for her, to be sure—and she'll give the restaurant the name of a taxi. The man next door to Mamma, the head of the family, if you can call him that, works at the taxi company. When he comes to pick her up, she tells him she lives in Marcus Hook, and he drives her to my friend Lino's house. You don't know Lino. He used to be a boxer. He has no heart for these *mulignani* trying to take over. He moved all the way to Marcus Hook to get away from them, and even that's not far enough these days. So the *mulignane* drives her to Lino's house, and when he tells her the fare, she says, 'I have no money,' and makes him come inside Lino's if he wants to get paid."

"*Gesù Cristo*," Antonio says. "Then what, you beat him up?

My brother can't be tied to this. Why does it have to be Mrs. Stella's she came from?"

"It's two blocks from my mother's house. He's the closest taxi, so there's a good chance they'll call him. If they don't call him, we keep trying different nights until they do. It might take a few tries, but the important thing is to make it look natural."

"Keep going," Buzzy says. "Let's hear the whole plan before Antonio tells us what's wrong with it."

"We don't beat him up," Renato says. "That's the beauty. Cassie has a much more elegant idea—"

"We get him inside," Cassie interrupts. "Lino's there, right? And Renato, and maybe Buzzy too." She glances at him. "In front of them, I tell the man, 'You won't be getting any money tonight. You drove me all the way to Marcus Hook to try to—' and then I tear my blouse and slap my face a little. I start to cry. The man is confused. Then he understands and gets nervous. He throws up his hands and tries to leave. Then Renato tells him—"

"Get out of Seventh Street!" Renato says, standing. He points his finger at Antonio as if he were the colored man. Cassie slides over to the empty seat. "If you and your monkeys aren't gone in one week, this girl tells the police what you did to her."

"I've got tears all down my face, and I'm screaming," Cassie says. She thrashes and musses her hair and runs her nails up and down her neck, making red marks. "I can't control myself."

"You see the quality of actress she is," Renato continues, still talking to the colored man. "Who's going to believe you over her?"

"So much for going straight," Antonio says, in Italian. He pushes his chair away from the table. "I don't know why you tell me these things. Stealing bracelets is different than—"

"What did he say?" Cassie asks. "Anytime you talk Italian, I know it's about me."

"After he's gone, my uncle from Naples moves in," Renato says. "He's been waiting to come here since the war. For a free place to live, he'll help take care of my mother. Cassie and I will stay here and kick Buzzy out. Everybody's happy."

"Except Buzzy," Buzzy says. "Where am I supposed to live?"

"You could buy all of Seventh Street with the cash in your mattress," says Renato. "You stayed with me this long because you're a tightwad."

"I don't want them in my neighborhood any more than you do," Antonio says. "Two of them come to my street. Every morning I sweep up their cigarettes, like I'm their maid. I'm so angry I can take the broom and—" He takes a swing like he's aiming for a baseball. "But your plan is not right. First of all, it's sloppy. A hundred things can go wrong. Second of all, it's dangerous for everybody."

"That's why I called you here," says Renato. "To give us a better plan. To improve this one. To do what you can for your friends and your people." He pulls his chair closer to the table and folds his hands. "Now, tell us how to make it work."

Antonio rubs his face. "I need to think it over for a few days."

"In a few days, ten more of them will move in. We need your help now."

"*Esagerato*," Antonio says. "Nobody moves this time of year."

"I like *this* plan," says Cassie. "I don't understand why Antonio gets to decide. He's too scared to even be there."

"He's the family man," Renato says. "His head is on straight. More straight than mine or yours. If he could get the beautiful

Maddalena to marry him, he must have something upstairs that we don't."

"Can you unlock the whiskey now?" Antonio asks.

"What, modest all of a sudden?" says Renato. "You walk into your village, pick an eighteen-year-old girl you barely know, and a month later she's your wife. Smile on your face when you come back here like you won the lottery." He turns to Cassie. "Even before, when we used to go out together in Wilmington, he would tell me, 'Renato, let me do the talking,' and a minute later, two girls come to our table with free drinks and invite us to some private party."

"And if my memory serves me," says Buzzy, "he worked some magic on you, too, Cassie."

Renato pretends not to hear this, but Cassie rolls her eyes. "Fine. I'm not going to talk anymore. I do all the hard thinking work, but no one cares about my opinion."

"I care," says Renato and gives her shoulder another smooch.

Antonio checks his watch. It's not late enough to use time as an excuse. "There's an easier way to do this," he says.

"Good," says Renato. "Then come up with one. Otherwise, it's Cassie's plan next week. Between Christmas and New Year's. I'm counting on you. This is bigger than Riverview Drive. It has to do with friendship—loyalty—not money. And who's to say that, someday, one won't lead to the other? That a favor now won't affect a favor later?"

The two coffees, and now Renato's threat, have set Antonio's heart going.

"You know who else is counting on you?" Renato continues. "My mother, in her bed right now with the covers pulled up to her neck, scared to death."

"We should go there this minute," says Cassie. "Make sure she's OK."

"Don't tell your brother anything," Renato says. "It's better if no one at Mrs. Stella's knows. Remember: everything natural, and no one gets in trouble."

So much for the beauty of Christmas, Antonio thinks. "Are we playing cards tonight, or what?" he asks. Renato stares at him. "How did everything get so serious all of a sudden? I come here to relax. If I can't relax in the pizzeria, where am I supposed to go?"

"We're not teenagers anymore," says Renato. "If we don't protect what we have, nobody will do it for us. You know that better than I do."

"I don't like this plan," says Antonio. "Not one bit. I'm telling you that as a friend, Renato. Someone's going to get hurt, and it's not going to be the *mulignane*."

"Then fix it," says Buzzy. "Knock some sense into these two." He yawns. "I'm going up to Marcie. I have a stomachache."

"He doesn't have the stomach for anything anymore," Renato says.

Buzzy's hair is going gray. He colors it with some sort of oil, but the roots of his curls are darker than the ends, and nothing about it looks natural. Before taking the stairs, he unbuttons his shirt at the collar to impress Marcie with his chest hair, which he also regulates with the oil. Buzzy has admitted his fear that Marcie will discover his secret and leave him for a younger man. This, Antonio thinks, is the sort of problem he could handle. He'd tease Buzzy a little, get him cursing, then remind him: not a single one of your women has ever called you the next Cary Grant, and look how you've scored.

But the kind of crime Renato's talking about? With that Antonio has no experience, and now it seems it might decide not only their friendship, but future business. He can't let Renato down again. In the past, he has tracked when and where the clerks at Braunstein's take their afternoon breaks. He has found Buzzy a free garage to hide his car in the weeks after a job. Unlike this plan, stealing from department stores hurts no one. He has to think fast.

Cassie watches him, arms crossed, as if she can see this plan turning over in his mind: vandalism. Rocks thrown at the window. A two-a.m. visit from an angry Officer Stanley. He doesn't like it, exactly—he won't do any of it himself—but it's less complicated, more direct, than Cassie's idea. It's what the coloreds should expect, anyway, living apart from their own kind.

Cassie's eyes dare him to speak. Buzzy comes back down in his underwear and shirtsleeves for a sandwich. Finally Antonio says, "All right, this is it. This is what I suggest." He stands in front of Renato and raises his right fist like a politician's. "Old-fashioned intimidation. We send these people a message. First, we paint GO HOME on a brick and throw it at the front door. Second, we slash the tires of the taxi and stuff an Italian flag in the gas tank." This will work over time, Antonio assures them. All it requires is a little patience.

"Teenage pranks?" Cassie says. "That's your smart family-man idea?"

They can't afford patience, Renato argues. He has been patient long enough. Besides, that race is very stubborn; too stubborn to let a few broken windows scare them off.

"This is the traditional way," Antonio counters. "And the traditional way always works. It's human nature. No man keeps his wife and family in danger for long. I promise: you hit them hard the first time, they'll be gone soon after."

"I thought of something like this already," Renato says. "For the same reasons. Then Cassie changed my mind." He's quiet for a while before he turns to her. "This is much easier, you have to admit."

Cassie shakes her head. "Too easy, if you ask me," she says. "What's fun about it? It has no imagination!"

"This isn't Broadway," says Buzzy, listening from the stairs.

Renato rubs her shoulder. "You'll get your chance, my little actress," he says, with a wink. "Don't worry. But maybe we try Antonio's plan first, and if it doesn't work, we try yours."

"That makes sense to me," says Antonio. "Go with the first idea you have. That's another tradition of human nature: trust the gut."

"Traditions are boring," Cassie says. "Not to mention a waste of time."

"Don't worry," Renato repeats. "You won't be bored for long. Not with me around."

At midnight, Antonio pushes through the front door onto the sidewalk. He waves to Officer Stanley, who sits smoking in the front seat of his patrol car, and struggles into his coat. An uneasiness comes over him, not only because he has stayed out too late again and will pay for it in the morning, but because he can't shake the suspicion that Renato and Buzzy agreed too easily to his change of plans. They may only be humoring him. He has to play both sides of this, make sure no harm comes either to Mrs. Stella's or to his friendship with Renato. He walks quickly, his head lowered against the gusting cold.

Before he realizes where his mind is taking him, he's reached the glowing neon sign at 522 North Union Street. He finds Mario out front, helping an old woman in a fur coat down the steps. "See you next week, Signora Finch," he tells her. "Or should I say next year?" He gives an exaggerated laugh that echoes through the streets. "Nineteen fifty-four! Can you believe it?" He guides the woman into the passenger's seat of an idling Lincoln, then waits as the car pulls away.

"Always the gentleman," says Antonio.

"*Fratello!*" Mario says. "Where'd you come from? What a nice surprise." He hugs him. "Did you see Mrs. Finch?" He rubs his fingers together to indicate her wealth.

"Listen," Antonio says, before he changes his mind. He takes out a handkerchief and blows his nose. Then, with one foot in the gutter and the other on the sidewalk, he tells Mario the details of Cassie's plan. Just in case they go behind his back. If they'd asked him for another tradition, he might have told them this: blood is thicker than water.

"Come in for some coffee," says Mario. "Looks like you could use it. You're not making much sense."

"It's Christmastime," Antonio says, as he follows his brother into the warmth of the restaurant. "There should be peace between us."

"I didn't know we were at war" is Mario's response.

7
Tombola

THE WEEK OF Christmas Eve, the women wake before dawn to shop and prepare the men's lunches. After work, there is the weekday dinner to fix, the gifts to buy and wrap, and every room to clean for the guests who will stop in over the next month. Every piece of silverware must be polished, every yard of drapery washed and rehung, every wall scrubbed. Maddalena sweeps under the stove and dusts the bulbs on the chandeliers and candelabra; she irons the tablecloths and napkins; she writes a card to her family and encloses the check for twenty-five dollars that Antonio has left on the dresser. She and Ida argue with the fishmonger over the paltry size of this year's catches, which stare up at them open-mouthed from their beds of ice. They buy and prepare flounder and scallops and smelts and anchovy sauce, batter for the apple and cauliflower *frittelli*, and trays of fried dough lightly powdered with sugar. They make twelve pounds of linguini by hand and dry them on the basement ironing table. The entire basement is smudged with flour—the floor, the cabinet handles, the stacks of pots and pans. Every few hours, they change the water in which the salt cod is soaking to achieve the perfect *baccalà*. The stink of raw fish—salty, intestinal—lingers in their clothes and hair, and Maddalena is convinced that everyone at the Golden Hem can smell it.

Maddalena and Ida leave work at noon on Thursday the twenty-fourth. On the bus they share a roasted red pepper sandwich, three apples and—a rare treat—a can of soda from the factory vending machine. Meat is forbidden until midnight. "Finally," says Maddalena, as she slides down the vinyl seat and stretches her legs. She closes her eyes. To her, the bus rides are like little vacations, an hour of guilt-free rest. There is nothing to clean or cook here, no one's hair to brush, no windows to clear of grime—though these could certainly use it. As darkness falls, an old woman at the back of the bus hums "Silent Night," and soon the other voices fade. Maddalena drifts off to sleep with a vision of Jesus' manger filling with snow, the baby shivering, Mary in her blue veil beside Him.

By six o'clock, the house is full. Ida's brother arrives with his family of boys carrying toy cars; Signora Fiuma from next door brings her niece and her new baby; Antonio's friends, Gianni among them, show up with their families in shifts through the night, one man with his tall American wife who drinks beer; before they sit down to eat, Father Moravia—who came over with Papà Franco in '31—blesses the table and wishes everyone a year filled with the love of Christ; Papà's widower friend, who might be a distant cousin if a certain photograph can be verified, sings "Tu Scendi dalle Stelle" out of key for the women putting away the dishes, and when the men hear how bad his voice is, they gather at the doorway to join in and rescue the melody.

On his own, Antonio has chosen to wear a coat and tie with the white shirt and gray pants Maddalena set out for him. He has even tucked a handkerchief in the front pocket of the coat. He keeps to his mother's side in the kitchen, helping to dry the good silverware before it is returned to its velvet-lined case. Maddalena catches him watching her, and for once he does not avert his eyes. He gazes at her, expressionless, unblinking, until she turns away. She cannot read him, but she senses that—one way or another—the silence game is about to end.

Mario shows up after dinner, stays an hour, and talks of nothing but the crowd at Mrs. Stella's. Ida and the girls gather around him as if he's Babbo Natale himself. He bounces Nina on his lap and twirls one of her dark curls around his fingers as he tells her how badly he's needed "on the floor."

"I'm on the floor, Babbo!" Nunzia says, and rolls around in front of the stereo.

"Get up!" says Ida, pulling on her arm. "You're wrinkling your dress."

Maddalena sets aside a plate for the man with the accordion. "Do you think Signor Fabbri could play a little bit while he's here?" she asks Mario. "Or will he be too tired?"

"Who?" he replies, the tail of a smelt between his lips. "Oh yes, Giulio. The Music Man. What do you think, should I invite him?"

"You didn't do it yet?" his mother says, from the other side of the kitchen. "What's the matter with you?"

"I guess I forgot," says Mario. "First thing when I get back, though, I'll ask him. If I remember. I'll tell him to bring the accordion if he wants."

"Make sure he comes," Maddalena says. "Nobody should be alone tonight."

After dinner, Ida brings a large gold tray stacked with espresso cups. Mamma Nunzia follows behind her with the *panettone* and cookies. Maddalena carries two pewter pots of coffee, still steaming. As she walks around the table to serve the guests, Ida and Mamma disappear into the kitchen. They return a moment later with two bottles of Asti and another gold tray, this one crowded with tall flute glasses.

Maddalena blushes. She rests her hand on the shoulder of Ada Martino, Gianni's wife. Please don't, she thinks. But they do.

"*Attenzione!*" Ida shouts. She hands one of the bottles to Mario and taps a glass with her fork. "Time for happiness!"

Antonio lowers his head.

Mario stands and takes his place beside Ida. He will do the talking now. "My wife and I just want to say that, for Christmas, God has given the Grasso family some very good news." The crowd quiets to a hush. Nunzia jumps up and down. Mario looks back and forth from Maddalena to Antonio. "After seven years of marriage," he says, "my brother and my sister-in-law are finally going to have a baby!" Upon uttering the word "baby," he pops the cork of the bottle, and the Asti spills out onto his hands and the tablecloth. The cork hits the ceiling, ricochets against the banister, and lands in Papà's coffee cup.

Everyone laughs. There is much clapping, and suddenly the supple arms of Ada Martino are wrapped around Maddalena. She kisses her cheek, and the cheeks of the parade of mothers who squeeze behind the table to congratulate her. The fervor with which they pinch her belly and tug her ear is sure to leave bruises. They point to their respective children across the room, and say, "Would you believe my Gabriella was only four pounds

when she was born?" and "Doesn't Stefano look just like his father?" as if Maddalena is seeing them for the first time. On the
other side of the table, the men shake Antonio's hand and clap
him on the back.

As Maddalena clinks her glass with Ida's, then downs it
quickly, she cannot help but feel triumphant. These women, all
Antonio's people in one way or another, have been cold to her
from the day she arrived in Wilmington. "Because you have
movie-star looks and they do not," Antonio explained, but
Maddalena knew that was only half the reason. She had yet to
prove herself to them, to give a satisfactory answer to their unspoken questions: are you good enough for the Grasso family or
just a prima donna? Do you refuse to have a baby because you
are looking for someone better? Did you marry Antonio just for
the free trip across the ocean?

Maddalena has wanted to answer them with these words: "I
walked onto that ship seven years ago like a mourner to her own
funeral. I gave up everything for a man I barely knew and did
not yet love. You should be comforting me." But she could not
embarrass Antonio, who turned their arrangement into a
romance—*The Dream of the Village Girl*, it might be called. "She
was so sweet, so innocent," he used to say upon introducing her.
"I picked her like a flower from the rocky soil of Italy, and now
here she blooms."

After this sort of introduction, Maddalena can hardly blame
them for disliking her, for taking a not-so-secret pleasure in her
failure to become a mother. By a certain age, don't all women
give up on romance and resent the young girl who still feels entitled to it? If only they knew that Maddalena no longer feels
entitled. She believes in romance, yes, in the man charging
across the drawbridge to burst through the castle doors—but

not for her. For her nieces, or her own child, or the American girls with their unchartable futures ahead of them. It is almost enough for Maddalena to live through someone else's love story; it frees her, at least, from the disquiet of her own decisions. Then, when the romance fades—as it always will; she knows this much about the world—she'll feel no guilt, no responsibility, only a vicarious and manageable heartbreak.

"I have some top-quality maternity dresses," whispers Elena, one of Signora Fiuma's daughters-in-law. "But you're probably too tall for them."

In the commotion, Maddalena and Antonio manage to avoid each other, and before long the room returns to normal. With nearly as much fanfare as he announced the pregnancy, Mario informs the guests that the time has come for him to return to Mrs. Stella's. He stands at the door, his coat thrown over his shoulder, and gives the crowd a big wave. The moment he's gone, Antonio pours himself a shot from the liquor cabinet. He drinks it in one gulp, then pours another.

Maddalena watches him from the kitchen. He stares into his whiskey the way a woman stares into a lake, as if seeking an honest answer from the reflection. If she dared, she could give him that answer, but even such knowledge will not settle him. For many years now Maddalena has been aware of Antonio's secret affliction, the poison in his blood that will never allow him the pure, peaceful health of men like Gianni or Mario. At first she called it ambition—to have more money, to drive a Cadillac, to own a three-bedroom house in Westover Hills. But ambition is a simple hunger. The demands of jealousy, though, can never be met. A green eye, she has heard it called; if that's true, Antonio has two. The eyes see everything he wants in the lives of other men but are blind to the joys of his own life. And yet these same eyes are fiercely protective of what he has, Maddalena above all, and see threats coming from all directions.

Antonio's jealousy of Mario is obvious to everyone—except, maybe, Mario and Ida, too busy with their own jealousy to notice—but Maddalena believes it has nothing to do with the success of Mrs. Stella's. If Mario lost the restaurant and got locked up in debtor's prison, Antonio would find something to envy in his desperate circumstances: his vacation from the daily aggravations of wife and family, the attention and help he'd get from their father, the challenge to rebuild his life from scratch. Antonio is jealous of men with five children, but surely he longs just as ardently for his bachelorhood—why else does he lie about the nights at the pizzeria with Renato? Why else did Maddalena's good news not soothe him?

She once resented Antonio for his affliction; now—in spite of the way he has treated her—she feels mostly compassion. Look at him: a man lost in his own house, afraid to ask for directions from the one person he can trust. He grips his whiskey glass, walks hesitantly toward the stairs, stops, rubs his face, turns back for a moment, catches her standing there, spins around again, and heads for the porch. Other women fear their husbands will strike them; Maddalena fears the damage Antonio might do to himself.

Strange that the first glimmer of love Maddalena felt for Antonio started in this room, on this same holiday, their third as a married couple. At the time, she still thought of him less as a husband than a friendly uncle, a grown-up for whom she had to behave like a lady so as not to displease her parents. She used to fix her hair and makeup early in the morning, so that when he woke he'd find a good young wife tidying up the bedroom, pulling back the drapes. He never saw her naked, as their love-making was accomplished in the dark, hastily, in decorous silence, and with her nightgown tucked under the pillow so that she could slip it on immediately afterward. She learned to separate this part of her life from the rest, often forgetting it occurred at all. Then she'd get her monthly bleeding and relive all the nights Antonio pulled the nightgown up over her head.

Antonio protected her, supplied her with enough money for groceries, and every few months surprised her with a new dress or a coat from John Wanamaker's to lift her spirits. Dutifully he mailed her weekly letters to Santa Cecilia, paid for photographs to be taken and sent over, and arranged scratchy, expensive transatlantic phone calls during which Maddalena could muster only an anguished weeping. "*Cara, cara di Mamma*," chanted her mother across the thousands of miles, with her sisters' voices echoing from the interior of the *municipio* where they had traveled to take the call. Her brother serenaded her, drunkenly, with old songs like "Madonna Fiorentina" and "Il Primo Pensiero"; her father described the snow and the rot that had withered their row of chestnut trees. During the precious two minutes they had together, each Piccinelli desperately repeated his or her own name—"*Sono io, Teresa!* It's me, Teresa! Teresa!"—as if to confirm with the unquestionable authenticity of voice that they still lived, they had not forgotten her. For Maddalena, the phone calls were torturous, a penance for the crime of abandoning them. She'd lay in the upstairs room for hours afterward with a cold towel on her forehead, and Antonio would knock gently on the door to check on her. He promised to take her back to Italy someday, once they had the money, but Maddalena knew she'd never see her family again in this life, and she couldn't promise her husband she could leave them if she did.

The week of this third Christmas together, Maddalena

learned of the marriage of her sister Carolina, who had not once traveled to the *municipio* to take her calls, and from whom there had not been a single letter. The news, and how she learned it, was so unbearable that Maddalena took to her bed for three days. She refused to tell anyone—not Ida, not Mamma Nunzia—what troubled her, and after a while they stopped asking. In the meantime, the women worked twice as hard on the holiday preparations, and Papà Franco wondered— loudly enough for Maddalena to hear, in his booming voice from the bottom of the stairs—what kind of woman Antonio had brought into their house. "If she doesn't shape up . . . ," he said, leaving the consequences to her imagination.

Maddalena wrote Carolina a letter, then tore it up. She wrote another letter to the man Carolina had married, then threw it into the fire. She pretended to sleep when Antonio crept into the room, quietly removed his watch and rings and set them on the nightstand, then slid into bed beside her. She did not flinch when he caressed her shoulder, sighed, and switched off the light. Then, the day before Christmas Eve, Maddalena gathered herself, took a bath, and joined her mother-in-law and Ida downstairs as if nothing had happened. She greeted Antonio's return from work with the same forced cheerfulness she had always displayed, and he kissed her hand in gratitude. "Women have unexplainable episodes, often caused by hormonal changes," he had once read to her in the Married Life section of the *Wilmington Morning News*. "It is best for a husband not to interfere by giving his wife the unhealthy dose of attention she craves. The episode, or fit, will then subside quickly, and the wife will have learned a valuable lesson."

"What does it mean, subside?" she'd asked him.

"Fade," said Antonio. "Go away. Disappear, little by little."

And it did subside, her sudden episode, if not the ache that occasioned it. Carolina's wedding. Maddalena had seen the actual photograph but could not bring herself to tell anyone where. She had seen the two of them kneeling in the front row of the church, she with the bouquet of flowers, he with the mustache and the satisfied grin. The blurry faces of the Santa Ceciliese behind them, the raging sunlight in the windows. How could it be the two of them, Maddalena thought: her sister Carolina beside Vito Leone, the boy she'd loved, who'd be her own husband if Antonio had not taken her away? Had the bride and groom settled for each other, or was there passion between them? What did it matter anymore, now that Maddalena had abandoned them both?

That Christmas Eve, she did not even try to make conversation with the other wives, unable to bear their coldness and distance, their secret alliances, for another year. She wore the same dress she'd worn the year before, though the wine stain on the sleeve had not been dry-cleaned. Antonio must have sensed these dramatic changes. As she'd waited at the stove for the coffee to boil, grateful for the few minutes alone in the kitchen, he came up behind her and wrapped his arms around her waist. He pressed his body into hers and rested his head on her shoulder. "Not now," she'd thought, with the house full of children and relatives, with the knife still being pulled slowly from her heart.

"Let's take the car," he said, to her surprise.

She turned around. His face was bright as a boy's, mischievous and eager.

"We need a vacation, don't you think?" He was whispering. "The food's all served. The kitchen's cleaned up. Ida can make more coffee. They don't need us anymore."

Maddalena gave him all the reasons to stay—it's not proper,

it's rude, you'll break your mother's heart—then stopped herself. The consequences would fall on Antonio, not her. "All right," she said, untying her apron. Antonio gave her a quick, celebratory kiss on the forehead. As she watched him scribble a note on a napkin, she felt the familiar thrill of collusive disobedience, and until this moment she had not realized how much she'd missed it.

Antonio grabbed a pair of old coats from the downstairs closet to avoid the crowd in the living room. Maddalena served the coffee just as the guests were assembling at the table for games. When Papà Franco asked her to sit beside him and play, she said, "I have a stomachache," and he rolled his eyes as if to say, "I give up."

Then she snuck onto the back porch, where Antonio was waiting. They rushed down the narrow alley beside the house and into the Chevy. Antonio took a deep breath. Then he steered the car away from the curb, over the patches of snow and ice, and raced down Eighth Street into the empty city. The colored lights blurred past. The bell tower of St. Anthony's stood proudly against the sky, and the traffic lights blinked and swung in the wind. Every once in a while, the street would be crowded with parked cars around an illuminated house, families visible in the windows, but there was no traffic, no one to prevent their escape.

"This is nice, isn't it?" Antonio said. "Nobody on the road but us? All of Wilmington to ourselves."

Maddalena nodded.

He turned on the radio and rolled down the windows halfway, though the air was freezing and neither of them wore hats. "You're not too cold, are you?"

"It feels good," she said.

Soon they were on 202 headed north into Pennsylvania. Would they end up in Valley Forge, where he had a great-uncle? City Line Avenue, where he used to go to nightclubs with his friends, before she arrived? Was he taking her to that park, somewhere in Philadelphia, where they once had a picnic and watched the ships?

He turned up the radio. His lips moved silently to the music, as if too shy to sing. "This is fun for you, right?" he asked, his eyes fixed on the road. "Better than staying at home watching me play cards." Between working the gearshift, he reached his hand across and rested it on her seat.

Antonio loved nothing more than playing cards late into the night with Gianni and his friends, the men around him cursing and cheating and telling jokes. He looked forward to this all year. And since he'd gotten the new job at Ford and worked double shifts, he'd had no time to see his friends. It occurred to her that he had taken this joyride as a gift to her, even though she had not told him why she'd been troubled the past week.

"You're missing your card game," she said.

He shrugged.

"We can turn around," she said. "It's already been a nice vacation."

"You're not having fun?" he asked, a note of hurt in his voice. The car veered to the right, over the line of the shoulder, as he turned to her.

"Yes, yes," she said. "Very much. But—"

"Then no turning around."

They drove another half hour, through the towns of Wawa, Black Horse, and Rose Tree. Route 1 grew wider. A grass divider appeared between the lanes, and the houses alongside—some made of stone—doubled in size. Manicured shrubbery and tall evergreens protected them from the highway, but Maddalena could still see flashes of gold chandeliers, floral wallpaper, staircases that circled up to the second floor.

They turned off onto a road Maddalena did not recognize, and soon darkened restaurants and department stores replaced houses on both sides. Then a row of car dealerships appeared, one after the other, flooded with light. Were they open? Who shopped for cars at eleven o'clock on Christmas Eve?

"Here," Antonio said, as he turned into one of the lots. The sign on the roof of the showroom said CADILLAC in script letters.

"It looks closed."

"Not for us," said Antonio.

A chain-link fence separated the parking area and showroom from the rows of cars behind it. Antonio drove slowly along the fence away from Route 1, around the back of the showroom. Here the road turned to gravel. Where the fence disappeared into the woods, he stopped, shut off the ignition, and rolled up the window. No one could see them here. The spotlights, arranged on steel towers, did not aim this far back from the lot.

" 'Now what?' you're asking yourself," he said.

"You read my mind."

"Button your coat," he said, with two quick pats on her thigh. He got out of the car, ran around to the passenger side and opened her door.

"Tell me where we're going first?" she asked, taking his hand.

"Just follow me."

He led her into the woods, still covered in an inch of snow. Her heels slipped on the rocky path that ran along the side of the fence. She wore no hat or gloves. Her legs below her knees were exposed to the cold, and her cheeks burned in the harsh wind. Yet she kept pace with her husband. At the top of a small hill, the fence ended, and he pulled her across. They made their way back down the hill on the other side of the fence. Then they stepped from the dark woods onto the brightly lit stage of the car lot.

Rows of Cadillacs stared them down. They were arranged by model—the larger ones closest to Route 1, convertibles in the middle. Antonio and Maddalena walked hand in hand among them, as if at a zoo or a graveyard. He tried every door handle, smudged his thumbs over the price lists in the windows, and ran his hand along the wings, but Maddalena was afraid to touch those perfect creatures. For a moment she worried the police could trace their fingerprints, then decided trespassing was not a serious enough crime. Still, it was always best to admire from a distance.

Antonio had come here many times with Mario, he explained. They'd brought the salesmen free pizza from Renato's and pastries from the Pasticceria Grasso before it went under. It was part of a long process of softening them up, of laying the groundwork for the day when the two brothers would show up with a wad of cash thick enough to pay outright for a new Fleetwood. By then the salesmen would have become friends, and would offer them a friend's discount.

"Mark my words," said Antonio, his palm flat on the hood of a Coupe Deville. "I'll be driving one of these before I'm forty."

He was twenty-eight, Maddalena twenty-two. It was easy to imagine their lives in nine years: gliding through the wallpapered rooms of their home in New Castle, three kids at play in the yard, Sunday trips to Eighth Street in the shiny Cadillac. They'd build up to this life little by little, with double shifts and borrowed clothes and the fatty cut of meat, but when the life finally commenced it would feel like a stroke of luck—like God appearing at the edge of the ditch to pull them up and out.

For fifteen minutes they walked among the rows, trying to convince each other they weren't cold. Maddalena's earlobes and fingers and the tip of her nose had gone numb. Only her palm, clasped tightly to Antonio's, felt warm. There was no sound in the lot but the *flap flap flap* of the American flag that hung above the showroom, and the occasional whoosh of a fast-moving car on Route 1.

Then Antonio tried the driver's side door of a convertible and, with a miraculous squeak, it opened. "Oh, baby," he said, and immediately released Maddalena's hand. He got in, reached over to unlock the passenger's side, then got out again.

"We shouldn't," she said, when he held open the door on her side.

"Don't be silly."

She slid across the soft leather. It was cold at first, but so soothing that she hardly noticed. The seats and floors were beige, the panels and dashboard a pale green, the console a gleaming chrome. Elegance, she thought; amazing how immediately and unmistakably you could smell and feel and taste it. All you needed was money. She settled her shoulders against the seatback, keeping her feet elevated so as not to track in dirt.

Antonio had no such concern. He stomped into the driver's side with shoes still muddy from the walk in the woods. He gripped the wheel and steered left and right, pretending to swerve around the trees in the back lot.

Maddalena's feet struggled to hover over the floor mat. She had nowhere else to put them. "Be careful," she said. "If you break anything—"

"This car is unbreakable," he said. Then he noticed her feet. "What are you doing?"

"I don't want to make it dirty."

"It's brown!" he said, with a big smile in the brilliance of the spotlight. "It won't show!" There was that eager boyish face again, but this time Maddalena noticed the faint wrinkles in the corners of his eyes. When had they appeared?

"And this isn't ours *yet*," he said. "You don't have to worry about cleaning it."

"It's so perfect—"

He was laughing. "Do it!" he said. He leaned over, grabbed her ankles, and tried to press them down on the mat. "Do it!"

She fought to keep her legs up, but he was stronger, and the soles of her gold high heels finally soiled the mat.

"There!" Antonio said. "Now you really did it. You better have three thousand dollars hidden in those drapes."

"I wish," said Maddalena. "Can you imagine?"

They sat there a while. The wind whistled and shook the cloth top. He said, "You know I would buy this for you, if I could."

"I know," she said. "But you know I don't pray at night for a Cadillac."

He shrugged. "I have too many dreams. I want us to have it all."

"We're not starving," she said.

"Sometimes I wonder." Then he shook his head. "Don't listen to me, please." He rubbed his face. "You feel better, though, right? This drive did you some good?"

"It did," she said.

"You won't be so sad anymore? Not tonight, at least?"

"I'll try."

He stared into the woods. "Because I love you, Maddalena," he said. "You still don't feel the same about me—maybe you never will; maybe that's why we don't have a baby yet, I don't know—but I always loved you. From the beginning."

She nodded. It was not the first time he said these words to her. Usually she kept silent and let the moment pass. But tonight she felt the urge to tell him that she might, in fact, have come to love him a little; that it may have started in the kitchen as she undid her apron. Something had happened in that moment. The image of Carolina and Vito in the church, so fixed in her mind that week, had subsided. She'd had her own husband there before her, and they were hatching a plan, an adventure, the way she and Vito used to do in the back room of her family's store.

She did not tell him any of this, not in the front seat of the Cadillac on Christmas Eve 1949. She did not have the words then, and either way, how could she be sure? So they drove the hour back to Eighth Street, snuck up to their room to make love under the warm blankets, and hoped God would look kindly upon them.

FOUR YEARS LATER the guests have gathered again, but this time Antonio offers no plan of escape. The women finish the dishes, the men suspend their games of *scopa* and *briscola*, and by ten o'clock they are all playing *tombola* at a penny a card. Every seat at the table is taken, every inch of floor space jammed with children. Maddalena shares her card with little Nunzia, who bounces on her knee and loudly repeats each number after Antonio calls it. No sooner does Maddalena notice that she needs only forty-two and nine for a win when, miraculously, nine is called. She points to the number, and Nunzia marks it by dropping a lentil on the card. A flutter rises in Maddalena's chest. She stares at the *42* printed on her card until her eyes cross, willing Antonio's hand to pull the number from the bag. But this is not her night. Antonio calls twenty-five instead, and everything happens at once: the table booms *Natale!*, each man kisses the woman closest to him on the cheek (a ritual Ida invented to celebrate the special Christmas number), Signora Fiuma wins the *cinquina*, and Mr. Gold walks through the door carrying two white poinsettias.

He is dressed for a funeral: black coat, wool pants, gloves and hat. But he is grinning, the plants like two trophies. He wipes his shoes on the remnant of green carpet used as a mat, lets out a deep breath, and looks proudly around the room. In the commotion of Signora Fiuma's win, only Maddalena and Ida notice his entrance.

They rush to him, Ida in front, Maddalena close behind. Ida takes the plants in her arms and thanks him for coming. They stand firmly in front of him to block the view of the men at the table.

"What a nice surprise!" says Ida.

"I make the effort to visit all my little ladies at least once a year," he replies, trying to move deeper into the room. "Also, I like to see the customs up close." He looks over their shoulders. "You're playing the game now, the one like bingo?"

"*Sì*," says Ida. "You buy as many cards as you can afford. Right now they cost a penny, but the longer the night goes, the more expensive they get." She goes on explaining, though Mr. Gold already wrote down this information at work. "We divide the money into four kitties, each one bigger than the one before. If you have a number that's called, you put a lentil on top of it on your card." She talks so fast that she's nearly out of breath. "First person to get three numbers in a row wins the *terno*; four in a row the *quaterna*, five in a row the *cinquina*. The fun part is that each number has a little saying that goes with it. We call forty-seven *il morto chi parla*, the dead man who talks; seventy-seven is 'an old woman's legs.' There are lots more." With Maddalena at her side, Ida keeps Mr. Gold penned near the door. He cannot step forward without meeting at least one of their elbows. "The first person to get every number on their card wins the *tombola*—the biggest kitty of all."

"And afterward, you make soup from the lentils," says Mr. Gold.

"On New Year's Eve," Ida confirms. "You have a good memory. The lentils are supposed to bring money."

"We rinse them first," Maddalena says. She rubs her arms and glances around the room.

"I'm watching our cards, Zia!" declares Nunzia, but Antonio has stopped calling the numbers. He rises slowly and walks toward the front, still holding the bag of wooden chips, shaking it like an instrument.

"Is that who I think it is?" Maddalena hears him ask.

A hum of anticipation fills the room, as more than a few players realize how close they are to victory. "Call the next number, Antonio!" Signora Fiuma yells. "I feel lucky tonight!"

"You've won enough," says Ida's brother. "Give us poor men a chance."

There is nowhere to move without stepping on the children lying on their stomachs in front of their cards. Maddalena takes one of the poinsettias from Ida, thanks Mr. Gold again, and kicks one of Nina's cards by mistake. Then she hears her name.

"Maddalena," Antonio says, for what seems like the first

time in years. There is no anger or pleasure in his voice. He could be reading from the front of an envelope.

"Mr. Gold, this is my husband," says Maddalena. "Antonio Grasso."

"Pya-chaireh," Mr. Gold says, a word Maddalena taught him last week, and which he wrote phonetically in his notebook. He sticks his hand through the narrow space between the two women.

Antonio fixes his eyes on Mr. Gold's face. He does not shake his hand. He sways for a moment, drunkenly. Then he drops the bag of numbers onto Nina's head. The wooden chips spill down her back and roll in all directions on the floor.

"Ow!" says Nina. "Zio Antonio!"

"Did I use the wrong word?" Mr. Gold says to Ida. He reaches into his coat pocket and pulls out the little notebook. The kids scramble around him on all fours to retrieve the numbers.

Signora Fiuma leaps to her feet. "Make sure thirty-three's in there," she says. "That's my number! *Gli anni di Cristo.*"

"No, no," Ida says to Mr. Gold. "You said it perfect."

Perry Como sings through the radio, as he has been doing since nine o'clock, but the rest of the room has gone quiet. Mr. Gold shifts his weight from one leg to the other, then ticks his head toward the console. "WAMS," he says. "I had this on in the car."

"Perry Como is Italian," says Ida.

Antonio leans in closer to Mr. Gold. "So, you're the man my wife works for."

"Well, it's my name on the paychecks," he says, with a laugh. "It's very good to meet you, by the way. That's what I was trying to say in Italian. Mrs. Grasso is one of my best seamstresses."

"That's good news," Antonio says, nodding. He pauses a moment. His neck is flushed red. "Let me ask you. Are you a married man?"

"I am."

"So, where's your wife now?"

"She's at home." Mr. Gold narrows his eyes, gives Antonio a bemused look. "Maybe you don't realize, but tonight is not our holiday. Otherwise I would not be here. Tonight is like any other Thursday to us."

"And your wife," Antonio says, a big grin on his face. "She knows you bring flowers to other women?" He nudges him gently in the ribs.

Gianni walks over and stands behind him. "The game is waiting, *uaglio*," he says.

"The plants are for all your family," says Mr. Gold, evenly. "Not just the women." He turns to Ida. "Maybe I'm not welcome here?"

Everyone at the table stands simultaneously, as if in church. The men start to walk toward Antonio and Mr. Gold. The kids scatter and assemble themselves on the stairs, balancing their cards for when the game resumes.

Whatever happens next, Maddalena will have to suffer the consequences. Better not to watch. Better to take a step backward against the brass banister, lower her head, and brush her chin against the white petals of the poinsettia. Antonio once insisted these plants could kill a cat or a small child if eaten, but she doubts this. He takes as fact every article in the newspaper, every secondhand story from the men at Ford.

"Why wouldn't you be welcome?" says Antonio, with a fake confused look. He comes toward him and throws his arms around his shoulder. "It's your money that keeps the roof over our heads, right? Take your coat off, stay a while. We're in the middle of a game right now, but the next round you'll play." His voice is friendly but unnatural and overloud. "Maddalena, get Mr. Boss Man a glass of wine."

Maddalena looks up.

"Oh, I can't stay—" says Mr. Gold.

"Don't insult us now," Antonio says. He tightens his grip on Mr. Gold's shoulder and pulls him close. He leads him past Maddalena, across the crowd of standing men, and installs him in his own seat at the head of the table. "You watch my father's cards with him. He'll teach you how it works." Then he turns to the rest of the table. "Let me introduce you to Maddalena's boss, Mr.—" He stops. "What's your first name?"

"Milton."

"Mr. Milton Gold! Uncle Milty!"

The guests sit, polite smiles on their faces. Mr. Gold raises his right hand in a tentative wave.

"Who's got the numbers?" Antonio says, brightly. "Maddalena, Ida, we're waiting for you."

Maddalena sets a glass of red wine in front of Mr. Gold, then resumes her place at the table with her niece. If Antonio calls forty-two, she doesn't notice, and Nunzia is too young to recognize the number. Instead she watches her boss look intently over Papà's shoulder, whisper questions in his ear, and not touch his drink. He appears comfortable, relaxed even, but surely Antonio is not fooling him. "Ante up, Uncle Milty," he says when a new game begins, and Maddalena breaks into a sweat. "You're on your own now."

Mr. Gold makes a fist whenever he gets a number. Then he loses the *terno* to Ida. "It's all luck, then?" he asks. "Am I wrong to say there's no strategy?"

"No, that's right," Antonio says. "The only trick is to keep your eye on your cards."

Mr. Gold plays one complete game. Then he pushes his chair away from the table and declares it time to go. "I have other ladies to see, from here to New Jersey," he explains, and gives a slight bow to the guests. "They might not all be night owls like you."

"You're insulting us," says Antonio, again in the overloud voice. "You play one little game, then leave without tasting our food or drinking a glass of wine? We're not good enough for you?"

Mr. Gold smiles politely and rubs the inside of his palm. "Of course you are, Mr. Grasso. But I really do have to go. Business, you know."

"We understand," says Ida, from across the room.

"One more game," says Antonio, his voice more insistent. "That's all I ask. Then I leave you alone. I'll loan you the penny for the card, if you need it. You can pay us back, no interest, next paycheck."

Nobody laughs. Slowly Mr. Gold sits back down and suffers through another set of numbers. He tries to make eye contact with Maddalena between the two red candles of the centerpiece, but immediately she looks away. Under the table her legs are shaking. Ida sits beside her and rests her hand on her knee. The guests whisper and stare and hide their grins in their wineglasses.

It would be much easier if Antonio just threw a punch; at least then someone would know what to do. Gianni would hold Antonio back and give Mr. Gold time to run for the door. He'd pour his friend another shot, then return to the game as if nothing happened. Instead Antonio has put everyone in this in-between place, just so he can show Mr. Gold who the real boss is and still keep Maddalena's job.

Though no words of accusation have been spoken, Maddalena feels the eyes of the men and the wives on her in judgment. It takes only one insinuation, false or true, to give people ideas, to turn them against you. On the way home, they'll giggle over Antonio's show. They'll delight in the scandal that would befall the Grasso family if he were right about the handsome Jewish boss. "Poor Antonio," they'll say, shaking their heads. "We could have told him from the beginning she'd be trouble."

Late into the third game, Antonio goes upstairs to the bathroom, and Mr. Gold sees his chance. It is eleven o'clock. He stands, quickly grabs his coat and hat from the rack, and waits at the door for his host to return. Maddalena stands beside him.

"I'm sorry we kept you so long," she says. "Will you take some food home to your wife?"

"No, thank you," he says, the irritation obvious in his voice.

"Milty!" says Antonio, rushing down the steps. "You weren't going to sneak out, were you?"

"I wouldn't leave without saying good-bye," Mr. Gold says. "Thank you for the games. And the wine and the delicious pastries."

"My pleasure," Antonio says. He slaps him on the back. Then, just before Mr. Gold turns to go, Antonio grabs Maddalena's hand and brings it to his lips.

"Merry Christmas to you both," says Mr. Gold.

Antonio glares at him, still kissing Maddalena's wrist, as the door slams and the man is gone. Behind them, the impatient Signora Fiuma has taken over the game.

"Twenty-two!" she says.

"*La carrozzella!*" booms the crowd. "The carriage!"

"Are you happy now?" Maddalena asks. With the women watching from the table, she pulls her hand away and rushes up the stairs.

Alone in her room with the door closed, she waits for Ida and Mamma Nunzia to check on her. She will explain her humiliation, and they will make excuses for Antonio. They'll beg her to forget about it, to remember her husband could always be worse. "Antonio's jealousy comes from love," they'll say. "You should feel lucky he still thinks another man might want you."

Through the floorboards Maddalena can hear the call of the numbers, the disappointed groans, the coins jingling in the hands of the winners. But there are no footsteps on the stairs, no shadows outside the door. Eventually, someone approaches. Maddalena lifts her head. But it is just a guest who needs the bathroom. She turns out the light, slips off her shoes, and climbs into bed still wearing her dress.

Under her pillow she finds a small, wrapped box. She draws back for a moment, as if it's a cockroach or a stain or some other unwelcome thing. But written in marker in the left corner of the striped red paper are the words *Per Maddalena. Con Affetto, Antonio.*

She should wait. She listens until the end of the song playing on the downstairs radio, then can wait no longer. She slides her finger under the tape, folds the paper for reuse, and carefully opens the box. Inside is an oval-shaped silver locket on a little cloud of cotton. She unclasps the locket, and a folded-up note falls out. *"I due amori della tua vita,"* it reads. The two loves of your life. In the left frame, Antonio has inserted one of the few precious photos of her mother. Its small size can hold only her face—the ringlet of black hair that falls against her cheek, her hopeful eyes, her lips in a thin, cautious smile—but it is enough.

The comfort of the face is what Maddalena misses most. In the right frame, Antonio has inserted another folded-up slip of paper. It says, in tiny meticulously scripted letters, *"nostro bambino."* Our baby.

Maddalena holds the locket open in her palm, the chain laced through her fingers. This is how life with Antonio will continue to be, she thinks. Her mother might have told her as much. He will torment her with silence and spite from an impassable distance, and then, just when her fragile love for him begins to crack, when she considers giving up on him completely, his good heart will show. The game they are playing will end, and they will never speak of it, never admit there was a game at all.

She can see it as clearly as if it is happening now. She will have her baby not in a hospital, but here in her marriage bed, on the humid third floor, with Antonio between her legs waiting for the little Jewish face. He will rejoice only when the baby peeks through the muck with his father's eyes, the wide Grasso nose, the almond-shaped birthmark on the back of his neck. There will be no trace of her family at all, no link to her past— only the picture beside the child's in the locket. For a time, joy will return to Eighth Street, and Maddalena will rest. Antonio will rush home from work to sit beside her. They will forget the months he ignored her and acted crazy and slept through her sicknesses, and she will be his beloved again, mother of his perfect child.

8

Mamma

JULIAN SPLASHES AFTERSHAVE on his cheeks and neck. He examines his skin in the bathroom mirror. The mole on his left nostril, which has tormented him for years, seems almost charming. He tests his left profile, then his right, declares it a draw.

He flicks the light switch off and on rapidly. "All the world's a stage," he says aloud, on his way into the hall. He can't remember if he read this line in a Shakespeare play or an Italian poem, but for the first time he thinks he understands it. Since starting at Mrs. Stella's, he feels at every moment—in the bath, at the kitchen table, in the yard raking leaves—the eyes of an invisible crowd upon him. Songs run through his head in an endless set, commanding his fingers to play the notes on the porcelain tub, a plate, the rake.

Even this house could be a stage, he thinks. It is sparse enough and absent of decoration: dark wood paneling, brown carpet, mud-colored sofa, cherry coffee table. Only his poster of Manhattan—black and white save the blue tint to the sky—interrupts the blankness. If he remembers, he will buy a plant, add a flourish of green. Or a red slipcover to hide the holes in his father's leather chair.

"Don't tell me you don't see it," he says to the smiling man in the framed photo. "Their eyes glow, these customers. They stop talking. They listen and sway. Listen and sway! I take them to a heavenly place."

He talks to his parents every day, as he has since their deaths, reporting developments like an anchor on *Midday Headlines*. Little Abraham has still not come home, he tells them, but—"Calm down, Papà"—he has begun to include him in his nightly prayers. Maybe that is why he invades Julian's otherwise happy dreams, floating on his back in the water, always naked, always dead. Sometimes he appears in the public pool, sometimes in a bathtub, but never without the same ghoulish bloodshot eyes staring up at nothingness. For this reason, Julian now keeps the hallway lamp lit through the night.

Even in death, his father cannot keep silent. "Don't forget the electricity bill," he says. "You're paying for that, too."

The Delluccis took out a loan, Julian says, eager to change the subject. They expanded their business to double the size, and bought a van painted with DELLUCCI ELECTRONIC REPAIR in big letters across both sides. Dellucci makes one delivery in the morning, then spends the rest of the day driving the van around the neighborhood to show it off.

Julian has learned six new songs just from playing them over and over on the phonograph. The notes have come easily, as if they've waited for years in the tips of his fingers, eager for release. He tells his parents about the woman who approached him at Mrs. Stella's last week. She'd crossed a bar full of customers just to talk to him. "You play with all your heart," she said, squeezing his elbow. "Your music fills me up—more delicious than any dinner." Then she offered her hand. "My name is Helen," she said, before disappearing into the crowd.

"You're doing this for a woman, then?" his father asks. "You can't make money and find a *fidanzata* at the same time? That cheap-skate Mario Grasso's taking advantage of you."

But Julian does not care that his wages are in meals. Soon he will propose that he perform Fridays as well as Saturdays and holidays, and maybe one of the slower weeknights to attract more business. Then maybe—if he finds the nerve—he will negotiate a different price with Mario. Not for himself, but to satisfy his father. And yet his careful explanation of this does not please the old man.

"Working for food," he says, with disgust. "In the Old Country maybe, but not here. Your grandfather did not come all the way to America so you could barter."

"Maybe I would have been better off in Italy," Julian counters. "You could have opened a little café. Our family could have run it. You could have passed it down to me and my children. What do the Fabbris own here, anyway, besides this house and this old furniture?"

"I don't see any children," says his father.

With his mother Julian does not argue. He rarely summons her voice. He cannot bear it. Only in moments of jubilation, or during a particularly happy dream, does he risk it, and even then he fears that his longing to share his joy with her might overwhelm him. It was she who used to walk him to the library and wait outside as he picked out the books that interested him, her to whom he read stories on the many nights his father spent at the racetrack. She would iron or sew or wipe down the inside of the refrigerator, and Giulio would sit on the arm of the couch and read aloud an entire mystery novel start to finish. She'd stop him every few minutes at first to posit a theory. By the middle of the book she'd announce, "I know who did it!" and not interrupt him again until the end, when the detective would often prove her right. If, at some point in her life, someone had told her she was a smart woman, she would have assumed she was being mocked. Giulio himself—to his shame—never told her. And yet he has never met anyone with as quick a mind.

Today, his conversation with his father ends the same as it always does. Julian turns away from the photograph, walks out onto the porch for air, and smokes a cigar. Then he remembers the date. He rushes back inside, rights the frame, kisses his two fingers, and presses them to the faces of his parents. *"Buon Natale,"* he says.

He arrives early for his shift at Mrs. Stella's. The place is glittering. Gold garland covers the molding from one corner of the dining room to the other, and makes an X across the ceiling; it wraps every painting and spirals around the wooden columns that divide the restaurant from the bar. In the center of each table, a tall, red candle sits on a bed of plastic holly leaves splashed with silver confetti. Shiny glass ornaments hang from the coatrack and on the branches of two small trees set up on either side of the columns. Julian, anticipating this festiveness, wears his father's red tie with his dark suit. When no one is looking, he plucks a sprig of holly and threads it through the buttonhole of his lapel.

When Mario asked Julian to perform on Christmas Eve, he did not hesitate to answer yes. He needed an excuse to turn down his widowed great aunt, who'd invited him to the house in

Philadelphia she shares with her widowed daughter. The women are short and humorless, with powdery skin and a fondness for jangly gold bracelets. Over time they have taken on each other's features—a sinking chin, bruiselike smudges under their eyes, white hair—and now it is impossible to tell which one is thirty years younger than the other. Julian knows the widows only from the four funerals they've attended together— their husbands, his parents—and so in his mind they are inextricably linked with death. He is too superstitious to risk a holiday with those dark angels.

At Gino Stella's request, Julian steps out from his usual spot behind the microphone and does a turn among the tables. Tonight there are mostly big parties of ten or more enjoying pasta, fish, and vegetables served family-style in oversized white bowls. The four-tops have been arranged into long rows that span the length of the dining room. The dessert cart has been rolled into the center of the room, covered with an iridescent gold linen, and transformed into a display of elaborately iced cakes and cookies. At the round table by the window, beside a tower of poinsettias, sits the most dazzling decoration of all: Helen. She wears her hair pulled back and a green velvet dress that bares her shoulders. She drinks red wine, laughs, folds her hands under her chin. With her is a bearded man roughly Julian's age, two grandmotherly women, and a young girl in a dress identical to hers.

Julian maneuvers through the narrow spaces between the chairs, keeping his eye on her table. He plays more softly than at the microphone and holds the accordion high so as not to smack the customers in the head. They applaud as he passes. At Helen's table, he flubs the refrain of "Inamorata," but she doesn't seem to notice. The girl reaches out and tugs on his jacket.

"Abigail!" Helen says, and slaps the girl's knuckles.

"It's all right," says Julian.

She does not love the bearded man, Julian imagines. He is the brother of her best childhood friend, Abigail, who died in a fall from a horse. Though they have named the child after her, she is mean-spirited, nothing like the dead girl at all. Now only Julian's music soothes Helen's troubled heart.

The hours pass quickly. Julian's mind returns again and again to his brown, empty house—no tree, no lights, no one to start a game of cards or *tombola*. Christmas Eve should be loud and drunken late into the morning. It should not end at eleven o'clock, as the celebration at Mrs. Stella's must, so the waiters and cooks can join their families. At that point, Helen will take Abigail and the bearded man home; the parties of ten will reconvene at another long table in someone else's living room; even the dark angels might still be detailing their various illnesses for their guests in the gloomy Philadelphia walk-up. The Delluccis or Rosa Volpe across the street would happily take in Julian for the night, but he cannot bear to show up uninvited, to throw himself across their doorstep like a beggar.

Julian plays until his hunger forces him to take a twenty-minute break. Marcello—the teenaged waiter, who has just arrived from Naples and speaks not a word of English—appears with his dinner. He sets the bowl of pasta and the plate of fish on Julian's little table by the window, lights his candle, and smiles.

"Have time to sit?" Julian asks in Italian, but the boy dashes off, his hands behind his back.

He hasn't twirled his first forkful of pasta before Mario pulls up a chair. "Leave plenty of room," he says. "After we close, you come to my house. My mother's cooking for you."

"Oh!" Julian says, his delight obvious. He blushes. "That's— *grazie*, Mario." He thinks a moment, rubbing the corner of the table with his thumb. Clearly the Grassos feel sorry for him. They presume he has nowhere else to go. "But of course I have to offer my regrets. To have another guest so late—it's too much work for your mother."

"What work?" Mario waves the idea away. "Your plate's already prepared. You'll be the one working, *uaglio*. My sister-in-law says, 'Tell that man not to come unless he brings his accordion.' She wants a private concert for the Grasso family."

"Your brother's wife?" asks Julian. "The one from Italy?"

"The blonde."

Julian waits the appropriate few seconds. "How can I say no to a blonde?"

"*Perfetto*," Mario says. He dips a napkin in Julian's water glass and blots a spot on his tie.

"You must be tired of my same old songs," Julian says, moving the rubbery fettuccine around the bowl. "You sure you want to hear any more of me?"

"No offense," says Mario. He dabs again at the tie. "But I'm too busy to pay attention anymore." He smiles. "You could be playing with your feet and I wouldn't notice."

Julian nods.

"But not tonight," says Mario. "I promise. Tonight I'll hear every note." He shifts in his chair. "I was thinking, though, and listen to me now. You know what would make this Christmas even more tremendous?"

"What?" says Julian, though he knows what's coming.

"If the accordion player did a little singing—just a little—to get us in the spirit. My brother and the blonde—they're not getting along so good right now. A song might bring them together."

"I'm sorry, no," Julian says, firmly, though his mouth is full. "I would like to help, but—I told you a hundred times I'm not ready. Not yet. I mean no disrespect, but—"

"I heard your voice," Mario interrupts. He leans in closer. "Last week, when you took a piss, that was me in the next stall. I sat there with my eyes closed, asking myself: is Mario Lanza in the toilet with me?"

"Everyone sounds good in the bathroom," Julian says. "It's something about the tiles."

"I'm serious," says Mario. "Think about it. Think how nice it would be for these customers. Most of them are drunk anyway. If you sound bad, which you won't, they won't remember a thing." He pauses. "But if not here, then in the living room of my house. That's a must."

Julian shakes his head.

The face of Gino Stella appears in the round window of the kitchen door. Mario rolls his eyes. "Sooner, not later, though, OK?" he says, and raps his knuckles three times on the table as he gets up to go. "Wait for me at eleven. We'll walk together."

MARIO'S ROW HOUSE is taller and more narrow than Julian's. Made of the same red brick, it is barely distinguishable from the house attached to it. An alley divides it from its next-door neighbors on one side; the other backs up to the hilly lawn of a Presbyterian church. The Grassos share a stairway with a family from Abruzzo called Fiuma, Mario tells Julian. Signora Fiuma is a cripple, her husband a drunk and a shoplifter. With them they also share a small plot of grass, on which they've planted a box hedge and a struggling rosebush. Many of the bricks in the steps have crumbled and separated from the mortar.

Three men stand talking in the bay window on the second floor. They look out toward the sidewalk but do not acknowledge Julian and Mario. Other guests cross behind the men, carrying drinks and chasing after children. Every window is illuminated, casting a fuzzy glow on the parked cars and the church and the marquee for DiNardo's Florist two doors down. He takes this road each week to replenish the vase of flowers at his parents' grave, but until now he has not known that the Grassos live here. Julian has always thought it a lonely block. Sit on your porch and you face not neighbors but a barren lot and a patch of thick pines. You watch the trash gather along the edge of the lot and the wind kick the cigarette butts up and down the street. Julian would never trade his little house for this—no matter how many Negro families sprung up around him.

He follows Mario inside and sets the accordion on the radio console, which is tall as his waist and spans half the length of the living room. It is made of dark wood and features two large speakers on both ends, a cabinet to store albums, and a phonograph in the center that's currently playing a scratchy Perry Como record.

No one seems to notice Julian and Mario's entrance. Antonio Grasso calls forty-seven, and the dozen people crowded around the dining-room table lower their heads over their cards, searching and hoping. He does not see the blonde from Italy who requested him. There are kids everywhere, on the floor with their cards, racing toy cars on the stairs, sprawled on the sofa asleep.

The interior of the house—this Julian might consider trading for his own. There is color here: a powder-blue sofa, pristine under its plastic slipcover; ivory armchairs with plush cushions; the sparkling tree; poinsettias along the banister; the red and blue oriental rug that divides the territory of the living and dining rooms. A mirror in a gold frame spans the entire wall behind the sofa. Three brass sconces mounted to the wall display red, green, and white candles, each burnt halfway down. The unblemished furniture, free of nicks, has been recently polished. A woman's handiwork, Julian thinks. Only a woman can create and maintain rooms like this. No wonder his own house is falling into decay.

Julian does not immediately notice the piano jammed cruelly into the corner of the dining room. Crayon drawings—scribbles, really—are taped where the sheet music should be. Framed photographs and doilies centered under vases of silk flowers are spread across the top. The piano is old, yes, probably out of tune, but it is fashioned from a shiny blond wood so pleasing that Julian feels a sudden urge to rescue it.

Two girls run up to Mario yelling, "Babbo! Babbo!" and lock their arms around his waist. He tousles their long brown hair, which has unloosened from rhinestone clips in the shapes of butterflies. The girls eye Julian suspiciously, then giggle and rebury their heads. One is older than the other by a few years. The baby sister clutches a naked doll by the foot, dragging her head along the floor.

"He's here!" says a woman's voice, and all heads turn to Julian. Smiles and halfhearted waves from the *tombola* table. Then Antonio calls twenty-two, and they turn with determination back to their cards. Ida and Signora Grasso rush out from the kitchen.

"You came to us!" says Ida. "Welcome, welcome!" She gives Mario a quick kiss on the lips, then takes Julian's right arm. Signora Grasso grabs the left. They pull him away from Mario and weave him through the crowd, introducing him to this cousin and that; to the screeching, scattering children whose names he can barely hear, let alone remember; to the Fiumas and other neighbors from the block; and to Father Moravia—who squeezes Julian's cheeks as if he were a child, saying, "Little Giulio! A miracle to see you out of the house!"

They sit him at a card table in the surprisingly large kitchen and tuck a linen napkin between his neck and shirt collar. From this seat he can see and be seen by the game players and the rest of the dining room, though only Ida and the Signora pay him much attention.

Ida delivers with two hands a bowl of steaming pasta. As Julian eats—the anchovies are just salty and fishy enough without overwhelming the sauce; the linguine is fresh and al dente— they bring out platter after platter of fried fish and roasted vegetables from the refrigerator and the back porch and begin to reheat them on the stove. When he's nearly finished eating, they pile the other courses onto an enormous plate, arguing over how much he might want.

"Give him more *broccoletti*," says Ida.

"He has that all the time," says Signora Grasso. She spoons more *baccalà*. "He's never had this before. Not the way I make it."

"That's all right," Julian says. "I like everything."

The more he eats, the more intense his hunger. The fish is light and lemony, with a sprinkling of fresh parsley. Each of the *frittelli* is a surprise, filled with either cauliflower, apple, or cod. His mother's *frittelli* somehow went soggy minutes after she took them from the fryer, but these make a nice crunch when he bites into them. Ida and Signora Grasso stand over him, nodding and smiling.

Other guests— shapeless, faceless figures—go in and out of the kitchen for more wine or dessert. There are cheers and groans from the dining room, then the clacking of the wooden chips being dropped back into the bag. Another game is about to begin. "Each card double the price," Antonio announces.

Soon someone will ask me to join in, Julian thinks, and I will have to stop eating. For insurance, he grabs some roasted peppers with a folded slice of bread. The oil drips onto his chin as he stuffs the entire sandwich in his mouth. He reaches for more fish.

"What do you think of the flounder?" asks Ida. "This is the first year we made it."

He spears a piece with his fork, holds it up to the light, then devours it. "It's delicious," he says.

"Not enough batter," Ida says, her arms folded. "I told you, Mamma."

Julian smiles and sits back in his chair. "Everything is perfect," he says. And it is. It is peace on earth. He is so happy that he can almost convince himself that his parents are not gone, that his father has merely made the short walk to the Delluccis to deliver a plate of *ciambelline*, that his mother is standing at this moment at the top of the stairs in the house on Seventh Street. In his mind, it is still Advent, busy with plans and anticipation, and his mother has carried up the dusty box of garland and ornaments from the basement. By the time his father gets home from the Delluccis', she and Julian will have decorated the tree and strung the garland around the windows and mirrors. He'll stand with his hands on his hips, trying to disguise his grin with frustration. "Why's this mistletoe so low?" he'll mock-complain and swat at it with his elbow; "how much money'd you waste on these candles?" He'll tease them until he buckles, until he is forced to admit they have transformed his house for another Christmas. There is no vase of faded lilies, no stake through the center of Julian's heart; there is no dead Negro boy, no nightmares of hands at the throat. There is only glitter and Perry Como singing "Because" and a full stomach and his mother standing before the tree with her arms crossed, gazing at the lights.

Signora Grasso clears the plates as Ida wipes down the table. They combine, cover, and return the food to the refrigerator and the back porch. Only Julian's wineglass remains. Then comes the enormous bowl of fruit and three trays of cookies. "Now you're talking," he says.

Mario peeks his head in from the living room. "Don't get too comfortable. It's almost showtime."

"We never had a real musician play in our house before," says Ida. She removes her apron and sits across from him. "One year my brother brought his mandolin, but—" She leans over to peer into the next room, then whispers, "I make better music banging pots and pans."

"You couldn't even recognize the songs," says Signora Grasso. "'Sing along!' he told us, and everyone stared at the floor."

"What about the piano?" From his seat in the kitchen he can see it, untouched and overladen, shamed into the corner behind the dining-room table. He does not recognize the name—Kimball—but that is no surprise, considering he knows nothing about pianos. Maybe the Grassos dragged it here from the Old Country, he thinks. Maybe the one person who knew how to play it has died, and no one can bear either to use it or let it go.

"It came with the house," says Signora Grasso with a shrug. "The keys stick, and the sound—it's worse than the mandolin. Can you play?"

"No," says Julian, disappointed by the piano's unremarkable history. "But I always wanted to know how."

"We'll get it tuned, then," she says. "My husband knows a guy." She smiles at him, touches his arm. "So by next year—no, Easter!—you can learn. Then you'll play for us."

"All those famous Easter songs," Julian jokes. He clasps the old woman's hand between his. "But I thank you." He holds her there for a moment. "The invitation means a lot to me."

A young couple enters the kitchen to say good night. The husband's got his sleeping daughter slung over his shoulder, her bottom cupped in the crook of his arm. The woman, in a fur coat and hat, glances at Julian, yawns, and covers her mouth with a black-gloved hand.

As Signora Grasso tries to convince the couple to stay one more hour—"For the show!"—Ida leans in toward Julian.

"We need some happiness here tonight," she whispers, grimly, in his ear.

Before she can explain, someone calls *"Tombola!"* and people are banging their fists on the table and throwing their hands in the air.

"That's it," says Antonio. He slides a pile of coins over to a clapping fat woman in oversized glasses. "That's all she wrote."

Mario lifts the accordion case onto the coffee table and fiddles with the latches. He waves to Julian and mouths, "Now." He has already cleared the children from the living room and arranged them on the stairs. He nudges the adults aside and pushes the coffee table against one section of the couch, where an old man dozes. "There's a cot downstairs, Zio," he tells him, gruffly, but the man doesn't budge. He installs Julian in front of the window not only because it's in the center of the room but also so the neighbors and passersby can envy the magic of a Grasso Christmas.

Julian counts seventeen adults and nine children, all facing him. Eight of them—five kids, three adults—either sleep or are fighting an obvious battle to keep their eyes open. The fat woman holds her hand over her stacks of coins. A man about Julian's age shares his chair with his wife, who rests her chin on his shoulder. Father Moravia moves a potted fern out of his line of sight. Julian slows and deepens his breathing, and yet, over the loud chatter, he can still hear water boiling in the espresso pot, every scratch in the Perry Como record, the faint tinkle of the ornaments when someone brushes the tree. He tries to focus on Ida and Signora Grasso, who stand beside Antonio in the doorway of the kitchen. If he pretends he's playing only for them, maybe his nerves will hold steady.

"A small audience here at Café Grasso," Mario says. "Compared to the restaurant. But look: just as happy."

"And your sister-in-law?" Julian asks. "Didn't you say she—"

"Maddalena?" asks Mario, in a low voice. "Stomachache." He nods toward the upstairs, then turns to the crowd. "If I can have your attention, *Signore e Signori!*"

He succeeds only in waking his uncle. He kicks off his shoes, pulls his sport coat up to his neck like a blanket, and repositions himself on the couch.

"*Signore e Signori!*" Mario says again, loudly, and knocks on the coffee table with his palm. "*Attenzione!*" This time they hush. "Welcome to the grand opening of the Grasso Cabaret!"

Antonio stares expressionless at his brother while the women in the doorway smile amid the clapping and laughter.

"Ida," Mario continues. He ticks his head toward his wife. "Tell them if I'm lying. Don't I say to everyone: The day Signor Giulio Fabbri came into Mrs. Stella's was the best day since I became a partner?"

"That's the truth," Ida says.

Mario pats Julian on the back then checks his watch. His thick gold and diamond ring sparkles in the light. "Now that it is officially Christmas Day, in the Year of our Lord 1953, I want to give you all a very special gift. Those of you who have heard Signor Fabbri play know his beautiful music; those of you who have not heard him"—here he stops, puts on a puzzled expression—"*Why* haven't you heard him? Why aren't you at Mrs. Stella's?"

The crowd laughs.

"Too expensive!" someone calls out.

"Sauce is too sweet!" says someone else.

"*Silenzio!*" says Mario, with a grin. "We don't want you *cafoni* anyway. But seriously—"

A shadow appears at the top of the stairs. As the floorboards creak, the shadow dips and stretches along the wall. The sister-in-law. Maddalena. It must be. But why is she hiding? Maybe she is dying, Julian thinks, and the stomachache is the symptom that confirmed it. This would explain the stricken Antonio, the grim Ida. Or maybe Maddalena has just learned that her husband took up with one of the fast girls at Renato's Pizzeria. Now she must martyr herself in her room and leave Antonio to explain her absence.

"If we're lucky," Mario is saying. He pinches Julian's arm. "I believe Signor Fabbri will even sing a few verses."

"I'll leave the singing to Mr. Como," Julian says, lowering his head. His shoes are scuffed and dull. A thread sticks out from his right pant leg. Then he finds his courage. "The songs are for you to sing, not me," he says. "You will know all the words."

He slides his finger the length of the accordion keys. He's not prepared for how loud the instrument sounds in this room, which is less than half the size of Mrs. Stella's. "Sing along!"

They clap. Julian bows and begins the first verses of "Tu Scendi dalle Stelle"—the easiest and most famous song he knows—and immediately they join in. Mario crosses the room to stand beside his father. The old man is in his seventies now—older than Julian's father had been—but his skin is smooth and his hair thick, moon-white, and carefully parted in a rolling wave. He seems a decade younger than Ernesto Fabbri, who had been wrinkled and bald the last fifteen years of his life.

Julian plays "Some Enchanted Evening" and, as best he can, "Come on-a My House." Ida and Signora Grasso gaze at him eagerly, their smiles unflinching as statues'. The shadow at the top of the stairs does not move. Julian has fixated on it. Once, an arm reaches down and pinches the ear of one of the little boys, who is pulling the hair of the girl who sits in front of him. On the arm are gold bracelets. During the refrain of "Mona Lisa," when a leg slips below the line of the ceiling, he holds the final note longer than he should. She wears not a sick person's housecoat or a mourner's black, but a ruffled blue dress and heels. Possibly someone is punishing her, Julian thinks, and again finds Antonio's troubled face.

It is getting late, and the energy of the sing-along is waning. "I have one more song for you," says Julian to the crowd. "The finale!" They perk up. The problem is that he has not yet decided on the song. A full minute passes in awkward silence as he searches his mind for the perfect close. It is not until he sees Signora Grasso untie her apron that he decides.

"This beautiful song is for our hostess and spectacular cook," he says, extending his hand to her. "Because of you, Signora, tonight I am ten pounds heavier and a hundred times happier." He plays a flourish on the keys.

Mario raises his glass to his mother, and Ida rushes around

the table to pour refills. Julian waits for their full attention before he begins. He knows this song, "Mamma," so well that his fingers and arms move more by memory than will. He slows the pace of the first verse to extend the emotion. Everyone sings along with their full voices, which rise and fall more gloriously than the church choir's. At the chorus, Julian, too—unconsciously, at first—joins in. Once the words are out of his mouth, though, floating out over the table, to the ceiling, up the stairway, he cannot stop himself. Someone calls out, "*Bravo, Giulio! Finally!*"

Mario's mouth opens and closes and his arms reach across his brother's shoulders. It is the last thing Julian sees before the room blurs. He shuts his eyes. The tree lights become little stars. By the time he reaches the second verse, everything else has fallen away: the voices of the singers, the syncopation of their fingers on the table, the children giggling. He is alone with the music and the words:

> *Mamma, I miss the days when you were near to guide me,*
> *Those happy days when you were here beside me.*
> *Safe in the glow of your love*
> *Sent from the heavens above,*
> *Nothing can ever replace*
> *The warmth of your tender embrace*
> *Mamma, until the day when we're together once more*
> *I live in these memories . . .*

Maybe he sings the song all the way through twice, maybe three times. Or it could be just once. He cannot be certain. Whether he sings in Italian or English is also unclear to him.

Time passes, and he opens his eyes. Gradually the blur

comes into focus: the candles flicker in their sconces; the brass pendulum swings on the wall clock; tilted heads watch him, their eyes wide and glassy. Concerned. Mouths set in flat lines. Maddalena, now fully visible on the stairs among the pack of children, holds her hands over her face.

When Julian reaches the final, desperate cry of "Mamma!" the applause begins. He abandons the remaining notes and releases his grip on the bellows of the accordion. Waving a white handkerchief, Signora Grasso leads the pack that comes toward him. She dabs the handkerchief at his eyes. Apparently he has been crying. Still dizzy, his cheeks flushed and wet with tears, he shakes hands with the rush of strangers: bright flashes of lipstick, wide noses, a beard, voices declaring, *"Bravo! Bravissimo!"* They thank him over and over. One says, "I'm very sorry." An arm rubs his sweaty back. He tries to keep his balance. He glances up at the stairs again, but Maddalena is gone. The children point at him.

"Thank you" is all he can say. *"Grazie tanto."* Politely he pushes through the crowd toward the kitchen, his eyes fixed on his frayed pant leg and the wavy pattern in the wood floor. The guests are reaching for their coats.

Antonio recognizes the look on his face. "It's upstairs," he says.

Julian steps over the children and is grateful when he sees that the door to the bathroom is open. He shuts and locks it. Everything is white and clean as a hospital—the stacks of towels, the cabinets, the small porcelain sculpture of Venus on the ledge of the tub. In the lights from the bulbs around the mirror, his skin appears a sickly yellow. But maybe his skin is and has always been a sickly yellow. Maybe he is as old and sad and foolish as he looks.

He runs a towel under cold water and covers his face. Still the tears come. They are not for himself, for his humiliating display, but for his parents, Maria and Ernesto Fabbri. They are not alive. They are not at peace. They are not standing by the window in their little house on the other side of Union Street. They are anxiously wandering heaven, their eyes cast down, waiting for their son to make a life for himself. Never will Julian find their proud, familiar faces in a crowd of strangers. If only he'd been braver, less content, less lazy, while they lived, they might now be able to rest.

They pity him, those people downstairs knocking around, kissing each other, slinging their children over their shoulders. That poor lonely man, they're whispering, don't we know a girl who might let him take her on a date, someone plain and lonely herself, with a fondness for music? Surely the neighborhood has been talking like this since his first days at Mrs. Stella's, asking, Doesn't he have other family, in Italy, or Philadelphia? Doesn't he have anyone?

But Julian has never asked a woman on a date, nor does he have other family who matter—not in the Old Country, not anywhere. Only the dark angels, so far removed from his father's line that no one remembers how they earned the titles of aunt and cousin. Both his father's brothers, and at least one great-uncle, joined the priesthood. Julian's mother had been an orphan, raised by nuns outside Naples. His baby sister is long dead. If he invited all his friends in the world to dinner, he could seat them at the card table in Mario Grasso's kitchen and still have chairs left over.

He sits on the toilet, the face cloth cooling his skin. He asks his parents' forgiveness for the freedom he has felt the past three months—for the hours he passed on the porch in the pleasant late summer or at Renato's and Mrs. Stella's, without a single memory of them invading his thoughts. Once, he stood at their graves and worried about a character in the book he'd brought along for the walk. How could he have conceived of a happy life—playing "Santa Lucia" in a tacky restaurant!—in a world without them? His behavior has been shameful. When he gets back to Seventh Street, he will cover with black tape the new name he scratched into the back of his accordion. He will never play again for the customers at Mrs. Stella's. He will never play for anyone.

From the window, he watches the cars pull away from the curb. Mario and his father stand on the sidewalk, smoking cigars and waving to their friends. The house has gone quiet. Someone runs the kitchen sink. Julian hangs the wet towel on the rack and is about to turn off the light when he hears movement in the room next door. He waits, his hand on the switch. Someone walks from one side of the room to the other, singing to herself in Italian, opening and closing drawers. Maddalena. She comes closer to the wall they share, and he recognizes the song:

> *Mamma, solo per te la mia canzone vola*
> *Mamma, sarai con me, tu non sarai più sola . . .*

It is slow, mournful, more of a prayer or a confession. She lingers, as if she knows he is listening through the thin barrier of wood and plaster. He pictures her shoulders pressed against her side of the wall, her head turned toward the window. She has removed her blue dress, her bracelets and high-heeled shoes, and wrapped herself in a blanket. She is remembering Christmastime from her childhood, maybe, when she lay between her parents in their bed waiting for La Befana to fly in on her broomstick. She is not dying, Julian decides. It is not as simple as that. She is lonely. She has lost someone she loves, and cannot imagine how she will face the years ahead.

PART TWO

Prima

9

Epiphany

Through the windshield, Antonio sees Ida rushing down the front steps of their house, waving what appears to be a wooden spoon. He gets out of the car and carefully approaches her. She is a sleepwalker and has been known to wake in a bewildered rage. Once, she walked all the way to the flower shop in the middle of the night, rang the doorbell, and smacked Fran DiNardo across the face.

"Antonio!" Ida says, when he steps into the light of the streetlamp. It is May, the air warm and fragrant. She runs toward him, barefoot, waving the spoon. "Where have you been? The baby is coming!"

He shakes his head and smiles. "It's too early," he says, and lays his hand on her shoulder. At arm's length, he gives her a gentle shake. "Wake up."

"I'm not asleep!"

Antonio looks at her. She wears an apron, not a nightgown. Her hair is not up in pins. "She has another month to go, at least—"

"Tell that to her."

He rushes into the house, precious time already lost, but still thinking there must be some mistake. "It's too early," he repeats. "What's going on? Is Maddalena all right?"

"I don't know anything," says Ida. "Everyone's at the hospital, but do you think they call me? It's been over an hour."

He takes the stairs two at a time. He hears her ask, "Where have you been, anyway? It's one o'clock in the morning."

Quickly Antonio removes his clothes and grabs one of his good long-sleeved dress shirts from the closet. As he's buttoning, he reconsiders. Maddalena would want him to save this shirt for church. So he puts the first shirt back on. "Finish making it dirty," she would say.

He gets to Wilmington Hospital in five minutes. He doesn't remember the roads he takes or where he parks. He pushes through the glass doors, past the women in white gathered at the reception desk. They must notice his grease-stained work pants, the mud he's tracked onto the marble floor. After one of them pleasantly directs him to the maternity ward "on three," he breaks into a run, nearly colliding with a gurney left in the middle of the hall. Repeatedly he presses the up arrow on the elevator, then takes the stairs.

The maternity nurse is less agreeable. Possibly she smells the liquor on his breath, the foul odor steaming from his armpits. Can she blame him for sweating? Does she not know his baby came too early? If he's here now, how can it matter what he's been doing the past few hours?

"Grasso," he repeats for her. "*G-R-A—*" She flips through a thick stack of clipboards. Is every woman in Wilmington having a baby tonight? Then Antonio sees his father emerge from a room at the far end of the hall. He goes to him.

His father's face is serious, his hands deep in his pockets. The room from which he has come is not one in which Maddalena lies on a bed, cradling their baby at her breast. It is a waiting room. His mother sits in the corner, eyes closed, lips moving, her rosary pinched between two fingers. Strangers are scattered around her reading newspapers, arms folded, asleep, staring.

"What's going on?" Antonio asks. His mouth has gone dry. "Where is she?"

His father takes his arm and leads him away from the room, down the narrow hallway. Up here the floors are cheap linoleum, speckled ivory and tan. It is a gloomy place, unfit to welcome new life. They lean against a closet door beside a piece of chrome medical equipment the size of a safe, with an octopus of plastic tubes sticking out from the top. Antonio shudders. What use could there be for this contraption in a maternity ward?

"You have a healthy daughter," his father says. But there is no joy on his face.

A daughter. A girl. A healthy baby girl so desperate to see the world that she came four weeks before her time. He lets out a deep breath and steadies himself. He grabs the back of his head with his hand, squeezes, and looks down. "And Maddalena?"

His father is silent. Then he clears his throat. Antonio raises his head.

"Not so good, *figlio mio*." he says. "After the baby came, there was some kind of problem. Bleeding inside. Could be a small problem or a big one, but the doctor doesn't know for sure. He doesn't know how to stop it."

God forgive me, Antonio thinks. Everything is my fault. If I'd been with her, there would be no problem, big or small. If I'd been a better husband, she'd be safe.

"The baby came too fast, is what I think. Less than an hour and it was over. The doctor said Maddalena was very brave. But now—"

His mother emerges from the waiting room, tucks her rosary in her dress pocket, and comes toward Antonio with her arms outstretched. She has never looked so irreversibly old. Even her palms are streaked with wrinkles. *"O Dio!"* she says, clutching his face.

"She won't wake up," says his father.

ANTONIO BEGAN THAT year, 1954, in darkness. On New Year's Eve, all of Eighth Street lost electricity, and for three nights he and his family wandered like mummies through the candlelit house. Arms out, they tripped and collided with each other, and before it was over they sent crashing to the floor two wine decanters, a lamp, and a vase of silk flowers. The kids huddled with Ida on the couch, whimpering, afraid of every ghostly shadow that appeared on the wall.

"It's only Zia," Ida would say, as Maddalena creaked slowly down the stairs. She had trouble sleeping. One of the nights, as she tossed and turned, she said, more to herself than to Antonio: "I miss the radio. The voices calm me down."

"I'm not an electrician," Antonio told her.

Secretly, he was in no hurry for the power company to rescue them. A generator provided heat and hot water; the gas oven cooked their food. Why did they need to see one another? So his mother could tell him he looked tired, or ask, "What's bothering you, anyway?" As if one simple answer could explain his troubles.

Antonio no longer worried about Milty Gold. It was clear the moment he met him that the man was no Buzzy, not with that bush of hair in his ears, his feminine chattering with the women, his dainty fingers fumbling for the pocket notebook. Antonio almost felt sorry for him. But he'd been forced to make a point, and the point had been made. He and Gianni had had a good laugh about it afterward, remembering the captive look on Gold's face, his mad dash out the door, his near-tumble down the icy stone steps.

The day after Christmas, Antonio had sent Maddalena back to work armed with a bottle of Chianti as a gift, though Gold had not taken a sip of the very same wine two nights before. It mattered little to Antonio whether Gold saw the Chianti as a peace offering or as a reminder of his rudeness in leaving a full glass on the table. In fact, Antonio wanted Milty Gold to puzzle over the gift, just as he had wanted him to puzzle over the avalanche of kindness he showed him on Christmas Eve. The way to control people like him—most people, actually—was to keep them guessing whether you loved or hated them. You had to give them an equal number of reasons to think either way. People were cautious in such circumstances; they went back and forth as they weighed the evidence; and in the meantime, you got what you needed from them. You failed only if you let on too soon how you truly felt. Then they had something on you— your love or your hate for them an easily exploitable weakness— and could play you for all you were worth.

These were Antonio's thoughts as he sat in the living room

amid the shadows and flickering candlelight. At the other end of the couch, Ida sang songs with the girls, but their voices might just as easily have come from the radio. The darkness put a comfortable distance between everyone, and suddenly the house seemed larger, almost cavernous. He did not need the long walk to the pizzeria, the adventures of Renato and Buzzy and their girls, to distract him. Maybe all he ever needed was to be left alone—a few days, a few hours, even a short drive up the coast—so he could listen to his own voice.

But the world had become very crowded. Men could not keep to themselves as easily as they used to. Peace and quiet came only at night, when you were too tired to enjoy it, but obligations came at all hours and from all directions. No matter what route home Antonio took, he was bound to run into a coworker, a neighbor, or a face he recognized from the pizzeria. Someone's cousin from the Old Country was always just arriving, and he'd have to spend the better part of an hour listlessly nodding to the tale of his voyage and his wide-eyed impressions of America. "You'll come to my house for dinner once you get settled," Antonio found himself saying, often just for an excuse to walk away. And though he welcomed the boom in population—it would help turn Wilmington into a real city; it would feed his base of customers once he opened the trattoria—he resented the responsibility he felt for every Italian who stepped off the boat. Most of them came from the South anyway—Naples and Sicily and other places that made his people look like a race of illiterate pickpockets—and lacked even the rudimentary education Antonio had received in Santa Cecilia. It occurred to Antonio that having an elegant wife had turned him into a snob. He sometimes forgot he grew up not in Roma or Milano, not even a northern town, but a central Apennine village of three streets, where they'd stopped turning the pages of the calendar in the middle of the last century. The only virtue of the place was its peacefulness. People drove from all the major cities of the country just to sit in the olive groves, breathe the fresh air, and luxuriate in the silence.

At home on Eighth Street there were his nieces pulling each other's hair and skittering across the living room like windup toys. There was the newspaper to read. "How to Live with the H-Bomb" was the title of Bill Frank's editorial, helpfully accompanied by a bull's-eye map that showed the decimation of much of Delaware if the Big One struck the center of Wilmington. There was Maddalena casting a disapproving eye on his grease-stained fingernails, his mother begging him to take an immediate look at the icebox because it didn't seem as cold as it did last week. When Antonio did not say much at dinner, there were questions; when he talked more than usual, there were different questions. There were always questions. And little jobs and favors. Requests for advice. Unable to reach his brother, who ate all his meals at Mrs. Stella's, they all sought Antonio.

Aloneness. That was what his life lacked. No wonder he took the roundabout route home from the pizzeria. No wonder it seemed as though everyone was in his way. If only he had time to sort and plan, to weigh and negotiate, he would stay out of trouble. He would figure out exactly how to make good on his ideas and dreams.

The power company restored electricity after five days, just in time for the angry phone call from Renato that Antonio had been expecting. With his wife and mother watching from the stairs, he hung up without saying a word, and mumbled, "Mario needs me" and "no emergency." Then he grabbed his coat and headed to the pizzeria.

"You have some nerve," Renato said, when Antonio walked through the front door. "I didn't think you'd show your face in here again."

He and Buzzy sat smoking cigars at the back table. Cassie was between them, arms folded across her chest, the corners of her mouth turned downward. She shook her head in disgust as Antonio approached. The deck of cards in Buzzy's hand suggested they were not so angry that they couldn't play a game or two of *briscola*. He stopped and held out his palms. "I have a good explanation."

Buzzy and Renato stood.

"Please. Listen to my side."

They stared at him. Over the spitting and knocking of the radiators, the phonograph played Mario Lanza.

"Yes, I did tell my brother about your plan," Antonio said, holding the men's stare. "My gut told me you'd try it anyway, no matter how much I warned you. Turns out my gut was right." He looked at Renato. "If it was your brother, *uaglio*, you'd have done the same."

"Someone's loyal to me, I'm loyal to them," he said. "End of story."

"I only told Mario so he'd call me if Cassie ever came to the bar by herself. At first he thought I was playing a joke. Then last night, there she was in her little skirt and all that makeup. At midnight the phone rang. I ran out of the house, but by the time I got to Mrs. Stella's, the taxi was already at the curb. I saw Cassie on the sidewalk and tried to stop her, but she wouldn't listen. So I grabbed her arm. She squirmed like an animal and kicked me in the leg. She pulled my fingers back, I lost my grip, and she ran to the taxi. But I caught her in time. 'Keep moving,' I told the driver. 'I'll take the girl home—'"

"'And don't come back here tonight, no matter who calls you,'" Cassie said, mimicking his voice. "'If you know what's good for you.' He scared him off for good. He ruined everything!"

"My wife is home by herself in the dark—my three-months pregnant wife," Antonio said, "and I'm running up and down Union Street with a girl? And then afterwards I have to lie to my family about where I've been? I took a big risk."

"For no reason," said Renato. "Why you didn't mind your own business, get a good night's sleep next to your wife, and let us do our work is a mystery to me. You care so much about that *mulignane* that you turn your back on us?"

"I was doing you a favor—"

"Look at my arm!" said Cassie. She pulled up her left sleeve to reveal finger-shaped bruises. "Is this what you call a favor?" She lifted her leg and showed a gash just above the ankle, a perfect arc of crusted blood.

"I did not do that," Antonio said. He turned to Renato and said in Italian: "You know I'd never hurt a girl. Especially yours."

"You pushed me into the fire hydrant," Cassie went on. "I tore my leg up. Then I fell in the gutter. You don't remember. You were the one like an animal. Drunk as a skunk!" She presented her palms, red and swollen.

"I was not drunk," Antonio said. "I was home in my pajamas. She did this to herself. It's obvious to me." But it did not seem obvious to Renato or Buzzy. Renato looked through him, as if at a stain on the wall just behind his head. Buzzy kept shuffling the cards.

"Get the fuck out of my shop," said Renato calmly, his eyes still fixed on the stain. "From now on, stop by the *nero*'s house after work. Maybe he'll cook for you."

Cassie giggled.

"You don't mean that," said Antonio. "Come on, pour me a whiskey." He sat in the empty chair. "We have other things to catch up on. It's been too long, with all these holidays. And my electricity's been out. What do you say, Buzzy? You're quiet tonight."

"Indigestion," he said, and downed his shot. "This isn't helping."

Cassie pushed away from the table and crossed her arms, as if afraid to sit too close to Antonio. What an actress, he thought. Did Renato really not see? Had her *fica* turned him crazy? It was good enough, Antonio remembered, but nothing special. Their few nights in bed together, he and Cassie had tickled each other for a while before she undid their clothes, climbed on top of him, and straddled his waist. She'd arched her back, and he'd closed his eyes so as not to stare at those bird tracks on her chest.

"Whatever you do to make those people leave, you have to stay invisible," Antonio said. "If they see your faces, they can always come after you. They have friends, too, you know. That was the problem with Cassie's plan. Too much exposure."

Renato stood behind her and rubbed her shoulders. Antonio continued to think out loud, trying to restore their faith in him: they could plant stolen jewelry in the taxi; they could follow Waters until he broke the law, as he would eventually, and then report him to the police. He talked on and on. Cassie's eyes fluttered in half sleep. Mario Lanza sang love songs. Renato lit the grill and threw on some eggs.

"No, forget all that," Antonio said. "We have to think more simply. Like I told you from the beginning. If you just scare this man enough times, sooner rather than later he won't want to live there anymore."

"It has to be sooner," said Renato. "My uncle—"

"Tonight, then," said Cassie, suddenly awake. "I still have the energy. Nothing else to do on a Wednesday."

By this time, Antonio had gone twice to the cabinet to pour himself shots.

"A brick through the window," said Renato. "It can't hurt."

"We can wrap the brick with a note," said Cassie. "It can say 'Die, niggers, die.'"

"*Gesù Cristo*," said Antonio. "Where'd you find this girl? You can write that if you want. Not me. *Go home* is good enough. Or maybe you throw some broken glass or dump black paint on the porch, smear dog shit on the windows of the taxi."

"They'll laugh at that," said Cassie. "They're *used* to that. If we don't try something bigger, they'll stay fifty years. In"—she closed her eyes for a moment—"in the year twenty-o-four we'll be the only white people in Wilmington. Then they'll be throwing stones at *us*."

"Not if you keep at it," said Antonio. "Once a week, every week, at different times of the night. In the morning even, or in the middle of the day if you can. You'll wear them down. It won't take long, I bet you, before they give up."

Buzzy held his stomach. "I'm going to sleep," he said. "First I'm going to throw up, and then I'm going to crawl into my bed and pass out. All by myself. No rocks and dog shit for me tonight. But good luck."

"Another chicken," said Cassie. "Ask me if I'm surprised. Put your coat on, Antonio." She touched Renato's sleeve.

"*Amore*, finish your eggs. We should go this minute. It's time we accomplish something."

"What's this *we?*" said Antonio, with a smile. "I don't speak French. There's just you. No *oui*."

Renato glared at him. "You owe me," Renato said. "You don't come tonight, you erase ten years of friendship. Next time I need a restaurant partner, I won't turn to you. I'll tell someone else what I heard the other day from my buddy on Lincoln Street. That space we lost on Riverview. The Greek—" He stopped. He scratched his head in mock contemplation. "Oh, shit. I can't remember now."

"Come on," said Antonio. "What about him?"

Renato shrugged.

If he'd been brave enough to refuse Renato then, six days into January, the day of the Epiphany, maybe Antonio would have avoided all that came afterward. Maybe he would have been at home, where he belonged, when his baby was born. But this sort of courage did not come easily. He had less faith in his own principles than in the insurance of long friendships, of keeping on good terms with men who knew him well enough to hurt him. One day, he told himself, he'd call in favors from all the years he played on other men's teams—not only Renato's and Buzzy's, but his father's, Mario's, Mr. Hannagan's. They would reward him handsomely for his allegiance.

"To keep us warm," Cassie said, as she downed a shot. "I'm ready."

So the three of them, in winter coats and scarves and dark hats, walked to Seventh Street. At the railroad tracks, they stopped to fill an old pillowcase with stones and twisted steel nails. Antonio carried the nearly empty bottle of whiskey he'd opened at the pizzeria. With every swig, he reminded himself to keep calm and play along. He was not guilty if he tried to talk them out of it, if he never threw a single stone. "It might be too early," he said. "This time of night, people are still out."

"Think about it," Cassie said. "Anyone walking around this neighborhood probably lives here, which means they're probably an Italian. They'll look the other way if they see us."

"She has an answer for everything," Renato said, his arm around her waist.

"You won't like that so much when you're married," Antonio said.

"No, no," Cassie said. "I'll be the perfect Italian wife. The day after Renato marries me, I'll put on my apron and sew my lips shut, like his mother and sisters. That's our deal. But until then"—she kicked a tin can into a chain-link fence at the corner of Sixth and Union—"I'm an American girl to the bone."

"Let's try not to talk," Antonio said, as they turned onto Seventh and slowed their pace. The farther up the hill from Union they walked, the darker it became. There were no street-lamps, and only a few Christmas trees remained lit in the front rooms of the row homes.

"As soon as we're done," Renato reminded them, "we run to St. Anthony's and hide. I know one door that's never locked. Go through the park, not down Ninth." He took a deep breath, dropped the bag on the sidewalk in front of the Waters house, then stared at it a moment. The wind shook the dead plants in the flowerpots, making a hissing sound.

To his amazement, Antonio had not considered this obvious hazard: if they threw a sharp steel nail at the window, might it not hit the head—or the eye—of one of the kids asleep on the floor? If they blinded one of them, or caused some other serious bodily harm, how could he live with himself?

Before Antonio could voice this concern, Renato had already crossed the street. At the front steps he turned, faced Antonio and Cassie, undid his belt, pulled his pants down to his knees, and squatted. He moved to the lower step. Then back up to the top step. After he finished, he came toward them with a broad smile, his belt jingling as he relooped it. "Fried eggs," he said, and covered his mouth to muffle the laughter.

Antonio's stomach tightened. "That's enough for this time, probably," he said, turning toward the glow of Union Street. "We'll come back another night."

Cassie reached into the bag and pulled out three big rocks. "I'm just getting started," she said, and ran into the yard.

"Wait!" Antonio whispered.

The first rock shattered the storm door. Then she hurled the other two, one after the other, with all her might, at the front windows. The crash was so loud that the three of them instinctively covered their ears, as if watching fireworks. Then they ran, leaving the pillowcase on the sidewalk.

The next minutes passed in a blur. Antonio saw only his feet, pumping over asphalt, grass, concrete. He heard a door slam, then another. Someone was calling "Abraham!" again and again, and the name echoed across the field. By the time Antonio reached the church, chased by no one, breathing hard, his drunkenness had evaporated. He felt only fear. His ankles throbbed. He pushed through the back door into the room behind the altar, where the priests dressed, and found Renato and Cassie rolling around on the floor in a fit of giggles. They kissed and tickled each other.

"Do you think he followed us?" Antonio asked.

No answer from the lovers. Soon their coats were off and the straps of Cassie's dress pulled down to her elbows. Antonio paced in a wide circle around them, trying not to look, until Renato—nuzzling hungrily at her neck—declared it time for him to go home to his wife.

ANTONIO'S DAUGHTER, WHO will not have a name until Maddalena wakes, lies just beyond the glass. She is kept warm by four round coils embedded in her see-through crib. She is too fragile to be held by anyone but the doctor and nurses, and it will be weeks, Antonio is told, before they allow him to touch her translucent skin. He can only imagine how it might feel to cup her delicate head in his hands and press his lips to her cheek. They keep her separate from the babies who arrived at the right time, who did not threaten the lives of their mothers. Her chest rises and falls almost imperceptibly, and once in a while her leg or arm spasms. She rarely cries. Her eyes remain closed, two little slits above a nose the size of his fingernail, two bluish lips. Cracked skin around her fingers and toes. She seems as much his child as Eisenhower is his president.

Maddalena has been unconscious for twenty-four hours. She has been given a private room, away from the other new mothers. Ida sits calmly in the chair beside her bed, knitting a blanket for her niece. "I'm not worried," she says, the needles clacking between her fingers. "God is giving her the rest she needs. When she gets enough, He'll wake her up and put her to work again. Until then, she's building her strength."

Antonio grows increasingly impatient with Ida. He can't bear her sunny face, her blind faith. If she weren't his sister-in-law, he would grab her by the shoulders and shake her. What do you know about anything? he would say. He directs his rage—at Ida, at God, at himself—at the blanket, which Ida has already ruined by using three different colors of yarn of varying thickness. One side curls and twists under itself. He takes the blanket and stretches it as hard as he can, unraveling it from the blue corner. He throws it back in her lap, and she resumes her work as if nothing happened.

The doctor enters the room, lays his hands on Maddalena's face like a priest, checks her heartbeat, nods, and leaves. He wears a gray suit, and his hair is an unnatural terra-cotta color, his cheeks freckled. Dr. McMenamin. Irish. Antonio follows him, pleading for an explanation, a clear diagnosis, a timeline. But the doctor's information is as stubbornly repetitive as Ida's. "We're in a wait-and-see period" is his favorite answer. Or: "It's still too soon to worry."

"How long until it's not too soon?" Antonio asks, but he only purses his lips.

Antonio does not miss work. He has no choice. Mr. Hannagan rests his hand on his shoulder. "It's a tough test," he says, then reassures him that doctors know what they're doing nowadays, that it's not like before. Before what? Antonio wonders. "Just be grateful we give you insurance," says Mr. Hannagan.

The workforce at the Ford plant has more than doubled in the past year, and now Antonio has not only his boss to answer to but a hierarchy of supervisors who parade up and down the assembly line with clipboards. They take turns keeping watch on each man, standing behind him and off to the side, masking the seriousness of their inspection with small talk and dirty jokes. In the meantime they scribble on the clipboards. No wonder Antonio's performance rating—posted for all to see on the bulletin board above the card-puncher—has slipped from an "Excellent" five stars to a merely "Good" four; he is too busy feigning delight in the supervisors' cleverness, telling them how funny they are, how he will have to remember to tell their jokes to his brother. His rating will slip further now, in his distraction. Lunchtime provides no relief, as the men are packed into aluminum picnic tables in the musty break room, where the din is so loud that many never remove the earplugs they wear on the line. This week, Antonio sits on the floor in the corner, in the cool draft of the window. Though the radiator is turned off, the place swelters with the throng of bodies.

Antonio goes from work to the hospital, the hospital to work. He sleeps in the metal rolling chair beside Maddalena's bed, one arm touching hers at all times. His mother brings him clean clothes in the early morning, and he changes in the men's room at the other end of the maternity wing. People stop by in the evening: Gianni and his wife, the Fiumas, Ida's brothers, Father Moravia with his sprinkler and bucket of holy water. Antonio repeats the doctor's words and sees on their faces the same fear and disbelief the doctor must see on his. On the second day, Renato and Buzzy appear without Cassie or Marcie, having heard the news from Officer Stanley, who heard it from Mario at Mrs. Stella's. Antonio cannot look them in the eyes. It seems that all of Wilmington, the network of cousins and uncles and strangers from the Old Country, is whispering about Maddalena. They stand around her, shaking their heads, talking across her pale and unresponsive body. Her arms hang at her sides, and her hands are turned outward. She wears a hospital gown tied loosely around her waist and thick stockings up to her knees. Around her neck her Christmas locket, on her finger her wedding ring, on her face an unchanging and impenetrable blankness.

Three full days pass. Antonio crosses the city from the hospital to Eighth Street. The late-night walk feels familiar, almost instinctual, by now: the screech of distant cars, the milky light from the streetlamps, the men wandering with their dogs.

It is sometime between midnight and dawn. He makes his way through the dark living room of his father's house, unplugs the radio, and sets it on his shoulder. It is heavy, unwieldy. He carries it back to the hospital, sets it on the floor beside his wife, connects it to an outlet on the other side of the door, and switches it on.

The radio gets no reception on any station. Only static. Still he turns up the volume, brushes the hair behind Maddalena's ear, and climbs into bed beside her. He will stay here until someone tells him to leave.

The radio does not soothe Antonio. His mind is too thick, and the static makes him only more anxious. He thinks back to that first attack on the Waters house on January 6, now almost five months ago. After Renato cast him out of the church sacristy, he rushed home to Maddalena. He wanted to talk to her, to confess. If he told her about the piles of shit on the step, the shattered windows, the steel nails in the living room, she could absolve him of his guilt, remind him he didn't cause any of the damage himself. She would understand how he could hate both the colored man and the cruel tricks Renato and Cassie played on him. In the end, she might say that he was helping to teach those people an important lesson. Many times, peering through the curtains at the boys on the curb, she had agreed with him that blacks should have their own place to live, just not a neighborhood where the Italians or Irish had already put down roots. Surely there were vast tracts of America that remained to be settled; why not seek them out, establish a community of their own?

He found Maddalena sitting up against the headboard, in

the dim glow of the bedside lamp, her box of stationery on her lap. Asleep. He shut the door quietly, removed her reading glasses and set them on the nightstand. Her pen had slipped out of her fingers and leaked a stain the size of a dime onto the ivory sheets. Above her lips was an angry red pimple she must have recently squeezed. When did her face change? he thought. Her cheeks, neck, even her ears seemed fleshier. Older, but no less beautiful. Her lips were parted slightly, as if she'd fallen asleep in the middle of something she wanted to say.

He switched off the radio and took the box of stationery from her lap. *Cara Mamma*, her letter began. She had written about Giulio Fabbri, the accordion player, crying for his mother in front of the Christmas Eve guests. His song had broken her heart. It had made her feel like an orphan. It had made her want to run down the stairs, throw her arms around the man, and tell him "I understand you." Since she'd come to America she had been hiding her sadness from everyone, "even you, Mamma," but the accordion player did not let her hide anymore. She felt that if she didn't stop hiding, she would no longer be able to get up in the morning. "My only happiness comes when I think of my baby," she wrote. "If it weren't for my baby, I would drink a bottle of poison."

Antonio read this sentence many times. *If it weren't for my baby, I would drink a bottle of poison.* He turned the page over. She had added to the letter every night for two weeks and marked each section with the date. His name did not appear anywhere. Did he matter so little to her? She apologized for her state of mind and said she would probably never have the courage to mail these ugly words. That night she had been writing about the unforgiving cold, the taking down of the lights on Union Street, and then, presumably, she'd drifted off.

Antonio had thought of the bewildered faces and the snickers in his living room as Giulio Fabbri played "Mamma." He had felt embarrassed for the man, bleeding in front of a room full of strangers, but Maddalena had found it moving; she'd suffered along with him but could not turn to her husband for comfort.

She stirred. "You're back," she said, so quietly he could barely hear her, and rubbed her eyes. Sweat beaded on her forehead and matted her hair, though the air was cool. Frigid, actually. She kicked off the covers. Having a baby must confuse women's bodies more than Antonio understood.

"I was thinking about our new house," he told her, though that had not been on his mind at the moment, and she would probably not remember anything he said. "I like the ones across from Wanamaker's, up on the hill."

She slid down from the headboard onto her side. Her nightgown rode up her thigh, revealing her supple legs. "Those are nice," she said.

"We don't have quite enough yet, but it can be done. Somehow."

"Anything can be done," she said, dreamily. The pillow muffled her voice. Then: "Are you drunk?"

"No."

"I smell whiskey."

"I *was* drunk. I stopped by Mrs. Stella's."

"That's good," she said. Still her eyes were closed. "You should be closer to your brother."

"He's a pain in the neck," said Antonio, and laughed. "But who isn't."

They were quiet for a while. Then she said, "Do what you want, with everything." Her face was turned away from him.

"The money, the job. I don't care. I'm not going to bother you anymore."

He stroked her hair. "What do you mean by that?"

She didn't answer.

"The city's not safe," Antonio said. "It's not like it used to be. We'll raise our children somewhere better. When I first came here, you could walk anywhere at night and no one would bother you. You could play bocce in the street at three o'clock in the afternoon and not see a car for hours." He shook his head. "Those days are over."

"That's the village," Maddalena said. "You want empty streets, go back there."

He caressed her foot, her ankle, the length of her calf up to her knee. Still she kept her face turned away. Her chest rose and fell. "I wish we could," he said. "For you more than me."

"You feel guilty," she said. "You only talk like this when you feel guilty."

He sat there a while, his head throbbing, his hand limp on her foot. It felt cool as marble, though the rest of her body burned in a near-fever, and patches of sweat had formed where her nightgown clung to her skin. He had questions for her. Explanations. He wanted to bury his head in her chest and ask forgiveness. But there would be plenty of time for that, he thought, and let her sleep.

10

A Concerned Neighbor

AT DINARDO'S, JULIAN chooses a cheerful prearranged vase of pink, blue, and yellow flowers. Before he can ask, Fran pulls out the white lilies and replaces them with tulips. Maddalena is in danger, but still alive, and so there can be no suggestion of death, not even between florist and customer. Fran DiNardo has known Maddalena all seven years she has lived on this block of Eighth Street. Julian has known her only the past few months, a long enough time to start a friendship, too short for it to end.

"Never a dull moment, is there?" Fran says. "Good for business, bad for my heart." She is a short woman of indeterminate age with a leathery face and a voice deepened by years of smoking. Never married, she's worked in her father's shop for as long as Julian can remember. He has never seen Fran without her green apron and an assortment of rubber bands around her wrist. In fact, he has never seen her outside this damp, humid store. She and Julian have a standing appointment here on Saturdays, when he picks up the fresh flowers for his parents' graves. Surprised to see him on a Wednesday morning, she buzzes around like she would for a new customer, spritzing the jungle of tall leafy plants that crowd the floor and the blooms that droop from the hanging pots. When she cranks open the front windows to let in the fresh spring air, Julian notices the muscles in her forearm.

"When Signora Grasso wakes up, tell her I made something for her," says Fran. "Let me show you."

From the top shelf of the refrigerator she takes out a small white box. Inside, wrapped in tissue paper, is a delicate spray of violets attached to a plastic hair clip. She lifts it carefully and holds it up to her ear. "I don't know if people wear violets in their hair," she says. "But they're her favorite flower. And I had a few left over."

Julian looks at the tulips, irises and astra-somethings waiting for him on the counter.

"She'll love yours, too, don't worry," Fran says. She closes up the box, affixes a gold seal to the flap, and places it back in the refrigerator. "Have I steered you wrong before?"

"Never," he says. He walks to the register, takes out his money clip, and starts counting. Sun streams in from the skylights, forcing him to squint.

"You're in a hurry," says Fran, crossing the room. "I understand." Without looking up from the numbers she punches into the cash machine, she says, "You know Signora Grasso from the restaurant?"

Julian hesitates. "Yes and no," he says, hoping that will end it. But Fran looks at him expectantly.

How can he explain the strange course he and Maddalena

have taken? On Christmas Eve, he sang a song that moved her. Upstairs, through the wall between bedroom and bathroom, he felt a certain unspoken connection to her. Over the past few months, she and Antonio visited him many evenings at his house, where they talked and played records. Once or twice a week Julian has met Maddalena and Ida at the bus stop, accompanied them home, and stayed for dinner. "She is my friend," he would say, if it were not so peculiar for a single man advanced in age to befriend a married woman in her twenties. Instead he says, "Franco Grasso worked with my father. I'm just paying my respects."

"Ah," says Fran. "May he rest in peace. A good man, your father. I always said so." She hands him his change. "See you again Saturday, yes?"

All morning the flowers sit wilting on the windowsill in Julian's kitchen. He lifts the shade and changes the water, but they refuse to resurrect themselves. He should have brought them straight to the hospital for the early visiting hours. Instead he stopped at home for a glass of lemonade and twenty minutes of walking in and out of the rooms with the curtains drawn. He cannot bear the idea that his friend is in the sort of coma Mario described: her face pale and frozen and fearful, as if she'd seen a ghost the moment her body shut down. But Julian is already two days late with his respects. If Maddalena wakes and learns that all these strangers have come to visit, but not Julian, she might never forgive him.

He arrives at her room just after seven in the evening. Standing in the hallway, he can see only a pair of bare feet at the end of the bed. He is grateful when Mario appears beside him.

"Don't be afraid," he says, his hand on his shoulder. He leads him in.

Maddalena lies there in a lifeless trance: eyes closed, lips parted, chin lifted as if about to call for help. Julian draws in a breath and looks away. His hands tighten around the vase.

Antonio sits in the chair beside his wife, slumped so far down that his shoulders are even with the arms. He rises slowly to greet Julian, takes the flowers, and sets them on a table with the others. No one has brought violets.

"I am so sorry," Julian says to Antonio, and then, when he remembers the baby, "Congratulations."

"Thank you."

"I don't—" Julian says, and holds out his hands. "In this kind of situation—"

"Nobody knows what to say," says Mario. "That's why it's so quiet in here."

"There's nothing to say," says Antonio. "We just wait."

Julian has always felt discomfort around Antonio, as if the man secretly disapproved of him and was only waiting for a good reason to admit it. At his most optimistic, Julian believes that Antonio cares so little about him that he has no opinion one way or the other. Even in these awful circumstances, it still concerns Julian what Antonio will say about him after he leaves.

Mario offers him one of the chairs that line the side of the bed opposite Antonio. Julian sits and crosses his legs. He wears dress pants, a collared shirt that's too tight around his neck, a dark-blue tie, and thin socks that don't smell (as far as he can tell), though he doesn't remember the last time he washed them. The only sound in the room is the humming of the enormous machine attached to Maddalena. Mario slowly and silently taps his foot. Antonio's eyes flutter, fight, and close.

What good is he doing here? Julian wonders. Can Maddalena sense him, and if so, does she need his panic hovering over her? How useless they all become—the men on both sides of her bed, the doctors, the apple-cheeked nurses—once God puts His hands to her throat.

Julian notices the radio on the floor. Should he have brought his accordion? Maybe one of his songs would wake her. Something happy—"Funiculì, Funiculà," or another of her favorites, "Terra Straniera." Maybe she needs the music to guide her back from that place between life and death—not quite purgatory, but some sort of foggy cave God puts you in as a test. Julian believes in this place. If you want badly enough to live, you run through the maze of tunnels until you find your way out. If you want to die, like his mother in her exhaustion and his father in his loneliness, you simply lie down in the puddles and mist.

He wonders if Maddalena knows that the child she's longed for all these months lies safe and healthy in the other room, and if that knowledge alone might be enough to bring her back. Should he ask to see the baby? What is the proper length of time for him to sit in this room—an hour? Until the next visitor? He is not family. He has no rightful place here. Yet he feels he knows Maddalena better than any of these people.

Twenty minutes pass. Julian pleads in his mind for Antonio and Mario to leave and give him some time alone with his friend. He needs just a moment, long enough to whisper something in her ear. No improper confession, no "I love you" for the nurses to giggle over, though he has, indeed, come to love Maddalena in his own way. He has news she's been anticipating since that night almost four months ago when she and Antonio first showed up at his house, and he longs to share it with her, to see her cover her face with her hands in happy astonishment. He was waiting to tell her until he was certain, but now wishes he'd had more faith. He gives her a quick glance, thinks, *You'll be so proud of me*, and lowers his head again.

MADDALENA AND ANTONIO's first visit came at eight o'clock on a Friday evening in mid-January. Julian lay in bed, the covers up to his chin, when he heard the bell. Through the curtains he watched them waiting on the stoop: she in a long coat, her belly not yet visible, carrying a tray of cookies; he in a black derby and leather gloves, a bottle tucked under his arm. They stomped their feet against the cold and peered into the living room windows.

Julian put on the pair of pants he'd thrown across the radiator an hour before, then grabbed a sweater from the trunk in his closet.

"Surprise!" Maddalena said, when he opened the door.

Julian was suspicious. Since Christmas, Mario had been begging him to return to Mrs. Stella's. After the daily telephone calls failed to convince him, the afternoon drop-ins began. Soon he grew hostile. "You promised me!" he'd shouted from the street, like a lover, as Julian pulled the curtains. Had Mario now gone so far as to send his brother and his pretty blonde sister-in-law to make his case?

They offered no such explanation for their visit. They sat at his kitchen table and passed around the tray of cookies. Maddalena and Julian drank coffee while Antonio drained the jug of homemade wine he'd brought. For the first awkward hour, Julian and Maddalena did most of the talking, trying to fill the painful silences, as Antonio sat back in his chair with his glass resting on his chest. Maddalena had a heavy accent that made each verb sound present tense, and often unconsciously replaced the English word with the Italian. Neither she nor Antonio mentioned Mrs. Stella's. They complained about the patches of ice on the sidewalk, the plumbing in city houses compared to what it must be in the new suburban neighborhoods, and the new priest with the whiny voice who'd just been brought in to assist Father Moravia. St. Anthony's parish was growing fast, and the old pastor couldn't handle the needs of his congregation alone.

Not until Julian brought up the vandals did Antonio come alive.

"I heard about this," he said. "I didn't realize you lived somewhere with a front-row view. Did you see who did it?"

"I sleep through everything," said Julian. "If they drop a bomb on the house, I won't notice until the morning."

"That could be next," Antonio said. He thought a moment. "If you did see something, what do you think you would do?"

Julian shrugged. He had asked himself this same question several times. "Honestly? I don't know."

Maddalena leaned forward. "What is it like? Living so close to them?" She was whispering, as if Abraham Waters and his family could hear her through two brick walls and across a windy street.

Immediately Julian thought of the boy, still unfound, still invading his dreams. But how much of his fixation on little Abraham, his sympathy for Waters, did he want to admit to the Grassos on their first visit to his house? Surely they already thought him *pazzo* at best after that display at Christmas and had come here not for Mario but on a sort of charity mission to comfort the lonely. "I don't think about them anymore," he said. "To me, they're invisible."

"They won't be around much longer," Antonio said. He stood and, hands in his pockets, walked to the front window. He parted the curtains and gazed into the street.

"I never knew what they looked like until I came to this country," said Maddalena. "We used to hear about the Ethiopians all the time back in the village. *Selvaggi*, savages, they called them—the people on the radio and the soldiers who came back from the war. They made them sound like monsters: skinny arms, big, round eyes, skin so dark they could hide two feet in front of you at night and you wouldn't know they were there. But I never saw a picture of one. Not once. And now look at me!"

"Mussolini was an embarrassment," Julian said, with greater conviction than he intended to convey. "What did he want with Africa, anyway? To go against America and the entire world for a piece of desert—and then to lose. To retreat in shame!"

"I agree with you on that," said Antonio, from the living room. He was sitting on the couch now, alone, his back to them. He'd left the curtains parted about two inches.

"We loved him at first," said Maddalena, dreamily. "That voice he had—it was like music, so strong and *feroce*. I knew nothing, really, about the war or what he was doing in Africa. I didn't even know where Africa was on the map. Just that voice. *Una voce incantevole*, my mother used to say." She looked away. "There was a man in the next town who got captured in Africa, spent four years a prisoner in Addis Ababa—I'll never forget that name—and when he got back to Italy, you know what he said? 'For Il Duce, it was worth it.' It was shocking to me, how he could still love a man like that after what happened."

"And you wonder why we moved here," Antonio said. "The Italians have no sense. They believe the last thing they hear."

"Sometimes I think . . . ," said a still-dreamy Maddalena.

She cast her eyes over his shoulder, and Julian could see she was thousands of miles away. "What would my mother do if she had to live like me, seeing the *neri* all the time on the bus, in the stores, and now down the street from my own house, mixed in with the Italians? She would run screaming back to Italy, I think. When she put me on that boat, she had no idea this is the America waiting for me."

Julian smiled at her. "It's a very different life, that's for sure. Two lives, really."

"It is," she said. She looked over at the back of her husband's head. She lowered her voice. "Sometimes when I remember something that happened to me in the village, it's like I'm re-membering one of my romance books. Or a radio song. Then I think: that was you, Maddalena! *You* used to make up plays in the olive grove, not the peasant girl in your book."

"I know what you mean, in a way," said Julian. "There is the life when my parents were alive, and the life after." He looked down.

Antonio had no comment on any of this. The three of them were quiet for a while. Julian stacked the espresso cups and brushed the crumbs from the table. After Maddalena rubbed her arms, he excused himself to turn up the heat. On his way, he noticed that Antonio had closed his eyes. Julian took the empty glass from his hand, and he sank deeper into the couch. "Should I wake him up?" he mouthed to Maddalena.

Maddalena shook her head. "You have to excuse him. He worked all day."

Julian put on more coffee and sat with Maddalena at the table, waiting for it to boil. Her husband falling asleep did not seem to bother her, and he wondered if he did this often. "Can I tell you something?" he asked her.

"OK."

"I changed my name," he said. "After my father died, I was not the same person, like I told you. My name is Julian Fabbri now—the American way, with the *J*—not Giulio." He shrugged. "But nobody calls me Julian. It's like they're afraid to. Or maybe they don't realize."

"I didn't realize," she said.

"I used to think: maybe the new name will help me forget. Make my life easier. But it didn't work."

"I wish I could forget," she said, and again traveled far from Julian's little kitchen, with the squeaky faucets and the rivers of cracks in the tile. When she came back moments later, her eyes brightened. "But I have so much to look forward to." She put her hands over her belly. "That's what I tell myself every day. You should say it, too, Julian, believe me. After a while, you can get used to anything."

The coffee was bubbling. Julian reached over to switch off the burner.

"Can I ask *you* a question?"

Julian nodded, ready for the Mrs. Stella's conversation she'd been building up to all night. It was a smart tactic: send in the blonde to do your dirty work. He poured the steaming espresso into two cups. From under the sink he pulled out a bottle of anisette. "You want a shot first?"

"No, *grazie*," she said. "Two glasses of that wine . . . it's very strong."

"It is."

She folded her hands in her lap. "I was just wondering," she said. "You don't have to tell me, but—"

"It's OK," Julian said, ready to explain that he still could not—and would never—be able to put the embarrassment of

Christmas Eve out of his mind. It was hard enough just to sit and talk with her, who'd seen him make a fool of himself. "What is it?"

"Did you ever want to get married?"

This he did not expect. And though he'd asked himself that same question many times, the answer he gave Maddalena surprised him. It was something he did not know about himself until the moment the words left his mouth. He said, "I'm not what you'd call a passionate person."

Maddalena had no verbal response, but on her face was a look of great concern, as if he'd just told her he had an incurable disease.

He thought a moment. "Maybe I should say it like this: Giulio was not a passionate person. And for Julian, it's probably too late."

He sat back in his chair. Because such statements deserved a laugh, he gave her one. How else to avoid allowing her to indulge the self-pity of a grown man, the blatant plea for sympathy? Maddalena should have shrugged him off, said, "How silly you are, Signor!" Instead her silent concern hung like a shadow across her face.

So he put a Jerry Vale record on the turntable, and they made it through the first side before Antonio woke.

Good-byes were said, plans made for the next visit, and still the shadow lingered on Maddalena's face. It followed her out the door, down the steps onto the sidewalk, and when she turned to wave to Julian there it was again, dark and grave as a veil over her eyes.

*   *   *

Two mornings after Maddalena and Antonio's first visit, Julian walked onto his front porch and gazed upon destruction. This time the vandals had scorched the Waterses' tiny plot of dead grass, smashed the flowerpots, and splattered black paint across the driveway and sidewalk. The activity must have been witnessed or heard by someone on the block, but not a single man had been brave—or awake—enough to run out and stop it.

Waters walked around his yard, dropping shards of terracotta into a grocery bag. He'd parked his taxi at an odd angle in the driveway, as if he'd been in a rush to jump out. Like most days, he wore his enormous brown coat, overlong dress pants that trailed on the ground, and cowboy boots. He worked wearily, stopping every few minutes to catch his breath. He tried to put out the smoldering patch of black grass with the hose, but the pipes had frozen. He got on his knees, the wind whipping his hair, and poured some sort of chemical solution over the paint on the sidewalk. He scrubbed with a wire brush, and after a few minutes the stain faded.

Julian—in his slippers, housecoat, and layers of pajamas—held the newspaper under his arm and watched from behind the glass door. The spell of frigid weather would not break on this day, with the wind so strong it bent the antennae on the cars parked along Seventh Street. The few birds who'd remained for the winter had disappeared. It was too cold for snow, the newsman said, prompting Julian to wonder how that could be possible. What happened to the moisture in the clouds in this situation? It couldn't freeze up there in long, heavy sheets of ice. There was so much he didn't understand about the world. His most pressing question now, though: why, in the darkest and harshest hours of the night, had someone mustered the energy to inflict this damage?

It had to do with little Abraham, Julian decided. The boy must be in some sort of deep, complicated trouble he was too naive to comprehend, and this second attack must signal that the trouble would not end anytime soon. But did it mean the boy was alive or dead? Julian's mind raced. Usually he delighted in making up stories for the lives of his fellow humans, but for this boy only the same gruesome images kept surfacing. The harder he tried to imagine a happy ending, the less likely a possibility it seemed.

A fog came over the glass, then froze into a starry film of ice crystals that obscured his view. He breathed and rubbed two little circles with the balls of his fist, making himself a set of peepholes. But Waters was nearly finished. He stepped into his car. Now, except for the circle of dead grass and the taxi warming up for a day's work, his house looked as ordinary as the one beside it. A stranger walking by, on his way to the market in this gray early morning light, might not even wonder who lived there. It was not until Waters backed the taxi into the street that Julian saw the reason a stranger might stop, look closer, then hurry along. Visible on the concrete driveway, under the oddly parked taxi, was the faint but unmistakable outline of the words DIRTY NIGGERS.

Quickly Julian shut the door, as if the vandals had shouted the words at his face. "I live here, too, you know!" he said, to the empty hallway.

JULIAN WOKE IN his armchair, sure he'd heard a noise, but when he pulled open the bedroom curtains he found no commotion on the street. The Waters house seemed the same as the last time he'd checked, the view from the window flat and still as a photograph: telephone wires, parked cars, shrubs and grass seared with frost. He checked his watch. He'd nodded off again. But over the past two hours he'd missed nothing.

He returned to his chair, slapped his cheeks and tightened the laces on his wingtips. He deemed his inability to stay awake as a failure of character. He talked to himself like this: You have a job now, Julian: to guard and protect Seventh Street. Lie around in bed all day if you want to—it's not like you have to punch a card somewhere else—but don't sleep while you're on duty.

A different mind took over at this hour of night. It was as if the Julian who made the decisions the rest of the day vanished and left another Julian to run the graveyard shift. Usually the graveyard-shift Julian had nothing to do but turn the crank of dreams, but over the past week he had been put to work. These silly thoughts themselves—a man in his head turning the crank of dreams?—Julian might never entertain during regular hours. But here, half-asleep in the three-a.m. darkness, his thoughts made a profound sense. He recorded the more interesting ones on a sheet of paper, which he tucked into the dog-eared copy of *Walden* on his dresser. In the morning or afternoon—whenever he'd wake up—he'd read over the jottings and frequently throw them in the garbage. If he died in his sleep and people found these mad scrawls, half-English, half-Italian, slanted down the page, would they not think he'd gone *pazzo* for real?

This was the closest he'd ever come to defending his country. He'd been too old for Korea and the World War II draft and did not have the stomach to enlist. Besides, he found war distasteful, though he'd yet to develop a moral philosophy around it more sophisticated than Jesus Christ's, which taught him to turn the other cheek, or Thoreau's, which might have landed him in jail. When, in 1941, there was a call to replace the deployed Guard with a state militia composed of the over-age and the underage, he ignored it. All across Delaware, bright young students and half-deaf postmen and retired cooks signed up to be the last line of defense should the enemy reach our shores, but Giulio Fabbri kept to his house like an invalid, following the progress of the troops on the radio and in the newspaper. He'd ventured outside so rarely during the war years that people still thanked him for his service, thinking he'd been deployed.

It occurred to him now that, had he indeed volunteered for the state militia, he'd at least have learned what to do if he caught the vandals on his street. Maybe he'd charge after them, pointing the long gun at their behinds. Maybe he'd stick his head out from the hole in the middle of the tank and yell, "Stop or you're dead!" from a megaphone, his voice clear and incanta-tory as Mussolini's, and they'd have no choice but to throw up their arms and surrender. Then Julian would gather them on his porch and patiently explain to them that destroying property in their shared neighborhood was like setting your own clothes on fire—not only did you end up naked afterward, but you had scars and burns that may never heal.

His thoughts jumped to Il Duce himself. Yes, the man had an extraordinary voice, one that, like Julian's, could probably carry a tune. Maybe he gave up a career as a tenor just so he could run Italy into the ground. It would make a great poem: "Benito's Serenade." The idea intrigued Julian, so he wrote the title on the sheet of paper, along with the first two lines that came to him: *You could have stirred us to love, but you chose wrong; you could have saved your country with a song.* At three a.m., it sounded worthy to be read to Maddalena Grasso on her next visit. At three in the afternoon the day after, it sounded worthy only to be shredded into confetti.

For six nights, Julian kept watch. On the seventh, he was woken at dawn, pulled the curtains out of habit, and saw Waters running across his driveway. He carried a crowbar. He had the vandals in his sights. Julian quickly closed the curtains and peeked through the narrow slit in the middle. Waters made surprisingly long strides for a man of his age and size and waved the crowbar over his head as he rounded the corner onto Scott Street.

Strewn across the lawn were bags of garbage torn open and emptied: banana peels, aluminum cans, glass bottles, coffee grounds, rotting tomatoes, and heads of lettuce. One bag had been dumped on the roof of the taxi, and now a yellow liquid—soup? egg yolks?—streaked the back window and dripped onto the driveway.

Minutes later, Waters reappeared, the crowbar over his right shoulder, his other hand on his hip. He walked slowly, breathing hard. He was barefoot. He opened the passenger door of the taxi and tossed the crowbar in the front seat. He looked up and down the street. Julian froze when his gaze lingered on his window, afraid any movement would give him away. But Waters just shook his head and went inside.

The cruelty of the vandals astonished Julian. He had never witnessed such heartlessness. As he watched his neighbor cross and recross his lawn, scooping another man's trash into a bag, it occurred to him that the vandals might next harm Waters himself, or another one of his children. Who knew how far they would go? There was the old lady, too, who sat for hours on the porch rocker in the summer in her floppy hat, knitting. Danger hung over them all, and, if recent history were any indication, Julian would not be able to stop it.

If he could talk to Waters, he would advise him to move out of this neighborhood as soon as he could, stay in a motel if he had to. Whoever wanted to force out his family would not stop at broken pots and burnt grass. "I have nothing against you or your people," Julian would explain, as calmly as he'd lecture the vandals themselves. As evidence, he'd tell him of the nights he'd made himself a sentinel at his bedroom window.

That morning Julian commenced on a trip across Seventh Street, ready not only to express his sympathy to Waters but to ask if there'd been any news about his son. Then, as he waited on the sidewalk for a car to pass, he lost his nerve. He turned toward Union instead, and ended up on a shivering winter promenade around the block. Any personal involvement with Waters would incur all sorts of obligations for which he wasn't quite prepared. His neighbors would line up outside his door: Rosa Volpe, the Delluccis, even Antonio and Mario Grasso. By the time the promenade was over, Julian convinced himself that Waters did not need him to solve his problems for him. He should have known the day he moved in that Seventh Street was rocky soil, no place for a family like his to plant itself.

And so Julian wrote a letter. It was the least he could do. When evening came, he crept across the street and left it on the Waterses' porch beside the gift of a new flowerpot, which he'd bought that morning at DiNardo's. The letter, signed "A Concerned Neighbor," asserted at least three times that the author was not the man destroying their house. But the author did see clearly that this was a battle the Waters family could not win. "You don't know me," said the Concerned Neighbor, "but you can trust me. I don't know you, but I care about you and your family the way I care about all God's children."

Julian waited two hours in sentinel position before the taxi pulled up and Waters found his gifts. He paged through the letter—not long enough to read it thoughtfully—stuffed it in his back pocket, and carried the flowerpot inside.

When Julian heard a knock at his door the next night, he immediately prepared himself for Waters. Should he invite him in? Should he admit he wrote the letter? But it was only Antonio and Maddalena Grasso on his front stoop, jolly as salesmen, with their cookies and wine. He had not even realized the weekend had come.

"Surprise!" said Maddalena.

Their shoulders and the tops of their hats were dusted with snow, the first of the season though it was already February. The snow fell delicately around them on that windless evening, settling on the bare trees and telephone lines.

The Grassos' visits with Julian followed the same schedule: they'd eat the delicious amaretti and *pizzele* prepared with love by Maddalena and her mother-in-law, make small talk about politics and weather, and avoid any mention of Mrs. Stella's. Eventually Abraham Waters would enter the conversation, and they'd argue again over the morality of the vandals—a topic on which they disagreed more in degree than spirit. Both men thought the Waters family would be better off in their own section of the city, but Antonio had more sympathy for the vandals. He was convinced they were a group of Italians who merely wanted to keep their neighborhood safe and had no connection to the missing boy. "I don't approve of destruction as a means of preservation," Julian would say. "It's like setting your clothes on fire . . ."

"I don't understand what that means," Antonio would reply. "I want you to tell me a better way to protect what we Italians have built."

To that Julian would offer a statement such as "It's a problem with a hundred solutions, and no solutions at all," which irritated Antonio further. He was not a man who enjoyed the complexities of truth. As hard as Julian tried to wrestle over the Trieste question, the merits of the Korean War, or the recent arrest of Sonny Boy Thompson—sometimes taking positions that he himself did not hold, in the interest of debate—Antonio rarely played along. Most discussions ended with him shaking his head and saying, "Nobody said life was easy," or "It's just destiny."

Eventually Antonio would drink too much of the strong homemade wine, wander over to the couch, and fall asleep. Julian and Maddalena would remain at the kitchen table, and he'd ask her opinion on the topics Antonio had dismissed. She did not read the newspapers—Julian assumed she did not know how—or listen to the news, but she had gleaned enough to assert that Trieste should belong to Italy and not the Slavs; that communism did not treat fairly people like her, who worked harder than others; and that the mother of Sonny Boy Thompson deserved sympathy for the actions of her son. She never took a position without immediately discrediting herself afterward, which prompted Julian to say, "You're smarter than you think."

Like her husband, Maddalena did not enjoy discussing current affairs. Mostly she wanted him to tell her stories from his childhood, and every once in a while she'd share a memory from her village. At the end of the night, she'd go to the couch, stand above Antonio, shake his shoulder, and say, "Hurry up! You're late for church!" or "Antonio Grasso! You fell asleep on the job again! This time you're fired!" He never laughed at these same little jokes, but the ritual delighted her.

On that first snowy night in February, Maddalena did not remove her scarf, a signal to Julian that he kept his heat too low. In contrast, Antonio rolled up his sleeves and smoked one cigarette after another. "I have a message from my brother," he began, as he uncorked the wine. "Believe me, I don't want to get involved, but now that he knows we see you, he begged me to tell you a few things."

"Don't waste your breath," said Julian.

"The main thing is that he can't keep making the same argument to get you to come back to Mrs. Stella's."

"That's the good news," said Maddalena.

Julian could sum up this argument of Mario's in less than ten words: "More money for us means more money for you." On each of his visits, he'd offered a small—then incrementally larger—percentage of the profits the nights Julian performed. But 100-percent profit could not erase from Julian's memory the pity in the eyes of the Christmas Eve guests, the sense that they had seen him not only naked, but on the toilet with his pants around his ankles.

"I appreciate your brother's kindness," said Julian. "But this problem is between him and me."

"According to him, he's seen the light," Antonio continued. "These are his words: at first I thought Giulio was acting like a big baby, but now I see he has pride. And pride is a quality I admire very much, a quality I share."

"*Julian*," corrected Maddalena.

"I was being Mario," Antonio explained. "Didn't you see the way I stuck out my chest?"

Julian laughed.

"But this pride that makes us," said Antonio, again with the puffed chest, this time with a fist over his heart. "It also ruins us.

We are blind to our own situations. You can't see how deeply you are loved at Mrs. Stella's, Giulio Fabbri. Missed, the way you miss your dear mother and father. My customers still ask—so often it's starting to annoy me—when you will be coming back. We tried a new guy, younger, better-looking if I have to say, but he didn't have the"—here Antonio searched for the word he clearly already knew—"the *passion*. He sang in a nice voice and didn't miss too many high notes, but what we got from him we could have got much cheaper from a record player."

"Bravo," said Julian. "If something ever happens to Mario, you could take his place, no problem."

"Can I try?" asked Maddalena. She put her hands flat on the table and leaned in eagerly. "I know the speech, too."

Antonio turned to Julian. "She wanted to be an actress once," he said.

Julian rubbed his eyes. All this talk of Mrs. Stella's made him want a drink. If he could pry the bottle from Antonio's hands, he'd enjoy a glass of wine instead of coffee. If not, he had a case of red in the basement left over from the funerals.

"I insulted you when I came to your house all those times, with my offers of money," Maddalena began. She paced from one end of the kitchen to the other with her head bowed and her hands behind her back, the way Mario did when he got nervous. "I understand that now. So today I ask you not in the spirit of your wallet, but in the spirit of truth, of love, of *famiglia*. And, if I can say—" She cleared her throat. "Because I am concerned."

Julian looked up. "Concerned?" He'd grabbed the bottle from Antonio and was reaching for a glass.

Maddalena's lips pursed and turned downward. She folded

her hands and extended them toward Julian. "Look at how you live," she said. She walked to the counter and ran her finger along the top. She held up the finger, black with dust. "It's the middle of the afternoon, my friend, and you're still in your housecoat. A single man needs purpose. If not *la musica*, then what? If not a pretty girl who might walk at any moment into my restaurant, fall in love with your voice and your talent, then what? *L'amore è la vita, amico mio.* Love is life! Life is love! Forgive me if I'm saying too much. I consider myself your friend. If I don't look out for you, who will? You are still grieving, I know, but you can't grieve forever."

Something passed between Maddalena and Julian then. She may have been repeating one of Mario's speeches, in a skilled imitation, but her confident performance made it clear she believed every word. She was not so talented an actress that Julian couldn't see through her charade. Who was she to tell him how to live? How did she know what purpose his life did or did not have? In their talks, she was always trying to get him to reveal something about himself, some secret he might be hiding. The moment Antonio fell asleep, she'd start with the questions. What did Julian think of so-and-so's widowed sister? Maybe there was a girl from his childhood who still wrote him letters?

Maddalena went on, but Julian stopped listening. He stared at the silver crucifix on the wall beside the refrigerator. Had he sinned by allowing the tips of the Lord's hands and feet to tarnish? Of course he'd considered keeping the house a bit tidier. For a few months after his father died, he'd regularly used the broom and dustpan. But before long he'd lost patience for the persistent effort that cleaning required. No sooner would he wipe the coffee table than dust would again settle there, dulling the sheen he'd worked so hard to achieve; no matter how many times he emptied and soaped down the inside of the refrigerator, he could not expel the lingering rotten-vegetable smell. The reason for this trouble eventually occurred to him: his parents wanted the house dirty. A son alone in their house pushing around a wet mop insulted their memory. He needed a woman to bring this place to life, a woman to make him better than the lonely old bachelors on their barstools at Mrs. Stella's. He needed a wife. So until one fell from the sky, the neat piles of rags in the linen closet, which his mother had kept clean as her own underwear, would remain untouched.

Mario Grasso clearly did not understand this. After the restaurant closed at night, he returned to the scrubbed floors and walls of his home on Eighth Street, embraced his wife and his daughters, and slept in peace. He did not walk through the rooms of his house like a scared child wishing that—when he turned his head—he'd find his mother standing at the sink, his father dozing in his armchair.

"Tell me how *you* live, then, Mario," Julian said, interrupting Maddalena. At this point, she was in the middle of a list of songs Mario suggested Julian might want to learn.

"How *I* live?" she asked.

"Yes." Julian crossed his arms. "You people talk like you have all the answers for me. Why not share them? Help a pathetic old man?"

Maddalena looked at her husband.

"We're just repeating information," said Antonio. "We didn't mean for you to get angry." He pushed his chair away from the table. "Maybe we should leave?"

Julian forced a smile. "No," he said. "Stay where you are. The truth is, I really want to know the answer. From you, from Mario, whoever the expert is. Tell me what it's like to have responsibility—for a wife, children, a business. When do you rest?"

"We don't know yet," Maddalena said shyly. "But soon. A few more months." She sat beside Antonio and put her hand on his shoulder.

Did she always wear this much makeup when she visited? Her face had gone pale the moment he'd interrupted her, but two circles on her cheeks remained warm and rosy. She'd painted her lips a glossy red, and possibly thickened her eyelashes. Around her neck she wore a heart-shaped locket, and in her hair two rhinestone clips that sparkled even in the dim light of the kitchen. Maybe these trips to Seventh Street were her only chances to dress up, the only entertainment her husband allowed her.

"I never rest," Antonio said. "I'm at the plant before the sun comes up. I get on my knees and break my back all day, sweating through my shirt. Look at this—" He held up his right palm, revealing a rash of pink blisters. The biggest, just below his ring finger, was the size of a nickel. "For five hours this hand holds a screwdriver, turning here, turning there. The skin tears off like paper. Then for half an hour I sit on a folding chair and eat a sandwich with thirty other men and shoot the shit. After that, five more hours, me and the screwdriver and the inside of a Ford. I go home, eat some more, and then, if I'm lucky, I get an hour or two to take a nice walk, get some air, visit my brother. Let me tell you, the night I get six full hours of sleep, I'll throw myself a party." He glanced at Maddalena. "Soon the baby will come and cry all the time, and then I'll really be sunk."

"Mario doesn't have it easy, either," said Maddalena to Julian. "Ida and the girls never see him."

"Gino Stella does nothing," said Julian. "That much I saw for myself."

"Gino wouldn't know work if it bit him in his fat ass," said Antonio, with a laugh. He refilled his glass, and with it finished off the bottle. "My brother's his little dog. Without Mario, Mrs. Stella's would roll over and die. He's a big talker—too big most of the time—but he works hard for that dump. I give him that."

"I agree with you there," said Julian.

As if on schedule, Antonio rose and walked to the window, using the furniture to steady himself. The snow was letting up. An inch or two covered the ground, reflecting the moonlight and glow of the streetlamps.

"I have a secret dream," Antonio said, without turning from his view.

Julian and Maddalena waited. They exchanged glances.

"Are you going to tell us about it?" Julian asked.

"One day, I'm going to open my own restaurant, right across the street from Mrs. Stella's. Me and my brother. We'll put Gino out of business."

"That's brave," said Julian.

"And stupid, probably," he said.

"Since when do you want to open a business with Mario?" asked Maddalena.

Antonio shrugged.

"It's good to have ideas when you're young," Julian said. "When you get to be my age—"

"I have a hundred ideas," said Antonio. He described the L-shaped layout of the dining room, the flagstone, the white tablecloths and shiny wood floors. From his wallet he took out a small piece of paper that had been folded over many times; on it was written *Trattoria Grasso* in the fancy cursive script he'd designed for the marquee.

Maddalena watched him, her face blank as the snow. Julian

guessed that she was hearing all of this for the first time, that Antonio did not talk much to her unless he'd been drinking. By the time he finished—having gone through the new menu from *primi* to *dolci*—he'd exhausted himself. "You mind if I rest my eyes for a while?" he asked, as he lay on the couch and propped his feet on the cushions. Every week, this same question preceded the nap he'd never admit he'd taken, not even after Maddalena shook him awake an hour later.

"Be my guest," said Julian.

"I should be the one resting my eyes," Maddalena whispered, after Antonio's first snore. "I don't work nine hours a day? Then come home and cook dinner, and make his lunch and his father's lunch on top of that? He thinks I have it easy because I *sit* in front of the sewing machine, and he has to *bend over* in front of the car. But I don't complain." She shrugged, a defeated look on her face. "You know, in my village, I never had a job. A few hours in my father's grocery once a week, that was it. Just to give me something to pass the time. Now in America all I do is work. All everybody does in this country is work."

"Except me," said Julian.

"Because you don't belong here," Maddalena said, casually, as if this were a point they'd already decided.

"I don't?"

She blushed. "Never mind," she said, with a wave of her hand. "Don't listen to me. I want to hear more about what you started to tell me last time. Why you didn't join the army."

Julian narrowed his eyes at her. "No," he said. "You should tell me what country I belong in. I'd like to know."

"Antonio gets mad at me," said Maddalena. "Because I've been planning your life for you, and it's none of my business. I don't want you to be mad at me, too."

This did not surprise him. "I could never be mad at you," he said, though her pity had made him want to throw his wineglass across the room. "So let's hear it. Or should I get a drink first?"

"You should move back to Italy," she said, with an urgency that suggested she'd kept this in for a long time. She leaned her entire body forward and lay her palms flat on the table. "That's where your blood comes from."

"Oh, that's perfect," Julian interrupted. "Half of Italy crosses the ocean one way, and Julian Fabbri goes the other. Am I so backward?" He crossed his arms. "What can I do in the Old Country that I can't do here in the Land of Opportunity?"

Her face was serious. "You can forget," she said. "Pretend you never lived in this house, in this little half city. Pretend you never had a father or a mother. You told me one time: 'Nineteen fifty-four will be the year I change my life.' But how much can you change here, with all these ghosts?" Julian followed her eyes across the kitchen, half expecting to see the line of Fabbris along the wall: his Nonno and Nonna, his parents cradling a lifeless Caterina, the two cousins he lost in the war.

"I promise you," said Maddalena. "Walk into any village and the people will open their arms to you. Relatives or not. They'll find you a house to live in and a café to play your music. They'll find a wife for you, too, if you want, sooner or later." She raised her eyebrows. "You can change your name back to the Italian way, or pick a new one. I like Alessandro or Umberto. But Giulio is good, too."

Julian stared at her, disbelieving. How proud of herself this woman was, and what a sad creature he must have painted himself to be. He stood and brushed the crumbs from his lap. "The snow is getting worse," he said, and checked his watch. "You should wake your husband."

"You're not mad at me, are you?" she said. "The last thing I want to do—"

"No," Julian said, though his hands trembled as they reached for the coatrack. He stood in the hallway waiting for her to rise and retrieve her husband. Instead she crossed her legs and stirred some sugar in her coffee. She wanted him to tell her he liked her idea. "I'm an American," he said. "I know the history, the literature. If I don't have a life here, I don't have one any-where. End of story."

"Look at me," Maddalena said. "I lived through the war in one country, and now I'm in another. A little girl from nowhere. If you really want to, you can switch."

"And the switching made you happy? You wake up every day and say, 'Thank you, God, for my beautiful life in America, where I work my fingers to the bone?'"

"I do," she said, unconvincingly. "I have a good life. Of course we could always have more money, and a house to our-selves, but other than that, what more could I ask for?"

"You miss your family. You miss your village. Even after eight years, it feels like yesterday you left them. Did you forget I saw you on the stairs Christmas Eve, that I heard you singing through the wall? It was like someone told you they were dead."

Maddalena shook her head. "I don't think about the past. I try to forget everything. Work keeps my mind busy. No one here knew me when I was young. That's what I want for you: to live in a place where nothing will remind you."

"But to forget completely is an insult. A dishonor to the people who loved you—"

"Not if you don't have a choice," she said. She turned her face away. For a while she remained quiet.

He sat back down beside her.

"It's not right," she said. "But you're the only person I can talk to like this." She still faced the back of the kitchen: the flaking white paint on the door, the snow settling in the corners of the windowpanes. "I have nobody else. No girlfriends, no sisters. Ida wants everything pretty all the time. And I can't upset my husband. So if you get mad at me and don't want to see me anymore, I'll really be alone."

He reached over. The tips of two of his fingers touched her sleeve. "How many times do I have to tell you I'm not mad?"

"You're going to think I'm crazy," she said, "but all week before I come here, I plan what I'm going to say to you. All the stupid things tonight, I practiced in my head—at work, on the bus. To make sure we didn't waste time."

"But I do most of the talking," said Julian, with a laugh. "You make me tell all my stories. I never hear yours. You had a beautiful mother, a father who was smart and kind, a village where the air was cool; your greatest excitement was riding a bike up and down a hill. It sounds like a book to teach young children how to read. Not a real person's life."

"I have no stories," Maddalena said.

It was the most obvious lie Julian had ever heard. "You wanted to be an actress," he said. "That sounds like a story to me. Why don't you tell it?"

By two o'clock the next day, every one of Julian's neighbors had cleared the snow from their steps and sidewalks. The temperature was dropping by the hour, freezing the bottom layer of the snow into a sheet of ice. As hard as Julian bashed it with the tip of his metal shovel, the ice yielded only a few holes and a mess of shavings.

"You're too late," said Renato Volpe, stepping onto the clean concrete in front of his mother's house. "This morning, it was like scooping up feathers."

Julian scattered a handful of sand onto the steps. "Is that right."

Renato made good pizza, but Julian never cared much for him. When they'd been altar boys together at St. Anthony's, he'd skipped out after Mass more than a few times to join his friends, forcing Giulio to do twice his share of the cleanup. Immediately after the recessional, Renato would throw his cassock on the floor of the sacristy, say, "Hang that up, will you?" and run out the back after Gianni Martino and his pack of neighborhood kids. Renato was five years younger, and in his group were the little brothers of the boys who'd ignored Giulio throughout grammar and high school. The one time Giulio found the nerve to complain about Renato's bullying, Father Moravia, then young and curly-haired, sat him on his lap and asked him to show compassion. Derelict boys had their fun as kids, said the priest, but would be punished when they grew up. And though smart and quiet boys like Giulio suffered in their youth, God rewarded them with happy adulthoods, devoted wives, and more wealth than a boy like Renato Volpe would ever achieve.

Renato's car—a long white Pontiac, with a silver streak down the front—had been idling for the past half hour, pumping clouds of smoke onto Seventh Street. He readjusted the chains on the wheels, then sped away over the slick road. He slid and narrowly missed the curb as he careened toward Union.

Julian was not the only one watching him. Abraham Waters stood, arms folded, on his front porch. He'd driven his taxi through the night and arrived home near dawn. The slam of the door had roused Julian from his post, and then the scrape of his shovel kept him awake.

Julian walked to the end of his yard, balancing the bag of sand on his hip. He looked around. Rosa Volpe peered at him through the drapes of her front window. "Do you mind if I ask," said Julian, "is there any news on your son?"

"Nothing."

"I think about him," Julian said. Who could survive outside in weather like this? "I hope he makes it home soon."

"That's good of you to say."

Julian nodded and walked off. He scattered the rest of the sand onto his iceberg of a sidewalk. Patches remained, but what more could he do? If someone slipped, he'd offer him a shot of *sambuca* and a hot-water bottle and his most sincere apologies.

"By the way," Waters said, as he turned toward his front door. He carried the crowbar over his right shoulder. "Thanks for the pot. But my family's not going anywhere. Not now, not ever."

II

Sad Eyes

OPEN AND CLOSE your mouth, like a fish, like Sister Clark teaching you English, like an old woman who's lost her mind and sits alone, no longer responsive to light and touch; the sound you'll make, instinctively, the most natural sound in the world, is *ma*. Mamma. *Mamma*. Under God there are no accidents. He gives us answers as clear as letters on a chalkboard. When we are babies, our first reach is for the woman who bore us; eighty years later, in our loneliness, after our husbands and lovers and children have gone, our final cry is for her. This is how Maddalena, in the blackness and silence of her long sleep, outside her daughter's reach, comprehends human life. It is little more than the opening and closing of mouths—eager for milk, for kisses, for help, protection, explanation—a million hours of talk continuing ceaselessly, until God shuts you up for good.

She has more to say, but, for now, God presses His sweaty

hand to her face, and she struggles to breathe. His palm smothers her mouth and nose; His fingers hold down her eyelids. She is still and speechless under His immense weight. And yet she can sense movement around her, changes in pressure and smell. Bleach, violets, three-day sweat. The steady beat of what could be music, or a foot tapping, or her own heart. Her legs drop away, then reattach; waves of heat ripple up and down the length of her body. Her child is no longer inside her, of that much she is certain, though the knowledge is less a memory than an awareness of lack. What was one is now two. It is the opposite of a wedding. What once belonged only to Maddalena now belongs to the world, and mother and child will have to share each other with strangers for as long as they live.

UNTIL THAT SNOWY February night at Julian's, Maddalena had nearly forgotten her interview at the Bianca Talent Agency. She had never spoken of it, not even in her letters home. After Antonio revealed to Julian her dream of becoming an actress, it took her a while—well into her superb impersonation of Mario—to remember that steps had actually been taken to bring her to the stage.

There was a harmlessness about Julian that led Maddalena to believe he'd keep her secret. The memory of the agency was a source of shame, though she had not sinned—not exactly. She didn't know what she'd call the sin if Father Moravia asked her: *la vanità*, maybe. Vanity. Or selfishness. Pride. Whatever name she gave this disease, the priest would pull open the screen and tell her she'd caught it from American movies, on which he blamed every sin. Though he'd absolve her and grant her the serenity that followed confession, the longing for costumes and makeup and those first steps into the lights would remain.

She and Antonio had insulted Julian with their meddling, but he refused to admit he was angry at them. Though he did rise abruptly from the table to grab her coat from the hallway, it was possible he felt no anger at all, that he was one of those people who found themselves so undeserving of attention that they took any interest in their lives as flattery. Angry or not, he begged Maddalena for the story. So there, in the safety of his kitchen, she'd relived her donkey-walk down the hallway of the Bianca Talent Agency, the inspection of her non-European teeth, and the silent drive to the suburbs—during which it had dawned on her that Bianca would indeed train a donkey if it could afford the fees. Of the trip to the parking lot she made no mention.

"So they never called you?" Julian asked, when the story was over.

"No," she said. "I knew they wouldn't, but—" She rubbed the edge of the table with her thumb. "Still."

For weeks after that interview, Maddalena stopped cold when the phone rang. Everything around her faded—the clearing of the table, the brushing of Mamma Nunzia's hair—as the voice of whichever man answered grew louder. But it was always one of Ida's cousins or the electrician or Gianni who called, leaving her flushed and fumbling to continue whatever she was doing.

"Cretins," said Julian.

Though she did not know that word, Julian had uttered it with sufficient disgust for her to agree with him.

"If I were you," he said, "I'd report them to the Better Business Bureau. Hell, I'll report them myself." He sat up in his chair. "What we should do is send *me* down there for an for an interview. If they say they've found the next Marcello Mastroianni, we'll know for sure they're crooks."

She laughed. "You shouldn't say that."

"It's a shame, though," he added, quietly. "You'd have made a fine actress. And I could say I knew someone famous." He paused a moment. "Then again, you can think of it like this: 'Rather than love, than money, than fame, give me truth.' I read that once."

Maddalena nodded. "My brother Claudio used to read," she said. "But he never remembered anything."

"Words just pop into my head sometimes."

"I don't think my brother was very smart," said Maddalena. "He always had a book in his hand, but, for all we knew, he could have been illiterate."

She hadn't spoken of Claudio in years. She found herself eager to tell Julian more—about her other brothers, about *Il Sogno della Principessa*, which she had yet to finish, about whatever popped into her head. But the snow was falling more heavily, and the time had come to wake her husband.

They talked again the next Friday, and every Friday after that. One week she and Antonio would show up on his doorstep; the next Julian would come to Eighth Street promptly at dinnertime. He planned his visits to avoid Mario, who spent most of the weekend at Mrs. Stella's. The days grew longer, and soon it was still light when Julian walked Maddalena and Ida home from the bus stop, carrying their bag of Lamberti's rolls. He'd update them on the stories he'd read in the newspaper that morning—political scandals, weather disasters, tales of crime and misfortune. Out West somewhere, police finally found the body of a millionaire's missing six-year-old son lying in a shallow grave. What shocked Julian was not only that the grave was on the property of the millionaire's female gardener, but that this woman had been leading a double life as a gunrunning prostitute. "Who can you trust anymore?" he'd say, and throw up his hands. "Only yourself. And the good Grasso family." Then he'd move on to the next awful story—a strange disease called "parrot fever" currently spreading from birds to innocent humans; a poor family who'd survived the harsh winter eating garbage; the constant threat of Russia incinerating America with an H-bomb.

"They shouldn't print any of that," said Ida. "All it does is upset people."

Maddalena agreed. She'd rather not know the cruelty people could inflict, or what unpreventable disasters might befall them, but she would never say so in front of Julian. Talking about disaster seemed to soothe him, make him less afraid. Maybe he believed that if he had knowledge of a particular type of tragedy, it would avoid him.

"*Occhi tristi,*" Antonio called him. Sad eyes. Or, because of his half beard and the shape of his head, "the goat." He pitied him. No man should live his life alone, not unless he'd intentionally harmed someone, and Julian didn't seem like the type whom God had punished for some brutal act.

And yet Antonio's sympathy didn't stop him from poking fun when Julian wasn't around. "There's a certain kind of man who never gets married," he said once, a joke everyone at the table but Maddalena seemed immediately to comprehend. Mario chuckled, mentioned something about the army, and then the subject was dropped.

Julian may have considered himself too old to get married,

but Maddalena made it her mission to convince him otherwise. If he ignored her advice to move to Italy, then a wedding here in America would do just fine. He did not lack passion; she saw it in his songs, in his adoration of his parents, in his rage over the catastrophes of the world. Early in life she had learned that passion needn't be obvious to be real; it could flow like an electrical current just under your skin, live but imperceptible. It needed only a spark. Then came the shudder and the shock, the dizzying spin, the instant craving for the next jolt. This had happened to Maddalena in two countries. Julian deserved it, too—and one of these days she would convince him.

DR. BARONE HAD predicted the birth for June 25. She was blessed, he told her; she would not have to endure her third trimester in the discomfort of a humid mid-Atlantic summer. She could take the baby to the beach the day of its baptism, let the fresh air heal them both from the trauma of delivery. The doctor was pleased with himself, confident, giddy with plans. Maddalena resembled his daughter, who lived in Canada; when she left his office the final time, he called her by the daughter's name.

Ida worried that Dr. Barone was not paying proper attention to Maddalena's weight, that she was too thin to be as far along as she was. She had a big enough belly, Ida conceded, and a puffiness to her skin in certain light, but her own doctor (a Sicilian who'd treated her family since the first war) had told her a woman needed at least forty extra pounds for a healthy pregnancy. Maddalena had gained less than half that, too little to give the baby a proper cushion.

Maddalena dismissed Ida's concern. In the village, girls who'd gained hardly any weight at all gave birth to perfectly normal babies. Plenty more girls transformed overnight from beauties to monsters: buggy eyes, swollen feet, skin so bloated it stretched and left hideous scars. Twenty-five years old, and already these girls had wrinkles. Maddalena had seen no evidence that one sort of mother produced healthier children than the other, so why should she ruin her figure? And since her doctor (whose people came from Bologna, a university town) had no worries, she ate as much or as little as she pleased.

Mr. Gold kept a closer eye on her as spring came and it became increasingly difficult to squeeze behind the sewing table. He brought a pillow for her back, a wider chair, and a hot-water bottle. Not once, though, did he suggest she quit. In fact, he pressed her to work even harder.

"You're sewing for two now, Signora Grasso," he'd say as he passed her station, tapping his yardstick on the floor like a blind person. "I should see double the results."

"Next place you work, you're joining the union," said Antonio.

Business was booming at the Golden Hem. In March, Mr. Gold hired ten new girls and still needed more. He'd tried to reach Gloria, but her phone had been disconnected. When the letter Maddalena sent her (translated into English by Ida) was sent back marked NO SUCH ADDRESSEE, she hoped for Gloria's sake that she'd gone home to Cuba. Her people lived in shacks, but at least the shacks had belonged to them for generations. Gloria could walk to the town center after all these years away, and the grocer would recognize her.

She was telling all this to Julian one night. They were sitting on the porch at Eighth Street, an early Friday evening a few weeks from Easter. The men wore light jackets and smoked cigars; Maddalena had arranged a white cable sweater over her belly to protect the baby from the lingering chill.

"Cuba is no place for honest people," Julian responded. "The government is a bunch of gangsters."

"Are they like us? The Cuban people?" Ida asked.

"They're Catholics," said Julian. "So yes, in a way they are."

"The Irish call themselves Catholics, too," Papà Franco said. "I wouldn't say they're too much like us." Like Antonio, he enjoyed disagreeing with Julian.

"What are we like, then?" asked Maddalena.

"We're workers," Antonio said.

"The Irish don't work?"

"Not like us," said Papà Franco. He leaned forward and rested his elbows on his knees. The porch furniture was new: wide, gray, wrought-iron chairs with high backs and little diamond shapes cut out around the seats. "My first day in this country, I found a job. The next week, I had two jobs: one for the day, one for the night. If I didn't have to sleep, I'd find one more. 'What Depression?' I used to say to people. They never saw me waiting in line for food. Never will. In this country, if you want work badly enough, you'll find it."

"Altro che!" agreed Antonio.

"Hard work and family," Papà Franco continued. "The Italians were the first to put those two together; we're the best at it. Look at me: I'm almost seventy years old. I should sit on the sidewalk all day with the other old men. Play cards, watch the skirts. But I could never turn down a paycheck if I could still work, not with my wife still living, two grandchildren, one more on the way. I tell you: I'll be working at Bancroft Mill the day I die. I'll close my eyes and fall into the machines. Good-bye to Franco Grasso; good riddance!"

Mamma Nunzia crossed her arms. "I just love when he talks like this," she said. She sat on the ledge and turned her head toward the street. With her long, white hair unloosened, white nightgown, and white satin slippers, she looked like a weary angel. Papà Franco was not an easy husband, she'd told Maddalena more than once; he had a temper, like both his sons, and blamed her cautiousness for all the failed Grasso businesses. She'd warned him every time he'd sunk more of their savings into a new bakery or café, and each time he lost the money he accused her of putting a curse on him just so she could be right.

"Maybe I'm not really Italian," Julian said. "Never had a real job, never wanted one, not for long at least. No family either. Not anymore."

It was an attempt at a joke, but nobody laughed. Maddalena pulled her sweater to her neck. "We're your family now," she said.

"You only get one family, though," Julian said, this time without humor. "Only one that's flesh and blood."

"If Italians could stick together," said Papà Franco, "we'd rule the world. We came close! But you know what? We're a lazy people too, in one way. We don't want to fight; we just want to work—for somebody else, usually; that's why I want my own business—and then we want to come home to our wives and children. Government, military, who cares—let them decide and we follow along."

Later, as she walked Julian down the steps to the sidewalk, Maddalena admitted she did not know what a union was, or where to find Cuba on a map. She'd wanted to imagine Gloria there, but she had no images to call up. It was an island, Gloria once said, but was it warm there? Green? Was it further away than Italy?

"I should teach you geography," Julian said. "Remind me. Next Friday we'll look at the atlas. These days, it's important to know where people come from."

"Yes," Maddalena said. She wanted to learn as much as she could, starting with the meaning of the word *atlas*.

ONCE, JUST BEFORE Maddalena left Santa Cecilia, her brother had sung to her from the doorway of her bedroom. She was eighteen years old, standing at her window, memorizing the view of her backyard—the steep, rocky face of the mountain, the scatter of chestnut trees, the chickens circling one another behind the wire of their tiny coop. Claudio had taken her by surprise. *"Terra straniera,"* he sang, *"quanta malinconia, quando ci salutammo e non so perchè."* She kept her back to him, unsure if he sang in sympathy or resentment. Their two older brothers had gone missing in the war, and now Maddalena herself was about to abandon them. Their father's heavy footsteps ceased midway up the stairs. In the kitchen, their sisters stopped chattering. The house suspended its creaking, the better to hear Claudio's voice. After he finished the song, he slipped into the hall and slammed his bedroom door. Their father continued up the stairs, and the kitchen chattering recommenced. No one spoke of the serenade. Three days later, as Maddalena stepped into Antonio's car, her mother begged her to forget she'd ever lived in this village.

"Your new birthday is coming," she'd said. "You'll be born in Philadelphia, in the United States of America." She held Maddalena's hand through the window. Then, as the car pulled away, she fell to her knees on the dirt road and covered her face.

Maddalena thought of that song—which she had not heard since, not even on the Sunday Italian radio program—as she brushed Mamma Nunzia's hair. It was one of the few chores she enjoyed: one hundred strokes on each side to straighten the curls and give the hair its silky shine. The silent, repetitive motion lulled her, different as it was from the roar of a similar motion at the sewing machine.

She sat behind Mamma Nunzia on the sofa in front of the mirrored living room wall so they could look at each other as she brushed. They had just eaten a rare midweek dinner at Mrs. Stella's to celebrate Ida and Mario's tenth anniversary—March 17—and afterward Antonio and Papà Franco had gone straight to bed.

"What a beautiful meal," Mamma Nunzia said, with a long deep breath, as if just having stepped into the fresh air. The faint wheeze in her chest, which often faded by the time Maddalena finished brushing, was not audible tonight. "I have to tell you," she whispered. "We never thought we'd see Mario so successful. I'm very proud. I can finally say my sons are settled." She folded her hands on her lap and stared at her reflection. She wore the white nightgown again, buttoned as always to her neck, embarrassed by her wrinkles and sagging skin. In the warmer months she never left the house without a sheer silk scarf tied in a knot under her chin. "Soon Mario will buy a place of his own, Papà and me will be gone, and this house will belong to you and Antonio and your baby."

"That will be many years from now," Maddalena said, and smiled. "It won't be a baby then." She straightened her head and pointed it forward. "How's this over the ears?"

"You were sad tonight," she said.

"Tonight?" Maddalena said, her hands still on her face. I'm

always sad, she could have said, but she didn't want her to take offense. "A little nervous, maybe. About the baby."

"That's natural," she said. "Antonio didn't pick another fight with you?"

Maddalena shook her head.

"He talks to you now, at least. Here and there. I've noticed. He's not as stubborn as he wants to be."

"He has his nights," Maddalena said. "I'm not an easy wife, either. Always crying, always looking backward."

"You've done better than I would have," she said. "When Franco and I moved here, our parents had both been dead a long time. We had nothing left in Santa Cecilia, only debts—to your father, mostly, for all the food we couldn't pay for. If it weren't for Zio Domenico loaning us money, we'd never have been able to make the trip. It didn't matter that we knew nobody in Wilmington. But for you—to leave everyone behind, to start a life with a new family—not your flesh-and-blood family, like Giulio said—it's a miracle you didn't throw yourself off the roof." She tilted her head to the side. The wheezing in her chest started, and she undid the top button of her nightgown. "No matter what happens, you're still young. I'd take your trouble anytime to be twenty-seven again."

Maddalena smiled. "And I think how nice your age must be. To have that settled feeling—"

"Please, no," she said. "My sons are settled. Not me. I won't feel settled until they put me in the grave. And neither will you, I think, not with a Grasso for a husband. My only wish is to live to see what happens to all of you. Twenty years—that's all I need. Twenty years more than what God has planned for me."

After the brushing, they cut that day's loaves of Lamberti's bread into slices and spread them across the dining-room table.

Usually Ida would help, but they gave her the day off in honor of her ten years as Mario's wife. They topped each slice with cold cuts, lettuce, and onions, drizzled oil and vinegar on top, then wrapped the sandwiches in foil. They put each sandwich in a brown bag with a paper towel and a different selection of fruit. Everyone at Eighth Street was picky: Papà Franco ate only bananas; Mrs. Stella's stocked crates of grapes for garnish, so Mario never wanted grapes; Ida must have citrus, especially oranges; Antonio preferred raw tomatoes, sliced in half, with a thick crust of salt. These preferences changed weekly. Just last Thursday, Papà Franco had come home, set his half-full lunch bag on the kitchen counter, and declared he'd never again touch a green apple.

"Remember," Mamma said, when their work was done and Maddalena walked up the stairs. "A sad face makes a woman look older. Right now I'd put you at sixty-five."

Maddalena flashed a halfhearted smile and grabbed the banister for support. After every few steps, she stopped to rest. She could not remember a day in the last seven months when she did not feel dizzy—first with fear, then with discomfort. Strange thoughts overtook her and made her nauseous: that the baby had fingernails scraping against her belly, that the baby had hair, that the baby was burping and urinating inside her. Whenever the baby moved, and she felt an elbow or a knee pushing through the skin of her belly, she feared it would poke through and rupture her fragile body.

When she got to the bedroom, she found Antonio on his knees, in his socks, in front of their closet.

"Do you need something?" she asked, startling him. "I thought you were tired."

"My old pair of shoes," he said. "The brown ones."

"They're in the basement," she said, and held onto the edge of the dresser. "What do you want those for? They have holes. And they're out of style."

"They're comfortable," said Antonio. "I don't like to wear my good shoes all the time. They get ruined too fast, and then we have to spend money."

"What size does Mario wear? It might make sense for the two of you to share—"

But he was already halfway down the stairs. Quickly, Maddalena unbuttoned her dress and pulled her maternity nightgown—on loan from Ida—off the hanger. She didn't like for Antonio to see her in her underwear, not with her body misshapen like this. Other nights, either she waited for him to fall asleep, or she changed clothes in the bathroom.

He came back in the dusty brown shoes.

"You're going out?" she asked.

"My head feels like it's full of cobwebs," he said. "I need the fresh air."

"But it's so late—"

He got on his knees again and rearranged the boxes on the floor of the closet. The piles kept falling over because he'd mismatched the tops with the bottoms. In frustration, he smashed one of the boxes against the wall, collapsing it into a useless flat of cardboard.

"Are you in some kind of trouble?" she asked.

"Trouble?" He froze. "No, of course not. What kind of trouble could I be in?" He stood, put his hands on his hips.

"I'm your wife," she said. "You can tell me."

He seemed to relax a moment. "Renato Volpe," he said. His tone was tender, apologetic. "You remember him, from the pizzeria. You don't like him. But he's opening a new restaurant, and he needs my help. That's all."

"So you *do* still see him," she said. "That's beautiful news." She folded her arms across her chest. "Why do you have to wear old shoes for his new restaurant?"

"I've already told you too much," he said.

"You told me almost nothing!"

He stood and faced her. "I'm not in trouble," he said, and stepped away, all the tenderness gone. "I'm the one who stops the trouble. That's all you need to know. When you need to know something else, I'll tell you."

"Please don't walk out," Maddalena said.

The slam of the front screen door. The heels of his old, dusty shoes on the porch.

12

Riverview Drive

WHEN HE THINKS back on that spring, Antonio can't remember once worrying about Maddalena's health. In fact, he considered pregnancy itself a symptom of durability, and pregnant women stronger—more vigorous, more resilient—than non-pregnant ones. How else to explain the village women who toiled in the fields up to the last push, then delivered their babies in the mud? Pregnant women fattened, their cheeks took on a ruddy glow, their nerves calmed, and they settled into a state of focused serenity—all signs of potency and robustness. Yes, they felt some discomfort sleeping and the occasional upset stomach, but these seemed merely reminders to take care of themselves, to nurture the life inside them.

Maddalena's pregnancy set Antonio's life on one definite track, at least, and for that he was grateful. The weekday routine—work by seven a.m., dinner no more than a half hour after he returned, sleep by ten—pleased them both now that a reward waited at the end of the monotonous nine months. Only when Renato needed him did Antonio sneak off to Fourth and Orange, and of those nights he and Maddalena seldom spoke. Better just to turn up the music on the radio, Antonio thought, and pretend she could not hear him creak down the stairs.

Weekends, he slept late and spent the first hours of the afternoon in the bathroom. He grew accustomed to waking at eleven to find the newspaper neatly folded on a tray beside two empty coffee cups. The moment Maddalena heard his footsteps on their bedroom floor, she'd climb the stairs to fill one cup with a shot of espresso, the other with brewed Maxwell House the way he liked it: no sugar, lots of cream. Antonio didn't want to speak to anyone—including Maddalena—until he'd taken care of his business in the bathroom and caught up on the state of the world. He lied to his family about having digestive problems, and while they whispered about his eating habits, he enjoyed the safety of the close quarters behind the locked door, the comfort of his naked thighs against the porcelain, the sterilized quiet. He read slowly and always regretted reaching the final section, for he'd soon be forced to rejoin the chaos of the house. This was relaxation, he thought; the rest of you can waste your money on resorts and trips to Wildwood, but two hours alone up here is enough vacation for me.

Late March surprised everyone with a stretch of warm sunny days, and Antonio saved the final section of the weekend edition—classifieds, radio and television listings—for the less-reliable solitude of the back porch. By that time of year he was starved for light, catching only a glimpse of it on the early-morning ride to the plant, missing it by an hour on winter evenings. The weekend was his only chance to feel the sun on his face. So he sat in his shirtsleeves just outside the shade of the grape arbor.

The arbor ran the length of the back porch and half its width. Under it sat two wooden picnic tables painted red, at which the Grassos ate most of their meals in the summertime. At the end of the season, the tables will be blotched with squished purple grapes, staining many a pair of trousers. The fruit will fall on their heads or into the bowls of pasta they are eating; more than once, Mario will shake one of the vines and send a shower onto the heads of his wife and children.

The other half of the porch was part concrete slab and part vegetable garden, where the women grew lettuce, cabbage, tomatoes, green beans, and a few carrots. Behind the garden, a wire cage held live chickens. The chickens would live a while as Grasso pets, delighting Nunzia and Nina with their frantic clucks and old-ladylike waddling; and then, one at a time, Mamma would stretch them across a board and take a cleaver to their necks. The girls never witnessed this, never noticed there were different chickens each week; they were too busy playing in the pile of feathers Mamma left for them by the back door.

It was onto the concrete slab that Antonio dragged a chair and sat in the unexpected late March sun. Bunches of hard, green pearls were just beginning to appear on the vines. The fruit would ripen in just a few months, when Antonio and his father would again argue over whether or not to crush them for wine this year. Didn't it always turn out either thickly sweet or bitter as vinegar, good only to bring to someone like Giulio Fabbri and drink with a plate of cookies? Why bother trying, when they could get a case of Chianti wholesale from Ida's brother's store? Besides, there were worms. Antonio had seen a few already, squeezing in and out of the tight clusters. Ida let the girls eat the grapes once they were ready, even though they always complained of stomachaches afterward.

Kids chased one another across the lawn of the Presbyterian church next door, enjoying the break from six harsh months of cold. The air smelled damp and loamy, like freshly turned earth. The budding trees rushed to clothe themselves now that spring had come early, and people like Antonio had taken notice.

He narrowed his eyes at his paper. "KITCHEN EMPLOYEES for Concord Country Club," he read. "Experienced, sober men only." He was not looking for a new job but liked to know what was available just in case. He even read the "For Coloreds Only" ads, if just to make sure they didn't offer a better salary. He wondered why this particular ad called specifically for "sober men." He had never been to the Concord Country Club and imagined it must be grand—white pillars, rolling hills, valet parking—but was it so hard to find good help that they had to warn applicants not to show up drunk?

He looked up at the second-floor windows of the house and caught Maddalena watching him.

The kids on the lawn, a trio of out-of-breath boys in shorts and bare feet, staggered closer toward the chain-link fence that marked the border between the church and Grasso property. Antonio could distinguish their movements through the dead vines that webbed the fence. The boys tackled each other, rolled around for a while, then sat panting with their legs outstretched, hands on the ground behind them.

"Two-Ton Tessie, that's your type," one of the boys said. Antonio leaned forward to hear them better. When he looked up at the window again, the drapes were drawn.

"So she's got a little extra," said another boy. "So what? Least I—"

"More cushion for the pushin'," interrupted the third boy, and they erupted in laughter.

Antonio covered his smile with the newspaper, remembering how he used to gather like this with his own friends back in the village. Their favorite spot was the hill in the woods behind the spring, a steep, muddy incline that became a safe hideout from their parents and anyone else looking to busy them with chores. One summer, his last in Santa Cecilia, a group of older boys cleared a line of sight from a certain rock up high, so that when they sat on the rock they had an unbroken view of the women bending down to fetch water. Oh, the thrill of that flash of skin! The breasts falling against the sheer fabric, the delicious possibility they might escape the cruel confines of the blouse! How rare and wonderful to witness this unguarded moment, the one time of day this girl thought no one was watching. And if she threw her hair over her shoulder and bent lower to sip directly from the source—eyes closed, lips parted—a hush would sweep across the village; the sparrows would stop midflight, the leaves would cease to flutter; and the boys would harden into statues with their mouths dropped open, certain that life offered nothing more magnificent than this.

As that final summer wore on, the woods grew thicker and the boys took turns climbing the trees to reclip the leaves, pull the branches off, and maintain the line of sight. In September, on the boat to the United States, Antonio thought less of the country he might never see again than of the rush of beating his friends to the rock each morning, of not knowing which girl would bow before him.

Since then, when has he felt such a rush? Upon his return to Santa Cecilia thirteen years later, as an old man of twenty-six, when he saw Maddalena standing on the steps of the church.

He'd felt rich then, his pockets full with profits from the early success of the Pasticceria Grasso. Maddalena had been a child when he and his family left Italy, and now there she was: one of the young women he'd have longed to catch at the spring. And he was not a boy anymore, but a worthy suitor with an entire country to offer, and blind faith that the *pasticceria* would bring his family great wealth. He invited himself to her house for dinner, purchased chocolate and wine in her family's store, and soon found himself on the terrace with her father discussing the business of marriage. Two decades before, Antonio's family could not afford to shop in that grocery; now Aristide Piccinelli was promising Antonio the hand of his youngest daughter. According to Aristide, Maddalena was involved in an unfortunate romance—less an engagement than a teenage infatuation; puppy love, they'd call it here—and in need of quick rescue. "You came at the perfect time," Aristide had said to him, and they drank a toast to the future. Less than a month later, Antonio was a married man.

He rarely thought of Maddalena's first love, and of course never spoke of him to anyone. Though they'd grown up together in the village and Antonio once lost to him in a footrace, he attempted to scrub his name and face from his memory. He was not Vito Leone with the oval head, hairless chin, and surprisingly quick legs; he was merely the Infatuation. At first Antonio counted him among the many village soldiers who'd died in the war, though he'd somehow managed to avoid the draft. An ocean separated Maddalena from this man, but he did have family in Philadelphia—a father and two sisters—and no good reason, as far as Antonio knew at the time, to stay in Santa Cecilia. Who could say when he might show up on their doorstep?

In his darker moments, Antonio used to imagine the Infatuation crossing the water to work in his father's tailor shop and live close to the woman he'd lost. Once a year for the first three of his marriage, Antonio drove to the shop—a dingy little place on Market Street—and peered into the front window. No one resembling Vito worked behind the counter, only his elderly father and one of his sisters. Was he off on a delivery? Putting out the garbage? Just in case, Antonio walked around and around the block for the better part of the afternoon, casually strolling past the store, convinced he'd catch Vito walking hand in hand with Maddalena, back from the sort of midday rendezvous he himself had once enjoyed with lonely American housewives. Sometimes he blamed the Infatuation—the memory of him, mostly—for Maddalena's inability to conceive and wondered how long it would take for the curse of him to lift.

Then came the letter from Zio Domenico, the Grassos' last living relative in Santa Cecilia. Buried in the pages of sentences praising the virtues of Communism was the news that the Infatuation had married Maddalena's older sister. After a brief apprenticeship in Naples, he'd returned to Santa Cecilia and remained there. If he'd had any desire to follow Maddalena to America, he had not indulged it.

Antonio did not know what to do with this information. He had to communicate it to Maddalena, but he did not want to say the words himself. Surely she still felt something for the man. Separation, he knew, only fueled puppy love; it certainly did not kill it. Possibly Maddalena even entertained a secret wish for him to appear at her window and coax her down. It was the stuff of her novels—young girls shimmying down trellises, undernourished paupers who reveal themselves as princes—and Antonio had no illusions about a woman's enduring need for romance, or the revenge she might want to take on a poaching sister. The American wives had taught him some of that. But now that the book was closed on the Infatuation, her fantasies should come to an end. It was time for Maddalena to let go of the past and devote her full heart to her husband.

Just reading the name *Vito Leone* in Zio Domenico's elderly script and being reminded of the flesh-and-blood existence of a man who once had been his wife's *fidanzato* made Antonio want to smash his fist against the wall. Instead, he stuffed the letter in Ida's pocket and asked her to read it to Maddalena. "Take an afternoon," he'd said, handing her fifteen dollars, nearly half of his weekly salary. "Bring her to Merchandise Mart. Make her buy something nice for herself." Ida had given him a stunned look. But Antonio knew no other way to tell Maddalena that not only had Vito Leone married, but that, after a brief courtship, he had chosen Carolina.

According to Ida, Maddalena had little reaction to the news. They'd sat across from each other in the restaurant inside the Five and Ten, two young wives out Christmas shopping. As Ida read Zio Domenico's letter aloud, Maddalena had nodded and closed her eyes. Her hands shook a bit, nearly spilling her soda, but nothing more. She read the letter to herself, folded it, and handed it back to Ida without a word. Maybe she had prepared herself for this long in advance or knew already from one of her mother's letters, and the ink on the page merely confirmed a loss she'd already grieved. That night, and throughout the weeks leading up to the holiday, she showed no sign that anything had changed.

But, in Antonio's mind at least, something had changed. For the first time in his marriage, he needed Maddalena to declare her devotion to him, to say she no longer felt the infatuation for Vito Leone. Hadn't enough time gone by for her not only to forgive Antonio for taking her from her village, but to fall in love with him the way he had done with her? He was no longer the stranger watching her on the steps of the church, threatening to steal her from her family. He was the patient husband who'd indulged her the nights she turned away from him in sadness and rage, who'd comforted her through the locked bedroom door when he heard her sobbing. He'd proven himself again and again: by arranging expensive telephone calls to Italy, by trying to earn enough money to one day return for a visit, by taking her to costly doctors and specialists. He'd hidden his disappointment when, month after month, she held her hands over her stomach and shook her head. What more could be asked of a husband he did not know.

That was the Christmas they snuck out of the house and drove to Route 1 to look at the Cadillacs. He'd told her he loved her, with hopes she'd profess her love for him. But she'd only nodded—no differently, maybe, than she'd nodded to Ida upon hearing the news of her sister's marriage. How unreachable you are, he'd thought then, his hands gripping the wheel of the car. How hard you'll make me work, all my life, to deserve you.

THE WARM SPELL ended in late March, when winter played its final hand. Most Wilmingtonians, wind-battered, chilled by weeks of relentless rain, stayed indoors. The city was quiet, as if sleeping late in hopes it would wake to better weather. There seemed always to be a train passing, belching black smoke, hooting gloomily in the gray afternoon. Mud collected in pools along the sidewalks, splattering the cuffs of Antonio's good work pants. Rain leaked through the roof of the shed and soaked the few remaining blocks of wood. When lit, the wood smoldered and smelled of rotten fruit. In the hours after dinner, the Grassos would gather around the fireplace, Nunzia and Nina at the edge of the hearth holding their noses with one hand and reaching toward the flames with the other. Only Maddalena, to whom the cold weather was a great relief, kept her distance. She sat alone on the sofa at the other end of the room, fanning herself with a folded-up section of the *Morning News*.

One evening, a phone call from Renato summoned Antonio to the home of his mother, Rosa. "Mario," Antonio said, shaking his head, when he hung up the phone. "He needs my help with one of the waiters."

"Gilberto again?" asked Ida.

"Gilberto?" said Antonio. He reached for his hat. "Yes, that's the one." He did not look at Maddalena, but the rest of the family either nodded or went on with their conversations. It had become easy for Antonio to lie in situations like this, though he did it more out of convenience than necessity. If he told them all the truth, that Renato Volpe had breathlessly begged him to get to Seventh Street as soon as he could, they'd delay him with a hundred questions: Were the police involved? Did he owe money? Did he get some girl in trouble? They'd wait up for him or expect a detailed explanation in the morning.

This way, all he had to do was stop by Mrs. Stella's and tell Mario to make up some problem with Gilberto the waiter. This way, he and Maddalena had no reason to argue over the girls who may or may not have been waiting for him behind the counter of the pizzeria. When he got home, he could look her in the eye and say, "I told Mario a hundred times never to hire a Sicilian," and she'd play along by telling a story of a lazy woman from Palermo who'd just started at the Golden Hem. The further they extended the lie, the stronger the bond it forged. They could tell the truth to Ida or Mario or any of their friends, but with no one else had they established so many enduring illusions: the peace Maddalena felt in America, Antonio's long walks "for air," their confidence that God would give them a child. Without these illusions, they had merely an ordinary connection; with the illusions, they had powerful bullets to fire at each other when the time came.

Antonio had been to Rosa Volpe's house once before, in the early morning, after he'd watched Renato and Cassie soap the windows of Waters's taxi. He'd sat with them in the dark under the dining room table, careful not to wake the old lady, waiting for enough time to go by so they could head home. They had not hidden in Rosa's house often, fearing for her safety if they were followed, but that night they felt untouchable. The Waters house had been hit more than ten times—with stones, paint, eggs, trash, mud, and now soap—and Renato and Cassie were growing bored. Worse, the man hadn't budged. It seemed he'd stay at 1932 until the place burned down.

Even in the dim lamplight, the interior of Rosa Volpe's home strained Antonio's eyes. Every wall was painted a glossy red, bright and bloody, that took a few moments to fathom. Only a few decorations interrupted the onslaught of color: a small framed photograph of the pope in the hallway, a crucifix above the mantel, a bust of Saint Peter on a credenza by the front window. Dark wood molding, in an ornate pattern of spires and lattice, ran along the ceilings and around the entryways. Even the baseboards, ten inches high, had been carved into that same design. Mahogany chairs with plush red cushions surrounded the dining-room table; a red sectional couch formed an L around the living room; red velvet drapes shielded the window. Who could relax in here, Antonio wondered, as he stepped onto the red wall-to-wall carpet. Did Rosa expect a visit from Pius XII himself? It was like entering an enormous confessional. All that was missing was the kneeler and the screen and the dour face of Father Moravia.

"You knew my father was a carpenter?" said Renato, as he sat between Buzzy and Cassie on the couch. He gestured toward the moldings. "See what I mean about the property value of this place?"

"May he rest in peace," said Rosa, in Italian. She wore silk slippers, a nightgown, and her white hair pinned in a bun. She must have been in her eighties, but she sprang to her feet like a teenager the moment she saw Antonio, shuffled to the kitchen, and returned a moment later with a tray full of cookies.

"Sit down, Mamma Rosa," said Cassie. "I'll do that." Yet Cassie remained on the couch, legs crossed, biting her thumbnail. She had on shiny black boots and a series of silver bracelets on her right wrist. After Antonio took two amaretti, Rosa presented the tray to Buzzy and Renato then set it on the coffee table. She sat next to Antonio in one of the dining-room chairs and watched Cassie reach over and grab the last of the *ciambelline*.

Other than the poisonous looks between Cassie and her future mother-in-law, Antonio sensed no emergency in the room. He took two more amaretti as the conversation turned from the unpredictable weather back to carpentry. Renato told the story of his father's insistence on keeping a block of wood in the hospital bed with him, so he'd have something to carve as he waited to die. He pointed to the large crucifix above the mantel: a crude figure on two thick slats. The edges of the cross had not been smoothed, and the figure's hands and feet remained unformed squares shot through with nails. "He was working on that the day he went," said Renato. "It was in three pieces—the body and the two pieces of the cross. I nailed them together myself."

"*Lo verdrò fra poco,*" said Rosa. I'll be seeing him soon. She knew English well, according to Renato, but spoke only Italian tonight.

"You're not going anywhere," Renato said, in English, and translated her words for Buzzy and Cassie.

"Yes, you're not going anywhere," repeated Cassie.

"I'm ready," Rosa said. "I'm not afraid."

Buzzy shrugged at Cassie, and the two exchanged a smile. He wore a blazer and bow tie and had fixed his hair in perfect, shiny curls. Gold rings adorned his fingers. "Where have you been?" Antonio asked. "Dinner at the White House?"

"Close," Buzzy said. "Riverview Drive. That's why he called you."

Rosa set both feet on the floor and stretched her nightgown across her knees, making a sort of table. She nudged Antonio, and from her sleeve she pulled three slips of paper. She arranged them on her lap. Two were funeral cards, the other some sort of poem handwritten in ink.

"This was my Frankie," Rosa said, and pointed to the card with the image of St. Francis and his lambs. Above the picture was written:

FRANCESCO VOLPE

SEPTEMBER 6, 1862—SEPTEMBER 20, 1933

This was followed by a short prayer and the date and location of the funeral service. "Thirty-seven years together," she said. "You know I still see his face in front of me? Right now. I can touch it!" She held up her palm and laid it on Francesco's invisible cheek.

Antonio nodded. Renato was whispering something he could not hear to Cassie and Buzzy.

The other funeral card had a picture of a female saint, haloed and holding a spear. Rosa handed it to him.

ROSA MARIA MORELLI VOLPE
JANUARY 2, 1872—

"Dante Pavani made this for me," she said, referring to one of the two Italian undertakers in Wilmington. The Grassos were loyal to the other one, though they had yet to need his services. "It's all prepared. When I go, all Dante has to do is put the date on the card. Frankie paid for everything already. The grave, the service, the food. Everything." She dropped her voice to a whisper. "And I have a few surprises."

"He was a good man," Antonio said, though he'd never met him.

"The best!" Rosa said. "We grew up on the same street. I never lived a day on this earth when I didn't know him." She gazed across the room, her watery eyes fixed first at the empty hallway, then at Renato and Cassie on the sofa. Renato had his arms around her. Cassie leaned in closer, her hair falling against his cheek, their knees touching. Rosa jerked her head, as if to shake off a spell. *"Leggi,"* she said to Antonio. She handed him the handwritten note. "Read."

> *Rosa Volpe was a flower that bloomed in the soil of two*
> *countries.*
> *Like a rose, she wilted and died and came back to life.*
> *She blooms now forever in the garden of heaven next to her*
> *beloved Francesco,*

Where there is no death, only sunshine and nourishing rain.
To the young people, Rosa says: fall in love and forget about
　　tomorrow.
To the old people, Rosa says: stay in love and forget about
　　yesterday.
To everyone here, she says: do not cry for Rosa Volpe. She does
　　not cry for you.
She knows when you are coming.

"What do you think?" she asked Antonio. She sat up in her seat and lifted her chin, clearly proud. "I said these words myself. And then the poet across the street wrote them down."

"Giulio Fabbri?" Antonio asked.

"*Sì,*" she said. "He helped me a little bit, but the words are all mine. Don't let him tell you different. Renato will read it at my funeral. You'll be there?"

"Mamma," Renato called, from across the room. "Leave the poor man alone."

"Is that the eulogy again?" asked Cassie.

"*Zitto!*" said Rosa, waving them off. "You'll be there?" she asked Antonio again. "At my funeral? All of Wilmington is coming."

"That's twenty years from now," said Antonio. "Who knows where I'll be? I could be one of the flowers of heaven myself." He grinned and patted her leg. "But if I'm still alive, I promise: I'll be at your funeral in my best suit."

"Twenty years!" Rosa said, shaking her head, her face serious. "No, Signor. I can't wait that long. I used to cry to myself, 'Oh, Rosa, if you were only a young girl still, with a pretty face!' Now every day I beg God to take me in my sleep, in this chair, anywhere. I'm so tired all the time. And I—" She stopped and glanced in Renato and Cassie's direction. Then she leaned toward Antonio and whispered, "I don't want to see what happens to them. I want to remember him like a boy. Before she came."

Antonio nodded noncommittally, and turned toward his friends on the sofa. Renato was bringing out the good cigars. "You're celebrating something," Antonio said, taking one. "That's why you dragged me here."

"I had to get you out of the house somehow," said Renato. "You live like a monk these days."

"So you got Riverview Drive."

"Grand opening: May 21," said Renato, with his arms outstretched. "Fine dining for the finest diners in Wilmington."

"And you're in after all?" Antonio asked Buzzy.

"I just helped with the papers," he replied. He ticked his head toward Cassie. "This lady here is in for fifty percent."

For a moment no one said anything. Rosa tensed. "Now I've seen it all," she said, in Italian. "Where's a girl her age get that kind of money?"

"My father died," Cassie said, guessing Rosa's question by her tone of voice. "Heart attack at fifty-five. Same age as Papà Francesco was. And there's more money where that came from. First Bank of Bernie Donovan's Mattress."

At Cassie's use of Papà to refer to her beloved husband, Rosa closed her eyes. Antonio would be amazed if she'd heard a word after that.

"Condoglianze," Antonio said, skeptically. "Why didn't I know? My family would have bought a Mass card."

Her father had died two years ago, Cassie explained, and since then her mother had been hoarding all the mattress money, which was hidden not in a mattress but in a collection of old paint cans. While helping her move to a new house, Cassie had discovered her dear father's will, which stated clearly that Cassie—his only daughter, his princess—receive a large chunk of that cash upon his death. "It was like a movie," Cassie said. "I started reading the will to her, and her face dropped five feet. She thought she'd never get caught."

"Greed," said Buzzy. "It's an ugly thing to see up close."

Antonio wasn't buying a word of it. However Cassie got the money, though, didn't change the fact that she and Renato would run the restaurant—*his* restaurant—together. Had they brought him here to rub this in his face?

"We thought you'd want to know," Renato said. "We didn't want you to hear it from someone else, then come raging at us some night when we were too drunk to defend ourselves."

They laughed.

"What's to defend?" Antonio said, with a forced smile. "I was out. I made my choice. I have a baby coming, a family to support." He bit off the end of the cigar. "I wish you the best of luck. I want a table for me and Maddalena opening night. And I expect a seventy-five percent discount."

Buzzy pulled a page of blueprints from his jacket and spread it across the coffee table. He weighted it down with two high-ball glasses that made rings on the filmy paper. The space was eighteen hundred square feet, enough for fifty seats, with a large kitchen and a deck in the back. It lay there before Antonio like a color photo of a naked woman—irresistible, just within reach, but far out of his league.

"We see red, white, and green umbrellas on the porch," Cassie began. She drew on the print with her finger. "Round tables here, booths here, a long banquet on this side. Classy, but fun. *Warm* is what we're going for."

"And entertainment on the weekends," said Renato. "A real

band—not some sad-sack accordion player with a bald spot. We've got thousands of ideas between us. And now, thanks to Cassie, we've got thousands of dollars to make them happen."

"I'm charging them a fortune to do the books," said Buzzy. "Young Paolo gets his first chance to run the pizzeria by himself. Everybody wins."

"Even you, Antonio," Cassie said. "No more pressure to give up your money. You can save it all for Maddalena and the baby. The quiet life—that's what you wanted, right?"

"You'll want it, too, sooner or later."

Cassie shrugged. "Five years down the road, maybe. Depending. Can you see me with a kid now? I used to think—" She glanced at Rosa, then stopped.

She'd wanted to be the perfect Italian wife, Antonio remembered, but clearly the old woman would not give her that chance. He wondered how hard Cassie had tried, or if she had any idea how a real Italian wife behaved. Her first night in Rosa Volpe's house, had she sat on the sofa like this, legs apart, eating cookies and asking for puffs on the cigar? If so, it was no surprise Rosa had begged God to take her.

"I'm going to bed," the old woman said, rising. She turned to Antonio. "Visit me again, Signor. It's nice to have company." She kissed Buzzy on both cheeks, pressed her lips to Renato's temple, then drew his head to her bosom. She held him there for a moment before she released him.

Maddalena had been lucky with Antonio's mother, who'd always shown her the same affection she showed her sons. Unlike Ida, Maddalena had impressed her from the moment she entered the house. Instead of resting from her long trip, she immediately put on an apron and helped prepare the dinner being thrown in her honor. She plucked and deboned the chicken; she cut, filled, and sealed the ravioli; she dried the flute glasses that minutes before had toasted her arrival. When she'd seen Maddalena's eyes well up with tears, Mamma had put her arms around her waist and taught her the word *destiny*. Destiny had brought her here, she said, and Maddalena's only choice was to welcome it. An hour later, Maddalena vomited into the upstairs toilet, still seasick, her stomach weak from a month of starving herself. She resented her husband. This country terrified her. But she could not resent or fear his loving mother and father, her gentle sister-in-law; they welcomed her with gifts of good china teacups, a silk scarf, and a ring studded with rubies. They told her Antonio had struck gold.

Cursed with Irish blood, raised her entire life as an American princess, Cassie had no such luck. To keep the peace, she had to buy Rosa's favor. So far, the plan had not succeeded.

Buzzy was rolling up the blueprints. Rosa had disappeared into the hallway. "I've never been so in love," Renato said. It seemed to have just occurred to him. "I don't care about anything anymore. I don't care what Mamma thinks. I don't even care if you're disappointed by the restaurant, Antonio." He looked straight ahead as he spoke, at no one and nothing in particular. "Nothing sticks to me. All I have to do is think: Miss Cassandra Donovan and I will run a restaurant together. And if it fails, and I lose all my money, all I have to do is think: Cassie and I will still be together." He reached for her hand. "I never thought I'd go against Mamma for anything. But it's like she's already left us."

Cassie blushed at the declaration. "You always surprise me," she said.

Buzzy raised his glass. "The couple of the year," he said. "*Cent'anni! L'chayim!*"

Antonio did not stay much longer. He sat on Renato's stoop for a while, smoking. The light was on in Giulio's living room. He could have stopped by, but he was tired of talking, and besides, who knew what sort of tricks the man would pull once he got Antonio alone.

The poet, Rosa had called him. Antonio and Maddalena had visited him out of charity at first—at Mamma's insistence—but now that he'd won Maddalena's devotion, Antonio was stuck with him. The thought turned his stomach. Giulio was one of those unspeakable men who had a talent for entertaining women, but no interest in them as wives. Antonio had heard all the stories and seen men like this in movies, but, until this year, never in person. Never up close. He supposed he should feel grateful that Maddalena had made a friend, but why couldn't it have been a young mother from around the block?

A degenerate—a sad, lonely one at that—had no business acting superior, and yet that's just the impression Giulio Fabbri gave to people. He was always referring to books no one had read, or countries no one had heard of, and one day Antonio would inform him that some people actually had to work for a living. He, too, would spend all day in the library if he could afford it; better yet, he'd build a bocce court in his backyard or learn photography or help the poor. Yes, Giulio had been orphaned and deserved sympathy, but if he'd been normal he'd have a woman and kids to comfort him—not an accordion and a stack of books and another man's wife.

Antonio walked home and, without a word to anyone, took the car up to Riverview Drive. The sign in the window of the restaurant still read FOR SALE. Inside were a few scattered tables, a pile of fabric that must have been the drapes, and a three-legged chair, overturned. The steakhouse, run with such optimism by the Greek, had lasted only two months. It was the same story of every failed business, especially the ones that featured the Grasso name: too much overhead, too few customers. Now the Greek had gone back to the Old Country poorer than when he'd arrived.

Antonio cupped his hands over the glass to peer at the lovely exposed brick and marble-topped bar. The photos of the Greek Isles had been taken down, but the lion's-head fountain remained in the wall of the foyer. Water dripped from the lion's stone lips into a blue-tiled pool. It was tacky, this fountain, which was likely why Renato and Cassie paid extra to keep it; Antonio wanted to take a chisel to its sharp, bared teeth. Soon the two restaurateurs would inflict their bad taste on these naked, innocent rooms, and Antonio would lose his chance to stop them. They'd allow the gleaming hardwood floors to scuff, the stuffing to burst through the leather booths. One thing Antonio had learned is that the least deserving people always stumbled upon the hidden treasure. While they were busy digging in the right places, hardworking men like himself were off saving money for shovels.

He walked up and down the sidewalk, crossing and recrossing the sign in the window. If only Renato knew his secret: that for ten years he'd had enough money saved to take a smart risk on a place like this. He'd kept telling himself the right time would come, and that he'd know it by a feeling in his bones. Now Antonio had to admit what he'd always suspected: he was not a gambler. Worse, he was no better than the thousands of peasants who'd crossed the ocean to make a life here. He was just a scared immigrant clutching the few pennies thrown at him every Friday afternoon, unwilling to risk opening his hands. There was a good chance that the second half of his life would look much like the first: punching his card for big companies like Ford and Bancroft Mill, answering to American bosses ten years his junior, stuck in the basement while his bosses danced across the floor above him. And when Antonio died, he'd have nothing lasting to show for his life—a child, yes, maybe even children, but no wedge of earth other than the six feet they'd bury him under.

He had lived frugally. He couldn't remember the last time he'd bought himself a firsthand shirt or cigarettes or a bottle of whiskey. He'd stolen or borrowed or been given most of what he owned or enjoyed. After many years of this, the pennies added up. Between the bank and the drapes, he had saved enough to cover an initial investment in Riverview Drive and about six months of rent. There was even a little money that no one knew about, hidden in a safety-deposit box downstate. The truth—he had purposefully let it get away from him—was that there had always been enough money for not only a business and a child, but a modest ranch house in New Castle as well. And if he'd pinched even more, he may have even been able to afford Maddalena's lessons at the Bianca Talent Agency.

For these savings he had his father to thank. During his first few years in America, he'd given his old man every dime of his salary and lived on a weekly allowance of three dollars, which he rarely spent. After Antonio married, his father took the contribution Antonio and Maddalena made monthly toward the utilities and secretly deposited it in Antonio's bank account. He saw no reason Antonio and Maddalena should pay an equal—or even close to equal—share as the reckless Mario and Ida. Plus, despite the money he himself was spending on the failed restaurants, Papà had emergency money saved for both sons—a wad of bills hidden in a secret place in the house Mamma told him about. He had taught his sons to live in poverty no matter how large the numbers on the bank statement. But only Antonio had learned this—so well, in fact, that he'd come to believe he had hardly any savings at all. And when he did remember the truth, at moments like this, he reminded himself that life was long, that he had never known a decade without war, and there was no telling what harm twenty years would inflict on his own health and that of his wife and children. What kind of man would squander the only money he might ever earn and put his family's future in jeopardy? In a heartbeat, he could end up like the Greek, back in his village begging distant cousins for food and shelter. No, Antonio was not a gambler, no matter how sure the bet; he would die with thousands of dollars sewn into his drapes. Then, finally, his wife and family, secure for their remaining years, would appreciate his wisdom, but not until then.

When Antonio left Riverview Drive that spring night, he did not plan to return until the grand opening. He had plenty of excuses ready for when Renato called to ask him to come to supervise the renovation, offer his opinion on the brands of liquor to stock, or tell Cassie she was wrong about the layout of the tables. Renato seemed to believe him, though he did question why Antonio needed to help his father fix the radiators now that spring had come. "There's always a shot of grappa waiting for you here, my friend," said Renato. "This is your trattoria as much as mine, even though you're too cheap to spend a nickel on it."

The first time, Antonio drove quickly past the space, then kept going down New Castle Avenue back toward the city. After doing this two or three nights in a row, he got braver. He made a U-turn and passed the space again, at half the speed, before hitting the gas to make the light. Work had begun inside,

but Antonio could not see the results from the road. He did notice Renato's car, and, once, the silhouette of Cassie sitting on
the windowsill with her chin on her knees.

He returned home from these trips with no feeling of satisfaction, only a resurgent restlessness. He opened the jar of cher-
ries soaked in grappa—a Christmas gift from Ida's brother in
1950—and ate three at once. He took Maddalena on one of
these trips, just to help settle her nerves, but didn't point out the
space when they passed it. They talked not of restaurants, but of
names for the child.

After a while, Antonio found himself parking in the neighborhood across from Renato's trattoria. It took a few tries before he found a spot hidden enough from the road but offering
a clear view of the entrance. He sat here for hours at a time,
watching men carry chairs from one end of the room to the
other. In the span of a week, the floor plan changed at least
three times. Renato liked to stand on a barstool and bark out orders to all corners of the restaurant. Buzzy visited now and
then, but only long enough for a shot and a cigar. There was a
different girl on his arm each time, always a head taller than
him, always left alone at the bar when Buzzy and Renato disappeared into the kitchen.

Other nights, Antonio would put on his old shoes and sneak
around to the muddy field behind the restaurant to examine
what the men were putting in the trash bins. It was not rare for
him to return to the car and fall asleep in the front seat, then
wake to find the restaurant dark, the parking lot empty. He
stored a blanket in the trunk for the chillier nights and cracked
his window so as not to steam up the car and call attention to
himself. Groggy, his neck sore, he'd make his way back home to
Eighth Street and promise himself this was the last time he'd

play spy. The risk of giving Renato or Buzzy the smug satisfaction of finding him was enough to convince him he would never return. But then, the next night, he'd find himself on his way here again.

Antonio woke in his car close to one a.m. the morning of May 21. "Goddamn it," he said, rubbing his eyes. He tossed the blanket in the backseat and sped home to Eighth Street. As he approached the house, he noticed the lights in the front windows, the absence of the Fiuma's Ford. He saw Ida on the stairs, waving the wooden spoon. Sleepwalking again, he thought.

MARIO STANDS, ARMS crossed, at the window of Maddalena's room in Wilmington Hospital. "The girl needs a name," he says. Ida and Mamma stand beside him, Papà paces the other end, Father Moravia half dozes in the one comfortable chair. They're all thinking it—have been for nearly a week— but Antonio's opinion is the only one that counts, and he will not change his mind. Until Maddalena wakes, the baby will remain unnamed.

He sits on the bed beside his wife. He sees little resemblance between her and the baby, despite the nurses' constant comparisons. "Trust us," they say. "She'll be as beautiful as her mother." Maybe Antonio does not want to see the comparisons. It would be easier if the baby's features were as common as those on Nunzia's plastic dolls, but they are not. She is a Grasso.

And yet the baby belongs to the nurses. According to them, Dr. McMenamin has handled her only once, the night he brought her into the world. It is the team of nurses who keep her warm, make the formula, feed her, give her oxygen treatments. She mostly lies alone, untouched in her heated cell, as if to trick her into thinking she is still in the womb.

One of the nurses, whose name is Brenda, has more than once told Antonio that his baby is stronger than the doctors think. She may weigh only three pounds, but her signs and her color are good. She takes food well. She responds. Brenda says that doctors are too cautious, that she herself has personally seen babies smaller than this one leave the hospital healthy as a normal child. Sometimes, Brenda says, she has more faith in the sick than the healers.

It is Brenda who appears late on the fifth night, after the visitors have left, when the hall is quiet and Antonio is alone in the room with his wife. "Shh," she says, as she nudges Antonio awake with her elbow. She shuts the door. In her arms she carries his precious daughter, covered head to toe in white blankets. Only her nose and eyelids and lips are visible. Brenda lays her facedown on Maddalena's chest. "The heartbeats," she says. "They might spark each other." The baby squirms for a moment, then settles into the groove of her mother's bosom, into the familiar rhythm of the blood. Antonio helps to hold her there, his hand on her bottom. Even through the blankets he can feel the life in her.

He and Brenda wait for a miracle, for Maddalena to open her eyes, to lift her arms and embrace her child for the first time. But there is no miracle. Mother and daughter go on sleeping. After a few minutes, Brenda grows nervous, gathers up the baby again, says, "We'll do this again," and rushes out of the room.

"The human engine's not like a Chevy's," Dr. McMenamin says dismissively the next day, when Antonio asks him whether physical contact with her child might help wake Maddalena.

The doctor does not know what Brenda has done and would likely fire her if he did. On the way out he pauses in the doorway, rubbing his chin. "I wouldn't rule it out, though," he offers. "It hasn't been proven, of course, but I believe brains can transmit signals to each other—of distress, of joy, of pain. And I never underestimate the power of the maternal bond. When the girl gets stronger, maybe." Then, with a wave, he wishes Antonio well.

Antonio feels a great fondness for this doctor. He trusts him, as he does most physicians. Their years in medical school, their seen-it-all nonchalance, win him over. To a doctor like this one, the human body is, in fact, simple as a car engine. Has he not opened the hood of the Chevy a thousand times and examined the same faulty parts, the expected wear-and-tear on the valves? What the Chevy is to Antonio, Maddalena is to this man in the white coat: a machine he will, after a few adjustments, eventually get up and running good as new. And that is how it should be: the dispassionate relationship between mechanic and machine, devoid of mystery, independent of faith. He finds this comforting. And, though he won't admit what he and Brenda have done, he trusts the doctor's instincts about the power of the maternal bond.

Until Dr. McMenamin tells Antonio he has never seen a case like Maddalena's before—and so far, he has not said any such thing—he will wait patiently, as he would if the Chevy needed a new transmission. He will keep reminding himself that his wife is still young, a farm girl healthy and strong as a horse. Women might still die in childbirth in the Old Country, but only because the calendar was stuck on a page a hundred years back. Here, Americans already lived in the future; and in the future, good health was not luck or even one of God's hard-won rewards. It was an expectation. A right.

None of this explains why you won't give your daughter a name, Mario might say. If you're so sure Maddalena will wake up, why not prove it?

Because, for all his faith in doctors, for all the calm he maintains, Antonio is far from sure. When he leaves the hospital at night, he no longer knows his destination. He has not slept in his own bed since Maddalena was taken here. He has slept alongside her on the hospital mattress, in the comfortable chair by the window, or he has not slept at all—just kept walking until the sun rose and it was time to make his way to the Ford plant.

Once, he walked all the way to the neighborhoods across from Wanamaker's and lay on the grass of a corner lot. The foundation of a new house had just been dug, the concrete perimeter of the basement set in a large square. He gazed into the dark hole and imagined the concrete floor being poured, the wooden beams multiplied and nailed together, the slathering of mortar between the red bricks. Now came the flowered wallpaper, the kitchen tile, Maddalena in velvet gloves and a sequined dress, opening the front door to greet the Christmas Eve guests. How cursed he has been with dreams! This little brick box, the trattoria, the son to carry his name, the blonde Hollywood wife who modeled in Philadelphia and earned per show twice the restaurant's monthly take. How greedy all these dreams seem now, when his only wish is for Maddalena to do what she's done every day of their seven years together: open her eyes, say "Antonio," lay her warm hand on his face.

There is something else he won't tell Mario, won't tell anyone. The baby already has a name. During that recent car ride, when he'd passed Riverview Drive so many times that Maddalena asked why he was driving in circles, they had decided. Primo, they would have called him, had she borne a son. The girl: Prima. Either way, it meant "the first." It was both the break from tradition—no Antonio Jr., no Franco, no Chiara, after her mother—and the bold declaration of hope that led them to the name. It thrilled them. But how could he bestow such a name upon the girl now, as hope faded, and she faced the possibility of being the only, the last?

13

An Unfortunate Romance

THOUGH JULIAN HAD bought the atlas with his own money and even scheduled the order of continents to cover, Antonio insisted on teaching the geography lessons. At first.

He liked to explain the history behind why each country maintained its particular borders. The problem was that most of the time he'd invent the reasons—a war that never occurred, a treaty that had never been signed—and give Julian a look that dared him to say he was wrong. Julian never dared, of course, though it pained him to hear this man tell his wife that Italy had been one unified power since the fall of Rome, that Belgians spoke Belgian, and that the vastness of the Atlantic and Pacific Oceans protected them from the threat of the H-bomb. "Look at this," Antonio said, tracing his finger eastward, then westward, from Moscow to D.C.; "by the time the bomb got here, we'd be halfway to Chicago in the Chevy."

"What if they bomb Chicago, too?" she asked.

It wasn't long before he grew tired of her questions. He spent ten minutes explaining the varied topography of the western United States, and she looked at him blankly, pointed to the Rockies, and said, "So those are mountains?"

Antonio shook his head. "Stick to sewing," he said.

After spilling wine on Australia—which Maddalena thought bordered on Germany—Antonio declared the lessons pointless and excused himself for the couch. Julian took over.

"I'm not a very good student," Maddalena said.

"Sure you are," said Julian. "It just takes time. The world is very big."

"Maybe having a baby makes you stupid," she said. "Lately my head gets fuzzy, like I just woke up, even though it's the middle of the day."

"It's nothing," Antonio said, matter-of-factly, from the couch. "It's just your nerves."

Julian could not find Santa Cecilia on the map, but Rieti and Avezzano—where Maddalena had traveled many times with her father and sisters—did appear as small dots north and east of Rome. He showed her Foggia and Lucera, the towns closest to the village near Pietrafitta, where he had spent the first four years of his life. He remembered little of the village, he said, only the sheep. His father used to hold him on the backs of the ewes and pretend they were horses. When he thought of Italy, Julian could still feel that tickle of wool on his bare legs.

Though Maddalena claimed to want to learn about other countries, she spent most of her time on pages 80 and 81: Italy-Sicily-Switzerland. With Julian's help, she traced the route she took to America: from an unmarked pocket of the Appenines near Sora, southwest to Frosinone, north to Rome, and up the coast to Genoa, over land she was seeing for the first and, in her mind, last time. From Genoa she'd taken the ship three thousand miles to New York City, then traveled 120 more to Wilmington. It surprised her that the distance from her village to Genoa was not much greater than the distance from New York to Wilmington. That second trip, gazing upon the endless expanse of fields and highway, had seemed much longer. When Julian flipped the pages to show the United States and Italy side by side, she drew back; "It's so small!" she said. Her eyes darted back and forth between the two. "If you compare, you think the people in Italy must be suffocating. But we didn't know any different. Santa Cecilia never once felt small to me."

Julian opened his hands as if to say, "Of course."

"Now when I tell people 'My village had three streets,' I can't believe it myself. It doesn't seem possible." She closed her eyes. "I've seen too much already, more than any of my sisters. Sometimes I think, if I went back, I'd feel like I was suffocating, too."

"Could be," Julian said. "But still you want to send me back there. You think I could breathe just fine."

"You," she said. "You're different." And while he waited for her to tell him why, she turned the page of the atlas back to Italy. Slowly she ran her finger up the Adriatic from Puglia to Abruzzo, then down the Atlantic side from Lazio to Calabria. "I had a friend who moved to Napoli. That's, what, a hundred miles?"

"A little less," said Julian.

She had mentioned this friend before, in the same breath as her family. He'd gone south to apprentice with a tailor, then returned to Santa Cecilia. His father and two sisters lived in Philadelphia, but Maddalena had never contacted them.

"Do you hear from him—the tailor?"

She looked over at the couch, where Antonio lay sleeping. "Oh, no," she said, sitting up straight. "Of course not."

Julian nodded. He saw in the way she tilted her head—forward and just slightly to the side—that she had a story about him, one she knew she shouldn't tell. Maybe this tailor had disgraced his family, and because of his actions the father did not open his Philadelphia house to him. Maybe he was the best tailor in Italy but felt he had to do his penance in the village. Julian imagined the Santa Ceciliese spitting on his shop window when they walked by but secretly paying him to mend their clothes. It seemed in Maddalena's nature to forgive and take pity on this man, who may have been a deserter or a thief but did not deserve the humiliations of scandal.

"Those villages can be cruel," said Julian. "Make one mistake, you pay for it the rest of your life."

Maddalena looked at him. "What kind of mistake?"

"I don't know," said Julian, surprised by her defensive tone, the accusatory crease between her eyebrows. "Anything. Desperate men in desperate times, crimes of passion, foolish choices. Take your pick."

Her face softened. "You made a mistake, then?"

"Me? No. I was thinking of your tailor. From the way you talk but don't talk about him, it sounds like he did something very wrong."

Again her eyes went to Antonio. His feet, in sheer black stockings, hung over the arm of the sofa. In the past few minutes, he'd begun to snore.

She thought a moment, walked over to the record player, and turned up Sinatra. Facing her husband, she brushed crumbs from her dress and straightened the waistline. By the time she sat back down, her face had changed again. Gone was both the crease and the softness; a shadow had fallen across her, as it had that first Friday night in this house. It seemed she'd either just been told sad news, or was about to deliver it.

"I said something to upset you," offered Julian.

"We talk about suffocating," she began, her voice a whisper over the music and the snores. "I'm suffocating right now, right here. When you don't say what you feel, what's in your heart—"

Julian nodded, and all at once her secret revealed itself, as clearly as if she'd written the words on a poster: the lonely Maddalena Grasso had fallen in love with him. With Julian Fabbri. His heart raced. How naive he had been! He folded his hands and set them gingerly on the edge of the table. Look at her gold necklace and earrings, her perfect hair, her makeup: all of it designed to impress him. Look at her bite her lip, blush, stammer through her stories. Julian had read enough to guess that a girl like her, separated at so young an age from her father, neglected by a distracted husband, might create another father for herself—someone to rely upon, to adore. Julian had become her teacher and treated her with kindness and respect; he'd even serenaded her, stirring up memories of her youth and the family she missed. The poor girl, he thought; now she'd have to sit before him like a schoolgirl and compose herself while the wise adult explained the roots of her infatuation. Julian knew well that this sort of exposure left scars. Exposure made you want to lock yourself in a closet and watch the world go by from two little holes in the door.

"Me and the tailor," Maddalena said, again in a whisper. "We were in love with each other. Before I was married, before Antonio came."

"Oh," Julian said. He let out a deep breath. He covered his neck with his palm, to hide his reddening skin. He had broken out in a sweat just moments before, and now his clammy hands cooled him.

"We made plans for the future," said Maddalena. "But we were very young."

"No wonder you wanted Sinatra so loud," Julian said, managing a smile. "Antonio doesn't know?"

"He knows," she said. "Everybody knows. Ida, Mamma Nunzia, Papà Franco, Mario. All the Grassos. Everybody. But nobody talks about it. I have to put it out of my mind, pretend there was no love affair, pretend I had no mother and father of my own." Her words came faster, but still so quietly Julian had to watch her lips to make them out. "I always lived on Eighth Street, you know. I always had a husband and worked as a seamstress. There was never a boy named Vito Leone who used to kiss me in the back room of the store, who crossed half of Italy, from here to here"—she slid her finger along the map from Frosinone to Genoa—"to try to stop me from going with Antonio, so he could marry me instead."

She shouldn't be telling me this, Julian thought. I am not a priest; I have no way to help her. Besides, it wasn't proper, not with Antonio in the next room, not anywhere. She was a young woman at the beginning of her life, about to give birth to her first child; he was an old man of forty, so ignorant of marriage and love affairs that he'd thought himself a part of Maddalena's. At least he had let her speak before admitting how flattered he was by her affections. Instead he put two fingers over his lips to signal that she'd said too much. But she kept talking.

"When I say I'm suffocating, Julian, it's not that I still love this boy—because that's what he'll always be in my mind, a boy—I don't want you to get the wrong impression. I love my husband. He's a very good man, better maybe than Vito was. Or is. Who can say?" She looked away. "It's just that the time goes by, and I remember less and less about him, about my family, my home. I'm scared one day I'll wake up and they'll be gone, no memories at all, that I'll have only this life, and not the other one. Tell me: if nobody let you talk about your mother and father, if you couldn't keep them alive with your stories, what would you do?"

"I'd die," said Julian, without hesitation.

"Then we are the same."

She told him more. He'd built that bicycle she told him about, from scraps he found lying around three towns, and let the girls ride it up and down the hill in Santa Cecilia. The bike rides had been her first taste of adventure—the wind in her hair, the danger of crashing—and, when she looked back, the happiest moments of her life. The war had seemed far away, her family and Vito within arm's reach; if she fell from the bike and cut her leg open, her mother would dress the wound, and Vito would kiss the pain away. Then the war came closer. She had been forced to flee to her aunt's farm, while Vito stayed in the village. The Germans vandalized her family home—not with bombs, but their bare hands—and Vito had repaired it from floor to ceiling. He'd patched the walls, restored the electricity, and even saved the portrait of her mother the Nazis had slashed. Despite this act of devotion, Maddalena's parents still did not consider him a proper husband for their youngest daughter. He had a sick mother, a father who'd abandoned them, and no trade to speak of. He was about to apprentice in Napoli when Antonio arrived, promising the riches of America.

"Now he's married to my sister," Maddalena said, matter-of-factly. "And I don't have to wonder, 'What would my life be like if I'd married Vito Leone?' If I wanted, I could write to Carolina, ask her. But I don't. My mother sends me letters, but she never mentions them. Carolina does not acknowledge me. She might as well be dead, except I know she is not. When I close my eyes, I see her feeding her children or sitting side by side with Vito at the tailor shop or planting flowers in the window boxes."

She jumped from memory to fantasy, then back again. Julian was not sure which was which. She had three sisters and two brothers—plus one who died in Russia—but the longer Julian listened, the harder it became to keep their names straight. She stopped whispering when the conversation turned less dangerously to tales of the village: the old *strega* who predicted doom for every passing stranger, the soldier who'd stolen her stamp money, the maiden aunt addicted to cigarettes, the beauty of snow on the chestnut trees. Always, though, Maddalena's stories found their way back to Vito. When they did, the color returned to her face; she'd speak more slowly and deliberately, as if painting a picture. It got so that Julian could almost see the boy—skinny, in wrinkled clothes—stepping shyly into the street the night she returned from the war, proud of the hard work he'd done on her house, certain the world would now make room for them.

"I have an idea," Julian said, interrupting her. He held up his hand. "Something for you to think about." It was past eleven, nearly time for her to wake Antonio. The Sinatra record had been flipped twice, and they'd reached the end of the coffee. Maddalena had stacked and restacked the little espresso cups as she spoke, and now one balanced precariously atop the other two. Many times over the past few months, she had sat across from Julian at this table and appeared happy. She had laughed at his jokes and done imitations of Mario; she had poked fun at

Antonio's drunken lope to the sofa and his inability to stay awake. But all of that had been an act. This, Julian thought, was the real Maddalena: confessing, unburdening, removing her makeup to expose her scars.

"You're the luckiest person I know," he said.

She stared at him.

"Do you thank God every day?"

"I do, yes."

Julian shook his head. "I don't believe you." He tried not to appear angry, though a part of him wanted to shake her. "You asked me once if I ever wanted to get married. The answer is yes. Of course I wanted to get married. You might as well ask, 'Were you ever thirsty?'"

"I—"

"It's ugly to have nobody," he said, waving her away. "All my life, until now, I had two people. It was only us, Mamma and Papà, and that was enough. I read my books. Every morning we walked my father to work at Bancroft Mill. We'd spend two weeks every June in Wildwood. The time went by. I looked around at the girls, but none of them looked back." He shrugged, unable to meet her eyes. "Do you know the Delluccis?"

Maddalena nodded.

"One summer, they brought their niece to our house. Papà arranged it. She was a nice girl, six or seven years younger than me. We sat beside each other at the table, and Mamma made lasagna and roasted peppers and *broccoletti* and *palla di neve* for dessert. She wore glasses, this girl—Amelia was her name—and wrote poetry. That's what her father said, at least. She hardly spoke at all. She was the oldest of five sisters, all of them married before her. I was her last chance. And even though Mamma called her a snob and noticed a stain on the collar of her blouse,

I liked her a little bit, I think. She reminded me of a governess from a British mystery novel. I could see how maybe Papà would buy us a house across the street and we'd all live nice and quiet, have dinner together every Sunday. I'd find a job in a library or a school, and we'd have two or three kids. But—" Here Julian took the empty espresso cup from the top of the stack and rolled it between his palms. "She didn't want me at all. Not even one date. Between me and nobody, she picked nobody."

"Something was wrong with her, then," said Maddalena.

"Now she lives in a convent," Julian said. "But she's not a nun."

"You still think about her."

"Not really," said Julian. "Not until now. Not until I hear you complain about all this love in your life." He smiled. "A boy in Italy builds you a bike, rebuilds your house. A man in America thinks you're Marilyn Monroe. In a few weeks, you'll have a child, someone else to adore you. This is what I mean by lucky." He gestured toward the living room. "Look out the window, Maddalena—there's no woman on the sidewalk waiting for me. No girl who used to watch me from her terrace, waiting for me to notice her. You and Antonio are the only ones who think twice about me."

"That can't be true."

"It is. Come to this house in the middle of the day sometime, when it's just me, talking to ghosts. See for yourself. I lie in my bed worrying what will happen when I get old and there's no one to take care of me. I can't even read anymore; it reminds me how much life I haven't lived, all the people I'll never meet. Every noise I hear outside, I think, what did they do to that little black boy? What kind of world is it when someone can just disappear, and nobody cares? I get so sad when you and Antonio leave every week. I don't even realize it until I start to clean the coffee cups, and then it hits me like a slap in the face." He looked down. "A man of forty years old, and you're my only friends. You'd think I'd have more to show for such a long life."

Tell me to stop whining, thought Julian. But Maddalena was too good a person, too compassionate, and—like most women, he imagined—too easily swayed by a man in pain. This was what had brought them together, after all, on Christmas Eve. He covered his eyes with his hands. "I'm sorry," he said. "Forget what I just told you."

She touched his sleeve then, two fingertips on the sheer white fabric of his shirt. Her nails were painted pink, her hands slightly swollen, noticeable only in the snug fit of her wedding ring. "Think how long you had them," she said. "Your parents." She drew her hand away. "I'd trade places with you, if I could. I had my Mamma and Babbo only nineteen years. When I left them, I was still a girl. Never once in nineteen years did I think I'd live somewhere else—the next village maybe, but nowhere I couldn't walk a few miles to find them. When you're young, you think only little things will change. You don't plan for a different country. Or a man like Antonio. Or a war."

Antonio must have heard his name. His right foot, still hanging over the arm of the sofa, scratched the sole of his left. The springs squeaked as he turned onto his other side. If they trusted history, they had no more than five minutes before he'd wake.

"Forty years you lived here, under the same roof with them," Maddalena continued. "Do you thank God every day for that?"

14

Easter

WE HAVE YOUR boy, said the note that Abraham Waters held to Julian's face. The letters, of identical size and spaced evenly apart, were written in black marker on a piece of thin cardboard. YOU LEAVE HE LIVES.

Julian stood on his porch, the noon sun stinging his eyes. He had just woken. He tied his robe across his middle, conscious of Waters's wife staring at him from her own porch across the street.

Waters had one foot on the bottom step of his stoop, the other on the walkway. As far as Julian knew, this was the first time Waters had ever come onto his property.

He looked over at Rosa Volpe's house but could not tell if she was peering through the drapes. The rest of the street was quiet—no cars passing, no wind, just a few robins scurrying across the yard. It was Good Friday, and not even the Lord's looming death had inspired sympathy in the vandals.

"You see who left this?" Waters asked. "They taped it to my door. Right to my front door."

Julian shook his head. "No," he said, looking closer. The letters had been drawn so precisely that at first they seemed machine-made. Then he noticed that the writer had pressed down on the marker more forcefully for some words, more lightly for others, and that the lines sloped downward at an angle. There was a stain, oil or grease, under the letter *W*. They'd used electrical, not household, tape to affix the paper to the door. These clues led him to no conclusions, but they were clues nonetheless.

"It's a fake," Waters said. "Gotta be. You tell me they got him seven months ago and now they bring the sign? It's bullshit."

"I didn't see anybody," said Julian.

The wife crossed her arms. Julian had never seen her up close, but from this distance she seemed younger than Waters, thinner, certainly, but not by much, with matted hair and cheeks round as a cherub's.

Waters shook the sign at him. "How much more can we take?" he said. His face contorted with a jolt, and his knees buckled, as if someone had just stabbed him in the leg.

"He won't tell you," the wife called out. "Will he?"

"Take this to the police," said Julian, taking a step back. "They can do fingerprints. They can't let this go on. It's against the law."

"No police care," Waters said. He walked off, the cuffs of his pants dragging on the concrete.

"I've been watching for them," said Julian. "From my window there."

Waters turned around.

"It's got to be teenagers. But I haven't seen anybody. If I had, I'd—" He searched his mind for the course of action he'd likely have taken, then said something less likely: "I'd have chased them down. Wrung their necks. Or called the cops right then."

"It's not teenagers," said Waters. "It's two men. A woman, too. I saw all three of them, from the back. They're lucky I don't know their faces."

The old lady—Waters's mother? Mother-in-law?—appeared on the porch in her wide-brimmed straw hat and handed the wife a screaming baby. It was the first time Julian had seen her since last summer, when she'd sat knitting in her rocker all hours of the afternoon. She must have been making booties or a blanket for this new child.

"Jesus Christ," said Waters. "That one never stops."

"Your youngest?" Julian asked.

"Yeah."

"How many do you have?"

"Four. With Abie."

A car approached, slowed, then continued on. One of the Lamberti brothers. Waters stood in the driveway, watching him go.

"I don't believe in it," Julian said. "What those people are doing. I just want you to know. It's my neighborhood, too."

"You're right," said Waters. "It's your neighborhood. That's absolutely right."

Back in his living room, with the drapes drawn and the newspaper before him on the coffee table, Julian tried to count the Waters children. There was Abe, of course. There was the new baby. He'd seen a girl once, too; she had braided hair, shiny shoes, and an unremarkable face. He could not recall setting eyes on a fourth child, but it was possible there were two girls close in age, and he had simply never seen them together. One of them, the younger perhaps, may have grown too afraid to attend school, so she stayed at home to help the mother with the new baby and the old lady. Julian imagined the girls lying beside each other at night, worried that if their brother could be kidnapped, so could they. Whenever they heard a noise—the egg against the window, the wind, the creak of their father's pacing across the floorboards—they clutched each other and promised never to separate. Then, when morning came, one caught the bus for school, and the other pulled the covers up over her head.

LATE AFTERNOON THE next day, Holy Saturday, Julian spotted a familiar-looking woman at the deli counter of Angelo's Market. He hid behind a tall display of lemonade cans and watched her. She squatted in front of the assortment of cold cuts, pointed to the turkey, and asked for a half-pound. "As thin as you can get it," she said, enunciating every syllable, as if Angelo's teenaged son did not speak English. It was Helen, from Mrs. Stella's. In profile, she looked older than Julian remembered from the nights he played for her. She had heavier eyes, and fine streaks of gray in her hair. He'd last seen her on Christmas Eve, when the lights in the restaurant were playing tricks, and the candles flickered between her and that bearded man she'd brought to dinner.

Today she wore slacks, a formfitting black sweater, and a light jacket. A gold pin in the shape of a musical note was affixed to the jacket. She pointed to the boiled ham, requested a half-pound, and consulted her shopping list. As she read, she bit the tip of her thumbnail. Julian hoped she was planning a

big Easter dinner, just so he could watch her stand there, order-
ing, for a while.

He sneezed, but Helen did not turn around. He cursed Angelo Montale for his dusty store. If the man owned a rag or a
broom, Julian never saw him or any of his employees use it. He
relied on the heavy foot traffic and high turnover to keep his
grocery store looking fresh, but the quarter-inch layer of dust
on the less popular items—jars of mayonnaise, bottles of maple
syrup, the lemonade cans behind which Julian crouched—told
the tale all too clearly. There was such a thing as loyalty, though,
and Angelo had run this store for as long as Julian had been
alive. The five separate times in the '30s when he'd been laid off
from Bancroft Mill, Julian's father had even worked here part-
time at the meat counter. There was no other Italian-run grocery in the neighborhood, unless you counted the fruit vendors
who pushed their carts up and down Union, or Arienzo's Fish
Market, or Three Little Bakers on Lancaster Avenue. The
prices at the A&P were a few cents lower, but you had to risk
the chance someone would catch you and curse you for patron-
izing the place. Once you crossed the line into the A&P, what
would stop you from getting your bread from anyone but Lamberti? Your cigarettes from anywhere but Arturo Cozzi's Smoke
Shop? You could not plead poverty as a defense, since Angelo
was known to offer half-price to any Italian immigrant who'd
lost his job, or found himself with a new baby, or gambled away
his savings.

Julian's mother had taught him to bring his own dust rag to
this market. When no one was watching, he'd wipe off the
packages of dried pasta, the tops of the orange juice bottles, the
cans of tomatoes. He put these in the wire basket, which he'd

also cleaned. A trip to Angelo's took a great deal of time, as Julian always felt obliged to stop and talk with one or another of his parents' friends. They'd ask the same question—"How are you getting along?"—and he'd offer the same answer: "*Bene, bene.* Just fine." They'd say they heard he was playing the accordion at Mrs. Stella's, and he'd answer with a lie he'd told so many times that he almost started to believe it: he'd broken two fingers shoveling snow that winter, and they still hadn't healed.

"What a shame!" they'd say. "My nephew told me you played very nice."

"Time heals all wounds," Luigi Dellucci liked to say, in reference to the fingers. He'd offered the same condolence at both his parents' funerals. He might have said the same thing to Julian as an apology for the daughter who'd rejected him.

"Signor Giulio Fabbri!" said a voice behind him.

Ida Grasso.

This time, Helen immediately looked over at Julian, and expressed—he was almost sure—an unannoyed surprise. The surprise may have even been called pleasant, if he'd had the time to consider it. Instead he had to contend with Ida, who'd grabbed his arm and slipped hers through it. She talked on and on in her throaty Napolitana dialect: Did he want to meet them at nine o'clock Mass tomorrow morning, or was he going to the *vigilia* tonight? Did he prefer cauliflower or broccoli with his roast? Did he like the wine her brother had brought him week before? It was expensive Chianti, triple the price of the kind they normally drank; the only problem was it stained her teeth and gave her gas. She wondered if maybe she just wasn't used to the good kind.

"Could be," said Julian.

Helen tilted her head at him, smiled, and walked toward the other end of the store. She picked up an onion, examined it, and put it back on the pile.

Ida's basket held only her purse. "You want to hear something funny?" she asked. "I forgot why I came here. We need two things for tomorrow, but I can't remember which two. I never write anything down."

"If you walk around a little, maybe it will come to you," said Julian.

"That's what I was doing," she said.

"Well, *buon fortuna!*" Julian said. "Good luck!" He broke free, patted her shoulder, and kissed her on both cheeks. "I need onions."

"Oh, we have plenty of onions," Ida said, and headed in the opposite direction.

Ten steps and there was only a bin of potatoes between him and Helen. "Excuse me, Signora," he began.

She turned to him.

"I meant to say good afternoon before, but—you know Ida Grasso, don't you? Her husband is the owner of Mrs. Stella's—she was talking to me first, and now—I didn't want you to think me rude, or that I didn't recognize you, so—" He bowed slightly. "Good afternoon. Happy Easter."

She nearly succeeded in returning the greeting, but Julian interrupted her. "I didn't know you shopped here. I never saw you anywhere but the restaurant. Do you live in this neighborhood? I thought for some reason you had a house maybe in the suburbs? Somebody told me that, I think?"

"Oh, no," she said. "I live in Forty Acres."

The Irish neighborhood. Just a few blocks east, the other

side of Pennsylvania Avenue, but a land foreign as Cuba. "And you come here for—" Julian looked in her basket. In addition to the ham and turkey, she had bought ground beef and a pound of lamb shoulder.

"I don't like our butcher," she explained. "Henderson's, on Delaware Avenue. Don't ever go there. He cheated my husband out of money once. I tell everybody I meet not to give him any business."

"Well, my heart belongs to Angelo," Julian said, his hand on his chest. In his mind he had a picture of the bearded man with whom Helen had eaten Christmas Eve dinner. They did not seem like husband and wife, though; they spoke too formally with each other, like boss and secretary. And the girl—Abigail, he remembered—looked nothing like him.

She smiled, balanced her basket on the pile of potatoes, and folded her arms. "So why don't you play anymore? We all miss you. They didn't fire you, did they?"

Julian scanned the aisle for Ida. No sign of her. He nearly told Helen the lie about his fingers, then stopped himself. "I wasn't fired," he said. "I just—"

"It took too much out of you."

"Yes."

"I could see that."

"You could?"

She pointed to the gold pin on her sweater. "I'm a music teacher. Piano, violin, some guitar. To kids mostly, and a few adults. I can see when someone feels every note. Never tried the accordion, though."

Julian said, "It's not a lady's instrument."

"No, I guess not," she said, and laughed. "I miss hearing you, though." She looked over his shoulder. "We go to Mrs. Stella's quite often, and I always tell Abigail—she's my daughter—wasn't it much nicer when that man was playing?"

"That's very kind," said Julian.

"I'm a terrible cook, you see. And Abigail deserves to eat well once in a while. She turned twelve last month. March 14."

"I met her," said Julian. "You probably don't remember. On Christmas Eve. She pulled on my jacket." He smiled.

Helen covered her mouth. Up close, Julian could now see that every one of her fingernails had been bitten down. She wore only one ring—an emerald on her right hand. "I'm sorry about that," she said, and picked up her basket. "You have a good memory."

"She's a beautiful young lady," said Julian.

He helped her find the right onion and advised her against the smallish and bruised tomatoes. They were the last of a bad bunch, and besides, the vendors on Union always had the freshest produce. The difference was night and day. But she was too timid to bargain with the vendors, she explained. Half the time she didn't understand them; the other half they flirted with her.

"I can help you some weekend," said Julian, head down, eyes fixed on an almond that had fallen into the barrel of walnuts. "I know how they work. I can get you a good deal."

She didn't say anything. Not yes, not no.

They got in line. She set her items on the counter beside the cash register, and at that moment Julian decided he, too, had finished his day of shopping. He would walk her out, gentleman-like, to her car or the bus or maybe all the way to Forty Acres.

He could feel Angelo and his nephew watching him from the deli, on the opposite end of the store. They had their arms around each other, snickering. Ida had disappeared. Helen's purchases, which included a lot of meat, a carton of cigarettes, and a swirled candy stick, came to $6.33; his purchases—a can of grapefruit juice, a box of pretzels—to forty-eight cents.

"That's all you're getting?" Helen asked.

Julian shrugged. "It's all I need."

"You should talk to my mother," said Helen, as he escorted her out of Angelo's. It was a warm evening, and Fifth Street was crowded with people. The men wore short-sleeved shirts; the women carried their fur wraps on their arms. "'You spend too much money,' she says—on food, on restaurants, on clothes. She'll be happy you helped me save a few pennies. I don't mind it, either."

"They have the good stuff on Sundays," said Julian, which was not a lie.

They talked for a while on the corner of Fifth and Union, near the bus stop. She was to wait here for her brother to pick her up. The streetlamps were lit, and the shopkeepers stood in their doorways with their hands on their hips, waiting for six o'clock so they could close. Julian shook his head "no, *grazie*" at Rocco Lamberti, who held up a small bag of rolls for him. His arms were growing tired from carrying Helen's groceries, but he wasn't yet ready to give them up.

Helen talked openly about her life. She and Abigail lived with her mother, in a small apartment above the home of her sister, brother-in-law, and teenaged nephew. The Rileys had lived in Wilmington for a hundred years, she said, and just now they'd begun to move up in the world. Her father, who'd passed away not long ago, had gone into law. Her son was a sophomore at Salesianum, a private Catholic school for smart boys. She had a cousin who worked for the district attorney, another studying

to be an engineer. The brother-in-law she lived with was a police officer, as her own husband had been.

"He was killed," Helen said. "My husband. I don't know if
you knew that."

"I didn't," Julian said. "I'm very sorry." He set the bags on the
ground. "I met him, too? Christmas Eve?"

"Oh," she said, confused for a moment. "No. Jerry died in
the war. In Poland. That man at Mrs. Stella's—well, let's just say
that when you're a widow at forty-three, all the old men think
they're your Prince Charming."

Julian looked out at the street. "I'm sorry," he said. "I didn't
mean, when I said I would help with the vendors—"

"Not you!" she said. She touched his arm. The wind whipped
through her hair, unloosing it from the clip in the back. "Gosh,
what am I saying? You—I feel like I know you already. I always
tell my students: once you see someone perform, they belong to
you forever. And I saw you many times, Giulio."

"Julian," he said.

"Julian?"

Eventually, after the explanations, a squad car pulled up, and
a blond officer rolled down his window. He eyed Julian. "Helen!" he called. "You all right?"

"Of course," she said, picking up the bags.

The back door opened, and Abigail ran out. She hugged
Helen around the waist. "Mommy! What'd you buy for me?"
she asked.

Helen pulled the candy stick from her pocket. "Cherry. That
OK?" To her brother-in-law, she said, "And before you ask, yes,
I got your cigarettes."

"Good girl," he said.

Helen and Julian made plans to meet on this same corner

next Sunday at nine a.m., before the best produce was picked over. If tomorrow were not Easter, he might have suggested they meet then. She'd come straight from church—St. Anne's— and bring Abigail.

Julian's dinner that night consisted of chickpeas and pretzels. There was no other food in the house. He dressed the chickpeas with a little olive oil, vinegar, salt, and pepper. The pretzels he dunked in white wine. He ate alone at the kitchen table, and though the radio was tuned to the Bob Hope Show on WDEL—its usual spot at nine o'clock on Saturdays—Julian grew impatient. He flipped through the stations and came first to the WAMS Barn Dance, then WILM's Country Time, and finally to WFIL's Dancing Party. He left it there. All the lights were on, the drapes drawn. He sat on the arm of the couch for a while and listened to the quicksteps, the sambas. Somewhere in Wilmington, a crowd of couples was gathered in the room where this band played. The men were leading the ladies across a shiny floor, and someone was taping it all for the poor souls unlucky enough not to experience it live.

Mamma, Papà, and Baby Giulio watched him from the end table, concerned. How he wished they really could see him—not just here, standing and extending his arms, practicing the one-two-three of the Viennese waltz, the one dance he knew—but in eight days, on the corner of Fifth and Union, when he took Helen by the arm and gave her a tour of their neighborhood. How he wished his mother and father could assure him that letting someone new into his heart, as he had once prepared to do for the Dellucci girl, was not a betrayal of their memory. At this moment, it did not feel like one. At this moment—a little drunk, quite hungry—he could imagine no better way to honor them than to prove himself worthy of love.

* * *

For the first date of his life, Julian Fabbri chose opening night at Trattoria Renato. Friday, May 21. The place was booked for a week solid, but Renato cut him a deal: a table for two in exchange for one night of accordion music one Saturday before the end of the summer. Because, in May, the end of the summer might as well be the end of time, Julian accepted. Had Renato made him wash dishes, he'd have agreed to that, too. His plan required Renato's restaurant; without it, he had only himself to impress his date, and he feared that would be far from enough.

He learned that Antonio and Maddalena had reservations for seven p.m. and would just be eating their dessert when Julian arrived. He'd wear his best suit, and walk arm in arm with the lovely brunette. Who's that woman? Antonio would ask Maddalena. How could Julian have kept this news from us? They'd signal to him from across the restaurant, and Julian would say to his girl, "Oh, look! My friends are here. Let me introduce you."

And then how deliciously he would wind his way among the tables, nodding to faces he'd surely recognize from the neighborhood or Mrs. Stella's. All the whispering they'd do, huddled over their dinner candles—surely Helen would sense it, and feel she'd made the right choice in accepting Julian's invitation. He'd keep his shoulders high and his feet straight, as Maddalena had taught him; he'd take slow, careful steps, careful not to rush. The trick was to pretend the world adored him and envied this new woman on his arm; the trick was to forget that, without Maddalena, he'd never have had the courage to ask her to dinner in the first place.

"Antonio and Maddalena Grasso," he'd say, his voice steady and formal. "This is Helen Riley."

"Molto piacere."

"She's Irish," he'd say. "Believe it or not." Everyone would laugh.

"Nobody's perfect," she'd say, squeezing his hand, and immediately they would fall for her, as Julian had.

But the night did not go as planned. First, Officer Stanley greeted them in the parking lot and asked if they'd seen anything suspicious around here the past few weeks, which made Helen nervous. "Is this a bad neighborhood?" she asked.

Then he led her into the safety of the trattoria: his head high, her hand clasped firmly in his. Though the ad had promised a romantic setting, it was louder here than Mrs. Stella's, with a great deal of dishes clanking in the open kitchen. Julian scanned the crowd, and instead of finding Maddalena and Antonio, a sea of unfamiliar animated faces stared blankly back at him, chewed, rolled their eyes, blinked, sipped their wine. He stood beside the lion fountain, unsure what to do.

"What's wrong?" Helen asked.

It was not until Renato greeted him that Julian learned what had become of them, why another couple now sat in their booth. According to Renato, Maddalena had gone to Wilmington Hospital the night before, and though the child—a girl— came out healthy, the mother was in great danger.

"It was too early," said Julian.

Renato nodded, folded his hands and raised them up to God. "It's in His hands now."

"The poor woman," said Helen. "How old is she?"

Julian was shaking. His mind raced. How terrified Maddalena must have been when the labor started, and she realized the danger she faced. How he wished he'd become a doctor—a scientist, a surgeon, a man of substance—someone useful to the world. What good did books and music do in this case, in most cases? Why bother loving people, if you couldn't save them?

"I'm sure she'll be fine," Helen said, and stroked his arm.

Renato was holding two leather-bound menus. "Life goes on," he said. "Let's get you to your table."

15
The Sign

WHEN A BLIZZARD hit Wilmington many years back, Antonio woke two hours early, walked six miles through the storm, and still reached the Ford plant on time. In nearly a decade, he has kept pace on the assembly line through two broken fingers—one on each hand—and chills from fevers over a hundred. He has put his name in the hat for every holiday shift, including Easter and Christmas Eve, and has never eaten Thanksgiving dinner anywhere but the wobbly card table in the break room. But today, Thursday, May 27, 1954, for the first time in his life, Antonio Grasso does not show up for work.

Maddalena's condition has not changed, nor is there the promise of change. The doctor will not commit to a prediction; the nurses will not say anything the doctor has not already said. Meanwhile, the baby grows stronger. The color returns to the doctor's face when he mentions her. It is something of a miracle, he says, how she maintains her weight. Father Moravia declares that Mamma and Ida, who have prayed continually for her, have helped achieve this miracle—in partnership with our Almighty Father. The doctor can neither confirm nor deny this. He can only stand in the doorway and order the nurses in and out.

What prevents Antonio from going to work is that he simply cannot get out of his chair. He cannot remember the last time he has slept, though it may have been while driving. When he tries to stitch together a sequence of events from the past few days, he finds many stretches of hours unaccounted for. He sees Nunzia and Nina on the floor of the waiting room, banging the heads of two dolls together. Through the glass he sees the inside of his daughter's screaming mouth, her lips and gums pink as ham. There is Father Moravia kissing the cross on his necklace; spittle in the corner of Giulio Fabbri's lips; the stoplights on Union going red, green, red, then green again, as cars honk and drive around him. A fat woman steps in front of Renato's nephew as he sweeps the outside of the trattoria; yellow petals fall from the tulips on the windowsill; black stubbly hair appears on Maddalena's legs. Those pale legs. It seems there is no life in her at all. And yet the hair grows.

Until now, Antonio has stayed strong. He has worked from six to six, eaten a brief dinner at home or at Mrs. Stella's, then returned here to the hospital, where he paces and fades in and out of sleep. More than a few times, he has gone for a drive. "To clear my head," he has told his mother, who spends the evenings at Maddalena's side with her rosary beads. He went once to Westover Hills, once to Battery Park just to stare at the water. But mostly he drives up and down Riverview Drive.

Five days after the grand opening, a banner announcing GRAND OPENING still draped the entrance to Renato's restaurant. Yet there was no prominent sign to indicate which restaurant had opened so grandly. From the road, passersby could see tables, a bar, and waiters carrying trays, but for all they knew it was another steakhouse run by a Greek. During his brief visit to the hospital, Renato had explained that the neon sign he'd ordered had been delayed. Furious with the two men who'd designed it, he told them that for every day that passed without the sign, he'd knock ten percent from the total price. The men were brothers who'd just immigrated from his mother's village, and Renato had promised Rosa he'd give them the business. In the meantime, Renato had tried writing the name of the restaurant in black marker on the GRAND OPENING banner, but the ink didn't stick to the slick surface, and by the next day the rain had washed it off completely. Until the two brothers came through, Renato had to settle for the name written in big letters on the inside of a pizza box and taped to the window beside the main door.

Last night, after the guests left and the busboys had just begun to mop the floors, Renato, Cassie, Buzzy and—was that Marcie, in gloves and a feathered hat?—gathered on the walkway outside the entrance to the trattoria. They faced the drawn blinds of the front window. Antonio watched through his windshield, as if at a drive-in movie, from his spot across the street.

Buzzy held a newspaper over his head as protection from the light rain that had just begun to gather strength. The wind lifted his curls, revealing in the harsh light of the streetlamp the bald patch at the crown of his head. Cassie wore a dress that fell at her knees in a ruffle, probably to show off her legs.

A young man peeked through one of the blinds and gave them the thumbs-up. Cassie raised her right hand and extended one finger, then two, then three. At three, the blinds came up, revealing the bright neon sign—TRATTORIA RENATO—that spanned the entire window. TRATTORIA was lit in green script and formed into a semicircle; RENATO was in red and connected the ends of the semicircle in a straight line. In the space between the two words glowed the bright white outline of a wineglass and a loaf of bread.

Cassie was clapping. The light danced across her face in the rain.

The two brothers appeared in the window and bowed.

Renato put his arms around Cassie and walked her back inside. They disappeared among the waiters and busboys as one by the one the lights went off. Buzzy and Marcie drove away. The sign remained lit. Before getting into their car, Renato and Cassie stopped for a moment to admire it. Renato traced the letters through the glass with his finger.

After everyone left, Antonio drove around the back of the trattoria, into the neighborhood of Collins Park, and waited. It was one o'clock in the morning. The rain let up. Clouds raced southeast, streaking across the moon, toward the Atlantic. He sat in the car with the headlights off, the windows rolled down and WFIL on low. He heard June Valli's "I Understand," and Jo Stafford's "Make Love to Me." *Everybody's sleepin' so it's quite all right.*

Collins Park was a quiet, unfinished neighborhood of ranches and small two-story duplexes and split-levels; each house had a quarter acre of property if it had an inch. Soon the lady peering through her drapes at the stranger in the idling car would send out her husband to ask questions. Before that could happen, though, Antonio drove to a different spot, cut the engine, opened the trunk, grabbed the crowbar, and stuffed it down the leg of his pants.

He marched through the tall grass of the empty lot that bordered the back of the restaurant. It was a mess back here: scrap metal, trash, discarded magazines, cigarette butts. A place for the kitchen workers to throw dice or fight or catch some air. Antonio gripped the crowbar through his right pocket and limped his way to the front of the trattoria.

He had stopped in for a visit a few times during the renovation, just to pay his respects to Renato, but this was the first chance he had to see the finished space up close. The tables, draped in crisp white cloth, were arranged in neat rows of two- and four-tops and set with gold-colored plates. The liquor bottles sat on illuminated shelves behind the bar. The floors had been buffed and polished. The bulbs of the elaborate chandelier above the maître d' station bloomed from multicolored glass petals. Circular booths, upholstered in black leather, lined the left wall. It made Mrs. Stella's—its muraled walls plagued with cracks, its oil paintings hung crookedly—seem all the more dismal. Any customer walking in here would feel inspired to open their wallets, if just to live up to the decor.

According to Renato, every table had been booked for the first four nights. He had reserved a booth for Antonio, Maddalena, and his parents. Ida refused to come without Mario, who referred to the trattoria with the same words Renato used for Mrs. Stella's: "the enemy." Papà believed in staying on good terms with everyone, especially your competition, because you never knew whose help you might need in the future. "Wilmington is big enough for two pasta-and-gravy places," he told Mario, but there was no convincing him. He protected Mrs. Stella's with as much force as he protected Nunzia and Nina. Any threat to it was a threat to the future of those two little girls.

Papà would not approve of what Antonio was about to do. He would remind him that Renato had been his best friend for nearly half his life, that if Italians didn't protect each other, they had no chance in this country. He would tell Antonio to think of how well Renato had treated Maddalena the day he'd brought her into the pizzeria. Had not Renato remembered Maddalena's birthdays more reliably than Antonio himself, and made sure to steal him fresh flowers to take home to her?

Antonio hesitated. He ducked around the corner of the restaurant, suddenly convinced he'd misjudged his good friend, that he was no better than a jealous and ungrateful child. Then he remembered Renato's relentless teasing after that first visit with Maddalena, and the knowing looks he'd exchanged with Buzzy whenever they brought up the subject of her beauty. As the years of their friendship unfolded before him, it became clear that Renato had never failed to undo his few acts of kindness. "Go talk to that blonde in the corner," he'd said one night on Market Street, long before Maddalena arrived. "I hear she won't put up a fight." And then just as Antonio had convinced her to take a walk with him, there came Renato dragging him off to some emergency that turned out to be a card game with Buzzy. Countless times Renato had pulled these stupid tricks, and Antonio had put up with them.

It had occurred to Antonio over the past few months that his own nights with Cassie must have played a part in Renato's sudden show of love and devotion. Cassie was the only girl the two of them had shared; though they never spoke of it, they knew they had come within months of each other, first Renato, then Antonio. Now Renato had reclaimed her for good, a victory of sorts over the man she'd turned to when she'd grown tired of him the first time.

All this was in Antonio's head as he huddled on the side of the trattoria the night Renato and Cassie unveiled their tacky sign. This and the fear that God, after all the songs and blessings and kissing of crucifixes, had grown as cruel as the lowest of the men He'd created. The murderers and kidnappers, the swindlers and thieves. There was no hope, not in heaven or on earth, if not even God could show mercy. Antonio wiped his face with his sleeve. The stale smell of the hospital clung to him.

Like Maddalena, he believed in destiny. Some force stronger than himself had led him here, just as it had led her to America and the two of them to each other. This same force—unmanageable, unpredictable—dictated even his unimportant everyday decisions: the blue shirt over the white, the king of diamonds over the four of spades. If he did not call on destiny, he had no nobler way to explain that he did not feel in control of his body when he stepped from the shadows on the side of Trattoria Renato, glanced once at the road to make sure no cars were passing, and smashed the glass of the front window. With the crowbar, he pulled apart the neon sign. The words unraveled in loud pops. A fizz of light, a slow hiss, one letter after another shattering. This time, when Antonio fell to his knees and wiped the tears from his face with his sleeve, all he could smell was whiskey.

Headlights appeared on New Castle Avenue. Antonio stepped through the window and ducked, praying for the slow-moving car to pass. He kept still, the crowbar quivering in his hand. The temperature had dropped ten degrees since the rain, and he shivered in his wet shirt. Eventually, the headlights faded. He gripped the crowbar with two hands, gave what was left of the sign one last stab, and pulled the blinds.

He jumped through the window and ran to the empty lot. He crouched in the mud among the thick weeds and tried to catch his breath. His armpits were damp, his underwear twisted and bunched. He must have cut his leg on a nail. He waited in those weeds for a half hour at least, shifting his weight, conscious of every flicker of light on the neighborhood side of the lot, the whoosh of every car as it zoomed down New Castle Avenue on the other side. Finally, when his knees could take no more, he returned the crowbar to his pants and walked to his car with his chin up, at the nonchalant pace of the innocent. He even waved hello to a man setting out his empty milk bottles.

His hands shook as he put the keys in the ignition. Even after he drove off, removed his shirt, and wrapped the blanket around his naked chest, he could not stop shivering. He circled the neighborhood and passed the trattoria twice—once coming north, once coming south. Unless you looked closely, and you knew a neon sign had been put up two hours before, it was impossible to see any damage from the road. No police would investigate until morning at the earliest, he told himself. By that time, he would be at work, where it was impossible to concentrate on anything but the secure attachment of armrest to seat.

And yet he finds he cannot go to work. He has not slept at all, not even after the bath he took in the middle of the night, or the change of clothes, or the cup of warm milk he fixed himself in the kitchen. He has pushed the chair closer to Maddalena's bed and lays his head on her arm. He closes his eyes. People move in and out of the room. He should call Mr. Hannagan, explain his absence, but he doesn't. He will keep completely still, his muscles throbbing, his bones fragile as chalk. If he moves, as Brenda tries to get him to do—her hands on his shoulder, her cheek against his ear—he will break into a thousand pieces.

16

Old Women

When Maddalena wakes, she finds an old woman asleep in the chair beside her. A blanket is pulled up to her neck. She still wears her shoes. Her fingers clasp a rosary. At first, Maddalena does not recognize her. The old woman's face is turned toward the window, and the light is poor. It must be the middle of the night, but there is no clock on the wall. There are only unfamiliar shadows: squares of lattice, an umbrella shape, an inch-thick line slanted from floor to ceiling. Maddalena tries to lift her shoulders, but they are too heavy. She smells roasted chicken, applesauce, detergent. Beyond the fuzzy glow of the doorway sit a desk and a large metal crate on rollers. A figure passes, then another. They move like women, swaying their hips. *Sashaying*. One of them stops at the desk. She gestures with her hands. Her mouth opens and closes. She pushes the metal crate away, but the wheels make no noise as they glide across the floor. Her footsteps, too, are silent.

Maddalena turns to the old woman. Her vision blurs, but the gray hair under the scarf and the knotted hands stay in focus. "Mamma," she says. She hears only a dull moan in her head, nothing like the word at all. The moan throbs behind her ears. She tries again to wake her, to the same effect. It has been so long since she has seen her face. If only she could make a sound loud enough, Mamma would turn to her. If only she could crawl out of this bed, kneel beside her, and lay her head on her lap. But Maddalena is buried in the sand, like a child at the shore, and no one will come to dig her out; the waves, foamy and swirling and cold, inch closer. If she screams, she will drown.

She remembers Mamma's skin, creamy-white and soft as a girl's. She used to say she had not laughed enough in her life to deserve wrinkles. She has lost the velvet black of her hair, the smoothness of her fingers. *Tell me where I am*, Maddalena begs, but her mouth no longer moves, and this time not even the moan pulses through her head—just a staticky silence, a low roar, like the beach in winter.

She does not know if she has slept hours, days, or months, but later, when she wakes again, the silence has broken. A phone rings; voices murmur just out of reach; something beside her clicks and hums. The blanket sits folded on the chair, but Mamma is gone. For the first time, Maddalena notices the vases of flowers. Light pools around them on the windowsill, breaks through the parted drapes. There is a girl standing in the doorway. She wears a white cap, white shoes, white nylon stockings, and a white dress. The girl is a nurse. This is a hospital room. She is in a hospital bed.

"Mamma!"

The nurse turns to her. "Mrs. Grasso?" she says, and rushes into the room. "Mrs. Grasso!" She is thin and pretty, her face flat with eyes wide and set far apart. She grips Maddalena's shoulders and leans down so close to her face that their noses touch. "Can you hear me?" she says.

Maddalena nods.

The nurse presses a button on the wall, then reaches for the blood-pressure device that Maddalena recognizes from her many visits to Dr. Barone. She wraps it around Maddalena's arm and pumps the little black balloon. "Good," she says. "I'm Nurse Morgan. I've been taking good care of you."

"C'è Mamma?" asks Maddalena. *"L'ho vista."* She tries to point to the chair, but she cannot move her arm. And yet there are no straps restraining her. *"L'ho vista nella sedia. Dov'è andata?"*

"I don't understand," says the nurse. Her pink cheeks go pinker. "I'm so sorry." She presses the button again. "We're going to find someone for you to talk to."

"Cosa mi è successo?"

She ignores her.

"Il mio bambino. Cos'è accaduto al mio bambino?"

The nurse bites her lip. "Bam-beeno," she says. "I know that one." She looks toward the door over one shoulder, then the other, as if about to steal something. "Baby, right?"

"Cos'è accaduto al mio bambino?" She feels a tingle in the tips of her fingers and toes, then a sharp pain between her legs, behind her knees and elbows. The sand is giving way.

"The doctor should be the one to tell you, but—" The nurse looks again, drops her voice to a whisper. "Oh, what the hell. You have a healthy baby girl, Mrs. Grasso. Looks just like you, too. She's been waiting for you." She grabbed her hand. "Now, don't tell anybody I told you, OK? This place would love to fire me as it is."

"*Una bambina?*" Maddalena says.

"You just hold on," says the nurse. Her face contorts in great frustration. "Joanne!" she calls, so sharply Maddalena flinches. "Get somebody in here, for God's sake! She's waking up!"

"*Mi sento male. Che cos'ho?*" Maddalena asks. She searches for and finds the English words, but they don't come out. "*Dov'è la mia bambina? Con Mamma?*"

"What you should do is try to stay calm," says Nurse Morgan, and smoothes her hair behind her ear.

More strangers enter the room: a nurse, a young doctor, another nurse, an old doctor. They ask her for her name and address over and over, take her temperature, and rub her arms and legs. They stand on all sides, smiling. Where is my family? she asks, but no one seems to understand. How could they leave me here? All the people can tell her is that her loved ones are on the way.

"This is a day of great joy," says the young doctor. "Are you a religious woman, Mrs. Grasso?"

"You didn't see the mother-in-law with the rosary?" Nurse Morgan says to him.

Maddalena has never known exhaustion like this. The talking overwhelms her, and the parade of doctors and nurses, and the swiftly hardening sand. Her hands and feet go numb again. And though she fights to keep her eyes from closing—so she can see Mamma again and her baby girl, just once, before the Lord takes them—she cannot.

PART THREE

The Light Around Him Changes

17

The Viewing

THE LINE IN front of the Pavani Funeral Home extends for a block down Bayard Avenue. Julian arrives alone and later than he intended. He takes his place behind an old couple he does not recognize, greets them with a somber nod, and waits.

Services are scheduled to end at eight-thirty, but unless this line moves swiftly Dante Pavani will have to keep his doors open past ten. Only a few of Rosa Volpe's mourners seem familiar, and Julian wonders, with some resentment, where they'd all been last year and the year before, at his parents' funerals. Have so many new Italians moved to Wilmington since then? When did the old woman make all these friends? In the years after her husband's death, she rarely left the house. Julian knew her as a disembodied face in the front window, peering between the drapes. She'd come to him once last summer, in the middle of the afternoon, to ask for help with her eulogy, then never spoke to him again. She had Renato for everything else: to bring her groceries and cut her rosebushes and keep her company when she needed it. If she attended Mass at St. Anthony's, she must have gone in the early morning, then shut herself back in her house before Julian woke.

It is not until Julian sees Paolo lift a young boy on his shoulders that he realizes who all these people must be: Renato's regular customers. When you own two successful restaurants, you eventually create a loyal following—not friends, not family, but people who feel close to you because you have fed them, because they have spent birthdays and wedding anniversaries under your roof. At first, Julian is relieved; the turnout at his parents' funerals now seems respectable. But then he feels a pang of regret. Even this *vecchietta*—mother of the arrogant Renato, suspicious and angry in her final years—deserves a long line of grief-stricken mourners at her passing. Anyone who lives a decent life deserves as much.

It is a humid August evening, and Julian can already feel the sweat under his arms. He removes his jacket and shuffles forward in his shirt and tie. When he reaches the entrance, he will put the jacket back on and ready himself for Renato. What will he say to him? You're never too old to feel like an orphan. Or how about: when the second one goes, you feel five years old again, lost on a busy street, running through the crowd in between cars and buses, screaming for your mother to find you. But instead Julian will say what everyone says: "I'm so sorry," and "She was a good woman," before he kneels at the body itself, prays for her soul, and goes home.

In the stale air of Pavani's viewing room, Julian finds not only Renato but his fiancée. She stands beside him in a sheer black dress and an oversized diamond ring, her hair pulled tightly back. Julian recognizes her from the early years at Fourth and Orange and his one visit a few months ago to the trattoria, where she complimented Helen on her shoes.

"I've got a house to sell," Renato says, jovially, after Julian offers his condolences. "You know anyone who's buying? It'll cost them a fortune, while I can get it."

Julian smells whiskey on his breath, which is not uncommon either for Renato or for the grieving here at the Pavani Funeral Home. Before each wake, Dante invites the loved ones into a private room in the back, where he provides an assortment of liquor.

His uncle was supposed to come from Italy, Renato explains, but he changed his mind. He and Cassie want to get out of the city before it's too late, put their money on a house in Collins Park, down the street from the restaurant. They'll have the house built from the ground up. No more apartments, no more creaky row homes.

"No more smelling like grease," Cassie says.

"Your mother was happy in that house," says Julian, though he has no evidence of this. "And Seventh is a good street."

"Most of it," Renato says. "Mark my words, Giulio. In ten years, you'll be surrounded."

It is when Cassie pinches Renato's behind—surreptitiously, and with a purpose more punitive than playful—that Julian first suspects that the vandals might not be teenagers, or kidnappers, or hoodlums from the East Side, but Renato Volpe himself. He looks the man in the eye, for a giveaway, but there is only a watery blankness. No guilt. No shame. God will punish the derelict boys, Father Moravia promised. But when?

If there were not a lifeless body at the front of the room, illuminated by soft lights and surrounded with flowers, no one would guess the sad circumstances of this event. Chattering ladies and families walk among the cushioned chairs facing Rosa Volpe. They wave to one another, shake hands, and trade news of marriages and children. They speak in respectfully muted tones, but the effect in the room is one of a hushed roar, like the one immediately following Mass. "Have you met Maurizio?" Julian hears someone say. "He's buried three wives already." There is stifled laughter as the woman beside Maurizio—the fourth wife?—raises her eyebrows and shrugs.

No one is crying. No one falls on her knees and wails. No one even looks in Rosa's direction after he makes the sign of the cross over her body and turns toward the audience. Angelo Montale takes the framed picture of young Rosa from the table beside the casket and says to Julian, "This is how she looked when she first came into my store. Francesco Volpe was a lucky man."

"And old age is very cruel," says Angelo's widowed daughter, who had once been beautiful herself.

Julian scans the crowd for Maddalena and finds her in the back row, behind the loud and fidgety Dellucci teenagers. Antonio talks with Buzzy Fisher on the other side of the room, but Maddalena sits alone in the aisle seat with her head down and her hands in her lap. As Julian approaches, he sees that her eyes are closed.

She wears a dark dress and a hat, with a half veil that conceals her eyes. In her fingers she clutches a rosary and one of Rosa's funeral cards, on which is printed the poem Julian helped compose. She has regained most of the weight she lost after a month in the hospital—eight days unconscious, twenty to recover—and now looks much as she did when she first came to visit him. But she is not the same woman he knew in February.

She no longer shows much interest in geography or the newspaper. The few times he visited the Grassos this summer, she talked mainly of her own health and the progress of Prima, and though Julian understood this, he could not help but feel—how can he put it?—*unnecessary* around her. He has sat across the table from her and thought, I have not survived a threat to my life. I have no child. What is my love story compared to yours?

He lays his hand on her shoulder. "Wake up, Signora," he says, gently. "You're late for work."

"*O Dio,*" she says. She straightens her back and looks nervously around.

"Don't worry," says Julian, smiling. "Nobody saw." He crouches in the aisle as a little boy runs past. "You remember our little joke, I hope."

"Of course," she says.

Most of the color has returned to her face, and she has gained weight. "How are you feeling tonight?"

"No pain, thanks to God," she says. "Just—I'm so tired. The headaches don't let me sleep."

"Why don't you go home?"

She glances at Antonio. "Respect," she says. "Mamma and Ida left two hours ago, but since six o'clock we've been here. I haven't seen Prima since this morning." Her eyes brighten. "You wouldn't recognize her, Julian—what a little *cicciotta* she is."

Four months after her birth, Prima remains in the care of the nurses at Wilmington Hospital. Maddalena visits her every morning, stays through midafternoon, and returns in the evening. For a few hours she is allowed to hold her baby, triple-wrapped in blankets to keep her warm, but then the nurses return her to her incubator or give her oxygen or some other treatment to strengthen her. In Prima's short life, she has undergone a blood transfusion and more injections than Maddalena can remember. She has gained weight, then lost it, then regained it again; her lungs have fully developed; she has battled and overcome infections, and bleeding in her brain. Still, the doctors want to wait before they release her. September 1, they say, is a possibility. Two weeks from tomorrow. "We'll throw a little party to welcome her," Maddalena says. "You'll come, yes?"

"How could I miss such a happy day?" says Julian.

When the family in front of Rosa's casket moves to one side, exposing her body for a moment, Maddalena turns sharply away. "I never look," she says, and grips her rosary. "I don't even get close. She can hear my prayers from here."

I miss you, Julian wants to say. Instead he folds his arms. "Helen tells me an Irish viewing is very different," he says. "But she won't go to one since her husband's. She doesn't believe in them."

Maddalena nods. She rarely asks about Helen, so he doesn't press. And yet he needs Maddalena to read her mind, to interpret the signs she's sending him and keep him from making mistakes. Julian does not even know what to call Helen, this woman who is certainly more than a friend, but not by much. All the many terms—sweetheart, baby, steady, dolly, *fidanzata, innamorata*—seem too young or too old, too serious or not serious enough.

Maddalena leans in and whispers, "What did you think of the invitations?"

"Invitations?"

"To come here."

"There were invitations?" Julian asks, loudly. The woman next to Maddalena shoots him a look.

From her purse, Maddalena pulls a small envelope addressed in slanted and shaky handwriting to La Famiglia Grasso, 2121 W. 8th Street, Wilmington, Del. Inside is a card made of thick ivory paper, the kind used in wedding invitations. Printed at the top of the card in fancy script is Rosa's name and date of birth, followed by the inked-in date of her death. Below that:

See Rosa One Last Time
___th _____, 19_____
6–8 p.m.
Pavani Funeral Home
Bayard and Lancaster Avenue
Rosa and Francesco are Reunited!
Time to Celebrate!
__th _____, 19_____
_____ a.m.
St. Anthony of Padua Church
901 N. DuPont Street
Wilmington, Delaware
Reception Immediately Following
Trattoria Renato
3 Riverview Drive
New Castle, Delaware
Be Happy and Love Life
"For You Know Neither the Day nor the Hour" (Matthew 25:13)

"You didn't ask yourself, 'Who are all these people?'" Maddalena says. "She must have sent these to the whole city. Not just Italians, either."

"But not to me."

She thinks for a moment. "Must be a mistake," she says, and shrugs. "Or it got lost in the mail. Or she just forgot. You always forget the people right in front of you."

Julian turns over the envelope. "I've never seen anything like it," he says. "So these people are mostly strangers?"

"I think so. They probably still wonder how they knew her."

"When my time comes," Julian says, "I hope I'm as ready as she was."

The woman next to Maddalena stirs. "Whatever's next," she says, "it can't be worse than here." She clutches her purse to her chest and stares straight ahead.

"I'll never be ready," says Maddalena, turning away from the woman. "Not anymore. There's too much I want to see." She leans in toward Julian, and for a moment he feels as though they are alone again in his kitchen, and the snow is falling, and she is about to confide in him. Instead she says, "You can't bring a baby into this world and not want to live a hundred years."

"Just you wait," says the old woman. She puts her hand on Maddalena's knee and laughs.

By ten o'clock, the crowd has thinned, and Dante Pavani stands beside a slouching Renato at the front door. "See you to-morrow," people say, on the way out. Julian, Maddalena, and Antonio leave together. They walk briskly so that Antonio can get home and drive Maddalena to the hospital. She will sleep there tonight, she says, on the chair in the hallway outside the glassed-in room, to make up for the four hours wasted at Rosa Volpe's viewing. She will wake early, attend the funeral, but skip the interment and the lunch. She refuses to celebrate anyone's death, even Rosa's, while her child fights for life. Antonio does not argue.

They stop to part at Eighth and Bancroft. "We'll see you at

the party," Maddalena says, as she kisses his cheek. "Mamma loves to cook for you."

"Leave him alone," Antonio says. He winks at Julian. "Don't you know he's a busy man these days? What's he want with our parties?"

They turn down Eighth. Watching them, Julian finally remembers to say, "I'm praying for little Prima!" but they are already a half block off, rushing arm in arm toward the car.

IN THE THREE months since Julian's first date with Helen, they have seen two movies, shopped for produce on Union, and drunk wine many evenings with her family in the living room of their home on Franklin Street. He has sat beside her on the piano bench as she played, though he has yet to sing along. Her son, Michael, still eyes him coolly, but this Julian understands. He has better luck with Abigail, who calls him Mister Fabbri and shows him her schoolwork. They play checkers, and she giggles when he says, "Go ahead and king me" in an Irish brogue.

On Helen's front steps, she switches off the porch lights and kisses him, briefly, before sending him on his way. She waits on the porch, in the dark, until he turns the corner. This happens at the end of every trip to Franklin Street, and is worth every awkward silence, every suspicious question from Helen's mother, Barbara.

All through Rosa's viewing and funeral and the party that followed, Julian worried what he would serve Helen the following Saturday—the first time she was to come to his house. He had sent her a card through the mail to invite her for "drinks and dessert," which he thought was a gentlemanly way to suggest that he could not cook for her. But should he buy a cake? Fine chocolates? How would he fill the hours afterward? What should he wear, now that she'd already seen all his good clothes? He made a special trip to Wanamaker's to buy a new white dress shirt, but not until he got home did he realize it was identical to the one he already owned.

He spent two days sweeping the floors of his house and wiping surfaces with a damp cloth. The more he cleaned, the more he found to clean. He emptied and restocked the refrigerator, mopped behind the stove, and rid the windows of streaks. He brushed the inside of the toilet. He fluffed the pillows on the couch and shook dust from the drapes. And yet when he stood back to admire it all in the light, he saw only dinginess and grime.

Now Saturday night has finally come, and Julian has nothing left to clean. He has not eaten in twenty-four hours. One plate of Three Little Bakers cookies waits on the kitchen table, another on the coffee table, but he does not want to disturb the careful arrangement. On a tray, beside two clean glasses, breathes a bottle of Chianti. Though he'd prefer a chilled white wine on this muggy night, he defers to Helen; white wine makes her sneeze. The espresso is already packed in the percolator, which sits on the burner. For music, he chooses Sinatra. Helen has never said she likes Sinatra, but Julian can't imagine how anyone could not.

At ten past eight, the lights of her brother-in-law's police car appear in the front window, silently swirling. He opens the door to find Helen walking toward him. She wears a simple green dress that shows her figure, her music-note pin, and her hair up, the way he likes it, though he has never told her. In high heels, she is as tall as Julian, but tonight she does not wear high heels. She has worn them only once, in fact—the first night on her porch, when she slipped them off to kiss him.

Inside, she drinks her wine quickly, and it occurs to Julian for the first time that she, too, might be nervous. "Let me guess," she says, as he leads her on a tour of the house. "Brown was your mother's favorite color."

"She used to say it hides the dirt," says Julian. "But she was always cleaning, so I don't know what dirt there was to hide."

"You kept up the tradition," she says, and rubs her finger along one of the bookshelves.

In the living room, she holds his family photograph in her hand and says, "You can see it in their faces, what proud people they were," and sets it back gently on the coffee table. "You must miss them very much." She lingers in front of the poster of Manhattan, pointing out buildings, and talks wistfully of what it might be like to live in a big city. Unlike Julian, she has been to a Broadway show and even glimpsed one of the actors afterward, buying a newspaper like a regular person.

At the closed door to his bedroom, which he has not bothered to tidy up, Julian stops and turns around. "Well, that's it," he says. He opens his arms. "You've seen King Julian's palace."

They sit side by side on the couch, drinking more wine than usual. Before too long, the bottle is nearly empty, and neither of them wants to be the one to finish it. The windows are open, but there is no breeze—only the flash of passing cars, the sputter of engines, and occasional footsteps on the sidewalk. Julian is grateful for the beginning of every new Sinatra song, as it gives him and Helen something to talk about: whether or not they like this particular one, and why. If Julian talks slowly, he can stretch the conversation for half the length of the song. It is never like this at her house, or at the movies; only here.

The end of side B comes, and in the long, scratchy silence Helen says, "Tom told me not to tell you this, but—" She looks down. "Last night? They found that little colored boy, the one who was missing. But you can't tell anyone I told you, because Tom could get in trouble—"

"Abraham?"

"Was that his name?"

"The boy across the street, yes. Abraham Waters. That's who they found?"

"I think that's the name."

"Is he alive?"

She shakes her head. "The boy they found, no. Tom said he's been dead for a month, at least."

Julian stands, but he has nowhere to go. He walks to the front window. "Where?" he asks. He parts the drapes. "When?"

There are no lights on in the Waters house. He hasn't seen the father or the taxi in a while—weeks, maybe—but the truth is that he hasn't been paying much attention. His mind has been on Helen and Maddalena and Rosa Volpe. He doesn't remember the last dream he had of the boy. He has mentioned him to Helen only once, in passing, as if his disappearance meant little to him. He wasn't sure of her stand, if any, on the Negro question, and was afraid to be on the wrong side of it.

They found him lying in the woods near the Brandywine River, Helen says. The police were looking for someone else and came upon his body by mistake. The smell had led them. Tom wouldn't say what he'd died from, only that it was not an accident. Until Tom pointed out the house when he dropped her off, Helen didn't realize that not only was there a colored family across the street from Julian, but that it was the same family who was missing their son.

"Does he know, his father?" Julian asks.

"I'm not sure," says Helen. "But I would think so, by now."

"What could they want from a little boy like that?" Julian says. He folds his hands across his chest, to steady himself. "Money? He doesn't have any money. He was good in school, the father told me. He liked music. Never got out of line. Never hurt anybody."

"You talked to them?"

"Sometimes," Julian admits.

Helen is quiet for a moment. "That surprises me," she says. "But it shouldn't, from what I know of you."

"The father gave up on him too soon."

"What do parents know anymore?" Helen says. "Even the teenagers have secret lives nowadays. When I was a girl, I never left the house without my mother. I'm sure it was the same for you. But we're a different generation. By the time Abigail's grown up—it's too scary to imagine."

"I read the paper every day," Julian says, his eyes on the dark windows, the empty driveway across the street. The world turns on cruelty, he might tell her. Not love. Not generosity. There are only two kinds of people left on earth—those whom grief has touched, and those it is coming for. If he could lift the roofs of the houses in his sight, of all the houses in Wilmington, and catch the people unaware, he'd see the desperate faces they try so hard to conceal. Instead Julian says, "I've read a thousand books, probably. But I don't understand one bit how the world works. Sometimes I think I was never meant to live in it."

The needle skips at the end of the record again and again, like a heartbeat. Helen lifts it, blows the dust off the tip, and replaces it on the holder. She comes up behind Julian. She puts her hand on his elbow, her arm around his waist. She pulls him toward her and rests her head on his shoulder.

"You're better than most people," she says. She kisses his neck. Her breath is warm and wine-sweet. "That's what you don't understand."

18

The Other Brother

MARIO WALKS UP and down Eighth Street, a bottle under his arm, talking to himself. Antonio watches from his bedroom window. He ducks behind the drapes each time his brother passes. It is eight-thirty at night, much too early for him to be home from the restaurant, and Antonio wonders if this means that the day and the hour have finally come for Mrs. Stella's. The news may surprise the customers, but not anyone who has heard the neighborhood gossip the past few months.

On the last day of September, Gino Stella drained the restaurant bank account and disappeared from Wilmington. With him went a year's worth of profits, and any hope of Mario retrieving his share. The same day Gino skipped town, someone robbed his mother's house on Sixth Street and tied the old woman to her bedpost. She hasn't spoken since and refuses to give any hint of what might have happened to her son.

After learning of all this, Mario visited Roberto Fante, who would soon expect the latest installment of protection money. Roberto said that he had nothing to do with Gino's debts. "Every minute Gino Stella's not at his restaurant," Roberto told him, "he's at the racetrack or some all-night poker game. They see him coming a mile away. *Che peccato*, what a shame, to see a hardworking man throw away his money." He put his hand on Mario's shoulder. "Tell you what: you're a nice boy. I'll give you one free month. By then, you'll figure something out."

When the regulars asked why they hadn't seen Gino or the adorable Mamma Stella in a while, Mario told them there'd been a death in their family, and they'd both gone back to the Old Country for the funeral. If Gino ever did reappear, Mario had a stack of condolence cards waiting for him.

"Something happened," Antonio says to Maddalena now. She sits in the rocking chair on the other side of the room, cradling Prima.

"You should go down there," she says.

"If Mario's in trouble," Antonio says, "he'll come to me." He moves away from the window and changes into his pajamas. He pulls the quilt up his neck and settles in for whatever rest he can get. For now, at least, his days of wandering the neighborhood are over. Sleep—not a card game at the pizzeria, not girls like Cassie Donovan—is the adventure that's now missing from his life. His daughter wakes up five times a night, every night, and though Maddalena always takes her immediately downstairs, Antonio can still hear her. Instead of cursing the girl, though, he lies alone on his side of the bed and thinks, Forgive me, Maddalena, but every time Prima wakes, I thank God; I say, don't let her stop crying. It means she's still alive.

Just after Antonio switches off the lamp, there is a knock on the door.

"*É Mario,*" he says. "*Scusa il disturbo.*"

"Come in," Antonio says, and there is his brother: red-faced, coat half-buttoned, shirt untucked, holding a full bottle of *sambuca.*

"We can talk?" he asks. He holds up the bottle. "Mamma's making espresso."

"I'm in bed," Antonio says.

"Did something happen?" Maddalena asks.

"Yes," Mario says. He steps inside. "Something good."

They wait, but Mario offers no details. He looks back and forth at them, then says, "It's too complicated to explain in a few words."

"Then it can't be that good," says Antonio, stepping into his slippers.

At the kitchen table, Mario tells Antonio what he already knows about Gino's disappearance. The way he sees it now, Mario says, he and Gino have pulled even. Without Gino's initial investment and contacts, Mrs. Stella's could never have opened. But in the past year, Mario has worked day and night for no salary other than a percentage of the profits. Even if he counted the money Gino stole, they had contributed roughly the same amount. They owe each other nothing, and, as far as Mario is concerned, he'd be happy never to see the man's face again, though he wishes him well. "God have mercy on his soul," he says, just in case, and crosses himself.

"Congratulations," Antonio says. "You're now the single owner. If I didn't know you so well, I'd think you sent those goons after Gino yourself." He laughs and sips his espresso, which is too weak and oversweetened.

Mario finds this very funny, too, and reminds Antonio how much he misses talking like this, just the two of them, bullshitting, with no women or kids to interrupt. If the Grasso brothers don't stick together, he says, they might as well rip out their father's heart with their bare hands. And what is the point of making money, of raising children, if they don't share everything with each other?

"How much closer can we get?" Antonio says. "Your wife sleeps ten feet from me."

Again Mario laughs very hard. He pours another espresso, but this time Antonio refuses the *sambuca*. He holds his hand over the cup and yawns.

"You're still waiting for the good news, aren't you?" Mario said. "You're thinking, did my brother really drag me out of bed to tell me he's the new Gino Stella?"

"Yes and no," said Antonio. He has his suspicions of what is coming next but would never suggest it on his own. He wants to hear it in Mario's own words.

"We have an opportunity," Mario begins, and tells him, with careful attention to his words, that he can't run the restaurant by himself, not if it means adding the books and Roberto Fante to the hundred things he's already responsible for. He has no stomach for it. The part-time cook, Settimio, knows only recipes, not business. And Papà—here Mario lowers his voice—Papà is too old for all the hours it will take. "And one other big thing," he says. He folds his hands on the table. "Money." He shrugs. "To keep it going, I need more money. To replace what Gino took, but also to—how can I say?—give it the Grasso stamp."

By the end of his speech, Mario has the disgraced Gino Stella on a ranch in Argentina and the young Grasso brothers rich co-owners—equal partners, of course—of the restaurant that will put Wilmington, Delaware, on the map. "Me and you, we'll be famous up and down the East Coast," he says, standing. He walks from one end of the kitchen to the other. "We'll be an Italian American institution robust for generations to come." In time, he says, they will break through the walls of the neighbors on Union Street, and gobble up the laundromats and bakeries and shoe repair shops like a hungry fish.

As Mario talks on, dreaming bigger every minute, the be-mused and skeptical expression on Antonio's face changes to one of apprehension. He knows that when his brother finally stops, takes a breath, and asks him in no uncertain terms to in-vest his savings and his future in the restaurant, he will have no good reason to say no. He has enough money in the bank and in the drapes, with some to spare. Soon Maddalena will go back to the Golden Hem, and bring home the extra income they've come to rely on for security. Their house in New Castle will have to wait a few years anyway, since they'll need Mamma to watch Prima during the day while Maddalena works, at least until she is old enough for school. The only reason for saying no that Antonio can give Mario—if he ever stops talking and asks his question—is that he is afraid. And at this moment, with the *sambuca* working its charms, and Mamma and Papà in their fi-nal years, and having lost a chance like this twice before with Renato, and, most of all, with his wife and daughter safe and healthy and rocking upstairs (he can hear the lovely creak of the chair through the ceiling, the murmur of Maddalena's shy lull-aby), it seems a great failure of heart to be afraid.

Mario folds his hands on the table. "So," he says. "*Fratello*. What do you think? Where would you rather be in twenty years? Taking orders from me or from that Hannagan?"

There is already so much pride to swallow. To give Mario an answer right away, to give him that much satisfaction, would make him unbearable. Years of negotiating begins now, Antonio thinks, with how he handles his brother's proposition. He cannot say what he really feels: that he is grateful, and terrified, and relieved, and that this all comes as close to perfect as he could have imagined. He cannot say he is proud of Mario for the chances he's taken over the years, for never giving up on all those Grasso businesses, and for the hard work at Mrs. Stella's that brought him to this table tonight.

"One thing," Antonio says. "The day you order me around is a day you'll regret."

"I can say the same to you."

"Except," Antonio says, and sits back in his chair. "Without me, there is no restaurant."

Mario smiles. "Again, I can say the same."

"A lot would have to change," says Antonio. "The name, first of all."

"You think I want Gino's name on our family restaurant?"

But this conversation is already too much too fast. Antonio appears too cooperative. So he stands, his heart pounding, his face as serious as a banker's. "I can't tell you anything for sure right now," he says. "Maybe not even until the weekend. But I will say this: it's not the worst idea you ever had."

"Of course," Mario says. "I wouldn't expect . . ." He looks like a teenager: his tie undone, his hair a mess, that eager smile. "Take your time," he says, and holds up his hands. "But do me a favor."

Antonio clears the coffee cups. He puts them in the sink and runs the water. "What?"

"Don't turn your back," Mario says. His leg is shaking. "Make your brother proud."

ANTONIO'S FIRST CALLING is to paint over the murals in the dining room of the old Mrs. Stella's. He chooses a glossy gold, dark enough to cover in two coats the cartoon renditions of gondoliers and pigeons that Gino loved so much. Across the far wall he and Mario hang a large, beveled mirror, bought wholesale, to hide the cracks in the plaster and open up the room. They fill the other cracks throughout the restaurant, shampoo the worn red carpet, and polish the wood floors in the bar area. In the corner where Giulio used to stand, they install a jukebox. Fifty songs are now at their fingertips, at five cents a song. With pleasure they dismantle the neon sign in the front window and throw it on a pile of trash. In its place they mount a charming green awning, made of quality canvas with scalloped edges. RISTORANTE AL DI LÀ it says, in white block lettering. Below that, in small script you can read only up close: MARIO AND ANTONIO GRASSO, PROPRIETORS.

When the day of the grand opening finally comes—December 31, 1954—Antonio slicks back his hair, puts on his best suit, and tucks into the vest pocket the speech he'll make in the minutes before midnight. He arrives at noon, six hours early, though he has no particular job to do, and is greeted with "Good afternoon, sir" by one of the waiters, an older man named Bruno whom he has known since he was a boy. Twice over the course of the day, the new cook asks Antonio to sample the sauce, and adds more salt when he declares it *sciapo*. As night falls, the candles are lit, and the guests begin to appear, Antonio looks over the reservation book again, though he can recite each name from memory. Thanks to the holdover customers from Mrs. Stella's, and the signs he put up in Angelo's Market, every table is reserved. And yet, despite all this respect shown to him, and the hard-earned savings he's sunk into the renovations and the operating costs, Antonio feels out of place.

Compared to his brother, he is an amateur. Antonio needs only to watch Mario for one minute to see that he is no longer the frantic baker of the long-bankrupt Pasticceria Grasso, with flour in his hair; or the fumbling waiter of Café Grasso, afraid to carry more than two plates at once. Gone is the arrogance he showed during his brief adventure at Mrs. Stella's. Look how gracefully he crosses the dining room, straightening silverware and tucking in chairs as he goes, winking at guests as if they're in on some delicious secret, motioning from a great distance to the bartender—in a sign language Antonio has yet to grasp—for a certain table to get a bottle of *spumante* on the house. It is beautiful, this choreography.

Meanwhile, Antonio stands uselessly at the front door, so befuddled by the taking of coats and the showing to seats and the hundred other simultaneous demands of the dinner hour that he's forced to cede the bulk of his maître d' responsibilities to Ida. Ida! Even his *mezza scema* sister-in-law can maintain a confident and professional air amid the chaos. She seems to know each new couple by name and welcomes them with a "Happy New Year," a bright smile for the gentleman and a different compliment for each lady. Antonio can barely speak to the people he knows—Gianni, the Fiumas, Angelo—let alone these strangers. Ida hands them all noisemakers, promises them the meal of a lifetime and a room of friendly faces. "Start 1955 at the Al Di Là," she says, "and you'll have luck the rest of the year."

What's wrong with him? the guests must be wondering, as

they pass Antonio on the way to their tables. Surely they ask each other, Why does he stand there, arms across his chest, mute as a mummy?

It occurs to Antonio that he has worked too long on the assembly line. He is too accustomed to a steady paycheck, the predictable turnover. Every time he has been laid off from a job, he has found one exactly like it in a matter of days. The inside of every automobile plant looks the same; he needs only to take his place, learn one or two relatively simple motions, and repeat them over and over until someone tells him to stop. He has no practice making his own decisions for a living.

Maddalena comes toward him. She wears one of her fancy dresses for the first time since the spring, when she used to put on her finest clothes just to walk the few blocks to Giulio Fabbri's house. After tonight, she will have a more exciting trip to make. It will be she, not Ida, who will greet the customers and take the coats on weekends. She, not Signora Stella, will walk among the tables and tell stories from the Old Country. If Antonio does want to show her off in this way, which of course he does, he will have to buy her some new clothes. Jewelry, too. Makeup and shoes. But now that Renato, betrayed by the very existence of the Al Di Là, no longer speaks to him, Antonio has no access to the Insurance Closet. The thought of paying department-store prices makes him wince.

"Did you eat?" Maddalena asks. She leans against the jukebox, her hands behind her back, swaying to "Sh-Boom." *Life could be a dream, sweetheart.* "The sauce has a good taste," she says. "The veal, too. Like night and day, from before."

"You think these people even noticed?"

"Americans," she whispers, with a smile. "As long as they keep coming, who cares? We know the difference."

"Gino had no respect for the tomato," Antonio says, and they laugh.

Maddalena puts her hand on his stomach. "You have to eat."

"I will," he says. "I'm nervous about talking in front of everybody."

"Don't worry," she says. "They'll be drunk pretty soon."

Antonio folds his arms across his chest. He can't calm down, not even talking to his wife. The guests continue to push through the doors, someone knocks over the ceramic pot of poinsettias, the kitchen runs out of basil, the bartender—Angelo Montale's son, Angelo Jr.—spills a bottle of red wine on the counter. How can Antonio eat, with all these unrelenting, unpredictable needs around him?

"I came to help Ida," Maddalena says.

"You're tired," Antonio says. "Let her do the work for once."

"I heard that," says Ida, who comes up behind him with an armful of heavy coats. She dumps them in Maddalena's arms. "If you're just going to stand here doing nothing, Antonio, you might as well go sit. You're making me nervous."

Maddalena laughs. "We ladies can take care of everything."

"Better yet," says Ida. "Go home and get some basil."

"Yes," says Maddalena. "The fresh air will do you good." She points him toward the door.

It is nine-thirty. The city is quiet and cold, the sky thick with stars. Everyone with a place to go tonight has already arrived. Only a few cars speed down Union Street, late for the best part of any New Year's Eve celebration: these tipsy hours of anticipation and promise, when it feels as though, at the stroke of twelve, your heart will finally lighten and your sins will be washed clean.

On the windowsill above the sink Antonio finds the basil plant, pale green and struggling to survive the winter. As instructed, he takes from the freezer a jar of chopped leaves the women have saved from the plant's happier days. He carries one on each arm, breathing in the sweet aroma, glad to be of some use.

When he gets to the corner of Eighth and Union, it is the first time he sees the Al Di Là at night, busy and open to the public. He stops for a moment, gazing from the far side of the street at the colored lights on the door wreath, the shadows moving across the windows. He sets the basil, which can wait, on the sidewalk. He has never known such joy. It is as fragile as the wineglasses his customers are now lifting to their lips. Make one slip, and the glass crashes to the floor. Can they guess that on this night, the last of a dangerous year, the man on the sidewalk in his black suit—shivering, biting his nails—has everything he wants? He has his family gathered inside, at the round table under the mirror: his wife, their baby daughter in her arms; his mother and father; his nieces. And yet there is no telling what punishments God is devising. How can he relax? How can any man?

He thinks of his speech. He's practiced it over and over—the assurance that the cook uses the freshest ingredients and prepares all the food in the authentic Italian way, the pledge to expand the dining room and maybe even install a dance floor by the summer, the wish that 1955 brings peace to the world—but now the words seem all wrong. He considers tearing it up and starting over, but he's run out of time.

Inside, all of the guests are seated, including Maddalena and Ida. Mario leans against a booth talking to Giulio and Helen. Antonio manages to eat a chunk of bread with some salt and olive oil, but he's not sure his stomach can handle much more. Angelo Jr. hands him a glass of wine, and for a while he sits at the table beside his mother. When Prima wakes, Maddalena hands her to him. He holds her for a few minutes before she starts to cry.

"They don't love their fathers until they're five," says Ida.

Antonio watches the customers put on their party hats, twirl their noisemakers, and ready their bags of confetti. The jukebox plays "Secret Love" and "Young at Heart," and a couple he doesn't recognize slow-dances in the back corner, by the kitchen door. In time the room grows louder, a string of garland is pulled from the wall and wrapped around a woman's head, and before long most of the guests are on their feet and milling about. The waiters start to hand out the fluted glasses, and moments later reappear to fill them with *spumante*. Mario keeps close watch on it all, and makes sure the tables are cleared of empty plates and used silverware. At 11:40, he nudges Antonio. "You ready, or do you want me to do it?" he says.

"You."

Maddalena overhears. "But you practiced," she says. "Don't let it go to waste."

"Mario's good at speeches," Ida says. "He's done them before."

Papà shakes his head. "These people need to see both brothers," he says. "There are two names on that sign."

"I'm not a speaker," Antonio says, but he cannot ignore his father's advice, and Mario has already grabbed his wrist. He leads him to the other side of the room, pulls out two empty chairs, stands on one, and helps Antonio up onto the other.

"Attenzione!" says Mario, in his booming voice, and the room immediately falls to a hush. "It's almost time, and I want to welcome you to the best New Year's Eve party in Wilmington, and the grand opening of the best Italian restaurant in the United

States of America!" Everyone claps, and Mario takes an exaggerated bow. "Did you enjoy the food?" he asks.

"Yes!" they yell back.

"Tremendous!" he says. "You can stay a little longer, then. Just be sure to tell your friends and neighbors who fed you so good tonight."

They love him, Antonio thinks. Look how they laugh and take each other's hands, hanging on his words.

"For the big moment," Mario continues, "you each should have a glass of *spumante* on your table. It's free, so drink it. If you want another, you have to buy it yourself." He shrugs apologetically. "Now. I'm Mario Grasso. All of you know me, one way or the other, but until tonight maybe you never met my brother, Antonio. He's the older one, the tall and handsome one—" He holds out his hands, to stop the chorus of boos. "It's true; I'm not blind. I'm happy to be young and intelligent. But what I want to say is, without this man, there would be no Al Di Là restaurant. My heart would be in pieces on the floor. And worse than that, we'd all have to eat at Trattoria Renato tonight, where I hear the roaches do the cooking."

Everyone laughs. A waiter rushes over and hands Antonio and Mario two full glasses.

"Many people asked me the past month, 'Why don't you call this place Ristorante Grasso, if you're so proud of it?' And I can say, too, this is because of my brother. If it were up to me only, Grasso would have been in the name for sure. But Antonio reminded me of something. Back in Santa Cecilia, in the Old Country, the only restaurant in our entire village was called the Al Di Là Café, and he said, 'Mario, maybe the way to change the luck of the Grasso name is to honor the place we came from.' So that's what we did."

There is applause, and Mario takes another bow. Then, "I've already talked too long," he says. He turns to his brother. "*Fratello*, you want to say Happy New Year to these people who are paying our bills?"

"Eight minutes to go," someone calls out.

Antonio holds one hand against the wall to keep his balance. Though he has only drunk one glass of wine, he feels dizzy, and the sea of eager faces does not help. Mamma has her hand over her heart, as if to keep it from bursting. Beside her, Papà smokes a cigarette, which he does only when he's nervous. In the back corner, Signora Fiuma takes the glass from her husband, who has already begun to drink it. Ida's brother hoists his curly-haired daughter on his shoulders, and, behind him, Giulio Fabbri has one arm around his Irish girlfriend, the other around her daughter. Maddalena, more anxious than Antonio, hides behind Ida. Whoever is not in this room tonight—Renato, Cassie, Buzzy, Mr. Hannagan, Gino Stella—might as well not exist. Lock them in a closet, Antonio thinks, and forget you ever knew them.

"I don't know what to say," he begins, as he takes out the prepared speech from his pocket. The crowd laughs, and the laughter immediately relaxes him, though he did not mean this as a joke. "I did have these words written down, yes, but—" He glances at the paper, then stuffs it back in his pocket. "They're not so great. I'm not the speaker my brother is. I just want to thank every one of you for coming here. And one thing especially. I was outside a few hours ago, and I was looking at this place from the street, with all of you inside. And I was thinking, how did you get so lucky, Antonio Grasso? You come from a nowhere village. You didn't have much school. All your life you wanted two things. You wanted to open a restaurant for your father, to honor him. And you wanted your beautiful wife, Maddalena, to have a baby. Now look, here are the two things, right in front of your face. If you work twenty-four hours a day for the next hundred years, still you won't deserve this luck."

People point and wave at the Grasso table. Papà waves back, lifts his glass. But Maddalena, still half-hidden, covers her face. Ida pulls her to her side. If Antonio were braver, or more drunk, he'd tell the crowd the full story: how God had tried to take her, and that, if He'd succeeded, there would be no joy left in the world—no reason to eat or drink or welcome any new year. No reason to put hope in a restaurant, or any future at all. But he has already said too much, and, in these heady moments before the great promise of midnight, no one wants to hear a sad story, no matter how happy the ending.

"11:57!" Angelo calls from the bar. He turns up the radio, and they can hear the distant voice of an announcer through the roar of the Times Square crowd.

Ida grabs Maddalena's hand and leads her toward the front of the room. Maddalena stops, and goes back for the baby. They stand in front of Antonio and Mario, who remain atop the chairs. Nunzia and Nina appear and grab their father around the knees. The crowd rushes back and forth across the room, talking over each other, calling out names, clamoring to find their husbands and wives, reaching for drinks, stuffing bread and pizza and olives in their mouths, finishing off their wine. Mario raises his arms and waves them around like a conductor. "To me, this is the most beautiful music in the world," he says to Antonio.

"Fifty-eight!"

Antonio rests his hand on Maddalena's shoulder and, carefully, bends to kiss her. Now that he's made his speech, his hunger returns. Soon he will sit at the table like a king and have the waiters bring him a feast. "I didn't embarrass you, did I?" he asks.

Maddalena shakes her head. She wears the new perfume he gave her for Christmas, her first gift paid for with his own money. If he could, he'd buy her ten new dresses, walk her through Wanamaker's without looking at the price tags. He'd drive her to New York City and spend the night in a hotel. Someday, someday.

"Fifty-nine!"

"You covered your face," Antonio says. "I thought—I'm sorry to call so much attention."

"I wasn't embarrassed," says Maddalena. She looks at him. There is lipstick on her teeth, and she's missing an earring. "I was just crying a little."

Behind her, the throwing of confetti. A group of old ladies forms a circle, as if for a tarantella. They lift their arms above their heads, march around a table, and start counting down from ten.

"I was proud of you," Maddalena says.

19

Salta!

On Sundays in the summer, the Al Di Là is closed and the family drives to Wildwood. Soon they won't all be able to fit into the Chevy, but for now they make it work: the men and little Nunzia in the front seat; Maddalena, Prima, Ida, and Nina in the back. When Antonio or Mario can't get away—because, even on its day off, the restaurant is needier and more starved for attention than a baby—Julian comes along. On the days everyone can make it, Julian follows in Helen's brother's car, and Maddalena spends most of the trip checking the rearview mirror, thinking how strange it looks for a woman to be driving a man around. Mamma Nunzia always stays home, unwilling to miss church to make the early start to the Jersey shore. She uses the day to cook the tomato sauce for the week, change the linens and tend the garden. If she feels up to it, she will take a few minutes to sit on the porch with Signora Fiuma.

This summer, 1956, is the first without Papà Franco. One night last fall, at dinner, he suddenly turned his bowl of wedding soup into his lap and slumped in his chair. His lower lip drooped to one side. His eyes stayed open and his heart was beating, but he did not move. The ambulance took him to St. Francis Hospital, where he lay pale and unresponsive. Though the doctor offered little hope he would survive the stroke, no one believed him. They had seen what happened to Maddalena. They had faith. Over four nights at St. Francis, they brought his favorite dishes for when he woke: polenta with butter and sausage, fried eggplant, lasagna with extra hard-boiled eggs. The covered dishes sat untouched on the windowsill. On the fifth night, he was gone.

Papà Franco had loved the beach. The summer before, he hadn't missed a single one of these Sunday trips. Nunzia would ride on his lap, and he'd point out buildings as they crossed the Delaware Memorial Bridge. "I helped build that," he'd say. "In 1932, when I first came over." Or, "An Italian owns that tall one; can you believe it?" He never went in the water—the motion of the waves upset his stomach, and he couldn't swim—but he liked to sit on a bench on the boardwalk and watch the girls. He'd smile at the pretty ones, ask their names, and tell them he was the famous Italian singer Ezio Pinza. When the wind kicked up, he'd take out a comb and run it through his thick white hair. "Who needs money, with a free show like this?" he'd say to his sons, when they came to get him at the end of the day. "God knew what he was doing."

The beach is crowded today, the first Sunday after the Fourth of July. Wildwood seems to grow more popular each week, mostly with teenagers, and Maddalena wonders if they should try the Delaware beaches sometime. Or they could try

Atlantic City again, though in recent years its beauty has faded, and the once-thrilling horses diving at the Steel Pier now just make her sad. Maddalena does not enjoy crowds now that she can no longer fit into a regular bathing suit. She is forced to wear this polka-dot tent, with its high waist and long, flowing pleats, to cover her enormous middle.

Ida wears a suit that matches Maddalena's, though she is two months further along. She spreads an old white sheet on the sand, and Mario weighs it down with shoes and a cooler. He takes out six wineglasses from the pillowcases in which they've been wrapped for the journey and starts pouring. He waves hello to an older couple whom they have seen here many times before. Maddalena arranges her and Antonio's sheet beside Mario and Ida's, so that they are between Helen and Julian.

Giulio, Maddalena keeps forgetting to say. She will never get used to it. Helen has convinced him to change his name back to the one his parents chose, as if that will help soothe his heart. If Helen marries him, Maddalena thinks, then maybe she will have the right to suggest such a thing. Though Helen hasn't admitted it out loud, she's one of those women who believes her opinion matters as much as any man's, and that she's as aware as Julian of the state of the world. When the beach conversations turn to politics or integration or an article in the Sunday newspaper, she's the first to make a judgment. And Julian, who once argued with Antonio over the smallest point, never disagrees with her. Maddalena has seen him glance at Helen before taking a stand on an issue and, when she disapproved, immediately take it back. Look at him now: "You're right, darling," he says, about the ending of *The Searchers*, which they saw last weekend at the Queen. "I didn't think of it that way." All Maddalena can do is shake her head.

I miss you, she wants to tell him. I've always had a husband, but you were my first friend in this country. She wants to ask him about this beach: how it got its name, how many miles it stretches, the history of New Jersey compared to Delaware and Pennsylvania. She wants to show him the list of Prima's first words, which she keeps in the top drawer of her nightstand. But he must think her silly now, her and her questions. So instead she says, "John Wayne must be a millionaire, all those movies he makes."

For lunch they pass around fresh bread from Lamberti's— the exclusive baker for the Al Di Là—mortadella and pro- sciutto from Angelo's, and a large chunk of *parmigiano*. For dessert there are peaches and watermelon, and a dried-out cake from Helen that is some sort of Irish specialty. They dunk the peaches in the wine, the cake in a thermos of American coffee.

The outdoors, the beach especially, works magic on Prima. If only Maddalena had discovered this earlier in the child's life, she might have spared herself and Antonio many sleepless nights. But she'd discovered it only last year, just after Prima's first birthday, when she'd nursed her on the porch on the first humid evening of the summer. Indoors, Prima always had trou- ble feeding, but the moment Maddalena stepped into the fresh air of the porch, she'd relaxed. Quickly Maddalena learned that, when the baby woke in the middle of the night, only a walk outside under the grape arbor, or up and down the sidewalk, could calm her. On the beach last summer, Prima never cried when the wind whipped sand at her face; she simply shut her eyes and waited while Maddalena wiped the little granules from her cheek. Now that she has learned to walk, she is fearless. If Maddalena does not watch her at every moment, she will chase a seagull or another child or nothing at all into the waves.

This kind of work—the protection of Prima, the changing and washing of her diapers, the rubbing of cream on her rashes—has come as easily to Maddalena as sewing or greeting guests at the Al Di Là. Those other jobs, though, do not fill her. Only Prima fills her. She can get both of her little hands in her mouth at once and nibble them until Prima laughs so hard the tears come. Her fingers are plump and soft, her nails like perfect seashells. How could Maddalena have thought she had any purpose on earth other than to mother this girl and the children who will come after her? Let the men make the money, she thinks. Let the abandoned Russian girls model dresses in Philadelphia. When Maddalena leaves the Golden Hem each night, she does not miss the angry thrum of the sewing machines, or the musty air, or the ache in her fingers. What's to long for in Mr. Gold's barking, his frequent competitions, or even the bus ride she once loved, when she has this little miracle to feast on at home?

Antonio swims out far, too far for Maddalena's comfort. She tries not to panic when she loses sight of him. He teases her by staying underwater for many minutes, swimming off, then reappearing on the opposite side of the rocks that divide the two ends of this stretch of beach. When he reaches the other side, he jumps out of the water, calls her name, and opens his arms for her to join him. Maddalena shakes her head. Like Papà Franco, she has never liked the ocean. She stays on the edge of the surf, cooling her toes, letting Prima pull her along.

Antonio walks carefully toward her over the carpet of broken shells in the sandbar. No matter how many times she has seen him in his blue bikini, or less, she still has to turn away when his body presents itself. She cannot look directly at it— the hair on his upper chest, his long muscular arms, the bulge between his legs that gives everything away—and risk the thrill that pulses through her. Someone will see it on her face. Since Prima, her husband's beauty has had this effect. Since Prima, she has noticed that, at thirty-five, Antonio can pass for any of these American boys around her, wrestling and hoisting one another onto their shoulders. Only the slight recession in the hair above his forehead, and, if you look close, the delicate crease in the skin between his eyebrows, suggests he might not be twenty years old.

She hands him his towel and stares at the ground as he bends to dry his legs first, then his stomach, chest, arms, and finally his face and hair. "How's my angel?" he says, and lifts Prima high in the air. He holds her before him, spins her around, and nuzzles his face in hers. "Never says boo, this one," he says, handing her back. He glances over at Nunzia and Nina, who rarely let anyone but Ida or Mario touch them. "Her cousins could take a lesson."

"We got lucky," Maddalena says. "For now. We'll see in a few years."

"Does she need a change?" Antonio asks. He holds onto the ends of his towel, which is draped around his neck. "After you do it, I can take her up to the little pool."

"She's fine," says Maddalena. "You should relax. It's your day off." She smiles at him. "Go have some wine before Helen finishes the bottle."

He wraps one arm around her waist and lays a hand on her stomach. "You're OK in this sun?" he says. "You don't feel dizzy?"

"No."

"You ate enough?"

"As much as I could," she says.

"Good." He pulls her closer, squeezing Prima between them, though she makes no fuss.

"You can't worry all the time," she says. "Dr. Barone says there's a good chance—"

"Dr. Barone," he says, and shakes his head. "Because he's right so much—with Papà, with you the first time. I can't listen to doctors anymore. They make everything up as they go along." This is how he gets whenever there is talk of the new baby: his face flushed, his eyes wide. There is no reassuring him. "I won't stop worrying for one second," he says. "Not until it's over. Not even then."

"I'm not worried," Maddalena says. She has told this to Antonio many times, since the day they learned she was to have another child, but it is not quite the truth. She senses danger every time the child moves inside her. At any moment she expects the slash of pain, the fall to her knees, the long darkness. For comfort, she turns to Fortunata, the woman in *Il Sogno della Principessa*, which she has finally finished. Fortunata always believes that God will protect her, even at the end of the book, when she learns she is not a princess after all. Fortunata comes from poor, ordinary parents, but she doesn't seem to mind. She doesn't need money, or the castle, or the jeweled robes so cruelly stripped from her by the barbaric guards. She has her young son, and the memory of the slain prince who loved her, and God's hand in hers as she makes her way alone and barefoot into the thick woods. Maddalena has recounted this story to Mamma Nunzia, who believes in this same sort of God, even in her grief. If she told anyone else, Antonio especially, that this story soothed her, he would think her silly. Ida would give her a blank stare. Helen would laugh. Only Julian, if she could reach him, might understand.

Antonio releases her, gives Prima's cheeks a gentle pinch, then walks over to his family. He can sit still for maybe ten minutes, and then he will need to walk the boardwalk or find a group of young men with whom to kick around a soccer ball. Used to be, when they took trips to Atlantic City, he'd beg her to play in the waves with him. The one time she agreed, he tickled her thighs underwater and squeezed her behind and put his hand between her legs. She felt no desire for him then. Afraid and embarrassed, she ran out of the water in tears.

Now she walks up and down the length of the beach, smiling politely at the people waving and making funny faces at Prima. She tries to eavesdrop on conversations and pick up new words. Her English is better than it was when she first started at the Golden Hem, but after her weeks in the hospital she forgot much of what she learned. She has made no new friends and speaks mainly to Ida in Italian. At the Al Di Là, her job is to play the part of the young immigrant from the village, to hide the American in her. Sometimes the customers ask her just to talk, say whatever comes to mind in her native language, and she stands there at the table telling stories about Santa Cecilia, though they don't understand a word.

"You are so *vain*," a woman says to her friend, as Maddalena passes. It does not sound like a compliment. "What a *travesty*," says a man, his face blocked by the *Philadelphia Inquirer*, and shakes his bald head. She used to know that word, *Inquirer*. *Philadelphia* is hard enough, with its strange *phs*. She will never get used to how it looks, no matter how many times she has taken the bus into the city. What do Americans have against the *f*? In Italian, every letter sounds the same wherever you put it.

She stops to watch two couples standing on the edge of the rocks. The women seem to be in their late twenties, the men quite a bit older. They are having some sort of argument. Maddalena walks up the sandbar. The men speak clear English, but the women have an accent. They wear tight one-piece bathing suits with frilly skirts that don't cover their knees. They fold their arms across their chests, shivering.

"*Salta!*" says one of the men, and claps his girlfriend on the back. "*Salta!*" he repeats. Then, to make sure: "Jump, right? *Salta* is jump?"

"*Sì!*" says the girlfriend. "*Ma abbiamo paura!* We are afraid!"

Italians. Maddalena smiles, looks closer. There is something familiar about the women. She has seen their faces before. On the bus? In a photograph? Though plain, the women are pretty enough to be actresses. Maybe they have escaped New York City for the weekend to join their boyfriends here.

Suddenly one of the men—the bigger one, who has a tattoo on his forearm—grabs his girlfriend from behind and lifts her up by the waist. The rocks look slippery, and, out of instinct, Maddalena grips Prima's hand more tightly. The woman kicks her arms and laughs as the man carries her toward the edge.

"No!" she screams, and now many heads on the beach turn to watch them.

"In you go!" the man says, and tosses her into the water.

Before her boyfriend can do the same, the other woman leaps off the edge. Midair, she calls out "Silvia!" and immediately Maddalena realizes who they are. Silvia and Sandra Leone. Vito's sisters, who moved to Philadelphia twenty years ago. They resemble him: the shape of their heads, their skinny arms and legs. One of their faces is Vito's; the other takes after their mother. Though they could not possibly recognize Maddalena, she turns and rushes from the sandbar, pulling Prima along. She stops to look back only once, to watch them splash in the water, happy, it seems, with their American men. She wishes she could go up to them. "We come from the same village," she would say, and, lowering her head, tell them her name. They'd wrap their arms around her, marveling at their great luck in finding a sister in America. They'd insist that she visit them some Sunday on Market Street. They'd ask questions about her family, and then, all at once, their faces would go dark. They'd remember the story of their brother's first engagement, that it was Maddalena who'd traded his heart for a trip across the ocean, and the happy reunion would end.

"How long until we go?" Maddalena says, when she finds her family among the patchwork of blankets.

"I'm ready now," says Mario.

"What's wrong?" Antonio asks Maddalena. "You don't look right."

"I'm just tired all of a sudden," she says.

"We're going to stay a bit longer," Julian says, his eyes on Helen. "Right?"

The hours have gone by quickly. It is pleasant to get away from the city for a while, and Maddalena is always disappointed, even today, when it is time to pack their things. Still, she enjoys the ride home through the New Jersey woods, those miles thick with tall pines and the smell of campfires. The girls will fall asleep across her lap, and allow the grown-ups to discuss why Julian still hasn't proposed to Helen, and speculate that it is because he is waiting for Helen to propose to him. Mamma Nunzia will have Sunday dinner waiting for them when they get home, and at seven o'clock they will all gather in the living room to hear the Italian radio program.

As they walk to the car, Antonio starts in on their usual game. "All the way down there," he says to Maddalena, pointing toward the dunes. "With the sunflowers in the front. That's the one we'll buy."

"The porch is too small," Maddalena says. "Look further down—the gray one with the veranda."

"You know I don't like gray," says Antonio. "It's depressing."

Since he opened the Al Di Là, her husband has become a talker. Not only at the beach, but everywhere: in the morning before he leaves for work, in bed when she is trying to sleep. He walks her back to Eighth Street on Saturday nights, after the dinner rush ends and he no longer needs her to charm the customers. They take the long way home, stopping every few blocks to lean against the streetlamps and gossip about the regulars and the cooks and Bruno the waiter. He tells her his vision of their future, and the light around him changes. A house in Wildwood, a Cadillac, a grandfather clock, Catholic school for the children—they will have all this and more, he says, and Maddalena has come to believe him.

On the boardwalk, he stops before Papà Franco's old bench. He stands Prima on top of it and asks if she remembers him. Of course she does not. She can only squirm and clap and point at the teenagers hopping barefoot on the hot planks. Still, Antonio tells her about her *nonno*, how he loved this beach, this view. "Be good to me," Antonio says to the passing teenagers, his arms outstretched, in a perfect impersonation of his father's voice. "I might not be here next Sunday." Then he scoops his daughter back into his arms, lifts her over a scatter of broken glass, and sets her down in the shade on the other side.

Soon Prima will be a little lady, and Maddalena will have her to turn to and talk with, like a friend. They will speak English to each other in public, Italian at home or when they don't want the Americans to understand. They will have many secrets, precious as rubies. She will help her keep watch over the second child, who, if God chooses, will be the first Grasso son born in the new country.

Rarely does Maddalena allow herself the pleasure of such a thought. A son! But today, with so many ghosts hovering on the beach, she seeks the comfort of the possibility. He will be named Franco, unless Mario and Ida beat them to it; otherwise, they will call him Antonio. Totò for short. The pride of his father, who will teach him to run a restaurant and play *scopa* and drive a convertible. Life will be easy for him, Maddalena thinks, for all the Grasso children. They will lead lives unrecognizable to hers, never longing for stone or mountains or olive trees, knowing only brick and skyscrapers and perfect green lawns. Words will come easily to them. They will marry late and spend their long youths choosing. She wishes them not luck or money; they will have both, as much as they want, or is necessary. Instead she wishes them fearlessness in all things: in love, yes, but also in work, in expectation, in the leap from the high rocks, in looking back, and in forgetting.

Acknowledgments

MILLE GRAZIE, A thousand thanks, to the following:

My wonderful family and friends, for their constant encouragement. I am privileged to have such patient and loving people in my life.

Michelle Chalfoun, my first reader, for her vision, insight, and generosity.

Antonia Fusco, my supremely wise and gracious editor, for seeing into, through, between, and beyond the words I send her.

Mary Evans, the lucky authors' agent, for never compromising.

Elisabeth, Craig, Peggy, Michael, Ina, and everyone at Algonquin Books, for their hard work and dedication.

Everyone at Grub Street, first and foremost Eve Bridburg, for their glorious friendship, financial support, and for making this trip significantly less lonely.

Francesco Castellano, for his crucial help with the Italian words in this book.

Steve Almond, Jenna Blum, Scott Heim, Michael Lowenthal, and

Heidi Pitlor—amazing authors all—for happy hours, scandalous conversations, long lunches, and expert guidance.

Allison Adair, for her lovely translation of "Terra Straniera."

The Bread Loaf Writers' Conference, especially Michael Collier, for letting me grow up on that magic mountain.

The staff of the Diesel Café and True Grounds in Somerville, and the Singing Starbucks in West Medford, for the (almost) free office space.

Michael Borum, with whom the days pass happily, the nights are full of stars, and life is a grand adventure. What can anyone give me greater than now . . .

READERS GUIDE

FOR

CHRISTOPHER CASTELLANI'S

The Saint of Lost Things

Discussion Questions

1. When Maddalena has chosen to marry Antonio, a man she doesn't love, and cross the ocean to make a new home in America, her mother tells her: "Your new birthday is coming. You'll be born in Philadelphia, in the United States of America" (p. 226). How does Maddalena struggle against this rebirth? How do you think this relates to Maddalena's difficulty giving birth to Prima? Discuss Maddalena's symbolic "new birthday" in America. Has it occurred by the time the book comes to an end?

2. The characters in *The Saint of Lost Things* live in an Italian American neighborhood in Wilmington, Delaware, near St. Anthony's Church, named for the patron saint of lost things—which also lends the novel its name. Discuss what Maddalena, Antonio, and Julian have each lost before the events of the story take place. How do they come to find what they're looking for? Is it what they expected? Discuss in

a larger sense how the theme of "lost things" develops
throughout the story.

3. Maddalena's English teacher, Sister Clark, tells her students.
"[U]ntil you master your speech, no one will show you the
respect you deserve. That's all it takes . . . [t]hen America
will smile and open her arms, loving as a grandmother"
(p. 4). Is the mastery of the English language truly all it
takes to assimilate in this country, or do you think there are
other barriers immigrants face in the United States? Is this
the same for immigrants today as it was in the post–World
War II era?

4. After the death of his parents, forty-year-old Giulio Fabbri
changes his name to Julian. He says he "wants everyone to
see hope—rebirth is the word—in the flourish of the American letter, in the embrace of the new country" (p. 45). How
did people react to this name change? What makes him decide to change his name back to Giulio at the end of the
story? What can changing a name accomplish? Did anyone
in your own family change his or her name upon coming to
this country? If so, how do you think that changed their
experience—and yours?

5. How do each of the characters relate to Abraham Waters
and his family? Discuss what may have led some of the Italian immigrants in the story to want the Waters family to
leave, and to even go so far as to cruelly terrorize them. Do
you think this is similar or different to how immigrants are

treated today? Discuss why you think the subplot of the Waters family has no real resolution. Do you think the author is making a statement about the reality of racism through the 1950s and beyond? "[M]y family's not going anywhere. Not now, not ever," Abraham Waters tells Julian (p. 216). Why does he insist on staying? How do you think you would have reacted in a similar situation?

6. What keeps Antonio from stopping Renato and Cassie when they first tell him of their plans to drive the Waters family from the neighborhood? Why does he help them at first? The author writes that Antonio thinks he "has to play both sides of this, make sure no harm comes either to Mrs. Stella's or to his friendship with Renato" (p. 113). Why is keeping loyal to his friend so important to Antonio? What makes Antonio vandalize Renato's restaurant toward the end of the story? Would you say Antonio is at heart a good person?

7. Do you think that Maddalena and Antonio have a happy and successful marriage? How would Maddalena's life have been different had she stayed in Santa Cecilia and married for love? Do you think that was a true and viable option? Maddalena recalls her first knowledge of possibly falling in love with Antonio as being the Christmas Eve night when they snuck into the Cadillac lot, after being married for years. Yet that night Antonio remembers thinking of his wife: "How unreachable you are. How hard you'll make me work, all my life, to deserve you" (p. 240). Do you think

Maddalena expects more of Antonio at first because she did not love him? Does this story change what you think about arranged marriages?

8. Each character carries around his or her idea of the American Dream—and is surprised at how it does not easily fall into their laps. How does Antonio keep his dream of opening a family restaurant from coming true? What makes him decide he is ready? How does Maddalena's idea of the American Dream change over the course of the book? What is Julian's dream? Discuss how the American Dream relates to Americans and immigrants today.

9. Julian sings in front of others for the first time at the Grassos' Christmas celebration, and they are all witness to his outburst of tears while performing the song "Mamma." Afterward, humiliated, he retreats upstairs to the bathroom. He thinks "[t]hey pity him . . . That poor lonely man, they're whispering . . . Doesn't he have anyone?" (p. 160). But when Julian hears Maddalena singing his song to herself through the wall, he knows one person was truly listening. "She is lonely," Julian thinks. "She has lost someone she loves, and cannot imagine how she will face the years ahead" (p. 162). Does Maddalena pity Julian? How does Julian see his friendship with Maddalena, and how does it evolve once she gets sick? How does Maddalena think that she and Julian are the same? Do you agree? Does Maddalena still think they are the same by the end of the story?

10. The author writes: "Everyone is fighting their private battles for the same thing: a little square of land, a steady job, a child to pass his name to; but if they win, something invariably goes wrong. The land is in the wrong place; the job doesn't pay enough; the child disappears" (p. 55). Which private battles are won in this story, and which are lost? Do you think that any of the characters' battles were not worth fighting? Do you agree that you must fight to attain the things you want in life? Is that the same for immigrants as for those born in this country?

11. While working at the Golden Hem, people tell Maddalena where their hearts can be found. One person's heart is with poets and historians, another's is still in her home country, and another's is with her children. But Maddalena's heart "lives in many places . . . It beats with the child's inside her; it tumbles down the hills of Santa Cecilia; it quickens when Antonio lays his hand on her hip" (p. 66). What does the "location" of one's heart tell about a person? Where is Antonio's heart? Julian's? Where is Maddalena's heart by the end of the story? Does her heart still reside in multiple places after Prima is born?

12. Maddalena only feels fully accepted into Antonio's family once she is carrying his baby. Antonio blamed this on what he called her "movie-star good looks," but Maddalena knows that she's expected to prove herself to them. "Did you marry Antonio just for the free trip across the ocean?"

is what she imagines they each think of her (p. 119). Maddalena's response would have been: "I walked onto that ship seven years ago like a mourner to her own funeral. I gave up everything for a man I barely knew and did not yet love. You should be comforting me." (p. 119) Is Maddalena seeking his family's acceptance or her own? How does she come to terms with her regret?

13. When Antonio is faced with the opportunity to finally make use of the money he'd hidden in the drapes and open a family restaurant, he begins to see himself clearly: "He was just a scared immigrant clutching the few pennies thrown at him every Friday afternoon, unwilling to risk opening his hands . . . When Antonio died, he'd have nothing lasting to show for his life—a child, yes, maybe even children, but no wedge of earth other than the six feet they'd bury him under" (p. 253). How does each character in this story discover their own "wedge of earth"? Why is this important to Antonio? Is this more important to people who have chosen to immigrate to a new country than to those who are born there? Is this still important today?

14. According to Julian, "[t]here are only two kinds of people left on earth—those whom grief has touched and those it is coming for" (p. 313). How does grief change a person? How has it touched and altered each of the characters? Julian tends to connect himself with people who share an understanding of grief—Maddalena, Abraham Waters Helen. How do each of these people change him? Do you

think he would have been able to start a relationship with Helen before his parents died?

15. How does the author make use of flashbacks in this story? How does this structure reflect Maddalena's views on her lost life in Santa Cecilia? Discuss the balance of past and present in the story. The novel ends in the present, looking ahead at what might be coming in the future—how does this ending work for you? Does the story seem fully resolved? Discuss how, in your eyes, you think the Grasso family will evolve. How could the story continue?